"AT LAST"

Novel

by

BILLIE JEAN KING

"AT LAST"

BILLIE JEAN KING

"At Last"

Republished Edition

ISBN 978-0-615-33269-7

Printed in the United States

The author guarantees all contents are original and do not infringe upon the legal rights of any other person or work. "At Last" is a work of fiction, names, characters, places and incidents are the products of the author's imagination or are used fictitiously. Any resemblances to actual events, or persons, are entirely coincidental.

Published by BJK Publications

Book design by, Tyora "TY" Moody

At: Tywebbin Creations www.tyoramoody.com/

Originally published by Xulon Press

ISBN 978-1-60477-3361

www.billiejeankingatlast.com

This book is dedicated to my beloved Mother, who loved me

Unconditionally.

Mary Stokes-King, Home Going

Mother's Day of 1989

≈

Anthony (Tony) Keith Nelson,

A cherished Friend...October 2007

≈

&

Jordyn,

My

Pook! Pook!

~ *Acknowledgements & Expression* ~

All Praises to my Lord and Savior, Jesus Christ. I Praise him for the manifestation of my gift to write. I thank him for Christian Broadcasting that served as a constant source of direction, guidance and motivation. I thank Zig Ziglar for his book, *"Better Than Good,"* which was an additional basis for motivation and inspiration.

To: My daughter Shari Amour King-Ignont. Thanks Shari for being the first to recognize and encourage me in my writing endeavor. I know it wasn't limited to bias only. I value your expertise from being a well read individual. When you were a kid, to avoid trips to the library, I recall selecting [fifty] books thinking that they would last you an entire summer; you read them in [3] weeks. Thanks for the confidence that you demonstrated in my writing abilities while you were in college; I felt privileged when you'd ask me to review your term papers and reports. Remember my letters, and the question that you posed to me. [Well, *Voila*!] Thanks for being my personal cheerleader! It's your turn now; time to bring your prototypes to fruition, that's still with me, collecting dust. ☺

To: Jordyn A. Ignont, thanks for your prompting when you asked, "Why don't you work on your book anymore," after taking a break and placing it on the top shelf. At the age of eight, I enjoyed the interest that you expressed when you'd ask me to cite you various scenes on the days that I gave you a ride to school. I look forward to assisting you in making your story a reality. ☺

To: Virginia Sue Smith, Still tugging with notions of doubt after Shari's overwhelming endorsement; I felt the need to place my writing under a less biased microscope. Remembering the days of old, when I'd dash across the street to play with you; only to be disappointed to find your head [buried] in some book. Your reading interest remained off the charts ahead of mine when we tried to read every book from Ms. Burk's Library that bore the name of my sister Millie. Never classifying myself as an avid reader; is this irony or what? To date, you average [twenty] books a month. I knew that you possessed the necessary capabilities to give me the thumbs up or down. It pleased me to learn that you felt compassion for my character, Vanessa; it was my [aim]. Thanks for the thumbs up, in spite of you calling me a *hopeless romantic.* Didn't think I'd have the nerve to say it, did ya? ☺

To: Brenda Gayle Reese, Memory escapes me Brenda when I try to recall how we reconnected last year. At any rate, thank God for the internet that unites us from California to Georgia. Discovering that you too are a passionate reader as your cousin, and a woman of God; I knew it was a divine connection. I *blinked* back the tears when you referenced my characters saying, *"I miss them, they* *were my friends"* after you'd completed the manuscript. I'm glad that you found common ground with various aspects of the women characters. As a single Christian woman in their age group; you provided me the feedback that I was seeking. Thank you so much! ☺

To: Josie Marie Washington, In the thirty-five years that I've known you, countless times I'd go to the mailbox, and find a book from you; always in nature of enhancing my spiritual growth. Not forgetting the times that I'd raid your personal library when visiting, knowing that I'd find something beneficial for self growth. Choosing you as my litmus tester for content and biblical structure; I was ecstatic and humbled by your level of interest and content approval. It was music to my ears when you called saying, *"I can't wait until blank and, blank, talk and clear things up, or will they?* You satisfied my wavering doubt when you commented, *"I like the infusion of the scriptures."* Scripture content was of key concern. The fact that I consider you *wonderfully conservative*; it was an added bonus. Sorry! I sneaked the *mint* scene right on by you. The girls thought it was cute. With you in mind, I added a [Disclaimer]. ☺ Thanks for being my long standing prayer partner, and friend.

To: Denise Campbell-Smith, If I were to give out awards, you'd win easily for most enthusiastic. The others had read the manuscript last year. When 2008 rolled in, I was in need of a heat check and some much needed motivation, you didn't disappoint, Denise. Unlike the others, I *purposely* issued it to you in chapters; I wanted to test your interest level. I loved your excitement when you'd call screaming for more chapters, after you'd completed them in the late night hour. I adored your comments *"why is this or that going to happen?"* I knew I was on target. I'm pleased that Bill's character was a favorite of the men. Thanks, ***Tilmon,*** for letting her sneak from you in the late night hours to read. I couldn't pin your Mom down long enough to read it; however, she showered me with positive support and eager anticipation for the completion. ***Thanks, Walterine Campbell.***

Thanks guys, for believing enough in my writing to sacrifice your time while working, and caring for your families to read my manuscript before publication. I struggle to find the words to convey to the gratitude that I feel. The fact that you've avid readers and hold Bachelors and Masters Degrees; I am immeasurably humbled by your level of interest.

Thank God for the prayers and support from my church family, and churches throughout the Bay Area and other regions of the U.S. A special shout to my relatives and friends in Bastrop & Mer Rouge, Louisiana.

Thanks! Morehouse & Bastrop High Teachers, It would be careless of me if I failed to thank the sources that were instrumental in teaching me the fundamentals of grammar. A foundation of teachings that was essential in providing me the necessary components for writing.

To:Tyora "TY" Moody at: Tywebbin Creations, Thank you for brilliantly re-creating my book design. It was a pleasure to be engaged in the process. You were a joy; I was especially impressed with the timely manner in which you always responded.

To: JoAnn Green, JOANN'S Beauty Supply Salon & Gifts. Thanks girl..., for all your support; you've been a trooper from day one. Thank you so much for bringing me to Santa Maria; affording me the privilege to meet your clients, friends, family and church family. ☺

To: Donna Moses, Sistah's in Harmony/Sistah's in Conversation. Thank you for allowing me a platform to showcase, and discuss my book. You captured the message in its entirety. Every woman in attendance generated a spirit of warmth and sisterly love; just some down to earth Classy, and intelligent Sistah's, who love the Lord. Cheryl, you can count on seeing your [*spread]* described on someone's table in my next novel. ☺

To: Wanda B. Campbell, So many words parade through my mind when I think of you; making it difficult to express my appreciation. I ask daily, Lord, why you didn't allow our paths to cross earlier. Immediately, I am reminded that I wouldn't have *appreciated* you as much, and probably wouldn't have *listened* to you. ☺Nothing builds character better than *trial and error.* Thank you for a well evaluated review of "At Last". **Thank** you for the *high marks;* I value your opinions and comments. I especially appreciated your constructive advice and suggestions. Thanks for enlightening me on the various trends and resources within the industry that afforded me the opportunity to republish "At last." **Because** you're a ***woman of God***, who knows her ***identity***, and realizes that although we're both writers; God has a different ***agenda*** for each of us. It's evident in the manner in which you shared your knowledge, time and ideas that you felt would assist me in developing and marketing *"At Last."* Your level of generosity give me hope for unity with others sisters in Christ. ☺

To: My Readers, past and future one's. I pray that you'll enjoy reading my novel as much as I enjoyed writing it. Since this is the ***republished edition*** of "***At Last***", it affords me the privilege, honor, and the opportunity to thank each of you. I feel extremely blessed and humbled by the outpouring of your warm and generous support since the release of my book in April, 2009. **From** e-mails, books signings, discussions, and individuals; thank you so much for your kind words expressing your level of interest, and how you've been blessed by various topics and character portrayal. Your positive and encouraging reception is indicative of the fact that *"At Last"* was God *inspired*, and God *mentored*. I give him all the Glory. **Sharing** how you've been inspired to make your passions a reality; I'm elated that God would use a *novice* like me to inspire you to excel toward your dreams, and God given *purpose.*

I had no...idea that *my food selections for my meal scenes* would capture so much attention; I guess I should've included *recipes.* **As a** single woman, I join singles of all ages in prayer as we endeavor to *triumph* over the issues, and struggles that are shared in the life of single Christians.

Thank you,

Billie Jean King

www.billiejeankingatlast.com

atlastbillieking@aol.com

***Scriptures in parentheses are not part of the characters dialogue; they're used as a point of reference in support of the subject matter that's being discussed.**

Chapter 1

Barbara Jean Keller shivered, and fumbled with the keys as she opened her front door after arriving home from Sunday morning worship services. On a brisk December morning in the San Francisco Bay Area; she's putting together the final touches for her *Christmas Sunday Brunch.* Last year's brunch generated such an overwhelming response; everyone pleaded for a repeat.

Her guests will be arriving at eleven o'clock a.m. After attending early morning services, she's pleased with the progress. Now that everything meets her approval, she'll wait until her guests arrive before scrambling the eggs. After taking one final look, she whispered a prayer of thanksgiving.

Always getting pleasure from the fellowship of her friends and sisters in Christ, but, repeatedly, she secretly contemplates the idea of enjoying a similar setting with someone of the opposite sex. In keeping with tradition, she continues to tell herself, next year Barbara Jean, next year.

Regrettably, for Barbara Jean next year had turned into sixteen years without a relationship. Never married, she'll be turning forty-seven in three weeks. She has a twenty-four year old daughter named, Michelle. Preferring to refrain from focusing on the number of years, the reality of time eludes her; she finds contentment in taking one day at a time.

The doorbell rang breaking her concentration; rushing to answer it; she greeted Karen with an armful of presents and treats. "Hey, Girl," and reaches to assist her with the packages.

Inhaling the aroma of the food, Karen mumbled, "Mmm..., something smells yummy! Oooh and I love your dress." Karen complimented.

"Thanks! You're looking cute and festive in your outfit too." Selecting a turquoise Chinese Kimono dress, for added comfort, she's wearing her black mules. Barbara felt that it accentuated her now visible shape, and blended nicely with her dark skinned complexion. Gaining more confidence in her appearance since her weight loss earlier in the year, she'd also changed her hairstyle; settling on a neck-length flip. Bearing a surprised expression, "What in the world did you bring, girl?"

"Oh, just a few goodies, and presents for the tree." Karen Lynn Harding, a dear friend of ten years. Sharing a mutual commitment to God, they've pledged to practice *celibacy* while seeking God for their mate.

Rearing her fifteen year old Son named, Michael; she's forty-two, a divorcee with a flourishing event planning business. For a new look; she opted for a shoulder-length wrap. Her lean and slender physique allows her to experiment with trendy fashions. The form-fitted black skirt with pleats at the tail showed off her long shapely legs. Her smooth russet skin tone radiated against her red satin blouse, and black rhinestone pin.

Taking a brief glance of the room, she noticed that Barbara had combined the dining, and living room areas to accommodate the buffet style setting. With no chance of snow in the Bay Area, to achieve the winter wonderland effect; Barbara drew back the satin cream drapes, and sprayed the slider with snow-flakes.

"Everything looks so functional and festive, I need to bring you with me to some of my gigs; I could use your ideas for decorating." Karen said, as she placed the presents under the tree."

"Aw..., you're so kind." Now seated in her favorite chair at the breakfast bar; she decided to poke fun at Barbara.

"Who's coming today, how many men did you invite?" Pausing from checking on her rolls in the oven; she cocked her eyes in Karen's direction. "Girl, please! I've already gone there."

Slowly motioning her head, a look of disappointment emerged onto Karen's face. "Barbara, we've got to do better next year, this year is gone; the holidays are here, and we're still alone."

Tossing the potholder on the counter top, "hey, you'll get no arguments from me. We have to implement those ideas that we've talked about, joining the Christian dating website, becoming open-minded to meeting men of all races, and younger one's, remember?" She reminded her, in a matter of fact tone.

Fidgeting in her seat, "I know..., but we've *waited patiently* for so long, Barbara; it appears as if life is passing us by some days." With sagging shoulders, Karen doodled on a message pad.

"It only looks that way Karen, before you arrived I was reminded that it's been over sixteen years since I've been in a relationship, is that scary?"

"Yes!" Karen laughed and nodded. Ignoring her, Barbara smiled. "In sincerity Karen, I can't blame God or anyone. He gives us free will to make our own decisions and choices. I think we have to play an active role in making it happen, with his guidance of course."

"Yeah, you're right, after eight years of being divorced; I just figured that I would've met someone by now. I've been so busy focusing on rearing Michael until it hadn't been an issue for me; time just slipped by."

"Now that I can relate. I tell you Karen, I was so thankful that God brought me out of that world when he did; Michelle became a teenager two years later. And by the grace of God, I was able to break *three generational curses* in our family; *sex and pregnancy before marriage, and higher education."*

"Now you're talking. I have the same agenda for Michael. I know he's a boy, but the same Godly principles apply to him as well. But as a single parent; you have to feel a sense of accomplishment with Michelle, right."

"Yeah, I do, all *praises to God.*"

"It's ironic that you used that expression Barbara, just this morning a minister was teaching on *generational curses.* In times past; we never recognized them as being such."

"I know..." She paused. "Don't forget about *obesity* and *poverty.* You know Karen, I think it's because we've regarded them..."she paused. "As a way of life, or genetically related, or something, that's why they're so hard to break."

"You know, that's it in a nutshell Barbara, thank God we're learning to identify them. It speaks to the progressiveness of the teachings in our churches today; we'd never heard of *"generational curses"* in times past."

"What was I saying before we got sidetracked?" Barbara asked. "Oh, oh the husband issue," she babbled on, flinging her dishtowel mid air. "You can see my plate was full girl; a husband wasn't a priority at the time. Of course I thought about one, and even prayed occasionally, notice, I said occasionally."

"By the time Michelle turned fifteen, um..., I think I sort of gave up, Karen." Shifting her feet, with folded arms, she continued to jabber. "I guess I just didn't believe that I'd meet a man whom I could trust over her." Bearing witness to the dilemma that she'd faced, she motioned her head from side to side.

"You must've been content, right? When we first met; you appeared to be."

"Yeah, you're right; I was to a certain point." Barbara stated, somewhat unconvincingly, while removing the rolls from the oven.

Aiming to keep Karen hopeful, "Now, look Karen, don't let my singleness discourage you. You're doing well financially, your business is thriving; you'd be an asset to any potential mate."

Airing a somber expression, Barbara continued her thought. Resting her back against the counter with outstretched arms, "In past times, I went through two recessions while companies I worked for went bankrupt. Thank God for the child support checks. Girl, a man was the last thing on my mind. Securing a better future for my baby, and dealing with life's obstacles were the height of my focus."

Connecting with Barbara's efforts to keep her optimistic in her pursuit, Karen nodded, and responded in an appreciative and hopeful tone. "Now, that puts things into perspective."

In deep thought, Barbara shifted her shoulders. "This may sound a bit of a contradiction Karen, and I certainly do not expect you to agree with me. But, some nights, more than a few nights; I go to bed feeling...,"she paused. "um..., feeling this extra sense of peace and contentment; realizing that *I'm alone; but not lonely*. I guess it's an oxymoron feeling. I desire a husband, but I'm *content without one*. Does that make sense?"

Smiling, and nodding accordingly, "Yeah, it makes perfect sense; I feel the exact same way." She paused. "I mean, that's how we're supposed to feel, right, contentment within ourselves first?"

"Oh..., you mean; as opposed to looking for a man, or a husband to bring us contentment." Barbara clarified.

"Yeah, yeah, our primary *purpose* in life can't be looking for a husband." Karen joked.

Barbara let out a cackle before saying, "You're so funny, that's not your sole *purpose*. You have your women's shelter ministry, your business, our ministries at church, and that's in addition to rearing, Michael."

"I know," she voiced in a moping tone, and continued to chatter. "I think it's all the commercialism that's associated with the *holidays*, seeing the ads, hearing the songs *"It's the time to be with the one you love, Chestnuts roasting on an open fire."* Acting with hand movement, Karen dramatized, and fell over laughing.

"Here, try this silly," handing Karen a yeast roll.

"You can take this to the bank, Karen; he will definitely have to be someone extra special, a *mature seasoned* Christian man for sure. Karen, you always have some man chasing you."

Between bites, "Oooh, girl, this roll is yum! You know that they don't count, they're never Christians, and you know that." She reminded Barbara, scornfully.

Divorced for eight years; Karen is committed to waiting on God for her next husband. Fully understanding the danger in not waiting; in times of frustration she often allowed the *lifestyles* of other Christians to make her feel that she's missing out.

Unleashing a boisterous chuckle, "I tell you Barbara; it does get awfully tempting at times. Especially when they appear to have it all going on, the appeal, the toned body, and that swagger..., girl I have to get on my knees, pull out that bible, and totally devour *I Corth10:13.* I am serious; it gets hard to keep *resisting* that temptation."

Piercing with laughter, and in complete harmony with her, "I guess we can thank God that we know how to deal with it, ha."

"I know we go over this one a lot Barbara, but..., why is it that, well, I'll rephrase it. Why does it give the impression that some Christian's continue to be blessed, when they do whatever they wanna do, go where they wanna go?"

"You mean, they date whomever they want, they sleep with whomever they want, and it seems that they're getting over, and having fun; while we sit on the sideline, *drooling*, and wishing that we weren't so *obedient*?"

Cracking up with laughter and nodding, Karen confessed overwhelmingly. "You're being silly, but yes!"

After a moment of shared loud laughter. "Now.., Karen, you know..., just because a Christian does well financially, it doesn't always mean that it's a blessing from God, girl. It could be that they've managed well, set some goals, or made some prudent choices. But, I hear you; it's the *trick* of the enemy." She clarified. "Our obedience should be defined by our love for God, and not the blessings we may or may not get; but you know that. You've been talking to some of the women on your *job*; I can always tell."

"Yeah..., I know, you're right; I just needed to hear it. If he rewarded us according to our iniquities, and our little *self righteousness;* I guess we'd all be *naked and destitute."*

"You are so—crazy." Still standing, with folded arms, and back resting on the counter, she reminisced, "I remember Charles Stanley teaching on that very same thing some years back Karen, he said *"they're not getting away,"* and he supported it with our *motto scripture."* Unanimously, they said. "*Psalms 37:1- 2*."

"Don't worry, Karen; the *New Millennium* will be your year." Barbara assured her with confidence.

Acknowledging the encouragement, Karen echoed. "It's going to be our year, in the name of Jesus."

Barbara and Karen have this conversation at least three times a year. Every so often they think that the grass is greener on the other side; *Psalms 37:1- 2* always helps them to bring things into perspective. *"Fret not thyself because of evildoers, neither be thou envious against workers of iniquity. For they shall soon be cut down like the grass, and wither as the green herb..."*

"You know I had to vent a little."

"Your venting is well-founded, and received."

Kimberly Denise Montgomery was the next guest to arrive; she's the daughter of friends to Barbara and Karen. Years ago, they moved to Maryland to Co-Pastor a church. After graduating college, she returned to the Bay Area; Kim is twenty-eight.

In spite of their age differences; they share a lot in common. Practicing abstinence, she's still a *virgin.* They attend the same church of which they've recently joined; she desired to be married as well.

Seated along side Karen in her red two-piece suit, Kim removed her coat and gloves. Using a hair twister, she placed her past the shoulder-length hair with brown highlights in a ponytail; which corresponded perfectly with her smooth flawless brown skin. God didn't slight Kim on any part of her anatomy; her physique formed the shape of an hourglass.

Complaining, Kim stated. "You must've run to the parking lot after church, I didn't see either of you? "

"Yeah! I did, literally," Barbara replied. Realizing that she was taking a chance attending early morning services and hosting a brunch at eleven, she dashed to the parking lot without stopping to fellowship with anyone.

"I had to rush to drop Michael off with his Coach; they're watching the Lakers and Spurs game at a pizza parlor today."

"Nice Coach," Kim noted. Fully aware that their gatherings only consist of women, Kim teased. "Who's coming today?"

"No—men, so don't ask." Karen promptly interjected, and laughed.

"I knew that," Kim voiced with certainty. "No, I really meant…whose coming?"

Using her fingers to count, Barbara identified their names. "Let's see…, there's Joyce, Janice, Brenda and Sue."

Kim felt obligated to clarify to Barbara why she'd invited one of her friends. "I invited a co-worker Barbara; she doesn't get much fellowship. She has this secret boyfriend who keeps her on a tight leash, her name is Vanessa."

Turning her head, and smiling, "No, problem, there's plenty of food. Michelle may stop by later." Barbara shared. Michelle and Jordyn are visiting for Christmas and the New Year from Texas.

Inhaling and savoring the aroma of the food that'd saturated the area, Kim remarked. "Mmm…the food smells delicious, Mom and Dad send their love; wishing they were here for the holidays."

At 11:05, the doorbell rang. "Merry Christmas everyone!" In a cheery and spirited tone, Barbara welcomed them. Including Kim's friend, Vanessa.

Everyone had arrived, admiring the celebratory décor, Joyce pointed out, "Oh my, something smells good up in here, and she has it looking so festive; girl..., you must've been up all night."

"Actually, no, I got an early start on decorating this year. Since everyone's here, I'll get the eggs going. You guys are no strangers, so hang up your coats and sit wherever you feel comfortable."

Massaging her hands, Joyce spoke. "I'm going to get close to this fireplace; it looks so warm and cozy."

Barbara was happy to see that her guests took notice to her decorating efforts. Tree branches, fresh pinecones, and candles decked the fireplace. The heat from the wood burning fireplace generated an inviting aroma from the tree branches and pinecones; the flames in the fireplace enhanced the holiday ambiance.

For their dining convenience, two tables with four place settings were arranged in the middle of the floor, in addition to the formal dining table. Hunter green tablecloths, and napkins adorned the tables, poinsettias and candelabras with red candles served as centerpieces for each table. The area was spacious and provided room for a comfortable flow.

Admiring the Christmas tree, Kim remarked. "Look at that tree; it's so beautiful; it reminds me of a Macy's tree." Barbara indeed was going for the Macy's tree look. To attain the optimum effect, she used clear lights and red velvet bows only, ranging in sizes from small, medium, to large. It was elegant enough to take center stage in any mall.

Swaying and humming to the music, "I love this music, who is it?" Janice asked.

"That's Kenny G's Christmas CD." Once or twice a year Barbara invited over old as well as new friends. Not all believed in organized Christianity, however, they all did believe in God. Seizing the opportunity whenever, Barbara or Karen always managed to sneak in a little witnessing here and there.

"Okay guys, it's ready, we're dining buffet-style today." Surpassing last years menu, she'd prepared her favorite sausage cheese, and spinach quiche, along with smoked ham, homemade sage and garlic turkey sausage, shrimp etoufee, creamy grits, scrambled eggs with green onions, home fried potatoes, Michelle's homemade jams, cheesy garlic toast, and yeast rolls. For dessert, she baked pecan and sweet potato pies.

Hot and cold beverages of orange, apple, cranberry juice, Irish cream coffee, and hot apple cider completed the meal. Barbara asked Karen to say grace as everyone patiently waited. *"Lord, Jesus thank you for this day and this time of fellowship. Father we ask that you will be in our midst. Please guard our hearts and our minds....*

Being the comedian, Joyce got things moving. "Good, bread, good meat, good, Lord, lets eat." She shouted, getting expressed amusement from everyone. "Look at all this food; there goes my diet," Brenda alerted.

"Mmm..., I've had a craving for grits; I'm going to put some of this shrimp etouffee over them, *yummy.*" Janice voiced.

Being the perfect host, Barbara refilled breadbaskets, and beverage glasses. For a brief moment after everyone had prepared their plates, quietness settled the room except for sighs of mmm's, and polite requests for more bread please, more this or that, please.

"Girl, you need to open up a catering business, this food is screaming," Sue voiced, after taking a generous bite of the quiche.

Acknowledging her with a warm smile, Barbara replied. "Thank you, but no thanks. I only enjoy cooking on a small scale Sue. If I had to cook for large groups of people; I think it'd take away the enjoyment for me."

"I'll never understand why you can't find—a husband." Janice remarked, as she reached for another roll. Blushing and smiling, Barbara found it amusing. Halting in the middle of pouring coffee, Barbara replied. "I knew it was coming." Janice's question was right on target.

"You know the saying, the way to a man's heart; is through his stomach." Janice reiterated. Releasing a soft giggle.

"So they say, but I can never find anyone to feed, well anyone that I'd want to feed that is." Barbara explained, taking pleasure in the compliment. Receiving the same sentiments each year from the girls, she found it gratifying and complimentary.

Sue sided with Barbara; her frustrated expression was evident. "You're not the only one that can't find anyone to feed."

Since the men topic had been introduced, Kim tried a little probing tactic, combined with complaining. "I think it's a shame, there are seven women here, and not one of us has a significant other?"

Causing shock, they let loose nervous laughter. Wearing facial expressions that read, "*So what else is new?*"

Scanning the room for rebuttals, Kim waited patiently. Clearing her throat, Vanessa finally spoke. "Uh, yes, I do, he had to be at his church today."

Respecting Vanessa as her guest, Barbara stepped up to give kudos to her. "That's great Vanessa, at least you do have...someone, and he's a Christian. Why do you think we're without men in our lives?" Barbara asked. A brief silence ensued.

After careful deliberations, one by one they uttered phases such as *"Oh, I don't know, it's not enough men to go around, men our age want younger women, some fall short of our expectations, and on the other hand, maybe we're just too choosy."*

"Uh, not measuring up, too choosy, why should we have to settle?"

Barbara asked, and continued to elaborate. "We're far more empowered than we were in the seventies and even the eighties. I don't mean financial empowerment only; I mean *empowerment that comes from self-worth, and a high level of self-esteem.*" She conveyed with passion.

"It's a known fact that women have taken great strides in repositioning their careers to be independent of a man's financial support, nonetheless; it goes deeper than that."

On the edge of her seat, Barbara fervently communicated her point. "We laughed and agreed with Kim that it's a shame that we're without relationships, with the exception of Vanessa." She paused and flashed a quick smile in Vanessa's direction.

"Every woman in this room possesses enough finesse about her to go out and secure a relationship with a man on any given day." Heads nodded confidently, showing agreement.

"But..., what we'd get becomes the issue." She said, and smiled.

"Correct! Janice remarked, in affirmation. Barbara resumed in making her case. "With no *race* of women *excluded*; finding *"just a man"* is sufficient for a lot of women. With consideration to most of the talk and reality shows, *"having just a man"* is a reality for many women."

While walking to refill her glass, Kim mouthed, in agreement. "Now you've said a mouthful, girl."

Barbara theorized by saying, "When we consider some of the reasons why we're without a man, it's because we've chose *not* to *compromise*. Whether it's due to our values, our desires, and last but not the least, our personal *relationship with Christ*. There are *many women* without relationships, mainly because of the values and standards that they've set."

"You're right; it doesn't sound shameful when you put it in its proper context, Barbara." Brenda said, with an air of confidence, feeling more at ease.

"Exactly, these are indicators that there's some level of empowerment that exist within us." Karen assessed. "When we're out and about, we see women arm and arm with men everyday; our natural response is *envy,* but we have no evidence as to what *price*—some of them are *paying for that arm.*"

"Absolutely, you're dead—on it, Karen." Sue shouted, in an authoritative tone. "I'm feeling empowered." Sue concluded, with a power to the people *fist,* everyone humored her.

"Since we're discussing independence and finances," Kim said, "I am proud of the fact that I'm self-supporting, as we all are, on the other hand; I'm not opposed to having a mate that makes less—money than I do. I'm more concerned with his character, his—values, and more importantly, and if we're *equally yoked,—spiritually.*"

Brenda aimed a sharp—look in Kim's corner before saying. "Now you've opened up a new can of worms, girl, speak for yourself." She laughed, as the others joined in.

With a frozen voice, helplessly examining the room with her hands extended outward, Kim solicited support from anyone.

"Am I alone in my thinking?" she asked, wondering why she wasn't getting any amen's. Karen and Barbara were so engaged in laughter; they were late coming to her rescue.

"We've kicked this one around a few times," Barbara finally acknowledged, offering Kim relief. "I agree with Kim, ideally it would be good if the incomes were in balance; but I don't want it to be the deciding factor."

"Precisely!" Karen sided.

"I think Kim and Barbara would agree we're not talking a 70-30 percent ratio with us being the 70%, I've gotten used to eating three square meals a day for some time now." Karen added. Bursting at the seams laughing, everyone was in agreement with her response.

Securing her arms tightly folded, "I'm sorry! But I've acquired some expensive tastes and habits; it'll have to be a 50-50 for me, or a 60-40, with him favoring the higher *percentage.*" Brenda stated firmly, closing doors for any protest attempts.

Sue, Janice, Joyce, and Vanessa chose the middle ground along with Brenda. Barbara and Karen shared Kim's sentiments for the most part. They knew if they trusted God to direct them to their mates; they believed that the incomes would be in balance, making it an equitable arrangement for all.

For individual reasons, they each chose to uphold higher values in their choice of men; therefore, agreeing that ⌈not⌋ having a man wasn't a negative reflection on them as women.

Taking a sip of her coffee, Joyce threw in. "You, guys just ain't looking in the right places. You've got to go further than the Church honey. You know there's only one *little available deacon*, and he thinks he's died and gone to heaven from all the attention." Joyce wasn't popular for *filtering* her words. Tossing her head back, with out stretched arms; she laughed hilariously. Having shared opinions, some cheered her on.

"Joyce, you're... ah, so wrong."

Kim partially agreed with Joyce but felt that some clarification was in order. "As much as I hate to agree with you, you nailed it Joyce, a little *exaggerated*, yes! Women do grossly out number single men in the church. That's why we have to focus our attention to our relationship with Christ, the spoken word, and maintain fellowship with other Christians. You're right; the unavailability of men can become depressing if we let it."

"Exactly if we let it. If men were our main focus for church attendance, we'd probably become a group *of disappointed and sexually frustrated women*." Karen voiced, exuding honesty and sincerity.

"Amen to that!" Rallied Barbara and Kim. To their knowledge, only the three of them were abstaining.

"It does get discouraging at times guys, but not to the point of frustration, thank—God." Karen stated.

"I've been divorced for eight years now and haven't been involved in a relationship. I admitted to Barbara before you guys arrived how on occasion I feel as if time is passing us by." Saturated with humility, she chatted on with candor. "Generally speaking, Christians do tend to think that the grass appears greener on the other side."

"Passing us by, uh, that's putting it gently, the operative word is *past*!" Janice said sulking, causing a buzzing effect from the girls. Janice is a Christian but had *straddled the fence lately*.

"These feelings are valid guys," Karen stressed. "Your strongest and most *committed* Christian women experience them. Oh, we don't like owning up to it; we prefer to project a stronger and a more faith orient *stand."* But, c'mon, guys, we all have *bouts of discouragement;* and we have the scriptures to prove it." Karen said, chuckling.

"Yeah, but all Christian women aren't as open as you Karen. I've had Christian women to make me feel ..., uh ...that at the idea of me desiring a man is *blaspheme*." Brenda aired.

In rare form, Karen continued with sentiments discussed earlier with Barbara. Her motives were to lend some encouragement to some of the women present. Particularly those who were out of fellowship with Christ.

"You're not alone, Brenda, it's not an easy walk but when we've committed our lives to Christ, we can remain victorious in our walk." Karen confessed. "Amen! Amen!" Voiced Kim and Barbara.

Feeling that Karen was a strong believer in God, Brenda listened with intensity. Seldom, Brenda allowed her circumstances to discourage her faith.

"That's inspiring Karen, thanks for sharing; it's nice to see mature Christian women showing openness, I can lighten up on myself a little."

Quickly assessing her relationship with the Lord, Janice repeated. "Karen said something that bears repeating. She said that she's submitted her life to Christ; to me, that's the challenging part. It requires forsaking all your desires, and allowing him to be head of your life." She paused and sighed.

"Well.., this is the area that I find myself falling short; I'm not quite there. Pausing... "To be honest, um, I'm not sure if I really want to be." Stated in soberness, and boldness, looking downward.

"That's good Janice, Karen replied. Taking ownership for the need to *submit* is the first step. You can't change what you won't acknowledge; I'm hopeful for you."

Joyce knew that it was inventory time for her, but she wasn't having it. "Hey...! You, guys are making way too much sense for me today; y'all trying to spoil my, *fun!*" She screamed, setting free a devilish laugh.

Some laughed, expressing solidarity. Swiftly, but gently Barbara reminded Joyce that she'd sparked the dialogue. "It was your little comment that got us started with this line of conversation, Missy."

At age fifty-eight, Joyce's a vibrant attractive woman, closely identifying to a younger version of Sandra on "227." Before taking early retirement she was a department store manager.

"You, guys are too choosy for me." Joyce fussed. "Well, for me..., he needs to be a polished professional." Janice declared, with her head and nose turned upward.

Having a well polished look also. Janice is forty-five, and an interior decorator who's been divorced for ten years. Given numerous business opportunities to show off her petite physique, and cute facial features, at the end of the day; she still fell short of finding her man.

Several women united with Janice on desiring a professional man. Since all were business owners, held specialized positions, and had acquired homes and rental properties; they felt that their desires were within reason.

"I don't care if he's a *ditch digger,* as long as he spends his money on me." Joyce proclaimed, and slapped Kim on the knee.

"Ouch!" Kim screamed loudly. "Some of us have to be *accountable* to a higher authority." Kim said, playfully with a smile.

"I do, too! I just ask God for a little more *grace*." Joyce said, belting out her *naughty* laugh. By no means was Joyce looking for anyone to take care of her, but did love men that'd wine and dine her. Twenty years ago, her husband died in a car accident. His double indemnity life insurance policy provided more than a comfortable life for her and her son, Jerold.

Instead of her running to God upon his death, she went in the opposite direction. After meeting Joyce, and learning of her plight, Barbara chooses to keep in close contact with her; she wants to be there for her when she's *through running.*

Barbara couldn't have predicted that their topic of men would run so deep. Wondering if she should spice things up by sharing about their up and coming *quest;* she glanced in Kim's direction with a smile, hoping she'd follow suite.

"Kim, Karen and I have made a decision to be more open minded in the *New Millennium;* we're embarking on a *quest* to find our mates." Barbara said smugly, while smiling. Kim didn't disappoint.

"Yes! We're going to join an online Christian dating service." Flooded with excitement, she voiced.

Reclining on pillows by the fireplace, the floor and couches; they'd all repositioned their seating arrangements. Rolling over to fluff her pillow, Joyce asked. "Why be limited to a Christian Website?"

Flashing Joyce a quick look of unbelief, in an authoritative tone, Karen answered, smiling. "Because..., we..."losing her words, she stuttered. "We only want Christian husbands, Joyce." Karen finally mumbled.

Finding it amusing, Joyce asked. "So, you're gonna pray and ask God to send you a husband over the internet?" With the *New Millennium* fast approaching, Joyce had yet to connect to the W.W.W.

"What's wrong with that, God is *omnipresent.* With so many websites to choose from, apparently there's a market for Christian internet dating. Take us for instance, we're all internet savvy. We use the e-mail, IM's, we pay our bills, we shop, and most of us make daily business transactions.

Question, if one of us joined an online dating website, should the men be suspicious or doubtful of us?" Getting a revelation, Sue remarked. "Oh..., you mean they're everyday people, like us."

"Yeah...!" Barbara said, nodding and smiling, before saying. "The ones that we're looking to meet. So what about the men we may meet at the *post office*, or *grocery store*, guys, should we be afraid of them too, is there a difference? "

After minutes of assessing the thought, Sue gave her take. "You know, I never looked at it that way. I do use the internet for everything now that I think about it. The few men that I've dated, including my business associates; they too have internet capabilities. I guess it is conceivable to meet someone with a common interest."

Forty-two and an insurance broker; Sue loved golfing and the finer things in life. Her brown hair with gold highlights and light skin tone brought together a radiant appearance. Sue believes in God, but doesn't feel that it's necessary to congregate in an assembly environment. Her former husband was a preacher, who can claim partial credit for her decision. *(Heb.10:25)*

"The internet was an option for the three of us Joyce to sort of coincide with our commitment to become more open and receptive; it's not a desired or recommended option for everyone." Karen reiterated.

"I guess you have a point there, girl." Joyce caved. "

"On the other hand," Karen asked. "How well do we know anyone we meet anywhere, unless we meet them through an acquaintance, right? I think we need to be careful and investigate every Christian man." Advised, Karen.

Practically spilling her cider and bobbing her head, Kim leaped to her feet, and shouted. "Amen to that, I can tell you about an experience I had with a man in the church."

Kim related that two years ago she'd dated a man that was a Christian. He was a college graduate and held a professional position, a homeowner, polished, the *"complete package."* Kim knew she'd found her, husband.

They pledged a vow of *celibacy.* They attended bible study together, and never placed themselves in compromising positions to be tempted of each other. Suspecting that things were far too easy, one day while in his car waiting for him to return, she pulled down the sun visor to check her hair and make-up in the mirror.

Pieces of mail dropped to the floor, discovering a completed reply card for a subscription to a *gay magazine*, she was past mortified. Following the initial hurt, her emotions shifted to rage and resentment. Handing him the reply card upon his return to the car, she asked him when he was going to tell her. In the final analysis, his answer was *"I hoped that I could change."*

Informing him that she wasn't practice material; she encouraged him to seek spiritual counseling, and never saw him again. Sharing only with Barbara and Karen, she thanked God that it'd only lasted for six-months. To support the fact that you need to examine all men with a critical eye; she felt led to disclose it to the other women.

"You can't assume they're okay just because they're in the church." Kim added. "I later understood why it became so easy for us to resist temptation; I didn't turn him on, *at all*." She forced a smile.

"He had to be gay, and blind." Joyce exhorted.

"Aw..., thanks Joyce, you're so sweet. You know how to redeem yourself, don't you, girl?"

"Hey!" Joyce echoed.

"Is that scary?" Barbara asked. Quietness draped the room.

"Hmm..., we can see there are other benefits to remaining celibate in relationships." Barbara added.

Grateful that Kim had shared a matter that was so personal and devastating in nature; they were chilled at the thought of the possible health implications. Sue got the conversation back on track.

"Have you, guys considered dating outside of your race?"

Grunting, while almost dropping her teacup, "Oh my, goodness, Sue, that's our second strategy." Barbara shared.

It was agreed; they were ready to be more flexible. Everyone in attendance was forty and over, except for Kim and Vanessa; some were growing weary in their hopes of finding a mate or companion.

"Been there, done that," Joyce led out quickly.

"It was a pleasurable relationship; seriously. The problems we encountered were from our respective races that had their own issues."

"I can't believe I'm agreeing with you, Joyce, Brenda conceded. But I had the same experience; the problems that we faced were with others also. This was some years back, and *people attitudes have changed* you know."

"I never had a problem with interracial dating; no one ever approached me." Janice stated, and fell over laughing; everyone joined her.

"Approached is the *operative word.* We're simply saying to be open-minded in your everyday course of life; it's not to be viewed as going on a [*crusade*] to find men *outside* of your race." Barbara re-affirmed.

Realizing that she was pushing the glass with her next comment, Barbara attempted to lessen the impact. "Not in every case guys, but frequently I think we Black Sisters give our Black Brothers a bad rap when they date women of another race."

Treading carefully, We, hmm..., immediately think its preference based or that they've gone on a mission. When in most instances it's due to their *environment; whether it's work, sports, or a social event*. For me, it was a work setting." She paused, studying the room and waiting for comments.

Voicing unenthusiastically, Sue came clean. "Well..., I guess I have to agree, that's fair; for me it was a social event."

Barbara breathed a sigh of relief. One by one each reminisced on the circumstances that led to their past interracial relationship. Except for Karen, Kim and Janice, it was determined that all had dated outside of their race. Interaction from work and social environments proved to be the direct links to their involvements.

Eager to see the extent of their newfound liberty, Brenda did a heat check. "Who's dated a younger man? That'll definitely open up more possibilities." She asked; giving off a seductive smile, loaded with provocative appeal.

"I'm only twenty-eight." Kim stated. "For me, Um..., I don't know."

Charging in with boldness, Janice broadcasted. "Younger men have never been an issue with me, if the truth be told, they're my first *choice*."

"You go, Janice! I'll consider a few years younger, but it'll depend on their level of maturity." Karen clarified.

Barbara told of the last two guys that she'd dated were five and seven years her junior. One had lied about his age, but because of his maturity level, no problems occurred.

"Barbara's batting two out of two." Kim noted, teasing. "You had your *fun* when you went back into that *world* didn't you, girl."

"I did..., I really did." In a brief after thought," she added. "You know Kim..., I'm still plagued by the residual affects from my so called *fun of worldly living.* If I knew then what I know now, I wouldn't have gone back."

"Amen! I can help you with that one." Karen remarked.

"The way of a transgressor is hard," she nodded, and smiled. (*Proverbs.13:15)*
"You got it." On the edge of her seat, Kim clutched onto every word.

Barbara was younger than Kim was at the time she'd returned to the world. She'd previously shared her *backslidden* account with Michelle and Kim; with hopes of keeping them grounded.

Resting against the couch on the floor, Kim hugged a pillow, expressing feelings of deficiency. "As a teen, and now as an adult, I feel that I've missed out. I've never done the *club scene*, or dated men of the world."

Feeling that she'd led a sheltered life; her parents preferred to call it *a protected life*.

"My Mom said that *sins* from worldly living could become deeply ingrained in our beings. She said that if I feel the need to experience the *club scene;* I should wait and let my husband take me to one."

"Hello!" Barbara echoed. "She's right; I share the exact sentiments as a mother. Your Mom and I collaborated on that one, Kim. Our situation is a little different, you've developed a personal relationship with Christ Kim; and that wasn't the case for me." Barbara expounded.

"Oh, I knew my behaviors were outside the will of God for my life, but I hadn't made him, *Lord* over my life as you have. With that said, your *accountability level would be great."*

"I know..., you're right." Kim uttered, in a feel sorry for yourself tone "I'm without excuse, I was born in the *word*, I had a bib that said, *"I love Jesus."* I'm kidding, guys. I think my feelings are consistent to Karen's bouts of discouragement, the grass looking greener on the other side." Kim admitted.

"Michelle and I have these talks all... the time. We laugh about being *eighty years old;* sittin in *rocking chairs* still complaining that we never went to a *"night club."* They roared with laughter. Cackling loudly, Kim rolled in the floor with a pillow cradled to her stomach, resembling a woman that's in need of some *Midol's*.

"Karen, we need to share our "*motto scripture*" with Kim."

"Exactly! Chew and meditate on *Psalms 37:1, 2,* it'll get you back on track, in a hurry." Karen assured.

Sympathetic to Kim's statement, Barbara didn't want to provide Kim with a false sense of security, thinking that's its okay to have your *fun* and not suffer any consequences. She was confident that Kim was only experiencing discouragement.

Seated in her favorite place on the floor; Barbara clapped her hands to get them back on point. "Now, back to the younger men topic. My preference is seven years younger, my limit is nine. I'm open to meeting men my age, but men my age don't appear to be *into me*, they generally go for Kim and Michelle's age group. I'm usually more attracted by younger men." She explained, in a moping tone.

"You're right, Barbara." Brenda agreed. "When Morgan and I are out, men in our age group are giving her the eye, she's twenty-two. You know guys, I was never open to dating younger men until I signed up for an internet dating site. To my surprise, younger men were the only ones that responded to my profile. As Karen stated, it depends on their level of maturity. I'll go a little younger than Barbara, ten to twelve years is my limit."

"Whoo—hoo!" They shouted. Sounding surprised, Barbara remarked. "That's way younger, Brenda." Brenda didn't look her age, so attracting the interest of men twelve years her junior was a realistic option for her. She's forty-two; she works hard to keep her dress size in a range from sized six to eight. Being an Administrative Assistant; *she loved the dress for success look.*

"Since we're clear with our agenda for the upcoming year, Barbara said, "Let's consider journaling our experiences. I've kept one for a few years now; I think we've dealt with some pretty realistic issues here today. Since the brunch is turning into a trend; we can bring our journals and compare."

"That sounds like fun." Karen, and everyone agreed.

"Let's end with Prayer, *Lord Jesus, we thank you…*

Pleased with their topics of conversations for the day, Barbara was especially elated with the privilege to talk about their personal relationship with Christ. The opportunity to witness couldn't have gone better.

The Lord used Karen to demonstrate his faithfulness when seasoned Christian's own up to their periods of *discouragement.* Her transparency became a source of strength for Brenda and the girls. Barbara, Karen, and Kim were equally excited about their *quest* to find their mates.

In past years, they'd never exercised any initiative to see what choices or options that were available to them. As Joyce stated, they needed to branch out. Realistically, they knew that the chances of them meeting their mate in *their place of worship* was a slim to none possibility.

Each had their list of specified conditions and principles of what they were looking for in their Godly man. In the final analysis, only God would know the scope of their *liberalism.*

Chapter 2

Fifteen minutes late, Karen Lynn Harding dashed into the parking lot to find Michael and Coach Hansen sitting on his SUV, laughing and talking.

Apologizing copiously, she approached them. "I'm so sorry, please forgive me; we got carried away with our topics of conversations today."

"No, problem! It provided me the chance to meet you; I see you at the games and practices, and then you disappear." Bill remarked, teasing her. *If she only knew; I've dreamed of this opportunity.*

Karen smiled, lowering her head, admitting shame. She was surprised to learn that he'd noticed her coming and going.

"Is it that apparent?" Showing a half moon smile, "I'd plan on meeting with you." Michael suddenly remembered that they'd never met and introduced them. Extending his hand to her, they exchanged greetings. "Please, call me Bill."

"Terrific, you can call me Karen." Michael had mentioned earlier that he was hungry, since Karen was tardy; Bill hoped to spark a tiny guilt complex to gain her acceptance to dinner.

Glancing at his watch, "Its dinner time for me; would you guys like to join me?" Waiting anxiously for this moment, the timing was perfect; everyone had cleared the parking lot, giving him the privacy that he needed.

With arched eyebrows, she smiled and looked in Michael's direction for his approval. "Sounds good to me, can we, Mom, please?"

"Sure, am I forgiven for being late?

"Late? Who's late? You can follow me to avoid a return trip for your car. I hear you love Chinese food, Karen."

"Do I!" In route to the restaurant Michael went on a little snooping expedition. "Mom, I think Coach likes you, he always looks for you. If he can't find you in the bleachers, he'll ask, "Is your Mom here, today?"

"Oh, he's just considerate; he knows you're being raised in a single parent household."

"No! Mom, he asked the type of food you prefer." Karen was impressed that Bill had inquired about her cuisine preferences.

"What did you tell him?"

"I told him you love Chinese, What if he's really interested in you, Mom?" Michael was adamant in his innocent attempt to hook-up his Mom with his Coach-Mentor.

"Michael..., you're reading too much into this, the man's only concerned for you."

Michael turned to her with a taken aback look in his eyes. "Excuse—you; I am... not... the only player on this team that's being *raised* by their, Mother."

Responding with such an out pouring of passion, Karen had no recourse; she was forced to take a softer line. "Alright..., I'm sorry, let's enjoy the fellowship."

At age fifteen, Michael was a good candidate to be a great basketball player. In addition to being a team player, he received good grades. Standing 6'2 and growing, he was destined to be the height of Karen's father. After excelling in the game; soon he'd become a *starter.*

If Michael assessments were correct; it'd be a plus. Karen had to admit; Bill was quite a catch. Justifiably tall in stature, he looked to be about 6'5, slender form, with striking blue eyes. His silky black hair had been overtaken by shades of brown. He positively bore characteristics that she admired.

For some time she'd entertained the idea of looking outside of her race for her husband. Growing up in the suburbs; she'd attended school with a diverse group of people. In spite of her *quest* commitment with the girls; she still maintained a trace of reservation.

Within minutes they pulled into the parking lot of the restaurant. Bill hurriedly parked his car and ran over to escort them. Once inside, the owner's son greeted them. "Good evening! Mr. Hansen, it's so good to see you and your guests." Watching Lin grow into a fine young man, Bill was happy to see him. He helped his parents when he wasn't away at college.

"It's a pleasure to see you too, Lin." For years, this remained one of Bill's favorite restaurants. The food and the service were excellent; he hoped Karen enjoyed it also. Offering greetings to Karen and Michael, Lin ushered them to their table.

Since becoming an event planner; she'd acquired an eye for detail, and was impressed with the authentic Chinese Décor. Karen's cheery and pleasant smile assured Bill that she was pleased thus far.

Shifting her focus to his irresistible blue eyes, which were staring directly at her; she hoped that her edgy demeanor wasn't too apparent. Excited that she was on a date, but with Michael present; she couldn't classify it as a *real date.* Attempting to break the ice, she asked. "Do you come here often?

Rubbing his hand across his mid-section, he smiled. "At least once a week or more, I try to stay away as much as possible."

Karen smiled at his hand gesture. "I know what you mean, if it was up to me; I could eat Chinese at least three times a week."

Karen was pleased that Bill had invited them to dinner. *Could Michael be correct; is he really interested in me.* Noticing him on and off the court during games and practices, she did find him appealing. Based on his interactions with the boys, he appeared to be a compassionate man as well. Michael definitely liked him.

"What about you Michael, what's your favorite food or eatery?"

"Oh, that's easy Coach, cheeseburgers and fries. I like Chinese too." He voiced, willingly with a big grin. Bill nodded.

"Somehow, I knew fries would be included." Bill was delighted that things were going smoothly. By Karen's now sedate countenance; he sensed that she was feeling more relaxed.

The waiter appeared with menus, tea, hot soup and wontons. Since Bill was an expert with the menu, Karen asked Bill to make recommendations for his favorite entrées; he was thrilled that she trusted his choices. In addition to Bill's suggestions, they each selected an individual favorite for adventure purposes; collectively they chose a new entrée.

Spending over two hours dining and fellowshipping, the evening couldn't have gone better if he'd planned it. Karen and Michael headed for the freeway leading to their home.

Resuming his matchmaking efforts, "see Mom, I told you Coach likes, you." He said, smiling and teasing her.

"Okay, I think you maybe correct Michael." Agreeing reluctantly.

"What do you think of him, Mom?"

"I like him fine; he's considerate, generous, and easy on the eyes." Peeking to get Michael's reaction; she gave him a healthy looking smile. Michael was on a mission; but Karen needed time to process the recent occurrence.

"Does that mean you like him, Mom?" Ignoring his question, Karen did a little *prying* of her own.

"Michael, are you saying that you wouldn't mind me *dating* your Coach?" Instantly turning to her with widen-eyes, "Of course not, Mom. You said you only want to date or marry a Christian, he's a Christian and a widow; plus he's cool." Offering up a wide mouth grin.

"A widow—?"

In a washed out tone, he replied. "Yes, his wife passed away three years ago of cancer."

"Oh, how sad!" Bearing a sympathetic face, she looked in his direction. Perking up; in full anticipation, "Coach is a big believer in God, like us, he goes to bible study; that's why on Wednesday practice ends at five thirty."

"I thought Coach Wilson was the head Coach?"

"He is; he volunteers his time to help Coach Wilson. They attend the same church, and they're old college buddies. Coach Hansen is a former NBA player, also."

"Really!"

"Yeah, he had arthroscopic surgery on his knee for an injury that he'd sustained in his first year of playing; it wasn't successful; so it ended his career. Now he devotes his time to helping young boys, he's a nice guy Mom. He's sort of a *local celebrity;* he owns an insurance agency of some sort. He's invited the team to his church later in the week for a youth rally; can we go, please, Mom?"

"We will see, Michael; I'm happy that you have a Coach who's a Christian." This was a big plus in Karen's eyes.

With great hesitancy, "Mom..., ah," he paused, electing to cautiously select his words. "Have you ever dated anyone of a different race?" *This boy is covering all grounds; he should've been at the brunch today.*

"No! I haven't sweetie." She spoke with apprehension, shocked by his line of questioning; she wondered where he was headed.

"I'm certainly not opposed to the possibility if the right man comes along." That was music to Michael's ears, he remained quiet the rest of the way home.

Karen's candor had given him a reason to hope. She wasn't about to disclose their *"quest"* with her fifteen year old son. She wondered if meeting Bill was *destiny;* since they'd agreed to be open-mind to interracial dating. Assured that dating Bill would not pose any problems from her son; she felt relief.

William Jefferson (Bill) Hansen was ecstatic after having dinner with Karen and Michael. A while since he'd been in the company of a woman, he was excited about the fact that she too was a Christian. After realizing his attraction to her, he started to make subtle inquiries to Michael.

Since the death of his wife Sherrie, he'd consumed his life with his church ministry, coaching, and mentoring. Other single mothers would invite Bill to their home for dinner, generally with a personal agenda in mind. Obsessed with her career, Karen hadn't taken the time to even notice Bill in that way.

Michael played a huge role in Bill's continued interest in Karen. Bill knew values and characteristics as Michael's didn't just evolve; this made Karen even more appealing to him. He couldn't dismiss the fact that *race* may be a factor for her, or the interest simply may not be mutual.

Growing up in a diverse environment, his home was in the center of a Black and Asian family. Race had never been an issue for him, or his parents. Most of his best college and NBA friends were Black; Bill was the minority.

Recalling a slight blush during a shared stare with Karen, he felt a little more confident after tonight. Convinced by the fact that he'd Michael's approval, his father presented new concerns. Observing him at games and some practices; he wasn't particularly friendly toward Bill, and felt that he could pose a problem.

Bill was delighted with his decision to volunteer his time to train young boys in his favorite sport. The insurance agency venture proved to be a wise investment. At age forty-four, he was semi-retired.

Being self-employed provided him the flexibility needed for his boys. Having produced a book of business that exceeded millions, upon retirement, he planned to transfer it to his Son.

At five o'clock a.m., Barbara Jean Keller was wide-awake. Enjoying her usual routine of quiet time, and a cup of hot tea, she reflected on the conversations from the brunch as she logged on to her computer, and gazed from the window.

Some of the brunch topics discussed stirred up many memories for her, some good, and some not so good. Kim's statement concerning her return to the world and having a good time; reminded her of God's mercy and grace that he'd extended to her in rearing Michelle.

Embracing the same sentiments and emotions of deprivation expressed by Kim; coming from the south, she'd led a sheltered life also. Becoming pregnant in her first year of college, her church going experience hadn't been conducive to fostering a personal relationship with Christ. Buried in her thoughts, she *reflected on her past…*

In spite of her love and devotion to Michelle, when she was eight or so, Barbara began to experience feelings of lack. She'd purposed, I'm *gonna have some fun in life.* Eventually, Barbara Jean did have her fun. Fun to her translated to *not going to church*.

Having a clearer understanding of God than she'd as a child; nonetheless, she still lacked the knowledge needed for developing a *personal* relationship with Christ.

Believing that she'd lost her mind; her family was okay after they realized that she—wasn't going off the deep end. Deep end to them meant, *drugs*. Her idea of *fun* was limited to dancing at social events, and political fundraisers. She joined the NAACP and attended several of their functions.

Loving to dance, happy hour on Fridays in Jack London Square became a main attraction. After making a conscious decision to lead a life-style that was in direct contradiction to the bible; she couldn't find the value in attending church any longer. Understanding that many would argue the difference, she'd many debates on the matter.

With Michelle secure at her Moms, most times she never arrived home until one or two in the morning. The thought of rising early, and *stumbling* into church *attempting to fool other Christians* didn't appeal, or make much sense to her. Possessing some knowledge of the scriptures; she knew she wasn't deceiving God; she felt that it bordered on mockery.

Making it a priority to keep Michelle in Church attendance, on rare occasions they'd attend early morning services at Michelle's school. In spite of her risky decisions regarding her personal life; she remained committed to providing a stable environment for her. Michelle received a Christian education from grades K-12. *Straddling the fence* wasn't an option for Barbara; it was all or nothing.

For five years, she *"had her fun."* But God had his own agenda and timetable for her life. Michelle began to experience discomfort in her abdomen. Enduring pain consistently for over three months before the doctors were able to isolate it, became too much for Barbara to bear.

Wondering if it were a *sign* from God, out of obedience, she knew it was time to *hop back* on the other side of the *fence*; she did so with no hesitation or resistance. It was later determined that Michelle needed a hernia repair, that was in the mid eighties.

She'd heard that Corinth Baptist was different in the non-traditional sense. From the moment that she entered the sanctuary she liked it. She loved the architectural design, in a circular fashion; it was divided into sections. No matter where you sat in the sanctuary, you were close to the front.

The Sunday that she attended, the Pastor and his wife were on vacation; their Son delivered the message. The devotional period was anything but *traditional*. Divided into groups they *prayed* back the scriptures, engaging participation from everyone; it was definitely an innovative experience for her.

Following a high-spirited praise and worship segment by the praise team and choir; the minister stepped to the podium. Disclosing his text, topic and a little pulpit humor, he went directly into his sermon.

Instructing the congregation to various scriptures to support his topic, she was impressed by his pulpit mannerism and doctrinal knowledge. She recalled being on the edge of her seat during the entire sermon. Being hungry for the word made it all the better.

Appearing to be in his late twenties; he invoked a presence of a far more *seasoned minister.* During his evangelistic appeal, he didn't miss a class; beseeching to the unsaved, the backslidden, assurance of eternal security, and those seeking a church home.

Barbara knew she fell in the backslidden category. Having purposed in her heart to recommit, she wasn't ready to take that presumably *mile* walk to the front of the sanctuary.

Unrelenting in his plea, at one point he stated *"I know there's someone else."* Requesting the organist to play softly, Barbara knew she was one of whom he was referring. In light of his persistence, she remained seated.

She resolved that the decision she'd made in her heart counted most, confident that she'd take that walk later, and she did. Thoroughly convinced that if his Son was a chip off the *block;* she knew she'd ultimately enjoy the Pastor as well.

Completely different from previous churches that she'd visited or attended, Corinth Baptist was an entirely new experience. The Minister, whom they lovingly referred to as *Junior,* announced *"All ladies interested in attending the women's retreat should meet to the right of the sanctuary following service."*

Dashing over, she sat in the last row listening and admiring the women in their enthusiasm. Waiting for the meeting to adjourn, she asked if non-members could attend. She received a favorable yes from one of the facilitators named Lynn, whose skin looked as *smooth* as the taste of a Hershey's milk chocolate symphony bar, with long lustrous hair; and a gorgeous smile that was sure to make any visitor feel *welcome.* She was so happy to be amongst God's people; she whipped out her checkbook and registered.

The retreat would mark an era of new beginnings for her. Topics extended to commitments and re-dedicating their lives to Christ, which entailed getting rid of strongholds, excess baggage, and *unequally yoked relationships?*

It became a platform for repentance, renewed minds and hearts; enhancing old friendships, in addition to the formation of new ones. Barbara knew this was the place for her and Michelle. Pastor Crenshaw was a man with a *vision*, a vision inspired by God to grow, and disciple his people.

Challenging you in every area of your Christian walk, the curriculum consisted of foundational classes of Survival kit, Church membership, Lessons on Assurance, Christian Living, Discipleship, Levels of 1-IV, Evangelism101-106, Master Life, Bible Study, Sunday school, and Street Witnessing.

Having separate ministries for teens, young adults, children's and seniors; it was a ministry that invoked life changes for those who took heed, and there were many.

For the first time in her church going experience, until Wisdom Fellowship, she'd witnessed Christians that were serious in their *obedience to the scriptures.* The evidence reflected in their lifestyles, the choice of their mates for marriage, and their *evangelism and witnessing* efforts. They were fondly referred to as "*Corinth University,*" because of their broad curriculum of study that *pioneered* in the teaching, and evangelism ministry.

In excitement, she and Michelle enrolled in as many classes as their weekly schedule would accommodate. Serious about her new commitment, she knew some house cleaning was in order.

Facing an enormous task in severing an existing relationship, she knew it had to end; it became the temptation of her life. Barbara hadn't acquired much spiritual wisdom at that point; yet, she knew you didn't play with fire.

By mid August, Michelle had completed her camping excursions for the summer; this gave her the confidence she needed. By keeping Michelle home with no weekend sleepovers, she knew she could make it. In her limited amount of faith, she was counting on God to honor the *intent* and *desires* of her heart to be obedient.

Each time her significant other would call for a date, she'd say she'd an outing with Michelle; it became increasingly easier for her to resist his charm, and for her to remind him of her new *commitment* to God.

Because she'd been one of Satan's all stars; she knew her fight would be great. In a *"backslidden"* position also, he later realized that his fight was no longer only with Barbara's *flesh*, but, that she was being covered by the Holy Spirit as well. By God's mercy, grace, and claiming scriptures like, *I Corth 10:13, and Phil 4:13*, she *persevered* over six-teen years ago.

After three and a half years, she'd completed Evangelism 101-106 & Discipleship Levels1-IV including the foundational classes. Her area of service extended to an intake counselor, street witnessing, the home visitation team and a reporter for the newsletter.

Barbara's phone rang, cringing and grabbing it, she answered abruptly. "Hello!" With rudeness in her tone.

"Hi Barbara, this is Kim."

"Oh..., hi Kim, girl...you startled me." She uttered with thankfulness in her voice.

"Remember the patient I mentioned to you that needs a power of attorney executed?"

"Yes, yes, I do."

"Do you think you can make it in this morning to see her? It's not an emergency; she's not scheduled for surgery for two days."

"Um..., let me see, Kim." Pausing to check her appointments.

"No, I have to meet an appraiser at a client's home this morning, then I have to go to the Home Depot. Hmm..., my calendar is full for today; will tomorrow around mid-morning be okay?"

"Great! I'll leave her name at the nurse's station."

"Sounds good. Kim, I'm getting ready to sign up with the Christian dating website this morning."

"Cool, oh my goodness let me know how it goes. This is going to be so much fun." Kim stated, with excitement. Committed to her work as well as her patients; Kim assisted them with concerns that extended outside the realm of her duties.

Holding an MBA, she's an RN at Carson General Hospital. Due to the hideous congestion from commuting, she recently purchased a condo within minutes to the hospital; she rents her home in the suburbs.

Somewhat shy, and because of her relationship with Christ, she's led a careful lifestyle. Thinking the world of her Dad, she desires her husband to be *"just like him."* She remains Daddy's little girl. Not expecting to find a *virgin* as her, then again she didn't want anyone that'd made too many trips around the block.

Her Dad assured her that the secret to finding a good husband was to find a man that *loved God.* Sounding foreign to her as a young girl growing up, now she related it to the love that she has for Christ. Kim knew it was her love and reverence for God that had constrained her, especially in college.

Recognizing the crucial role a power of attorney played in an individual's affairs, Barbara was happy to assist a patient. Being a notary was one of many positions that she filled. After Michelle graduated college and married, Barbara didn't feel the restriction to continue in careers that she *dreaded.*

Working in sales she'd experienced one too many companies gone bankrupt, or being terminated for her strong principles on honesty and integrity. On the flipside of working in sales, she discovered that she could earn as much or more income without a degree; justifying *suspending* college after two unsuccessful attempts to complete. Juggling work, and transporting Michelle to her Mom's in the evening; exhaustion always became a factor before the end of a semester.

Equipped with various licensures, they afforded her business ventures to work as an independent contractor. Her notary license permitted her to work as a certified loan document signer, her property & casualty license authorized her to market auto and homeowners' insurance. Her life and disability license provided her to offer insurance and financial products. Her realtor's license she used to market reverse mortgages to seniors.

Before logging on to her computer, she talked to God. *Lord, I'm going to sign up with this Christian Website. I feel justified in my actions, what I feel and what you want are two different things. So, Father, I give you permission to override my desires if they become a conflict for your will for my life. In Jesus name, I pray, amen."* Checking herself. *Girl, you're only signing up to correspond with someone, calm down.*

Logging in, she listed her profile after completing other relevant information and questionnaire. It read. *Christian woman seeking friendship with a serious Christian man, open to the possibility to a more serious level in the future. Will provide photo and occupation later, presently interested in developing a friendship based on topics of personal interest, spiritual growth, future goals.* Choosing the name Zest, it captured her mood at that moment.

Chapter 3

Enjoying the scenic route on a sunny December morning, Barbara had completed her due diligence with the appraiser and was in route to the Home Depot. She loved the Bay Area, its home to the Oakland Raiders, Oakland Athletics, and the Golden State Warriors. Across the Bay is San Francisco, the second most densely populated major American city after New York, its home to the Forty-Niners and the Giants.

In the South Bay, renowned technological giants such as Google, Cisco Systems, and Intel made their home in Silicon Valley. The year is ***1999;*** interest rates are at an all time low. The median price of a home in the San Francisco Bay Area is ***$417,000***. The market had created *unprecedented levels of paper wealth,* predominantly due to technology stocks.

Dabbling in the stock market also, Barbara Jean was too chicken to let her investment ride for a long-term return. Benefiting from a prosperous year in sales, she'd gone on her NBA Cruise (National Basketball Association).

As the *New Millennium* approached, many feared the uncertainty of the *Y2K.* Stockpiling food and survival supplies, people were standing guard waiting to see the outcome at midnight on December 31.

Barbara was determined to build a toy chest for her five-year-old granddaughter, Jordyn. Earlier in the year she'd taken a keen interest in interior design, upholstery, and furniture refinishing; that added to her excitement level today.

At eight-thirty a.m., she was happy to see the parking lot was scarce, affording her the privilege to browse without the hustle and bustle of other patrons

At Christmas time, the Home Depot was a popular spot to purchase gifts for men. Visiting the store frequently, she was familiar with the store layout.

Still contemplating her wood selection, she stood with her finger resting under her chin. Favoring the cedar, she stroked a beam as she admired the smoothness. From her peripheral vision, she sensed that the man standing next to her was looking at her, and not the wood.

Turning to acknowledge his presence, she looked into the face of a man with the warmest and inviting pair of brown eyes that you ever want to see. Wearing an expression of curiosity, "What are you going to build?" Stunned by his question, after a brief pause, "I'm attempting to build a toy chest for my granddaughter." She answered, with an inkling of doubt in her tone.

With raised eyebrows, he smiled, "Is the cedar your choice of wood?"

"You know..., I think so; it's really growing on me, especially the fragrance." "Nice choice, it does generate a nice aroma." Nodding and smiling in approval. Suddenly, her wood selection had escalated to *difficulty.* His lean but toned physique had impaired her focus. Good at judging men's height, he'd to be at least 6'2. She was 5'4, her Dad was 6'6; she remembered exactly where she stood against him.

Wearing blue jeans and tan laced boots didn't take from his cool and clean-shaven presence. His Houston Rocket baseball cap and gold shirt suited well with his even toned brown skin.

Figuring his questions weren't from a snooping standpoint, she asked. "Your approval of the wood, is it professionally recommended, or a personal preference?"

"Both, I'm a general contractor." He spoke, in confidence as he handed her his business card.

Barbara's dream had come to fruition; she loved to fantasize about the future. One of her reoccurring dreams entailed meeting a building contractor while shopping at the Home Depot. Since her newly acquired interests in furniture refinishing, she felt that it would be a complimentary match.

Battling off choking, she eventually asked. "Are you a residential or commercial builder?"

"Mainly, residential."

Dying of anticipation, she had to talk herself calm. *Relax girl, the man is probably married.* With that possibility in mind, she settled down. Just in case, she was happy that she'd taken special time in getting dressed.

Glad to be back in her blue jeans that were once too small, she also enjoyed comfort in her burgundy boots, and leather jacket. Carefree with her hair, she'd just shampooed and blow dried it; giving it a nice lift and bounce.

"How will you cut the wood?" Distracted by his question, she paused before answering him; she was reading the dimensions from the tag on the wood.

"Here, I'm gonna have it cut here, in the store." Again, he smiled, and nodded with approval.

"Is this your first attempt at building?"

Now aware that he was a professional builder, she became *jumpy.* "Yes, and it probably will be my last."

"I'm so, sorry, my name is Gary."

"I'm Barbara Jean; exchanging pleasantries, and smiles, Gary extended his hand for a shake. "You can't get discouraged this soon."

"No! I'm only kidding, I'm actually eager to see the results. Well, I guess I'd better locate a dolly to get this wood over to the cutting station."

"Please, use this one; I only have a few items, it's large enough to hold your boards." He'd purchased a drill of some sort, nails and a small can of paint. She thanked him as they began loading the planks onto his dolly.

"Thank you for the use of your dolly, and your help, this wood is—heavy."

"You're welcome; you're gonna need it to carry the wood to the checkout counter, and your car."

Uttering a nervous snicker, "Oops, I guess I will, you can tell I do this all the time."

Smiling, "Aw..., you know what you're doing."

Carefully planning every detail, she knew the number of wood pieces needed, the diameter to cut them, the number of nails, screws, and hinges. She'd even sketched a diagram; presently, her new friend's presence had altered her focus.

"I'm in no hurry." Gary happily assured her. "I don't mind waiting for you."

"Are you sure—?" She asked; sounding more like, *you'd do that for me?* I can get store help."

With assurance and re-affirming any doubts, "I'm positive; I'm intrigued with your endeavor." He stood relaxed, leaning against the counter, with his arms loosely folded.

After thanking him again, she proceeded to give instructions to the cutting clerk. Amazed by Gary's overwhelming act of kindness; she was experiencing an arduous time in containing her poise. *Wow, he's so nice and attentive; a married man wouldn't be helping a woman he doesn't know in this manner. Hmm..., maybe he's not married after all. So, is he hitting on me, or is he intrigued as he said, this is his craft? This is way too much, I sign up with a dating website, and hours later; I'm meeting a man at the Home Depot, this is too weird."* Gary had definitely taken a keen interest in Barbara's project.

"Where will the building process take place?" He inquired, still at the cutting station. She felt as if she was his new *Apprentice*.

"In my back yard, I have tables out there; they'll come in handy for sorting out the materials." He nodded, and smiled.

Returning a restrained smile while trying to keep a straight face, she couldn't deny her attraction to this man, or the attentiveness that he'd showed toward her. *Would you like to help me build it?* She thought. With the fear that he'd read her mind; she felt her cheeks *flush,* and forced a quick but phony smile in his direction.

After paying for their purchases, Gary took charge and pushed the dolly out the door and to the parking lot.

"Which way?"

"Straight a head." Since she'd arrived early, she'd parked near the entrance of the store; providing little time to chat. Grumbling silently, *of all the days of coming here, today I get a park directly in front of the store.*

Pointing to her black and white older model Beamer, Gary took complete charge of loading the boards. Enjoying the attention, she watched him carefully place the boards in one by one, appearing to stretch every second, and that was fine with her. After consciously concluding that there was some attraction on his part, her heart beat at a steadier pace, and her composure became more tranquil.

"Would you like to join me for coffee or tea? He asked, as he closed the trunk of her car, and brushed the dust from his hands.

Pitching him a surprised look, he detected her facial expression, "I apologize, I'm so sorry for assuming that you're single. I'm outdated; I always look for a ring."

Barbara laughed, softly, "its okay," she waved her hand. "You assumed correctly, I'm not married." *It's starting to look a lot like Christmas.* She joked silently.

"Neither am I," they both breathed a sigh of relief.

"Tea sounds good!"

"I'll follow you." Barbara said.

"Great, let me get my truck." Pushing the dolly further down the parking lot to his truck, he unloaded his items.

After entering her car, she made sure the windows were securely shut before screaming in disbelief that she'd met a man; and was about to meet him for tea.

Now in need of more self-coaching, *calm down, Barbara Jean, I need to find out more about him, I will not start assuming"*

Finally, alone, she'd wrestled and tugged with the question that'd lurked in the back of her mind since she met him. The big *'C'* word, is he a *Christian?* For now, she'd enjoy the fascination.

Needing to check her appointment book, with no Gary in sight, she jumped from the car to retrieve it from the trunk. While scanning the book, Gary drove up behind her driving a black Hummer.

Walking toward him, she took notice that he was wearing a tan leather jacket, and that he'd removed his baseball cap; revealing his low trimmed haircut, that she loved. *How much better could it get?*

Glancing at her watch, she remembered that she'd cleared her day to work on the toy chest. Bearing a frown, "I'm sorry Gary, do you mind terribly if we get together another day, or later today? I'm getting a late start with my project; my plans were to complete it before Jordyn returns this evening. With her present; I'll never finish it." She explained, and dropped her hands to her side, expressing regret.

Pouring on the charm, "Only if you convince me that you're not trying to get rid of me." *Get rid of him, is he kidding, I want to take him home with me to help."*

Desiring to assure him that she wasn't brushing him off, looking him straight in the eye, "Of course not! You can come and help me build it if you like; is that persuasive enough for you?" Rusty with flirting skills, she thought she'd better top it off with a fine looking smile. Fearful of rejection, Gary had wavered in offering his services.

"Wow! You read my mind." Eyes bulging with excitement. "I'd love to see this through. I'd hoped you'd ask for my help, you lead the way." He spoke, exhibiting a sincere interest in her project and her. *Yes! She read me completely.* Forty years old, never married, and no children, Gary was equally relieved to learn that Barbara was not married. He'd done well as a business owner, becoming a General Contractor had been a rigorous process. His father and uncles were all construction workers in the south, overseeing and building their homes; Gary always assisted them.

His Dad desired to become a General Contractor also; unfortunately it wasn't an option for him in Georgia at the time. Gary majored in business at college; his father insisted that he and his siblings earn their degrees before leaving home. Since a kid, Gary knew he wanted to become a Builder; it was in his DNA.

After earning his BA in Business Administration, he moved to California to work as an apprentice in construction. His goal was to get into a *Journeyman* program; unlike his Dad, he was successful in his efforts.

Before exiting the parking lot, she asked Gary to wait. Walking to his truck, she informed him that she needed to make a call home to let *them* know that she was bringing company. In case he became lost in traffic, she handed him one of her business cards. There was no one at Barbara's home; for safety reasons she wanted him to think that there were others present.

Since they'd be in the back yard, she was content in her decision, especially since Michelle would be arriving shortly there after. Thinking the Home Depot had to be an ideal location to meet a man, still, she had to exercise carefulness as if she'd met him over the internet. Praying continuously, God *please let him know you, please let him be a Christian.*

Dialing her cell phone, she called Michelle screaming. "Michelle, Wake up! Wake up!" Giving her a play-by-play of what was taking place. Michelle, now fully conscious became just as excited.

Often, Barbara felt that Michelle desired for her to be married more than she did. She knew her Mom had some definite standards for the man she desired. Largely, that he'd be a mature Christian, and serious about his walk with the Lord.

Because she hadn't dated in years, she was proud of her for not compromising her principles. In her *teen years,* she'd observed her Mom never dating. She remembered her being strict; however, but, she was fair, applying the same strictness to her life. Michelle recalled her never watching "*R*" rated movies, and so, Michelle could only see "*G*" and "*PG*" ones, she taught by example.

Vividly recollecting being angry for not being able to attend various functions as other kids; she passionately conveyed her frustrations to her when she reached adulthood. Since adulthood and marriage, she later realized that her Mom was still a young woman when she'd graduated high school, therefore, finally appreciating, and comprehending the significance of how she'd raised her. Like all kids, she thought her Mom was *born grown.*

Throwing back the covers; Michelle hit the shower. She'd spent the night with Barbara's sister, Mildred. Giving her Mom time to get home; she'd have a cup of tea with her Aunt.

From experience, she chose not to divulge the happenings to her aunt; the idea of her meeting a man would've caused way too much excitement, too soon.

Barbara's cell phone rang while in route home. "Hello!"

"Hi, this is, Karen, can you talk?"

"Can I! Karen, you're not going to believe what's happening, right now, girl."

"What?" Karen asked, with excitement. Barbara tells of her occurrence with Gary. Beyond surprised, "Are you serious?"

"Yes, he's following me as we speak."

Dumbfounded. "Oh my, Lord, you literally picked up a man at the store?" She said, innocently.

Holding tightly to the steering wheel to keep from falling from laughing, Barbara was glad that she was wearing her earpiece. "You're being silly girl; I couldn't pass up this opportunity." He's a Building Contractor Karen, and he's going to help me build Jordyn's toy chest, can you believe it. I'm cautious, but I'm not stupid." She said, with high-pitched enthusiasm, causing Karen's excitement to rocket.

"What's he like, is he cute, is he a Christian?"

"Look, girl, I don't have that many details; we just met, Karen, is this any different from internet dating?"

Giggling, "I guess not, since you know nothing about him."

"It happened so fast Karen; we haven't had a chance to talk. We were going to have tea, but I'm late getting started with this toy chest. I guess I did pick him up, ha, or him, me? Are you calling me from home?"

"Yep!"

"Great, get a pen, let's do a little probing. Take down this name, and number, Gary Lloyd Russell; go into the State of California Board of Contractors, and look up his license number or name." Needing more details regarding his business, she started her investigative inquiry.

"Oh good, I'm at my desk now, you know I love playing detective, girl. Inspector Harding is on the case. Okay! I'm in." She announced.

"There's tons of Russell's ..., let's see, here. Gary, Gary..., Russell, I got it. Gary Lloyd Russell, doing business as Russell Construction, licensed since 1989, expires in January 2002, shows a business address in Pleasanton. He's a General Contractor Barbara, did you know that?"

"I know Karen, that's why I'm bringing him home with me, girl."

"Does he live in Pleasanton, also?"

"I have no clue, you know as much about him as I do. I know he's not a "*felon*," well, not a convicted one anyway."

"How do you know that?

"Because..., the State of California can't issue licenses to convicted *felons*."

"You're too much, I'm not worried; knowing you, you've already prayed over him. My concern should probably be for him."

"I'm signing off, silly, we're home now, come over later."

"You know I will, I need details, Goodbye."

Still at her computer, Karen sparked a dialogue with the Lord. *What's going on here, Lord? Barbara meets Gary, Bill takes me to dinner. As soon as we began to avail ourselves to meet someone, things start to happen. Is this you giving us a sign not to do the internet?* Her phone rang.

"Hi Karen, this is, Bill."

"Hi Bill, I was going to call to thank you for a lovely evening, it was awfully kind of you to take us to dinner."

"The pleasure was mine Karen; maybe we can do it again soon. Did Michael mention the youth rally at my church on Saturday night?"

"Yes, he did, I'm going to let him come." Bill wanted her present as well. "Will you be coming?"

"Yes, of course?" Spoken with hesitancy.

"Fantastic! I'll pick you up?"

"Perfect, I welcome the opportunity to be chauffeured.

"Let me give you my phone number just in case, I'll call for you around five-thirty."

Not realizing that he'd expected her to attend, she was surprised, but played it off; tickled that he'd included her. Things were moving a little fast for her; however, she felt the holidays were shaping up for them.

When directing Gary to her back yard, Barbara's cell phone rang.

"Hello! This is Barbara."

"Barbara Jean, this is Walter, how are you?"

"I'm good Walter, how are you, what's up?"

"I need your services in the morning; I have some client's coming to my office for a nine o'clock signing, can you help me? It's a purchase and a second; I need someone who knows what they're doing. Mr. works in the City, if he can't make it, we'll need to schedule for tomorrow evening."

"Only for you Walter, that's fine. I can go to their home or meet at your office, whichever works best for them. What are you doing Friday night?" She asked.

"Nothing that really matters."

"My friend is having her annual Christmas dinner party, would you like to come?"

"Sure, thanks Barbara Jean! Will any cuties be there?" Ignoring his question. "I'll give you the details in the morning Walter, later." She said, with a soft chuckle.

Walter Douglas Hines, entrepreneur, mortgage broker, realtor.

After completing the funding on a home, the clients desired to be in it for Christmas. For their convenience, Walter had the title company courier the documents to his office. Networking on previous loans, and real estate transactions, Walter knew he could count on his friend, and business associate, Barbara

Jean. Earning a reputation for being a consummate professional, he maintained strong principles on honesty and integrity. Having lived in the community all his life, he'd cultivated many ties; that were instrumental in his entrepreneurial success.

In spite of his business and social status, Walter still fell short of contentment within his personal life. He masked it well with material toys, keeping busy at the office, and good works in his church, and *women.*

Always appreciative, Barbara Jean would bring him Christian literature in workbook form or her notes from bible study or sermons. Discerning a genuine spirit about him, she made it a point to listen, and offer him encouragement and counsel whenever possible; in addition, he was easy on the eyes.

Arriving shortly after her Mom and Gary, behaving as a kid; Michelle ran to her Mom's bedroom to spy into the back yard. Lurking by the window, she watched Barbara Jean remove the power drill from its case; she'd purchased it as a Christmas gift to herself last year. *Wow, Mom looks great, the weight loss shows."* Michelle hadn't seen her Mom interact with a man on a personal level since she was a kid; she smiled and nodded in support.

Taking pleasure in her subjects, Michelle chose to monitor a little while longer. Following suite with Barbara, Michelle's mind began to speculate the same as her Mom's did. *I wonder if he's a Christian, which would be too, cool. He certainly seems to have some definite interest in her, the ultimate question is, what his interest is?"* Checking herself, *Oh, Michelle, let's think positive, there are nice guys still looking to get married.*

Previously feeling a sense of pride after sketching and designing the toy chest, now she was embarrassed to present it to Gary. Assured that it was adequate for her understanding, after learning that Gary was a professional; she now doubted her abilities.

Handing it to him with hesitation, "Here's my diagram," with apprehension, and tension in her tone. Reminded of her school days, she felt as if she was turning in a late project, or report to her school teacher.

Bearing a serious expression, he studied it intently. Fearful of his disapproval, she stood as stiff as her cedar boards. Noticing her edginess, he smiled in his attempt to alleviate her stress.

"Relax..., you did good, you want it to extend across the foot of the bed, I got it, it makes sense."

"Exactly," she voiced, with zeal and surprise. Barbara Jean was as happy as a student that'd gotten an "*A*" on a test.

Realizing that her task to build the toy chest was complex, it motivated her even more. She loved challenges, and the sense of fulfillment that she'd felt from previous projects.

At the beginning of the year. she'd re-upholstered two wing tip chairs. Impressed about the outcome, she was blissful to see the results of this project, and feeling blessed to have his assistance.

"Jordyn is not here all the time; so, I want the toys to be out of sight when not in use, and the toy chest to function as a bench seat."

"It will," he assured her. Impressed with her sketching, "I'm in the market for a raring to go Apprentice; I'm looking for women to join my crew." Half teasing her, he said, while smiling.

"Thank you! But, no thank you!" Turning her head, to express emphasis. Aiming to keep him humored. "How about I designate myself as your Honorary Apprentice." Showing a full-sized grin.

"Hey, I think I like the sound of that."

Bringing in his tool belt, and gadgets from his truck, they sorted the materials and tools in the order that she preferred.

Being ever so careful not to overpower her project, Gary asked. "Do we have everything that we need; are you ready to get started?"

"Sure, let me get out of these boots. Would you like something to drink Gary, Water? Juice?"

"Any kind of juice would be fine, thank you."

"I'll be right back."

Dashing into the house, she headed for her bedroom. Thrilled, Michelle continued to look on in approval. Halting abruptly at the door after seeing Michelle seated by the window; grinning like the little girl that she remembered; rendered Barbara speechless; it became a nostalgic moment.

As a single parent, Barbara remained strong-minded that her baby girl wouldn't become a *statistic.* Making good on her determination, she was elated and swollen with pride over Michelle's educational and career accomplishments.

Before accepting a pharmacy recruitment position with a major healthcare organization, she'd worked in banking as a branch manager, and a recruiter for one of the technology giants in Silicon Valley.

"Michelle, girl, what are you doing in here?" Still grinning from both corners, "Spying on you and Mr. Gary interacting, he appears to like you."

"And what are you basing your conclusions on, Missy?"

"Hmm, the attention he's giving to you and your project."She's smiling and motioning with her hands. "His facial expressions when he looks at you, the way he smiles at you, need I continue." Dismissing her coolness, she was sopping wet by suspense. She blurted. "Is he a, Christian?"

"I don't know, Michelle." Now on the floor, Barbara struggled to remove her boots.

"I had this conversation with Karen; the opportunity hasn't presented itself, okay..." She responded, with a hunch of frustration.

"I know it sounds crazy honey, but all I know is his name, he's a general contractor, and he's not a convicted felon, I'm sorry." Now happy in her sneakers, she lay on the floor rolling with laughter.

"Mom..., you're still crazy, just relax, and enjoy."

"I plan on it." Peeking in the mirror, Barbara fluffed her hair and applied lotion to her hands.

Stopping in the kitchen to grab two bottled cranberry juices, she shoved them into Michelle's hands for her to bring out to them.

Having the same physique as Barbara, Michelle's about one inch shorter, and two dress sizes smaller. Her thick and lengthy black hair is fashioned in a wrapped bob. Her crimson sweater complimented her light brown skin tone, her black ankle length boots and form-fitted black skirt highlighted her short shapely legs.

Loving her in red, every year Barbara would get her a red velvet dress for Christmas. Entirely opposite of Barbara, she possessed a more serene personality, packed with cleverness and humor.

Making her entrance carrying the two bottles of juice, in a cheery voice, she greeted, Gary. "Hi! I'm, Michelle." Showing her eye-catching and inviting smile. Extending her hand to Gary, she gave him a bottle of the cranberry juice.

"Thank you; I'm Gary, nice to meet you. So, this is your baby?"

"Yep, my one and only, one."

"She's gorgeous, I see the resemblance." In her adult years, Michelle noticed that she was looking more like her Mother.

"Did you come to help?" He asked.

"No,—I think I'm gonna let you guys claim the bragging rights for this one; I'll just watch from a *distance*." Little did Gary know, she meant it *literally*? For whatever reasons, or motives, Michelle thought it was a generous gesture of Gary to assist with the project; she felt compelled to return the favor.

"Would you, guys like some breakfast now or brunch later?" Barbara glanced in Gary's direction to see if he was open.

"Sounds good to me, I'm famished, give us..., oh, another hour and a half or so."

"Great, nice meeting you, I'll go and begin the preparations?"

"It was a pleasure meeting you, too."

At one o'clock, after two and a half hours the toy chest was completed. Inviting Gary inside, Barbara pointed him to the guest bathroom to freshen up; she continued to hers.

On his way from the bathroom, in the hallway, his eyes caught the attention of a wall of NBA basketball players, such as Dr. 'J', Ewing, HaKeen and Drexler, who were her favorite, *Wow, she's a basketball fan too, she has an autographed picture of my favorite player, Drexler, did she go to Barcelona, too? She likes to build..., hmm."*

The aroma of the food broke his concentration. Michelle invited him to have a seat at the table. In a warm and cozy atmosphere, he admired the festive environment. The tables were still in place from the brunch on Sunday.

In minutes, Michelle brought two platters to the table, one with an omelet big enough to feed five people, consisting of chunks of potatoes, spicy sausages, green onions, garlic, cheddar and jack cheese.

Gary's eyes became so big, they seem to have dilated. While in college, she'd gotten the recipe from the "*Frugal Gourmet."*

Astounded and surprised at the amount of food that she had prepared, "My, goodness, girl, you were serious when you said that you were going in to prepare."

"Ah, it's really quite simple; it's one of my easiest breakfast entrées to prepare." The second platter was filled with whole wheat buttered toast and yeast rolls, followed by a tray of fresh fruit, melons, berries, grapes, and homemade jams previously made by Michelle for Christmas gift giving.

After removing a rack of cinnamon rolls from the oven, she summoned Barbara to join them. Returning after changing her top to a hunter green sweater, Gary was waiting for the signal to eat; Barbara said grace. *"Lord, Jesus...*

"We have orange, apple, and cranberry juices, coffee and tea, what's your pleasure? Michelle asked.

"I'll have some orange juice and coffee please." Barbara asked for her favorite, cranberry juice.

"How did you do this so fast?" He asked, before taking a heaping bite of the omelet.

"Well, Mom made the cinnamons rolls last evening, they only needed baking. The omelet and toast took only fifteen minutes. Once you dice the ingredients, you're done; it only looked like I fussed." Maximizing food consumption, she built her menu around items that were still on hand from the brunch.

"It's tasting like you fussed." Continuing to tear into the omelet, "This omelet is screaming; it's like dining in one of B. Smith kitchens." Mission accomplished, she'd satisfied her Mom's new friend.

"Aw..., you're too, kind." Taking a gulp of his juice.

"No, it was kind of you to prepare it."

"It's my small token of gratitude for helping with the toy chest for Jordyn. Have you visited one of B. Smith's restaurants?

"Yes, several times, and my compliment stands." Speaking the truth regarding his undernourished appetite, Gary had second portions of everything. Taking pleasure in the compliment, Michelle was pleased.

Without Gary's help, it would've taken Barbara until dark to complete the project. Taking her first bite of the omelet, "Ooh, Michelle, this omelet is delicious; it's your best yet."

"Oh, it's been a while since you've tasted it, Mom."

"Um..., could be, it's still delicious. I can't believe that we're done so soon." Barbara spoke.

"Thank God for, Gary."

Desiring to praise Barbara's efforts, he stated. "You knew exactly what you wanted, and you knew what you were doing; so, why did you allow me intimidate you?" Nodding, and looking in her direction.

"Was it that obvious? You're right; I was bothered by your presence Gary, just a tiny bit." She measured by gesturing with her fingers. Gary was on target; Barbara Jean had felt inadequate in his presence. She tried to remain cool, but apparently, she'd failed.

"I knew it, it's only natural, that's why I kept engaging you in the process."

"I got that." Resonating appreciativeness.

"Maybe I shouldn't have revealed my complete occupation to you," he paused. "On second thought, never mind, that was my ticket to getting here."

"Uh, uh..." she burst into laughter."

"Your response is well taken," Gary added, laughing.

"Gary, you added features I never would've dreamed of implementing. Thank you, so...much."

"Aw..., it's called *perks*! Thanks for letting me help; it was fun. On the jobsite I'm mostly inspecting or delegating, it felt good."

"I can't wait to see it, have you selected a color?" Michelle asked." Sipping on her juice.

"Um..., I'm leaning toward pink or purple or both, to correspond with her color scheme. I may add her initials, or some decals, the cedar is so beautiful, it could stand alone."

Washing down the toast with his juice, Gary commented. "I was admiring the wall of basketball players, so, who's the big fan?"

"That would be her," Michelle pointed.

"I'm guilty!"

"The autographed picture of Drexler, did you go to the Olympics?"

"I wish, no, a co-workers friend got it for me."

"I love a variety of sports, but basketball, it's my *passion.*" He said. Noticing a traded glimpse, and smile between Barbara and Michelle, "Did I say or miss something?"

"No, no, you used the word, *"passion."* That's the word that I use to express my love for the game of basketball also."

"Oh..., okay, so I guess you go to the Warriors games?"

"Well, sort of kinda. Barbara explained that since the Warrior's performance had been inconsistent in the past few years; she only attended games when they were hosting teams that she favored.

"You're not alone, I do the same thing. I'm a season ticket holder. I give tickets away as gifts to some of the guys on my crew, they always appreciate them."

"I bet they do, I'm sure they're good seats."

"Oh..., yes!"

Prior to Gary leaving, they proudly presented their masterpiece to Michelle. Displaying a magnificently crafted toy chest, the dimensions were thirty-eight inches in width, thirty inches in depth, and twenty in height. The inside included a top shelf divided into four compartments for smaller toys, leaving an open space in the lower half for larger ones. It was equipped with rollers for mobility purposes and a safety latch to prevent closure on her hand.

For book storage, each side had two shelves. Extending perfectly across the foot of the bed, it was a true work of art. For, Gary, it was a piece of cake; nevertheless, he felt the same satisfaction he gets from his professional work.

"Oh my, this is so—neat, guys," Circling it to get a full view, Michelle voiced, "Jordyn is going to love this."

Admiring it with a look of surprise, she drew in the scent and mumbled. "Mmm..., I can smell the cedar."

"The drilling intensified the fragrance." Gary informed.

"You, guys did all this in that short of time, wow!"

"I did have an *expert* on my team." Claiming bragging rights, as she looked in Gary's direction, with admiration.

"Someone's at my front door, it's probably, Karen."

Sprinting to answer it. Shortly, Jordyn appeared running. "Hi Mommy!" Jordyn, yelled.

"J! What are you doing here so early?" Michelle asked.

"I got bored. Is this for me?" With excitement, she pushed past her Mom.

"Yes, it is." Barbara answered.

She was affectionately called, 'J.' after choosing to cut her visit short with her cousins, they'd dropped her off.

"You can thank this nice man, his name is Gary." She introduced. Bending, he offered to shake her hand. Looking up and blinking her big beautiful eyes, she said. "Thank You, Mr. Gary!"

"You're welcome! Look at those eyelashes." He marveled. Jordyn inherited Barbara's skin complexion. Her long coarse hair and facial features were like her, Moms. She'd long, but thick eyelashes that would put to shame any *Maybelline* eye model. Her Dad liked to take credit for the double dimples on her right cheek, which enhanced her beautiful smile.

"Do you think you can fill this up with toys?" Gary asked.

Grinning and nodding, "Actually, I can, at Christmas and my birthday; they're back-to-back."

Bulging in excitement, "Did you make this, today?"

"Yes!"

"How did you do it? Where did you get all this stuff?"

"Hold up..., one question at a time, please!"Michelle refereed.

"Never mind, can I help paint it?" Jordyn asked, prancing with anticipation.

"Yes..., honey," Barbara answered, reluctantly.

Extremely glad that they'd finished before her arrival, at the age of five, Jordyn was *wonderfully precocious,* and ahead of her time. They were fascinated at her ability to grasp words, and reuse them in their proper context.

At approximately two-thirty p.m., Gary Lloyd Russell had assisted Barbara in building a toy chest, and enjoyed a scrumptious brunch. His next task would be to determine, where he'd be laying his head tonight?

In route to Walnut Creek, he hoped that he'd not be disappointed. Delighting in the no stress sparse commute afforded him the time to reflect, and absorb the day's events.

Impressed with Michelle's culinary skills, to Gary, it was a true example of the old cliché *"the way to a man's heart is through his stomach."* In addition, he felt she was an attractive young woman; possessing similar traits of her Mom. Smiling, *I sure hope she learned to cook from her, Mom.* He hoped Barbara would be extending an invitation to dinner someday.

Twenty minutes later, Gary pulled into the driveway of a two story contemporary house. *Maybe I should have called.* Ringing the doorbell and entering, he yelled. "Hello!"

From the hallway he opened the first bedroom door. With contemporary furnishings, the room was immaculate. The full-sized bed was intact with an undisturbed look, probably used as a guest bedroom.

Walking back to the front he headed for the kitchen, and threw his keys onto the kitchen counter; he saw a note. *Thanks man, I was only in town for one night. I figured you'd need your space. Later, Tony."*

Pleased to find the note, Tony was a long time friend whom Gary let use his home when he worked in the Contra Costa area. Over the years, Gary took advantage of his craft by purchasing homes below market value that were in need of repair; he'd acquired two. Completely remodeled, the Walnut Creek home had four bedrooms, and an in-law unit.

For his Pleasanton home, only the baths and kitchen needed restructuring. Given that it had excess acreage, he'd build an in-law unit there also; providing privacy for his parents when they visit, it also increased the property value.

His third home was located in the valley; he calls it his *Baby.* Designing and building it himself, with the support of his Dad, brother, and cousins; he referred to it as a *project in motion* because of on going improvements; warranting his visit to the home depot.

Since it's in a remote location, he only visits when he wants to relax, and get away from the Bay Area. He uses it to entertain his family when they're visiting from Atlanta, and to host weekend sporting events.

Taking pleasure in the freedom that comes with bachelorhood, he'd entertain the idea of marriage for the right lady. If Gary wasn't overseeing the building of some homes, or volunteering his services, you could find him on the golf course or at a sporting event.

At four o'clock p.m., Barbara Jean's doorbell appeared to be jammed. To stop the annoying sound, she rushed to open the door.

With broaden eyes; Kim peeked from behind Karen. "Is he still here? Kim whispered.

"Well good afternoon to you too, ladies..., get in here." Barbara ordered. Karen and Kim sat in their preferred chairs at the breakfast bar.

"Why didn't you call and tell me about, Gary?" Kim asked.

"Kim, didn't you just complete your shift?"

"Yeah!"

"Girl, I wasn't about to interrupt you on your job, in a hospital, just to tell you that I'd met a man."

"Well..., you could've left me a voicemail. Thank, God I called Karen. I was checking to see if she'd signed up on the website. It looks as if I'm the only one that's gonna need the services." She complained, looking disappointed.

"You guys are on a roll, where's Michelle and Jordyn?" Kim asked, displaying a dejected spirit and tone.

"Oh, they're visiting our Aunt Elnora.

Kim was feeling like the Long Ranger. Karen had gone on a date with Bill, and Barbara Jean had met Gary. Placing a plate of warm cinnamon rolls in front of them with a quart of milk, Barbara asked. "What did I miss?"

Overly excited with Barbara meeting, Gary; Karen forgot to tell her about her dinner with Bill.

"Bill took us to dinner last evening." She announced, in a bubbly tone and with a beaming smile.

"What! Girl, why didn't you call me last night?" Barbara screamed.

"I guess..., I'm still identifying him as just a concerned Coach. He called today; he's picking us up Saturday night to attend a youth rally at his church."

"Girl, if he was only a concerned Coach for his players, he would've rented a bus, and picked up every boy and their Mama." Handing them saucers, napkins and utensils, "Kim is right; he takes you to dinner, too."

"Oh, I forgot," Karen, said. "He asked Michael what was my favorite kind of food."

"C'mon now," Kim added.

"I guess you're right." On that note, she jumped to the end of her seat with excitement, and proceeded to tell them how cute he is. "He reminds me of Kurt

Rambis, (*former Laker Player*) just a little bit, and he's a Christian! Can you believe that?"

"Certainly!" Barbara replied. "That's what we've prayed for, right?" Karen had finally accepted the idea that Bill was actually interested in her. Not dating since her divorce, she found his attraction to her difficult to absorb.

Karen was no chopped liver. As her confidence grew, she eagerly told them everything about Bill.

Taking a bite of her cinnamon roll, she added. "His eyes are the color of aqua blue water."

Barbara reminded her, "Remember, *the truth is in the eyes*." She said chuckling.

"Girl, these rolls are on hit." Karen praised.

"Is the verdict still out on Gary? Is he a Christian?"

Standing in her favorite spot, with her back rested against the counter, "I'm still not sure; it never seemed to be the right moment. In the back yard we were busy building the toy chest.

He did do the majority of the work; I sure wasn't going to interrupt him. It was the prime motive for bringing him home with me, well, almost" She corrected, and smiled.

"He certainly enjoyed the meal; he kept complimenting Michelle on the food. We talked about basketball. I want the time to be right; it's a serious issue to me; it's worth the wait. He left shortly after we ate."

In spite of her nagging curiosity, she refused to pose a direct question to Gary regarding his faith or his church attendance. She had a more suitable approach when the time was right.

"What did Michelle think of, Gary?"

"She liked him. Her exact words were, *he's cool, laidback, engaging, he appears to be attentive and sensitive*. She thinks he likes me."

"If Michelle liked him, he must be okay!" Karen said.

"He looks about forty or so." Barbara informed them.

"Oooh, a building contractor, and young." Kim teased.

Barbara reminded Kim of their *quest*. "We talked about the younger men thing at the brunch, remember?"

"In all honesty guys, he doesn't know if I'm a Christian." Barbara admitted. "I'll tell you this, if he's not a Christian, for him ..., uh, I'd consider *missionary dating*. I'd be willing to pull out the *Four Spiritual Laws, Survival Kit, Getting to Know*

Christ and everybody else," she said, trying to contain her laughter. Kim and Karen were hysterical with laughter.

"I heard—that," they mouthed.

Barbara knew little about Gary. She knew enough to know that he was someone she desired to keep in her life on some level. She was adamant about meeting a *seasoned Christian* man. She wants someone who desire to know Christ for himself. She wasn't up to the challenge to coax or force-feed him to study the word, or go to bible study.

Her sentiments were consistent with her feelings in a personal relationship with a man, if it's not mutual, don't force it. She admittedly was smitten with Gary. Joking with the girls that she'd be willing to make concessions, she wasn't willing to *compromise* God's will for her life. She'd pray and take one day at a time.

"How are the plans coming for the party? Barbara asked.

"Great! Mom is taking off work Thursday. You know her; she looks forward to this each year."

This was Mary's *gala event*. In their younger years, Mary and Gilbert would make their rounds attending elegant holiday parties. In the past three years, they'd turned their home into a festive affair.

"I'm looking forward to it. Mary said I could invite some guests. I invited Walter; he's a business associate of mine."

"He's the big mortgage broker guy, right?" Karen asked.

"Yeah, right!"

"I've heard you mention him, is he available, a Christian, is he cute?" Inquired Kim.

Answering in a matter of fact tone. "Actually, the answer is yes to all three questions."

Hesitating. "Um..., Walter may not be your speed, Kim, but he is a Christian." Now inquisitive, Kim asked. "What exactly are you referring to when you say speed?"

"Hmm..., maybe speed was a poor choice of words; let's just say many women think Walter is cute. He's a good man, I like him as a person and a business associate, he is looking for a serious Christian woman."

"Well, I'm going online tonight and sign up." Kim announced, with assurance.

"Barbara, have you checked your e-mail for a hit from the dating website?" Karen asked.

"Girl..., please, I haven't had a chance, I've been pleasantly distracted by Gary."She said, glowing.

"I'm meeting my girlfriend, Jo Ann for dinner," Karen informed. "We're making plans for our trip to Europe next year; I need to get out of here, let's have prayer before I go."

"Thanks Karen;" Kim said. "You reminded me, I only have a week to book my Jamaican Cruise."

"Please remember my friend Walter as we pray. Um..., let's just say it's an *unspoken request*." They joined hands as Karen led them in prayer.

"Lord, Jesus we thank you for this day and this time to come before you. We confess our sins and ask for your forgiveness. Lord, the past couple of days have presented unusual circumstances for some of us. We can only see what our eyes reveal, but Lord; you know the hidden secrets and hidden agenda if there be any. Lord we ask that you will increase our spirit of wisdom and discernment."

As Karen continued to pray, everyone joined in and began to agree. Upon completion, they'd shared a hallelujah; praise the Lord, tear jerking moment.

In spite of their laughter and jokes, they understood the seriousness of leaving God out of their plans. Their praying was a testament that they desired to be in the will of God.

Chapter 4

At ten o'clock a.m., Barbara had completed the signing process. With his hands buried deep within his pockets; Walter nodded for Barbara to come into his office.

Familiar with his body language; she perceived that his heart was heavy, and that he needed to talk. His tall slender frame stood propped in the doorway, wearing dark slacks, a white shirt and a *sadden face.*

"Thanks for the business, Walter."

"Thank you, Barbara Jean. You look cheery and lovely this morning,"

"Aw...thanks Walter, that's precisely how I feel." After meeting Gary and building the toy chest, she'd a good-nights rest. She was happy to hear that it was reflective in her appearance and wardrobe selection. Dressed business casual, she wore a cream cashmere sweater, a brown form-fitted pinstriped skirt, and cream suede calf length boots.

By the window, she sat at a round mahogany table, coated with a stained espresso, which was consistent with the décor of the furniture. Keeping with functionality and practicality, two chairs were in front of his desk for consulting purposes.

For comfort, he chose a high back brown leather chair. Behind his desk was a credenza; on the wall above the credenza were his diplomas, certifications, awards and licenses.

Joining her at the table, he wore a broad but forced smile. His smooth skin tone was identical to his mahogany furnishing. He could double for Isaiah Washington any day.

He loved referring to her as Barbara Jean, "Thanks for inviting me to the party Barbara Jean; I need the fellowship."

Relaxed, with his hands placed over his head, he smiled. "Barbara Jean, why haven't you ever gone out with me in the past?"

With a baffled look, she laughed, timidly before saying. "Walter, some things you put under the classification of "*Let sleeping dog's lie.*"

Walter exploded into laughter. "Well, said, Barbara Jean, well, said." His posture slipped to its previous disposition, *burden.*

"This party will be good for me. The fellowship will help take my mind off myself."

Barbara leaned closer with an affectionate look. "I'm listening Walter, what's wrong?" She asked, in a compassionate and concerned tone.

"Oh, Barbara Jean, I'm feeling convicted, I feel..." he paused, "Um..., this heaviness upon me to get more in the *word,* and to leave these *women* alone." Making a fist, he clinched his hand over it; giving her a swift smile.

"I was only kidding when I asked about cuties being at the party; it's the area of my life that God is convicting me. Women are the last thing that I need in my life, Barbara Jean." He voiced, in an affirmative tone, dripping frustration.

Leaning backward in his chair, his hands gripped the arm of the chair, he added. "Especially the women that I date."

Giving him her undivided attention, "What kind of women are they, Walter?" Dropping his voice, he lowered his head.

"They're Christians; then again, they," he paused, "like me, they don't apply the word of God to their lives either." Now standing with his hands in his pockets, he paced slowly near the table.

"Barbara Jean, I'll be the first to admit my shortcomings. I'm not casting any stones here."

Turning quickly to make eye contact. "I want to be the bigger one and say *no* sometime. I don't mean to be *cocky*, Barbara Jean, but they *chase*, me." He cried, resembling a kid who'd been falsely accused.

"I can't tell you when I've had the pleasure to pursue after a woman."

Barbara Jean smiled, adjusting to a straight posture. She was all ears. "*Well, do tell,*" she pressed, playfully.

Freezing in his pace, he looked at her, laughing. "Stop teasing me, Barbara Jean; I'm trying to share my heart with you, girl."

Tenderly defending her remark, while snickering. "Okay..., I'm sorry, I'm only teasing, Walter. I'm a little envious." She said, grinning.

"Don't be so hard on yourself, Walter. You got game; you're physically fit and toned. You're handsome; you have a successful business that generates you an income to afford nice cars and real estate."

"You walk around *exposed,* Walter. You need to arm yourself with the *word.* You know the scriptures. *(Eph. 6:11)* It's the only way you'll be able to resist their advances. As you stated, they're disobedient to the word also. They're only doing what comes *natural* for them, as in the *Survival Kit,* remember?"

"Yeah, the *old nature,* I guess I'm too nice."

"Nice is good, maybe you need to refine your definition of nice."

"You're a Christian woman Barbara Jean; do you put a *move* on men or wait for them to approach you? Why do these women behave that way? What happen to letting the man chase the woman?"

Hmm..., should I tell him about Gary approaching me in the home depot? I've never discussed a man with Walter before, Hmm..., never had one to discuss."

Barbara elected to answer Walter's first question and share her experience with Gary instead, beside, she wanted to get a man's perspective.

Grinning broadly, "Walter, I want to get your take on something. A guy approached me yesterday at the Home Depot, and no! I did not make a move toward him. I was purchasing wood to make a toy chest for Jordyn. To make a long story short, after I determined that he was a general contractor," Combating the laughter; "I can hardly say it."

"You can hardly say what, girl?" Showing anxiety.

"I took him home with me to help build the toy chest." She blurted, in a rapid but explanatory statement.

Doubling over with loud laughter; he re-joined her at the table. Amused by her experience with Gary, he'd forgotten how depressed he was when she'd first arrived. "Barbara Jean, you're too funny, girl."

"Well..., Walter, what do you think of what I did?" She asked with anticipation and grinning, while tapping her fist on the table.

Motioning with his arms, "Well..., did, did..., you get the toy chest completed." Stuttering, with lifted eyebrows.

"Of course we did, that was—the agenda, Walter." She spoke, in an absolute tone, venting a hint of resistance. "Oh, you should see it, Walter." Suddenly calm, showing an opened mouth grin. "It's so beautiful." With clasped fingers, his hands rested on top of his head, he smiled, and glared at his dear friend.

Slowly turning his head from side to side, "Barbara Jean...," he paused. "Why in the world ..., was that so hard for you to say; because you'd just met him?" Shrugging her shoulders, while frowning, "I guess!"

"On a serious note, in general women do need to be careful of men these days Barbara Jean. Contrary—to what we hear in the news; all men are not *dogs, and perverts.*

Sometimes in life we have to make judgment calls, rely on our *gut* instincts, and in your case, the *Holy Spirit.*" He said softly.

Rendering a smile exhibiting naughtiness, "Hmm..., don't know if it was my *gut, or the Holy Spirit*; but I sure—had a good feeling about him. His name is, Gary." She said, smiling.

"I can tell..." Based on her tone, and mannerism, Walter was entirely receptive to her attraction toward Gary.

"No situation is the same Barbara Jean, but the Home Depot, c'mon girl, the man was there for the same reason as you, to shop. It was smart to make him think that there were other people at your home; you made a good call." He said, smiling.

"Now, back to you." She reminded him. "We got off track when you asked me about approaching men."

"Oh, yeah, why do women *chase*, men?" He asked sorrowfully.

"Simple Walter, it's not enough of you to go around. As truthful as it is, [I am kidding]. Let's keep it about you. Earlier you said you want to be the bigger one. Keep in mind Walter, the *nature that you feed the most* will prevail as the *dominate one*.

"Tell me about it. Trust me, I believe you."

"I know you read the material and books that I give you Walter, but if you're serious about your desire to grow, you're going to need to take some—classes. Classes such as discipleship and bible study. You'll see, you'll be challenged in your every day walk."

Because of Walters's issues with women, and they being of the opposite sex; she felt that a male spiritual mentor would better serve him.

"Walter, you," she paused; "you really need a male Christian mentor." She finally pushed out.

"A man will better understand your position. Oh, I—can identify mind you, but you can be more..., um, transparent with a man. You need accountability," she smiled.

"Plus, you won't have to endure my teasing you." Showing a look of sadness, he sat with his head slightly tucked, knowing that he had no man to consider. With compassion, she gazed on, and listened intently.

"You're correct on every account. Your teasing me is not a problem, Barbara Jean; you make it easy for me to talk with you." He mouthed, gently.

"Aw..., thanks, Walter."

"I've been thinking about attending bible study at your church or just going to another one altogether. The things that I told you today, if I'd shared my *women issues* with the men in my church; uh..., they would've cheered me on." With a confused expression, she stared.

Responding to her facial expression, "For real, Barbara Jean, it would be viewed as a *good thing*."

"Aw..., Walter, you've obviously given some serious consideration to this. I bet you think leaving would be disloyal to your Church and family." Looking surprised.

"Yes! He said, as his mouth formed a huge smile. "How did you know, Barbara Jean?"

"I've been there, but not—for lack of teaching. Christianity is an individual walk, Walter. Sometimes we have to leave family and friends for personal reasons, especially when we've exhausted all available resources for growth; which definitely seems to be your problem.

"You're right, my Mom implied that once."

"Before you can become *rooted* Walter, there has to be a ministry in place for growth."

"Exactly, that's my dilemma Barbara Jean."

"Walter, some churches have curriculums in place to enhance your growth better than others, I credit Corinth for my spiritual growth in the word today; it's where Michelle and I became *planted.* We have deep roots there, and good friendships that still exist; but it was a necessary move at the time."

"Hmm, that makes a lot of sense Barbara Jean. I can't relate to any sentiments like that. Between going to college and working weekends; I guess studying the word was kinda put on the *back burner*."

"Oh, I can relate to that; Michelle was in college at the time. We both worked on Saturdays, to afford her adequate study time; we needed a church with an early morning service, or she would've ended up with your *back burner* scenario."

"It's certainly obvious that you guys continued to grow."

"Of course we did. At Corinth, Pastor Crenshaw challenged you to search the scriptures for yourself, and to build a personal relationship with Christ. As a result, you learn to discern sound doctrine when you hear it."

Walter nodded in agreement. Barbara recalled members from similar churches with less progressive ministries would often attend classes at Corinth; Walters's thoughts were on key.

"My problem is; my commitment is to my church, and family, and not the, Lord."

"Wow! That's bold and honorable of you to admit, Walter. *Seasons* make up our lives you know; *Ecclesiastes 3* reminds us of that. We change our careers for enhancement and enrichment purposes; our place of worship can be—*seasonal* as well."

Bending over with laughter, she added. "Uh..., some pastors won't admit or agree, but then they'd be *suggesting* that God only speaks to them regarding relocating."

"Right, Right," he said, with a big ear-to-ear grin. "I get you now. That's a good correlation, Barbara Jean. You're correct; my career move certainly enhanced my personal life. I've been so busy with my career; I haven't taken the time to cultivate *my spiritual growth.* I need to avail myself for God to direct me."

"It's not my intent to persuade you toward my way of thinking, I'm merely giving you some *food for thought*. I'll be the first to admit, I'm kind of *different*, for lack of a better word, Walter." She laughed.

"My family thinks I'm *weird.*" Walter laughed loudly. "Barbara Jean! Stop it!" "They do..., Walter, *not* Michelle." She said, snickering. "Oh, they mean it in an *endearing* kinda way. They're just not too partial to change as I'm. Unlike them, I'm..., not too good at following in "*traditions,*" and I say that with *endearment.* Whether it's church, jobs, or travel, I've never been afraid to branch out on my own."

Walter looked on with an attentive posture, she perceived that the Holy Spirit was dealing with Walter; he'd never spoken so candidly in the past. She knew that he wasn't getting the teachings that he needed for growth.

"I'm hearing little nuggets in what you're saying, Barbara Jean."

"I'll share this little story with you Walter, and then I have to get out of here. Some years ago, I attended a church *banquet* of some sort.

Prior to it beginning, we were saving seats next to us for friends. After closely monitoring our behavior, one of the deacons seated asked. *"Why do Christians worry about who's seated next to them, we're all sisters and brothers in Christ."* "I tell you, to this day Walter, I never forgot that statement. I think it's been instrumental in instilling within me the *liberty* that I feel in *Christ,* and where I *worship.*"

"I focus more on the um... *teachings* that I will receive, rather than potential *friends or family members* who may or may not attend. If the doctrine is *sound*, and they demand *accountability* from me," She paused, and elevated her shoulders. "It works for me."

"Wow! Barbara Jean, Thinking on his situation. "Hmm..., we do have our portion of family members and cliques at St. Hebrews." He said, and Chuckled.

"I grew up at St. Hebrews, Barbara Jean; it's all that I know. It doesn't take a bible scholar to know that I'm not getting what I need there." He spoke and dropped his head. Lowering his head indicated to her that he was shouldering all the blame for his lack of growth.

Taking a stab at attempting to encourage him, she also offered up a possible solution to his problem. "Walter, you're not giving yourself any credit, you're victorious in areas that you've taken the time to nurture. Look at your business; you've single-handedly turned it into a successful venture."

"Exactly, my business, but where's the evidence for my spiritual growth?"

"Well..., if you apply the same energy and commitment to your spiritual development, you can be triumphant as well."

Turning her head, for added emphasis, she continued speaking with carefulness. "Look Walter, I am not *advocating* that you leave, St. Hebrews, that's between you and God. However, I do think visiting another church for developing—your *spiritual growth* wouldn't hurt"

"I'm not receiving it that way, Barbara Jean; you've touched on the very thing that's been on my mind."

"Your pastor is also your cousin Walter, why not go and talk to him. Let him know that you'd like to take some classes at another church, maybe he'll be open to you teaching with St. Hebrews what you've learned."

"That's a good idea, Barbara Jean. You know, I've been watching my neighbor across the courtyard, he's an insurance agent."

"The tall guy, I've never seen him up close."

"Yeah, you've seen him; I think he's single. He used to play professional basketball; we're both season ticket holders for the Warriors. I see him reading his bible in the courtyard area, and in his car. We speak in passing, and talk about sports; we've even referred each other business."

"That's good; you should ask him if you can join him at lunch sometimes."

"You know, I think I will. He appears to be serious about his walk with the Lord, and he's fun to talk to, like you."

"Aw..., I love talking to you too, Walter; I admire your earnestness and *humble* spirit."

"Some Christians are so *"puffed up"* Barbara Jean, I don't feel comfortable approaching them."

"Hmm..., that's a tough one Walter. I know the feeling, I been there in years past. We've become so *intellectually pregnant* with the *word* these days, we take our classes, go to seminary school; get our little certificates, and degrees, and for what? She responded in a disturbed tone, with arched shoulders.

Since embarking on her Christian journey, she identified with Walter's comments. She too had experienced seasoned Christians with elevated and *standoffish* behaviors. Towing with the risk of appearing judgmental, she desired to keep Walter encouraged as well.

"In truth, we're supposed to behave the exact opposite as we grow in Christ Walter. Our attitudes should become *deflated* once we recognize that our *little righteousness* is as filthy as the *rags* mentioned in *Isaiah 64:6.*"

"Um..., so we should be combining growth in knowledge with application?"

"Yep!" Pondering the idea, she paused. "We are commanded to maintain a high standard, Walter, and to be *set apart*, but, there has to be a balance. If we set our bar *too high* for anyone to ask for help, or too far apart for anyone to share their heart; then we're not carrying out the mandate of being an *effective witness;*" that comes with *growth and wisdom*, not certificates or degrees.

"My point Barbara Jean, aren't we commanded to make *Disciples, meaning to duplicate oneself*, right. I've been reading the material that you give me."

"You're correct; we need to ask God to help us to always be sensitive to those around us that are in need."

Nodding her head, and smiling, "You're going to be just fine..., Walter. You've acknowledged the convictions that God has placed on your heart, when the *right* woman comes along; the two of you will want to behave in a manner that's pleasing to God."

"You know Barbara Jean, I think you're right, I have to be responsible for my actions and stop putting it off on someone else."

"See..., you're thinking with more clarity already." Standing, they embraced with a *camelback hug*, and a kiss on the cheek.

"See you, Friday."

"I'm going over to the cafeteria for breakfast Barbara Jean; would you like to join me?"

"No! I have to get over to Carson General, rain check!"

"You got it!" Attempting to encourage his friend, when she reached the door, he yelled!

"Barbara Jean! Gary's interest wasn't limited to building the toy chest." He gave her a *wink.*

Needing to confide in his friend, Walter had purposely orchestrated the signing to take place at his office. The meeting was divinely inspired; issues discussed were confirmations to the direction that God was leading him. Agreeing that she was correct, he did need a Christian man to mentor him; he thanked God for her wisdom and counsel. Admitting to a mutual attraction, Barbara Jean felt that he was much too young to be a candidate for a serious—relationship; in her *worldly days..., a strong maybe!*

In spite of his weakness concerning women, she knew that he was genuine in his desire to grow stronger in the word. Unfortunately, there was no accountability system in place for him to grow in his present church; consequently, he repeatedly submitted to the advances of women that came to the church; labeled, *"fine."*

St. Hebrews extended three generations for his family. Presently, his cousin was the Pastor. The pulpit selection was restricted to family members whomever they felt were ready. Because of his professional knowledge and affiliations, Walter was head of the finance department, having no real say; he served primarily in an advisory capacity. They were grooming Walter to become a deacon, a role he wanted no part. Walter Douglas Hines, at age thirty-seven desired a closer walk with God.

Seated in the cafeteria at Carson General, Kim waved to Barbara to sit with her. Dr. Josie Washington, a Black Pediatrician was there making her rounds for her patients. Karen's mother Mary, the head nurse of the 7th floor joined them. Before taking her seat beside Kim and Dr. Washington, she grabbed a juice from the vending machine.

"What brings you here?" Mary asked, in surprise.

"A patient needed a power of attorney; I knew I'd find one of you in here." Deciding to tease Barbara, flashing a broad smile, Mary asked. "Are you going to bring your new friend to the party on Friday?" Sipping on her juice, and entertaining the idea.

"Well..., it's nice to know that good news travel fast also; I hadn't thought much about it Mary." In an after thought, laden with skepticism in her tone, "Do you think I should?"

"Why not, it's up to you? He's certainly welcome." Still airing uncertainty. "I'm not sure what's protocol, I don't want to appear forward, or assuming; hmm..., I'll think about it."

Taking a sip of her black coffee, which contrasted closely to her complexion, Dr. Washington remarked. "Child, it's the holidays, everything's protocol."

Barbara had considered inviting Gary. Desiring to be careful and not make assumptions because he'd helped her build a toy chest; she would give it more thought. Dr. Washington was correct; it was the holidays.

"Who went on a cruise?" Barbara asked with excitement, after noticing Kim sort through a stack of photographs.

"These are Miss Vanessa's pictures from her three day cruise with her significant other." Barbara laughed, and remarked facetiously. "So, he does exist?"

"Okay!" Kim said, heavy with emphasis.

"I was starting to wonder myself. Hovering over Kim to view Vanessa's photographs, Kim had no way out.

"I don't think she'll mind me showing them to you, guys."

"Not bad! Maybe she has reasons to keep him a secret." Barbara joked.

"I know him," Mary acknowledged. "He's a deacon at a church we've attended; the name of it escapes me."

Placing her hand on her waist, Dr. Washington said. "Well, I know him as Thomas Martin, he's—married; and he's my pharmaceutical representative. He maintained whenever he and his wife have a baby; he wanted me to be their Doctor. It's becoming clear now. The last time he came by, I asked how the baby making was coming; he ignored the question. I didn't push it; I thought he was having a bad day, most days I can't get rid of him."

In shock, with her mouth held open, the muffin that she was about to bite into slid from her hand onto the table. With one hand placed over her heart, Kim asked. "Are you, guys sure?"

Things were beginning to fall into place for Kim. Vanessa never brought him amongst her friends; she never spent holidays with him, and very few weekends.

Scratching her head, and frowning with attitude in her tone, Mary asked. "When was this cruise, and how was he able to pull that off if he's married?" Remembering Karen's cheating ex-husband Ronald; it became a sore topic for Mary.

"It was only a three day cruise," Kim reminded her.

Dr. Washington clarified, as she tossed her long black hair over her shoulders. "That's easy, pharmaceutical rep's are frequent travelers."

Dr. Washington is a native of the area; she'd been Michelle's pediatrician also. Attending the same church, she and Mary are about the same age. She and her husband Dan have been married for thirty-five years.

In her no none sense manner, the community embraced her as a positive role model. She's short in stature, but stood tall as a professional business person.

Gaining respect from a diverse group of individuals, she rendered service to the entire community. She served on numerous state as well as local medical boards. Begging for answers, Kim asked. "What am I supposed to say?" Sounding distressed.

"Do I confront her, or pretend that I'm unaware that she's having an affair with a married man?

"What's the nature of the relationship?" Dr. Washington inquired.

"Well, it's a combination of both, work and personal. We talk about church, we do dinner and movies. We have lunch here everyday."

Dr. Washington suggested that she try the informative yet innocent approach. "In conversation, say, *Girl, did you know that Thomas is married?* Remain silent, and let her speak. Men are so daring these days; it's a possibility that she doesn't know he's married."

Exhaling a deep breath, "I hope it's the latter." Kim remarked.

"Sorry guys, I have to get going. I have a few more clients to see. I'm taking off early; I have a *Warrior's* game tonight, the "*Rockets*" are in town." Barbara announced.

"Gilbert and Michael will be right there with you." Mary informed.

"Yes, I heard; I'll see you guys Friday, right." Everyone responded, yes, and said goodbye.

Having a difficult time, Kim vehemently sorted through the alarming information regarding her friend and co-worker, Vanessa. They're not the best of friends, but were unified with respect to their dreams for the future, getting married and having children. Both enjoyed reading; they often exchanged Christian novels.

Never hiding the fact that Thomas spent nights at her place, Vanessa's cavalier attitude always rendered Kim baffled; in light of her openness of being a Christian. She could never find the nerve to confront her. Nursing a vexed spirit, Kim wasn't looking forward to the encounter.

She was glad that it was her last day at work; she's taking some time off before Christmas. After placing the photos in Vanessa's locker, she headed for home.

Moving from Jersey to California five years ago, Vanessa came to Carson General through a recruiting firm from her previous job. Faithful in church attendance, you could find her there every Sunday.

After moving to the Bay Area, she chose the closest church to the home that she'd purchased, it reminded her of her church back home; she loved the choir. She wasn't too interested in participating in bible study or foundational classes that were available; she found contentment in the eleven o'clock worship hour.

When she met Thomas Martin, she lacked the strength and the Christ centered life needed to resist the temptation. For some reason, the secrecy, the isolation from others gave her some false sense of comfort in believing that he was there for her.

Barbara's phone rang the minute she placed the key in her door, she rushed to the extension in the kitchen. "Hello," she answered breathlessly.

"Hey girl, you're hard to reach."

"Hi Gary, it's good to hear from you; I got your message."Checking her voicemail earlier, she'd retrieved his message. Not desiring to play hard to get, she also didn't want to get in the habit of calling him. She knew that if a man was interested, he wouldn't be offended if a woman didn't return his call.

She'd witnessed it with Michelle when she was dating her husband Mitchell. While changing clothes, Michelle would listen to her messages and dash to the kitchen to eat before responding to them. Without fail, Mitchell would call a second time, as Gary had.

"Thank you for your hospitality. Tell Michelle I know how she got her husband, the food was delicious."

"It was quite tasty; she enjoyed preparing it for you. Thank you so much for helping me, Gary, you were a life saver."

"Aw, it was my pleasure; I love it when people take on building projects; I think it speaks to your character and creative abilities, the finished product provide a rewarding feeling."

"Well said, obviously I hold your sentiments. One might accuse you of being biased, Mr. Russell."

He laughed. "One would be correct. Hey, I'm sure you're busy with the holidays, and your family Barbara, but I'm hoping you'll let me take you to dinner on Friday evening." *Hmm, I guess its protocol after all, Dr. Washington."*

"Well, how about I invite you, instead?"

"Whatever works for you?" Gary grunted, she laughed.

"Let me clarify that, my girlfriend's parents are having their annual Christmas dinner party on Friday night; would you like to go as my guest?"

"That sounds wonderful, what's the attire?"

"We usually make it a dress up affair. The women generally get a little dressier than the men do. Men typically wear a sports jacket or suit. A tie is optional. I have your card; I'll e-mail you the details."

"I'm looking forward to it. I got a call today from my baby sister; she's coming to visit for Christmas, and she's bringing a friend. She claims that she wants me to have a true Merry Christmas this year."

"How sweet," she teased. "She's thinking about her big brother."

"That's the part that scares me." Letting off a soft chuckle.

"She's never remembered me in Christmas past. Knowing her, she's up to something. I guess it can't be that bad; it'll be nice to see her. I'll definitely have you over to meet her."

"I'd love to meet her."

"Barbara, may I call you, BJ?"

"Sure...," she paused, "I think...I like that." She said, hesitantly.

"Hey, did I tell you that I love the way that you pronounce my name?"

"No!"

"Well, I do, you enunciate it the way my Mom intended, most people call me *Ger-ry*. You're blushing, I can tell."

"We're full of admirations today, aren't we?"

"I'd better quit while I'm ahead, you've blushed enough today."

"Goodbye, Gar-y!"

"Goodbye, BJ!" Feeling good about the holidays, it was becoming too much for her to ingest. She could hardly believe that she'd actually made plans with a man for a *Christmas Dinner Party*. She trusts that she was reading Gary's signals correctly. Turning forty-seven, but often thinks that she's naïve; Michelle constantly teases her.

Prior to Michelle getting married, Barbara took her to Vegas for a "*mother-daughter get-away.*" Leisurely walking the streets of Vegas, men were handing out literature. Barbara would take everything that was handed her and continue walking without looking at the contents.

Because they were being inundated with flyers, and the fact that they were all *grubby looking men*, Michelle became suspicious and intercepted one of them. In *disgust*, she handed it back to the man; it was *pornographic material.* Barbara Jean was entirely oblivious to its content. Getting a kick out of playing the *mother role,* Michelle still taunts her about it, today.

Now excited about the dinner party, Barbara was feeling like a sixteen year old who'd been in a time capsule. At her desk; she slumped in her favorite chair to reflect on her conversation with Gary.

She couldn't believe that he'd asked to call her, BJ. Years ago, she'd a manager that referred to her as BJ; she thinks he did it because he'd a lazy tongue, nonetheless, she liked it. She chose to reserve it as a "*pet*" name for her future husband to call her.

Staggered by his request to call her BJ; forced her to say yes. Giving her true explanation she felt would've been inappropriate; favoring more of a shameful and pathetic prelude to a marriage proposal. She concluded; it wasn't that serious. Discovering one more thing about Gary, she was excited that he wants her to meet his sister.

Noticing that she'd left her computer online, she checked her messages. Remembering the dating website, she quickly switched screen names to check for potential replies. To her surprise, she had two. One from someone named, Sober, smiling, *um...Sober, temperate, sedate, I like that."*

She'd chosen the name Zest, she was feeling zestful about her life; she felt their names complimented the other. Opening the e-mail, she read his message. *"Hi Zest, it was refreshing to see your profile. I have no problem with us not displaying our photographs. I'm also looking for a Christian friend to correspond. Never married, but it's a commitment I look forward to someday. I reside in the Bay Area. However, I will be in and out of town for an extended period. In the meantime, I would love to correspond by e-mail if that's okay with you. Hope to hear from you soon. Sober.* Considering she didn't post a photograph, she was pleased and felt it was better than she'd anticipated.

Meeting Gary, and now an internet correspondent, she was past tickled. She responded: *"Hi, Sober, it was a pleasure to hear from you..."* She revealed a little more about her and activities that she enjoyed. Before retiring for the evening; she scanned her closet for her clothing selection for the party. She also had a little talk with the Lord, about her newfound men friends.

Chapter 5

At five thirty p.m., Friday, Mary and the girls were finalizing the dinner preparations. Dinner would be served buffet style between the hours of six and eight o'clock p.m. As customary, Mary spared no expense. Catering in the appetizers, main entrees, salads and vegetables, she prepared the desserts.

To down play Kim not having a date, Barbara recommended that they arrive early, and allow their dates to meet them there.

On a quiet cul-de-sac, they resided in a charming split-level home. Including a wood burning fireplace, the living room floor plan was open, with a slider that opened onto one of two oversized decks with dramatic evening sunsets. The dazzling hung gold drapes accented the light gold colored walls with ivory crown molding.

Sparse by design, the mahogany baby grand piano was the focal point of the living room, surrounded by a cream and mahogany chaise lounge. A round end table with a lamp placed between two matching wing tip chairs completed the décor. A corner near the fireplace occupied the Christmas tree that looked to be seven-foot; a tree that only Gilbert could've decorated.

Adjoining rectangle tables extended along the living room wall to the family room served as the buffet station. White and red linen tablecloths draped the tables with poinsettias as the centerpieces.

In the center of the room were six tables with place settings for six. In the family room, a flat screen TV covered the wall above the fireplace. Piped in music played softly. For the Karaoke performances, a mini stage was set.

Wearing a red satin floor length sleeveless a-line dress, with silver pumps and rhinestone accessories, Mary made her entrance from the staircase. Gilbert was less formal in his black slacks, white shirt, black vest and black bow tie.

Karen was the spitting image of her Mom Mary, except taller, Mary could pass as Karen's older sister. Huge in stature, Gilbert stood about *6'6, 250 lbs*, with a dark complexion. Having successfully worked his way into management with a parcel post company, after thirty-five years, he looked forward to retirement at the end of the year.

Karen selected a gold satin semi-formal form-fitted spaghetti strap dress with a matching shawl and black satin pumps, and white gold accessories. Barbara Jean and Kim completed their assigned tasks and headed to the down-stairs guest quarters to change.

Desiring to look extra special this year, Barbara chose a black formal prom-look dress with a beaded sequin bodice with one strap; the skirt portion was form-fitted with a side split to the knee. She wore black satin pumps and black and rhinestone accessories.

Following suite with the same accessories as Barbara, Kim looked dazzling in her black form-fitted strapless satin dress, with a split on the right side; Kim closely resembled Cinderella, including her hairstyle.

Since the dinner was buffet style, they chose to ask God's blessing over the food for the entire evening. Gilbert led them in prayer as everyone gathered and held hands. *"Lord, Jesus, thank you once again for blessing us…*

At five-fifty, the caterers had completed the food preparations. Crab cakes, shrimp cocktails, pinwheels of cream cheese and smoked turkey, spinach dip in a sour dough bowl, a vegetable tray, a cheese ball and Buffalo wings polished off the appetizers.

A honey glazed ham became the centerpiece for the entrees, accompanied by a rack of rosemary and garlic lamb, roasted duck with a cranberry glaze, candied yams, macaroni and cheese, cornbread dressing, mashed potatoes and gravy, sautéed collard greens seasoned with smoked turkey, a broccoli salad, green bean casserole, and a tossed green salad.

Outdoing herself at the dessert table, Mary baked pecan and sweet potato pies, a lemon cheesecake, a three layer caramel cake, pineapple and German chocolate cakes. For the children, she made a gingerbread house and ginger cookies. Drinks of sparking apple and cranberry cider, hot apple cider, coffee, tea, milk and juice tied off the beverage bar. For the kid's convenience, the kitchen area was assigned.

To free up Mary and Gilbert to facilitate the flow of the party; Karen, Barbara, and Kim greeted and seated the guests. Karen was first in line to greet; making it perfect, Bill was right on time. Made speechless at the sight of Karen, "Wow! You look, gorgeous." *She looks better than gorgeous.* "Thanks, Bill, you look quite handsome yourself." Bill looked better than—good to Karen. In his black slacks, white shirt with a red sweater vest and black blazer was a huge contrast from his sweatshirt, shorts and baseball cap. Before he entered, Gary was directly behind him.

"Hi, I'm Gary, Barbara's friend"

"Yes, come in Gary." *Um...not bad, Barbara.*

"I'm Karen and this is, Bill."

"I remember you from the NBA, I see you at the Warriors games; we sit in the same section." Gary chatted, with exhilaration.

"It's a pleasure to meet you."

"No! The pleasure is mine, man; it's nice to be remembered." Bill added, shaking his hand. Seeing Gary, Barbara strolled over. "Merry Christmas, guys."

"Barbara, this is Bill," Karen said.

"It's so nice to meet you Bill; do you ever get told that you look like, Kurt Rambis?"

"I do, quite a bit; I left my glasses at home, just kidding." Barbara had to agree with Karen; Bill was a cutie, with stunning blue eyes. When the introductions were completed, Karen walked Bill over to meet her parents.

"Were my directions okay?" Barbara inquired of Gary.

"Your directions were fine," nodding and smiling. "My, my, you're looking extremely nice, I love your dress."

She smiled, before saying. "Let's just say the sentiments are mutual, Mr. Russell."

"Aw, thanks, you're kind." Gary replied.

Barbara was delighted with her dress choice. She'd found it over the internet from a little boutique in New York, falling in love with it; she'd purchased it for the cruise. *Boy, what a transformation from his work clothes.* His charcoal grey suit, white shirt, with a red and white tie was a big distinction from jeans and laced boots.

"Come; let me introduce you to Karen's parents." Following the introductions, she seated him with Bill.

The doorbell rang, Barbara yielded to Kim. Opening the door, Kim thought she'd opened the door to a prize on the *Price is Right*. Missing only was a red bow to wrap her tall slender dark skinned prize, with a fine-looking smile, and shinny white teeth. It was none other than pretty *boy,* Walter Douglas Hines, decked out in a traditional black tuxedo and white shirt. Clearing his throat after regaining his composure, caused Kim to release her stare. "Hi! I'm Walter Hines; I was invited by Barbara Jean."

"Oh yes, I'm Kim, please come in." Continuing to stand in the doorway smiling and blushing. He asked. "Kim, can I tell you how—breathe taking you look this evening?"

"I think you just did. Come in, come in." Using her hand to usher him. Spotting Walter, Barbara rushed over to greet him.

"Merry Christmas Walter, Oooh..., you look so handsome in your Tux."

"Talking about letting your hair down, you're looking good yourself, Barbara Jean."

"Yes, she does." Kim agreed.

"Thanks! Guys, I see you've met, Cinderella." Barbara complimented Kim. "Aw...," voiced Kim.

"Indeed we have." Walter added, still glaring at Kim. To bring Walter back to earth, Barbara took hold of his arm.

"Come, Walter; let me acquaint you with Karen's parents." Walking away, she gave Kim a *wink*. With his neck crooked, Walter continued to glare at Kim as he walked away.

Pairing him with Bill and Gary, "Guys, I'd like you to meet, Walter, he's a good friend and business associate."

"Barbara Jean..., this is Bill, my neighbor at work."

"Oh, you're one in the same; I've seen you from a distance." Barbara replied, in surprise.

After swallowing a bite of crab cake, "Nice to meet you, Barbara, again."

Cutting in, Gary said, "It doesn't stop there. A couple of years ago we built some homes in Hayward, you were one of the *lenders*, Walter."

"Oh—yeah, Russell, "*Russell Construction,*" right?" Shaking hands, they gave that *fake hug* that men do. "Good to see you, man."

"Likewise." Walter agreed.

"What a small world, I'll let you guys play catch up." Sprinting off to find Kim and Karen, Barbara cornered them in the kitchen.

"You're not going to believe this." Barbara said. Jumping in, Kim demanded. "You'd better be telling me that Walter is the same mortgage broker that's cute, available and a Christian."

"Yes, he is, and Bill's Walter's new friend, Bill's office is in the same complex with Walter."

"Oh my, goodness," Karen voiced.

"There's more, Walter assisted in the funding for some homes that Gary built." Bursting with excitement, Kim asked. "Do you think that he likes me?"

"Like you,—girl, please...,I pulled him away to keep him from salivating on you." Barbara said, grinning.

"I guess you didn't notice my *juicy mouth*. I am claiming him; he's my husband, guys. My *quest* has ended." Kim decreed, making an exclamation mark with her finger. Trading glances with Karen, Barbara uttered. "Well, La de da, I hear the doorbell, let's go."

Before the entertainment began, Bill and Gilbert engaged in an intense game of Chess. Gilbert would like nothing better than to see his baby girl with a special man in her life for the *New Millennium.*

Gilbert stood center stage and announced. *"It's show time*!" Everyone congregated to the stage area in the living room for the *Karaoke* performance.

The music to Charles Brown's rendition of "*Please Come Home for Christmas*" played. Grabbing the mic, Gilbert belted out "*Bells will be ringing*" in his deep baritone voice.

The women screamed as if they were at a Charles Brown concert. Gilbert followed suite with a concert scene; reaching into the crowd, he pulled Mary into his arms. Mary responded bashfully, while the women glowed with envy. "*You go man, you go,*" shouted the men. Gilbert did one more song. For an encore, he sang "*Chestnuts roasting on an open fire*."

The room overflowed with surprised compliments of his talent for singing. He could've quit his day job any day, and given Lou Rawls a run for his money.

"Everyone join in," Gilbert declared. They sang "*Walking in a Winter Wonderland*." The words to the song appeared on a wall above the piano.

Glancing in Bills direction, Karen observed him glaring at her with an affectionate smile, she reciprocated.

Barbara turned to find Gary next to her, grinning. Competing with the music, he whispered into her ear. "I'm having a great time; the Karaoke entertainment was a good idea, thanks for inviting me." Inhaling her perfume. *Gosh, she smells nice.*

"I'm glad you're enjoying yourself, I felt bad having to leave you as soon as you arrived." *Mmm… his cologne is familiar.* Gary grinned, before saying, "I'm a big boy,—no worries; I hung out with Bill, Walter, and Gilbert. Gilbert's great at Chess. It would've been nice to get to know you a little better," he admitted, smiling.

"I know…, we've hardly had time to talk." She said, softly. Busy with hosting; she'd completely ignored Gary. She made it a point to chat with him for ten minutes before disappearing again.

"Will you excuse me; I need to talk to someone that I invited." Gary opted to make her blush.

Bearing a straight face. "You mean you invited another man, BJ?" Nodding, and smiling, "Yeah…, ah, he's not a real man; I—mean; he's a friend." Sensing that he was teasing, "Are you messing with me, Gary?" Nodding and smiling in agreement, he'd accomplished his mission. His remark surprised her, blushing was her only recourse.

Sitting on the fireplace ledge; Barbara found Walter gazing in Kim's direction. Snatching her by her arm, he pulled her to sit beside him.

"Girl, where have you been keeping her?" Smiling, "Who on earth could you mean? Oh..., you mean Kim." She teased.

"This woman has stolen my heart."

"Are you sure it's your heart?" She taunted, in a sarcastic manner.

"Aw,—Barbara Jean, I'm being good. How well do you know her?"

Linking their arms in an engaging manner, "I'm teasing you Walter; calm down, the attraction is mutual." Walter eyes became so bright; he could've been an ornament on the Christmas tree.

"Are you serious, she likes me?"

"Yeah! She likes what she sees. I've known her since she was a little girl. She's the daughter of some friends of mine that used to reside in the Bay Area."

"If Michelle and she were friends, I know she's a Christian, which means, she was raised in the *word."*

Because of his overwhelming allure for Kim, to avoid previous mistakes with Christian women, he needed to be certain that she'd been planted in the *word.* She eagerly responded. "You're right on every account; her father is a Pastor, and a protective—one I might add."

"I can't believe she's still single."

"She's—waiting on God to direct her to her husband." Hoping that he got the *hint*.

"I knew it; it's something different about her. I can't explain it Barbara Jean; but meeting her tonight, is *destiny."*

"Walter, you may be onto something. I'm feeling a sincere spirit—about you." Squeezing her hand. "I'm so glad that I had you to talk to the other day. I took your advice, I had lunch with Bill, and then he showed up here."

"I know, isn't that something?"

"He's just the person that I needed Barbara Jean. He makes it easy to be transparent. You were right on it; we're going to have bible study together. I'm also going to be attending his church for early morning services."

Returning the hand squeeze, "Oh Walter, that's fantastic! I knew God would direct you, I'm so happy for you; he knows you're sincere about growing. Remember Walter, our weaknesses that's been a stumbling *block,* will continue to manifest itself until we *crucify it.* Not to worry Walter, you've met your *match;* things will be changing for you in the *New Millennium*. Gotta go mingle, Love Ya."

Walter decided to test the waters with Kim. Hearing a voice behind her. "May I?" Reaching, he removed the glass from her hand and poured the cider for her. Turning and gaping into his eyes, "Thanks!" She spoke, in a faint voice.

"My pleasure, I've been looking for you."

"I was busy greeting guest."

"I'm glad I came here first, I was supposed to attend another event." Charming him in a voice of anticipation, "Have your plans changed?"

"Entirely, this is my last stop."

Not attempting to shield her attraction, "Good decision."

"What do you like to do for pleasure? He asked.

"I love to read, play tennis, and take long walks. On week-ends, I enjoy eating out with friends, and take in a *feel good* movie. What about you, Walter?"

"I like to golf, play and watch basketball, take long rides and watch the cooking shows and cook."

Showing a surprise look, "Me, too!" *He watches cooking shows! I'm impressed.* "Maybe we can have a cook-off or something?" He offered.

"I would love that Walter, it should be fun."

"Kim, before you take off, may I please—get your phone number?" *I thought he'd never ask.* He handed her a business card, and pen.

"Sure, I'd better get back to see if I'm needed for anything." Holding one hand to his heart, he watched her as she walked away. *Oh my, Lord, is this a test? This one is different, Lord, I can tell."*

Believing that the attraction was mutual, he loved her subtle but confident air. Meeting Bill was timely; Kim definitely possessed the physical attributes that had rendered Walter weak in times past with women.

During Gilbert's last song, Bill had maneuvered his way beside Karen. "Your Dad sings great, it's been fun."

"I'm glad that you're enjoying yourself, my parents love to entertain. I'm so blessed to have them."

"You really are Karen. When my parents retired, they moved to Oregon; I miss—them a great deal. I get to see them at least four times a year; but I miss going over for a good home cooked meal."

"Oh, I bet." Karen felt Bill was also missing the loving care of his wife; she could only sympathize with him. The breakup of her marriage was painful, but it was no comparison to his circumstances.

Forever loyal and supportive, Karen wasn't surprised in getting the thumbs up from both of her parents after they'd talked to Bill.

"We're looking forward to the youth rally on tomorrow night." Karen informed him. That was music to Bill's ears.

"That makes two of us; I think you'll enjoy it. I saw Michael briefly; he said he's excited. Did I tell you how beautiful you look this evening?" In a voice that was low and inviting, "It's always nice to hear again." Laughing, Bill repeated it again.

The second half of the entertainment resumed with *Legends* being the *theme.* A group from the hospital did the *Temptations*. Dr. Washington and her husband, Dan performed *Peaches and Herb* rendition of *"Reunited."* Walter took his eyes off Kim long enough to sing "*Your Precious Love,* by Jerry Butler.

After Walter and Gilbert did so well, other's wanted to take their turn at the mic. Smoky Robinson, Nancy Wilson, Sam Cook, Tom Jones and Aretha Franklin were in the house. For the grand *finale,* acted out by none other than Joyce; she did Tina Turner's *"Proud Mary."* Tina's legs had nothing on Joyce. The young *interns* loved them some Joyce.

To end the Karaoke entertainment, Gilbert led them in singing "*Silent Night and "Away in a Manger."* Karen played the piano as everyone joined in singing. Mary dimmed the lights and lit the candles that encircled the room. The combination of the panoramic view from the living room, and the illuminated Christmas tree; it was a moment to behold.

In between songs Karen played softly as Gilbert offered Praises to God for the blessings that he'd bestowed upon his family; reminding them that it's because of Jesus birth that made all their blessings a reality.

Spotting Dr. Washington, and Dan getting ready to leave, Mary ran over to chat. "I'll bring the car around, Babe." Dan informed her. "You, guys leaving?" Mary asked.

"Yes dear, I have early rounds; one of my little sweet peas is in ICU. No wonder there's always a smile on your face, you're thinking about Gilbert, with that Lou Rawls singing voice of his." She teased. Mary slumped over with laughter. "You and Dan weren't so bad yourself, *Peaches.*"

Blushing, Dr. Washington answered. "Oh..., girl, you know, I think this was the best one yet Mary, the Karaoke entertainment was an innovative touch."

"Everyone said the exact same thing, honey that was Gilbert's idea; you have a *Merry Christmas* and a *Happy New Year.*"

"Oh girl, I almost forgot to tell you, my pharmaceutical representative, Thomas stopped by the day after we saw the photographs. I wanted to ask about his wife, so bad!" Waving her hand, she confessed. "Child, the Lord *convicted* me that I was being *mean* and *nosy*, so I didn't."

"He didn't tarry; I think he had some guilt going on. He gave me a present, some samples for a new drug, wished me a *Merry Christmas*, and got out of there." She said, laughing.

"Well, I invited Vanessa because she's Kim's friend, I guess it's probably best that she didn't show." Mary said.

"I guess..., well, good night!"

Stunned, when she opened the door short of hitting Thomas and Vanessa, she almost ingested her tongue. Dr. Washington forced a smile, and greeted. "Well, hello, Thomas, what a small world, I didn't know that you knew the Rose's.

"Ah...," he stuttered, "I don't, I'm with Vanessa." Thomas was past embarrassed.

"Dr. Washington, this is my friend, Vanessa."

"Good evening Dr. Washington, I see you at Carson General, the pediatric ward, correct?" Vanessa greeted.

"Yes! It's certainly good seeing both of you, have a Merry Christmas."

"A Merry *Christmas* to you too, Dr. Washington." For years he'd serviced Dr. Washington, their topic of conversation always centered on them having a baby. Dr. Washington had previously met Thomas's wife; from a professional standpoint, this wasn't looking too good for Thomas.

Being entirely innocent to his awkwardness, Vanessa was also clueless to the fact that Dr. Washington knew about their affair and cruise. Regretting that he'd let Vanessa talk him into coming; Thomas wasn't prepared to accept the ridicule for him *dumping* his wife for a younger model tonight. A model that he hoped would give him a baby.

Thomas wasn't considered your classically "*handsome man*," but had a *strut* about him; which made him more appealing to Vanessa. She loved the classic tall and dark skinned man, making his 6'3 slender built an added attraction to her. At the age of forty-four, he'd become obsessed with the idea of having a baby, especially after all his brothers and sisters had kids. Married for ten years; he felt that he needed to move on while he was still young.

Serving as a Deacon in his church, and head of the finance board, he never understood why they kept him in such significant leadership roles; especially since he traveled frequently. Revered as the *big cheese,* and consistent in paying his tithes and offering, any shortcomings on his part were pardon. He loved the attention and the power.

Eyeballing them as they entered, Barbara sighed. *Oh my Lord, it's Vanessa and her man."* Moseying over, Mary whispered. "Do you see what I see? For Kim's sake, it's good that she left." Mary informed Barbara.

"Did she? That's great; she's still stressed from Vanessa's dilemma."

"In order to attend the party, one of the nurses is spending the night with Kim." Mary shared, "She has to work the early morning shift, Kim left to avoid disturbing her sleep."

"Oh..., okay! Great, it all worked out." Being the perfect host, Mary greeted them graciously. "Merry Christmas Vanessa, it's nice of you to drop by. The entrée's have been put away. Can I have the caterers prepare something for you; or would you prefer some beverages? "

"No! Thank, you." Vanessa explained that she'd attended a formal dinner party with Thomas earlier, she only stopped by to say, hello.

"You look familiar." Thomas said to Mary.

"Do you attend Peace Fellowship?" She asked, finally re-calling to memory the name of the church. Thomas cleared his throat.

"Uh...Yes," wishing he'd kept his mouth shut.

"Our church attended a Pastor's appreciation a year ago." Mary said. Aware of his discomfort, Mary offered him relief. "It was so kind of you guys to stop by. Come; I'd like for you to meet my daughter, Karen, and my husband, Gilbert."

Recapping the evening events, Gilbert gave his take on Bill and Gary. "From a man's perspective, they appear to be level headed men."

Making fun of Barbara, "You kept leaving poor Gary Barbara, he was fine with it. He's going to give me some ideas on a project I plan to start next year.

I thought highly of Bill also. I'd observed him at a distance at Michael's games. He's good people; he's good at chess too. Let's see how things pan out." Gilbert excused himself and said good night!

Karen and Barbara exchanged a relieved glance, supported by a happy smile. Gilbert's opinions were valued as *nuggets of wisdom.* "I concur with Gilbert sentiments whole heartily." Mary agreed.

"Well, what did you guy's think of my friend, Walter?"

"I know all the available women were trying to get at him." Karen quickly remarked. "I think he's *fine,* Kim thought so, too. I talked to him a little; he's sweet, well spoken, you know, that complete package deal, again." Karen added, laughing.

"Oh, I get you, not to worry, he's no Ralph." Barbara assured.

"But with his popularity with women and all, do you think Kim is ready for him?" Karen asked, with concern.

"Huh," uttered Barbara, "Trust me on this one. After careful thought, at this stage of his life, she's just—what he needs." Karen nodded in comprehension.

"He's sweet, they would make a cute couple, she deserves a good man, she's had such disappointments." Mary noted.

The hour was late; everyone was exhausted. Mary had previously ordered that they'd be spending the night, dismissing Barbara's half-planned idea to have tea with Gary.

Dashing to catch her phone before it stopped ringing; she got there just in time to hear. "*This is Gary; I'd hoped to talk with you, I had a great* time; *thanks for inviting me. I really enjoyed the little time we shared together. I am heading for my home in the Valley. I'll have to bring you guys down for a weekend. Connie calls it my bed & breakfast resort; I call it my place to retreat. Take care." Bed & Breakfast, hmm... sounds interesting*

Barbara was okay with missing his call; she'd many things that she needed to do before Christmas. Reading e-mails was at the top of her list. Heading to her office, suddenly, she remembered Sober, her new internet friend. Instantly, she logged in and sure enough she'd two messages from him; one was as recent as this morning.

A call from Karen interrupted her. Waking up early, Karen meditated on topics from Sunday's brunch. Experiencing a range of emotions, her central focus was Bill.

Appearing to be a Godly man, she wanted to make sure that her behavior remained pleasing to God. She didn't want to fall short as she did as a single Christian woman prior to her marriage.

Recalling statements from the brunch, "*Some men test women.*" She didn't want to fail the test, nor did she want to be an obstacle for Bill or any man.

"Hello!"

"Good morning, Barbara!"

"Good morning to you Karen, what's up?"

"Oh, nothing, just thinking about last night. I think I'm starting to like Bill."

"That's a good thing, right?"

"I guess!"

"Okay, spit it out, what's bothering you."

"You know me, I always think ahead of the road before I get there. I'm wondering what kind of role model Bill would be for Michael; I mean..., he's not a Black, man."

"No, kidding!" Barbara voiced, as they both shared a laugh.

"If Bill wasn't a Christian, it'd be a greater concern. You've prayed for a committed Christian man, only time will tell if you're in God's will with him." Barbara continued to admonish, in a fussing tone. "Sometimes I think we take this *culture* thing too, far. He's fifteen years old; Michael should have a good grasp on his identity by now. Since your divorce, Ronald and your Dad have been there for Michael, they're both strong Black role models for him."

"Deep down, I'm probably—identifying how Ronald felt about interracial relationships. I recall him saying, "*Black Men should rear Black Boys.*" He said it was a culture thing."

"Girl,—the enemy started early on you this morning."

"You got that right."

"Ideally, it would be a good thing with respect to nurturing and developing his individuality. Ronald created this situation; you have to make the best of it for you and Michael. Beside, Ronald is still in his life, he'll be the *prevailing influence*."

"You're right; Karen agreed, in a repressed tone. You know that we're going to Bill's church this evening for the youth rally."

"That's right!"

"Have you talked to, Gary today?" Karen asked.

"He called, I missed it; he said he'll be gone for the weekend."

"What's your take of him, now?"

"It's improving; I did find out that he has a sister. She's coming to visit next week. The anxiety to know more about him is subsiding. I'm not losing interest or anything close to that. Since the party, I'm confident that he's the business professional that he represents himself."

"That's a comforting thought, right? What about him being a Christian?

"The verdict is still out."

"Why don't you just ask, or say something spiritual." She chuckled.

"You mean, like *Praise the Lord, or I'm blessed,* to get his response."

"Yeah, yeah! Karen said, snickering.

"Um..., I don't want to use "*Christian buzz words*" for the sake of determining if he's a Christian. Girl, the secular world uses "*Christian expressions*" all the time. Nah...that won't work.

"I know; I'm just anxious for you."

"I know you are, and I appreciate it. I'm not ashamed of the expressions; I mean; I use them daily as endearing terms." I just think that they have their place. *(Rom 1:16)* Hey, I did think about it." Barbara giggled and admitted. "We're supposed to be a *peculiar people,* right?"

"Right, right," Karen agreed.

"I believe in time, it'll become evident in our conversations, and behaviors. We've just met, we haven't had any alone time. So far his behavior has been consistent to that of a Christian."

"Yeah, this is true, he's certainly mild mannered, you know, easy going, no stress." Karen said.

"You're right; I sense that too, I have my plan when the opportunity presents itself." Barbara assured her.

"You're so analytical; in other words, stop asking if Gary's a Christian." She laughed.

"No! No! Not at all, I welcome your concerns. My child is just as anxious."

"In the case with me and Bill, Michael was instrumental in alleviating any speculations between us relative to our faith. Your point is well founded; Ronald is the perfect example of people who throw out Christian phrases to impress people."

"We were supposed to have tea after the party, but we spent the night at your, Moms. I kept an eye on him last evening. There were many attractive women there; he spent most of his time talking to Walter, Bill and your Dad. Since we're only friends, it's really not a factor at this point, Karen."

"That's putting things into perspective." Karen surmised.

"Did I tell you about the guy from the dating website?" Barbara asked.

"No! Who?"

"He calls himself, Sober. He's a Christian; it was a prerequisite in my profile. He's never married, but desires to be some day. He admitted to talking to a woman he recently met, he said they're only friends. He wants to continue to e-mail me."

"Does he live in the area?"

"Certainly, I restricted my search to the Bay Area. He said he' be in, and out of town until the middle of next year."

"You think its work related?"

"Oh, I don't know; we elected not to mention occupations. We want to develop a friendship based on character, interest, dislikes, and spiritual matters."

"Oh, that's neat. I hate it when they ask, "*What do you do?*", as soon as they know your name." Karen said, laughing.

"Yeah, I know; Gary gave me his card five seconds after introductions were made. In retrospect, I think it was to convince me that his opinions were professional; it's nothing arrogant or nosy about Gary."

"What about a photo, did he post one?" Karen asked.

"No!" Barbara laughed. "That was my request also, no photos, just someone to correspond, you know, like a "*pen pal*" sort of thing."

"Yeah, yeah, that makes sense. If you're looking for a friend those things shouldn't really matter initially. I think it takes off some of the pressure. Well, I know your occupation speaks to your personality, and character, but it must be nice to communicate without expectations." Karen added.

"It is." Jokingly, Barbara commented. "You know it's been a while for me, I need to ease into this dating thing."

"Um, hum, you're probably right. You bring up a good point Barbara, regarding restricting your selection to the Bay Area. That's a good idea, you can readily *verify* what their telling you; I'll keep that in mind."

"Yep! Take Walter and Gary, we didn't meet online, but because they're local, Walter validates Gary's past."

"Well, I am going to sign off now. I've been so preoccupied thinking about Bill; I haven't had a chance to do anything. I'm going to get off this phone and get ready for our date. And... I'm not going to focus on Ronald's opinions. "

"Great, let me know how it goes. Good Bye!"

Ronald, Karen's ex was the typical *carnal* Christian, not believing in the sanctity—of his marriage vows, but had the nerve not to believe in getting a divorce. Having been caught in the act, Karen divorced him after three affairs that were made known to her.

Deeply committed to his fatherly responsibilities; he was devoted to Michael. Being a history teacher heighten his position for being a proud Black man. The fact that he was tall, and possessed a muscular physique; at 6 ft; he was still shorter than Michael was. Michael inherited his dark skin tone from Ronald, and his athletic and slender built from his Mom. Ronald maintained his love for Karen.

Continuously interrogating Michael concerning his Mom's social activities, he'd also make frequent drive by's, looking for unfamiliar cars. When Michael visits him, there's clear evidence that he wasn't sitting by waiting for his Mom to return.

Michael had noticed his coach taking an interest in his Mom for some time, never mentioning it to her; he chose to perform a heat check for his Dad's reactions. He'd casually drop statements to him made by his Coach. Ronald never disappointed; his response was consistent with that of the jealous husband. As Michael grew older, he formed the conclusion that his Dad had been the *weak link* that ended the marriage. Karen refrained from revealing specifics to Michael to avoid compromising his relationship with his Dad. Ronald knew that Michael had formed an alliance with his mother.

Chapter 6

Bursting with excitement, Bill was right on time picking up Karen and Michael. She and Bill were excited as Michael was. Michael slid in the back seat of Bill's SUV, allowing his Mom to have the front seat beside Bill.

It'd been a while since she was close and personal to a man in a dating situation, as expected; she was somewhat uncomfortable. Bill, being receptive to her discomfort; to ease the tension, he provided them with highlights for the evening events.

Halfway there, relaxed in her jeans and grey sweater, they were laughing and talking. Bill wanted everything to go perfect for the evening. After attending the party in her parent's home, he was convinced that Karen was someone that he wanted to get to know on a personal level. Fond of her parents, he felt comfortable in their midst; they reminded him of his deceased wife, Sherrie's parents.

Praying and asking God if it was okay to move forward with Karen, he felt this evening would be the beginning of a new life for him.

Upon arrival, Bill directed them into the sanctuary. The event opened to the tune of Kurt Franklin's *Stomp.* The building swarmed with teens, young adults and parents.

Seated in front of them were some of Michael's teammates. While bobbing their heads to the music; they exchanged high five's. Bill appeared on stage to welcome everyone; comfortable in his khaki Dockers, and a navy polo, he led them in prayer. After several songs, the praise dancers performed.

Leaving the parents in the sanctuary, the teens and preteens broke into separate groups. Informing Karen that he was the facilitator for Michael's group; Bill left to conduct his class. Facilitators for the parents consisted of a married couple and a single parent man and woman.

Focusing on the importance of a *family altar*, the parents were encouraged to take the time to come together one night a week for prayer and bible study. Parents were advised that the kid's initial rejection was to be expected, and that they should not become disheartened.

To support their theory; they solicited the aid of actual parents who testified how God had blessed their home because of them implementing family time.

In Bill's group of teens, they were tackling topics of peer pressure, bullies, abstinence, and developing a personal relationship with Christ. Teens passed on how they'd come to the point of embracing Christ as their, *Lord and Savior*, along with the teachings of their parents; they collectively pointed out the difference it'd made in their lives.

Because of their disobedience to God, and their parents, teen speakers from Juvi voiced how they'd gotten into the wrong crowd. Vocalizing how times had been hard for them financially, more importantly, how they'd lost their freedom as kids. For added affect, teen mothers came with their babies.

Since the evening was young, Bill offered to treat them to ice cream. Upon entering the parlor, Michael became excited; seeing his Dad Ronald and Uncle Joseph, he waved to them. The host escorted them to their tables, which were two booths away from Ronald.

In passing, they stopped to extend greetings. Michael attempted to introduce Bill to his uncle and Dad. Remembering Bill from his NBA days and knowing that he was Michael's coach; Joseph was eager to meet him. Making no effort to hide his dissatisfaction with Coach Hansen's presence, Ronald sat and stared toward the window; ignoring them completely.

After Ronald refused Bill's handshake, Michael frowned at his Dad, and all pleasantries came to a halt. Bill gave a handshake to Michael's Uncle Joseph, and signaled for them to continue to their table.

In a state of total anguish, Michael sat slouched in his seat. Nestled close to him, in a compassionate and discreet tone, Karen asked. "Are you sure you're up for this, do you want to leave?

"No! But Dad's being a real jerk, Mom."

With firmness, Karen admonished."I realize you're upset, but you can't call your father names, Michael."

Making a brave effort to remain tactful, and caring, Bill rallied to defend Ronald.

"Go easy on him Michael; he's shocked to see the three of us together." Ronald's actions hadn't surprised Bill; they were inline with his standoffish behavior during practices and games. After a few forced mouthfuls of ice cream, Bill knew that Michael needed some time alone; and insisted that they leave.

Michael wasn't too surprised; he'd noticed his Dad's attitude toward him on the court. The other boy's fathers on the team would always shoot the breeze with him, not Ronald; the mere thought of any man taking an interest in his ex was unsettling to him.

Whispering a pray, Bill drove away slowly after dropping them off. *"Lord, my worst fear just came true. Lord, I ask that you will comfort Karen and Michael during this time of frustration. Give her the wisdom to see past Ronald's beha-*

viors. Help Michael to forgive his Dad. Give me the strength to accept your will for my life. In Jesus name, I pray, Amen."

Michael's wave from the window assured Bill that things were okay with them. Driving off, he spotted a car parked across the street; he knew it was Ronald.

Bill had looked forward to spending more time with them for the evening, he was thankful that they did enjoy the youth rally. What was supposed to be his big night became a night of regret. The thought of Karen backing away from him made him nauseous.

Karen entered Michael's room to find him playing with one of his video games.

"Share your heart, what are your feelings?"

Raising his shoulders, "At first...," he paused. "I was embarrassed at Dad." Lowing his head, while smiling, "He doesn't like Coach..., because he knows Coach likes you."

"And how does he know that, Michael?" Grinning and looking similar to a kid with their hand caught in a cookie jar. "Well..., I sort of told him that Coach asked about you."

"Michael! You're bad..., but I'm glad that you're okay."

"I'm fine Mom. Dad—dates whom he wants, he has women over all the time; when he thinks I'm asleep."

"That's your Dad,—I needed to make sure you're okay with his behavior tonight."

"I'm fine; I won't pay it any mind. I'm cool, Mom. Sorry for calling Dad a *jerk*. I sure hope his actions didn't bother Coach too much. How are you, Mom?" Embracing him. "I'm better now, knowing that you're okay. Don't worry, Coach's a big boy; he can take care of himself. We'll talk about the youth rally tomorrow. Good night! I love you."

"I Love you too, Mom, Good night!"

Darting to her prayer closet, she couldn't believe what she'd witnessed. *Ronald had his nerve, behaving so rude and disrespectful to Bill.* Karen had no idea Michael had been taunting Ronald with Bill's interest in her. *Thank you Father for guarding Michael's mind and heart from Ronald's foolishness....*

After making one mistake in choosing her mate, she was determined to be led of God for her next husband. Unlike before, this time Karen knew the things to look for. She knew you couldn't stop at the man, you needed to know about his parents, the environment he grew up.

What type of relationship he'd with his mother, his father. How did his father treat his mother, if he was present or absent in the home? What was his church experience, if any? Did he believe in tithing; what were his treasures? How does he spend his spare time, or is he a *couch potato*. Lastly, does he have *purpose* in life, and a *love for God*? She wouldn't be deceived by church attendance only the second time around.

Thinking that she'd found a good God-fearing man in that of Ronald, every time the door swung open; he was there. She'd learned; attendance couldn't serve as a gauge to determining ones level of commitment to Christ. Time would prove; he was committed only to his own selfish desires.

Attending a church with a strong bible-believing ministry, like a sponge, Karen drenched herself in the word. Fellowship and attendance were Ronald's only interest, he never completed any classes.

There was still a lot she needed to know about Bill. After tonight, she feared that she might never hear from him again. Now, entertaining second thoughts; she wondered if interracial dating was a good idea. Ronald's comments continued to raid her mind. *"Black boys need to be raised by their Fathers."* Sadly, that wasn't an option for Michael. Karen believed that everything happened for a reason. For now, she'd get some rest, and look forward to early morning services.

Squeezing hands to greet, Karen slipped into the seat beside Barbara at early morning services. God's presence had manifested in a double portion that morning. While basking in the presence of the Lord, Karen had missed the praise and worship portion. Throwing on a brown sweater dress, and boots; she got there just in time for the message.

By the delivery of Pastor Rama messages, it was evident that he spent an enormous amount of time in prayer and study. Surpassing the five fold ministries, healthcare, diet, and nutrition were major components of the ministry as well; along with a full curriculum of studies designed for spiritual nourishment and growth. Finally, yet more importantly, you were challenged to seek God in discovering your *destiny purpose* in his kingdom.

Leading by example as a faithful husband and father, he was a strong advocate of marriage and the family; causing the ministry to capture the attention of a diverse group of people within the community.

Sensitive to Karen's heavy heart, Barbara invited her over for breakfast after morning worship. Tossing her bible and green purse onto the kitchen counter, that matched her green two piece suit; she flipped the switch to the coffee pot. In a sluggish posture, Karen sat at the kitchen bar.

"Okay, what's going on? Barbara asked. "Wait; let me check this message, Karen."

"Hey Barbara Jean, Walter, I want to thank you for the invite. I'm still on cloud nine after meeting Kim. Ah..., thank you, thank you. I can't believe how God brought everyone together, Bill being present, and Russell, who turned out to be your, Gary. I always refer to him as "Russell." You made a good call, girl. Talk to you soon."

"Someone's happy." Karen echoed.

"Barbara, you wouldn't believe what happened last night after we left church." Cutting up strawberries and peeling bananas to serve with cereal, bran muffins, coffee and juice, Barbara stated impatiently. "I'm waiting!" Karen brought her up to date. "What? Girl, how do you think Bill will respond?"

"I'm not sure, he tried to defend Ronald's actions, it was so embarrassing Barbara. Ronald played the jealous—husband role, girl, coupled with rudeness. I stand corrected, as my Grand Mama would say, He *showed his bare behind."* Trying to contain her laughter, Barbara inquired. "How was Michael, this morning?"

"Michael's fine, thank God. He's spending the day with April and Maurice; they have something going on for him."

"So what's your biggest concern?" Taking a bite of her muffin.

"I don't know; I'm confused. Everything was going good with Bill, and now this with Ronald, I don't know."

"Let me understand this, you're confused because Ronald doesn't approve of you dating a man, or a White man."

"I guess; I worry about Michael. I want him to have some level of trust and stability from one of his parents."

Giggling, before taking a spoonful of cereal, Barbara voiced. "Correct me on this, since Ronald disapproves, you can't have a White husband; are you suggesting marrying outside of your race is irresponsible or unstable?"

"No! You're being silly," she laughed.

"I'm referring to stability as it relates to our, *culture."*

"That's your department to make sure he continues to be exposed to our *culture and traditions*. Your parents will be a big influence in that area, and Ronald, they're the best."

"They are; you're right."

"Girl, this is the first man you've dated, can't you see what he's doing." Pausing for another spoonful of cereal. "He'd behave the same way if Bill was Black."

"Now that's the truth," Karen agreed.

"If Bill's race is your concern you can cheer up; at least he's a Christian. What if Bill was Black, and not a Christian, would you prefer him?"

"I see your point, Christianity should *trump* race."

"Of course, we talked about this yesterday." Barbara reminded her. "Ronald is still his father, and will be in his life. Nothing will change between the two of them. Bill is for you, the fact that he may become a member of your household makes it an *issue*."

"Michael made matters worse; he's been telling Ronald that Bill's interested in me."

"Hush! Girl, for real, Michael's a smart young man; he knows what he's doing."

"I think this is his way of getting back at him for all the women Michael knows about, he only wants me to be happy; he thinks the world of Bill."

"Satan has gotten all the victory he's going to get from this *race* thing. Where was your little mind during church today? I think the sermon was for us. He talked about being in God's will when we encounter opposition; it doesn't mean that we're *out of God's will*."

"Remember he referenced Joseph, look at the challenges that he was presented." Seated with her head slightly hung, "I got that, you're right. Starting my business was very discouraging; I almost gave up on numerous occasions." "Let Michael be your litmus test."

"What do you mean?"

"Pay attention to his feelings regarding you and Bill. The fact that you value his feelings proves that you're not selfish in satisfying your desires only. God knows what best for the two of you; he speaks to us through our children, *if we listen*."

"I think I'm going to stop thinking so much, put this on hold, and revisit it after the holidays."

"Now, that's the smartest thing you've said all morning."

"Did I tell you that I got the bid on that big New Year's Eve Party in the City?"

(San Francisco) Karen spoke with excitement. "Really!"

"Yes! The dinner dance for the financial brokers, realtors and contractors, you go, girl!" Barbara reached for an envelope.

"I have an invite to that from one of my title companies."

"You can come with, me." Turning her head, "I don't—know, Karen; it's been over ten years since I've gone to a "watch night service" on New Years Eve, and a dinner dance..., huh, much longer. Concluding on New Years Eve, I have this little prayer and praise ritual that I do during the week." She said, enthusiastically.

"The entire week, I praise God as far back as I can remember as a child; I look forward to it." She said, smiling. "I believe it's those prayers that get me through each year? It's a great time for self reflecting and meditation."

"Sort of like *buying insurance* for the up and coming year." Karen noted.

"Yeah, I like that expression, Karen, *buying insurance*."

"You're not getting *legalistic* on me, are you?"

"Me! Oh—please! Barbara voiced.

"You know this is my first New Years Eve event." Karen reminded her. "Oh..., I'll go girl, just to keep you out of trouble. *Black and White Ball,* that means a new dress." She said, with glistening eyes."

"Have you talked to Kim lately?" Barbara asked.

"Yes, she called last night, I gave her the scoop. Your sentiments were mutual, as always. She was sitting across the aisle from us this morning. When Pastor said, *"things aren't always as they appear,"* she was grinning and looking in my direction." Karen told her.

"I hate for anyone to look at me after the preacher done made a comment; people near you know that you have issues." Barbara fussed. Laughing in agreement, Karen said. "I know, don't you just hate that; I'm going to kill Kim."

"Kim's quite taken with Mr. Hines. Jackie called asking *"who is this Walter?"* She said that every time she calls Kim she's on the phone with him. I think he invited her to attend a New Year Eve's Gala." Barbara informed her.

"How special, well..., she said her *quest* was over. They do appear to have a lot in common. Bill has been a blessing for Walter."

"I know..." Barbara mouthed. "Well, at least it's mutual. He called me regarding a signing, it's the second time that he's thanked me; we didn't have time to talk."

"So, is she going?" Karen asked.

"I think so; she said she'd to go shopping for a new dress. I can't imagine her finding anything that'll top that cute little number she had on Friday night." Kim had just purchased a gorgeous evening gown for the party; now she's pleasantly surprised in the search for another one.

"I know, wasn't she a doll." Karen praised.

"Well, if he's inviting her, I'm sure it's your event."

"Oh, finance brokers, you're probably right." Karen agreed, with exhilaration.

"Walter is really out to impress Kim, normally he's at his church "watch night services." Barbara shared.

"I'm usually at my, Mom's preparing black-eyed peas for the next day, it's our time to offer thanks to God and bring in the New Year as a family. That's why I respect your little ritual. My duties will end at midnight; we can leave."

"Sounds like a plan; it'll be nice to get dressed up again." Barbara said.

"Did Kim talk to Vanessa?" Karen asked.

"I think she's meeting with her today."

"Great, can you say, let's go shopping?" Barbara suggested, with expectancy. Clearing the counter of their dishes, they headed for the mall.

After cautiously deliberating, Kim decided to confront Vanessa regarding her affair with a married man; they're meeting at the Marina. While waiting, she reflected on Walter. Enjoying getting to know him, they'd been on the phone non-stop since meeting.

Appreciating his bluntness relative to his women struggles, and how it'd inhibited his spiritual growth; he was direct in telling her about the convictions God had placed upon him. She found comfort in the fact that Bill was his new mentor, and spiritual advisor.

Walter didn't meet the criteria of her dream man with respect to a commitment to Christ. Walter, like Ronald was committed to church attendance, only. She was looking for a man with more of her father's qualities, and one that loved God.

Knowing that he was serious about growing in the Lord, she also felt a deep sincerity about him, and therefore, felt led to test his re-commitment to Christ.

With consideration to Ralph's issues, she felt Walter's *weakness* for women paled in comparison. Because of her relationship with Ralph, her *tolerance level* toward Walter had increased.

Laid-back in her appearance, Vanessa arrived in her black sweats, and white sneakers. Taking pride in keeping her tall voluptuous frame of 5'9 proportionate to her weight; she exercised daily. Her light copper toned skin complimented her brown neck-length hair. Giving account to her physical beauty, and high intellect; she lacked self-confidence.

Being made aware of Thomas marital status on day one; she chose to overlook it. So flattered by his attention and attraction to her, to justify her actions; she convinced herself that "if a man strays, it was the wife's problem, not hers." Giving Vanessa his sob story of wanting a baby played to Vanessa's emotions, being thirty-five, she became gullible. As much as she desired a baby, she wasn't willing to have one out of wedlock. She became putty in his hands.

Vanessa shouted. "Hey, girl, so what's up?"

"Hi, Vanessa!" Ushering her over to a bench in a more secluded area. In a melancholy tone, Kim said. "I'm sure you're wondering why I wanted to talk to you."

"Yes!" Adding emphasis, with a neck motion.

"Remember the day you let me look at your cruise photographs? Well...," she drew in a breath..."I was looking at them alone in the cafeteria when Mary, Barbara and Dr. Washington joined me. Barbara picked up one and asked who went on a cruise? I said, Vanessa, and gave them permission to view them." With the wave of a hand, Vanessa indicated no harm, "that's okay; I didn't want you showing them to the other nurses."

"There's more to tell, Mary said she recognized Thomas, and said she knew him as a Deacon from another church. Dr. Washington said Thomas is her Pharmaceutical Representative, and he's *married*."

Crossing her legs, Vanessa stiffened. Studying her intently. *This is not news to her ears.* Now keenly aware that her information is not news worthy, "I'm not shocking you am I, Vanessa?" Lifting her head, with a look that said, *so what's it to you*? Vanessa responded. "No!"

"You've dated this man for over two years, and you knew that he was married?"

"That's why I never told you; I knew you wouldn't approve or understand." She blurted passionately, with a neck joggle, and one hand resting on her thigh.

"You're right about not approving Vanessa, but understand; I would've tried, as I'm now. Can we talk about this?"

Waggling her shoulders, "Sure!" Walking over to sit beside her, Kim pleaded with compassion. "Vanessa, help me to understand, how did this affair begin?"

"I met him at the hospital; it was a mutual attraction. Within a week, he was spending nights when he was supposed to be out of town."

"Did you know that he was married, initially?"

"Yeah..." She extracted, slowly. "But he also said he was going to be divorcing her." Letting loose rapidly, implying justification.

"He wants a baby, and after ten years she hasn't delivered."

Enduring two miscarriages, Mrs. Thomas, out of frustration gave up trying. Realizing that there was no acceptable explanation for her actions; Vanessa chose to resort to the defensive approach.

In disbelief, and filled with compassion, Kim protested. "Vanessa, so now it's your job to give him his, *baby*."

"What's wrong with that? I want one, too!" She launched, in a tone suggesting worthiness.

"Well…," Kim paused, as her thought iced up. "Find your own man, Vanessa. He belongs to someone else." Kim hurled, fervently.

Being the daughter of a Pastor, she'd over hear conversations with her parents regarding indiscretions with married men and single women that had occurred in the church. She knew the discussions were private; accordingly, she kept them to herself. On the other hand, she'd developed intolerance for women with behaviors like her friend, Vanessa.

In most of the cases, broken families were generally the result of the affairs. Hitting close to home, her uncle had divorced her aunt; which devastated her cousins. She'd witnessed many women in the church trying to get at her Dad; therefore this became a *thin-skinned* matter to her.

"Vanessa, you had no—right to compound the problems in that marriage. You go to church every Sunday, girl! Talk to me!" Kim uttered mercifully, with arms firmly folded; she paced back and forth.

"Girl,—I grew up in the church my entire life, just like you, and this is how it's been. Like my Aunt always said, "As Christians, we're still human," and God forgives, 1 John1:9 tells us that." Supported with scripture, Vanessa threw Kim a left jab, responding with an attitude of conviction, defensiveness, and feeling no condemnation.

Kim was thankful that she'd selected a secluded area. Trying desperately to hang tough with Vanessa; deep down she was fearful of the outcome. Feeling confident that she was doing the right thing, still, she waged war with fear from the enemy.

Knowing Vanessa desired marriage and a family, she also knew that she'd never be blessed with her desires if she continued to live her life in bondage and defeat. Until now, Kim had never tried to challenge Vanessa in her acts of *fornication.*

Now standing, after regaining her composure, Kim answered back. "Well, how many times do you want him to forgive you for the same sin, Vanessa? Where's the *repentance* Vanessa? You're not afraid that you may not be receiving the refuge that you're seeking in 1 John 1:9.

And since we're quoting scriptures, what about Psalms 119:11 *"Thy word have I hid in my heart, that I may not sin against thee, or* Romans 6:1 *Shall we continue in sin, that grace may abound?"* Do they ring any bells for you Vanessa? Or do you plan to continue to hide behind 1 John 1:9?" She pleaded with her.

With her head looking downward, Vanessa sulked like a spoiled brat. She murmured, "I've heard one of them."

"You can't choose the scriptures that you think will only benefit you, it doesn't work that way Vanessa."

Treading back and forth, Vanessa halted, "I know we all have to give an account for our actions. It...she paused, "It just feels..., so right. I'm thirty-five years old, and I want to be married, and have a baby; we love each other."

"Of course you do, but at whose *expense*. I desire the same thing Vanessa; I'm twenty-eight. You were at that brunch; you sat back and didn't say a word, girl. You listened as we expressed our desires; you led us to think that you had it all going on. Some of the women even envied you. So has he divorced her, Vanessa?" She asked in a tone, hoping that she'd say no.

"Yeah! Two months ago."

"So, when is your wedding day Vanessa?"

"Sometime next year..., I hope." Shifting her head, Kim felt defeated in her efforts.

"You hope, Vanessa; as in *faith*? You're not afraid that he's going to *dump* you for a younger model later on, as he's doing with his wife for, *you*. You know we *reap* what we *sow*."

With insecurity and uncertainty in her tone, "As long as I give him his baby; I believe that he'll stay with me." Having heard enough, Kim knew that she wasn't connecting with Vanessa; she reverently surrendered. Kim couldn't believe—that Vanessa thinks that a baby will keep Thomas committed to her only.

"Vanessa, I'm here for you if you want to talk, I'll listen; I'll even ask my Pastor to counsel with you if you'd like. Look, if you haven't heard a word that I've said, girl, please take some time alone and *reverse* the role with Mrs. Martin. Have you considered how she must be feeling? Vanessa..., you're a nurse; I've seen the compassion that you give to your patients."

In tears, "I hear you; I just don't have the strength to let him go right now. As terrible as it sound, I don't want to let him go; I love him."

Embracing Vanessa with a kindhearted hug. "Oh, Vanessa..., I can't say that I *understand* your feelings." Pausing, "But..., I...I do accept them as being *genuine* and *valid*—to you. Does that help?"

"Yeah!" She mumbled, sniffling.

"I'm here for you Vanessa." Hugging Kim, Vanessa walked away.

In a drooped posture, Kim remained on the bench to wait for Walter. Thankful for Vanessa's candor, it wasn't as bad as she'd imagined. She believes in her heart that if this information was made known earlier; things wouldn't have gotten this far. On many occasions she'd invite her to single events, women's ministry functions, bible study, and church services; Vanessa always refused.

To confirm picking Kim up at the Marina, Walter had left her a voicemail. At the conclusion of his church service; they'd planned to meet for lunch.

Arriving at the Marina, Kim waved to Walter. Watching her hair blow in the wind; her beauty captivated him as she moved smoothly to his car. Wearing black jeans, boots, a red cardigan sweater with a white blouse and, a black sweater coat; she dressed for warmth; knowing that they'd be spending the day in S.F. She'd also get to meet his parents today.

Enjoying a *cloud nine* moment, Walter had been meeting daily with Bill for bible study and prayer.

Sustained by God in keeping him faithful during the *lonely times* after Sherrie's death, Bill had testified to Walter. Gaining faith and confidence, Walter was assured that God would do the same for him regarding his *fleshly issue.* Desiring to submit to God's will for his life; Walter felt that Bill's friendship was divinely appointed.

Experiencing peace and contentment for the first time in his life; Walter's amazed by the reality that you could enter into a personal relationship with Christ. Since a teenager, he'd watched his uncles and cousins cheat on their wives with other women within the church, and other churches; including his uncles that were preachers and pastors. Loving his Dad, he knew that he'd remained faithful to his Mother; Walter desired to be like him.

After attending early morning services at Bill's church, he found it difficult to sit though an eleven o'clock service at St. Hebrews. He knew that it would be a matter of time before he'd have to make a decision.

Looking forward to the New Year's Eve event in the City, this would be the first time that he wouldn't attend a "watch night service" at St. Hebrews. After becoming a business owner; he'd usually be late in arriving. The women wasn't bothered, they'd a much later agenda in mind with Walter. Their attraction to Walter ran deeper than physical appeal only; he'd excelled in the financial arena as well; which made him a more sought after catch.

Traditionally, the watch night services concluded with refreshments. Decked in their holiday fashions, the women would parade near Walter. Never disappointing, their wish was his command. The question became, who'd be the lucky woman for the evening?

For the first time in his adult life he looked forward to waking up in his king-sized, bed alone! The thought of it made him say *"thank you, Jesus,"* which was new *dialogue* for Walter. He'd never experienced talking and praying to God without being on his knees. He'd learned to pray without ceasing *(1 Thess. 5:17*). Manifesting his presence in a mighty way, God had honored Walter's sincerity, one that Walter could not deny.

Chapter 7

Gary Lloyd Russell was finalizing his holiday itinerary for his sister's visit. He'd prefer to relax than to entertain her and her friend. The year had concluded on a prosperous note, but a vigorous one. He was confused as to why his sister, Connie was so excited and pushy about coming to visit. Forever a busy body in the life of her big brother; she advocated that he should be married. Naturally delighted to see her, he was in no mood to entertain. He chose to solicit his new friend, BJ to assist him.

"Hello!"

"Hello, BJ!"

"Hi, Gary, this is a pleasant surprise."

"Good, I'm glad you feel that way. I'm full of surprises today, how's your day going?"

"It's good, no complaints. I had a relaxing time at the Marina earlier this morning."

"Really, that's one of my favorite places to go when I'm in the area. How often do you go?"

"Um, at least three times a week, in the early morning."

"Now I know where I can *find* you. Would you like to join me on tomorrow night as I attempt to entertain my sister and her friend? I know its short notice, please? It's going to be at my place in Walnut Creek; you can bring a friend or friends if you like."

"Sounds like you need rescuing." She chuckled.

"Am I that obvious? I am not up for this holiday entertaining BJ. This is usually my time off; she's insisting on enjoying the nightlife in California. I'm surprised; she's generally in Los Angeles."

"Okay..., I'll come."

"They're planning on staying until the New Year. She wants to go to a party of some sort. I have one more favor to ask, this is a big, one."

"Cooking is not an option, Gary."

"Girl..., I thought you'd jump at the chance to show me you can out cook, Michelle.

"Ha! Ha!" She uttered, mockingly?"

"Relax, I have tickets for a dinner dance in S.F., will you come with us?" BJ grunted.

"Is it that, ridiculous?"

"No! I'm sorry; I was thinking out loud, I'm attending that function with, Karen."

"Great, then why don't you guys ride with us, I'm getting a limo."

"Um..., that sounds nice, how thoughtful of you."

"Trust me, it's purely *selfish*, I don't want to go anyway, it's a limo or stay home."

"Sounds good, but I'll get back with you regarding the transportation arrangements."

"Thank you, thank you," expressing relief.

"I'm glad that you'll be there. New Years Eve parties have never been a favorite of mine, even when I was young."

"I know exactly how you feel, *old—man*." She teased.

"Hey…, watch it!"

"We'll be leaving directly after mid-night; Karen's the coordinator for that event."

"Oh, really; sounds like a plan. Look, I'll be in your area tomorrow evening, why don't I pick you up around six p.m. They'll arrive at seven-thirty or so, she's renting a car from the Oakland airport, this will give us time to chat. If you decide to bring anyone, let me know. I'm not too keen on the idea of you driving back alone."

"Aw…, that's considerate of you, no worries. I worked in Walnut Creek for eight years; it's like driving to the mall. I'll confirm with you tomorrow."

"Good, familiar territory is always a good thing, night. BJ, thanks!"

"Goodnight, Gary!"

Gary was relieved that BJ would help him entertain his sister and her traveling companion. He'd several male friends that he could invite; he just wasn't up for the partying. At times, Gary behaved more like someone eighty instead of forty.

Excited that BJ had never called him, Gary was old school and believed that the man should *court the woman*. He did feel that the attraction was mutual; she appeared to be excited to hear from him each time he called. BJ obviously was old school too, he presumed.

Looking forward to the opportunity to get to know Gary better, meeting a family member would give her more background on him as well. She figured his sister was probably an overgrown brat, since he didn't sound too overjoyed to see her. Thrilled that he lived in Walnut Creek; she'd get the opportunity to spend the night with her girlfriend, Christine.

Corresponding frequently with Sober, she'd come to love his great sense of humor. He was a Christian, but confessed that he probably didn't fit her complete criteria. She felt that he was wise beyond his age. Both were upfront in admitting the truth about other individuals in their life.

Revealing to Sober her attraction and interest to someone else, she also explained her concern that she wasn't sure if he was a Christian; she was referring to Gary. Sober admitted to having an attraction and interest to another woman that he'd met, but he knew very little about her.

Before heading to Gary's, Barbara called to give Karen his information in case of an emergency. "Have you heard from Bill?" Barbara asked.

"Yeah, he left two messages; I'm going to call and thank him for a pleasurable and informative evening."

"Um..., sounds like he misses you, Karen."

"I miss him too, I really—do."

"Well..., girl, you need to dance with the one who *brung ya!*"

"Cute! Are you looking forward to seeing, Gary?"

"Am I, Yes? I'm excited to learn more about him. We'll finally get to talk. I've prayed and asked God to help me contain my emotions; I want to get it right this time, Karen."

"That's good, Barbara. God's gonna honor your heart. I've been thinking the same thing, more than ever after the brunch topics."

"I believe God honors our intent, Karen. I mean, I can't control my feelings for him, but I can—control how I respond to them, right."

"I agree Barbara; we do have to guard our hearts. Girl, mine hurt so once; Huh! I thought it'd literally broken into pieces."

Laughing, "I know; I've had to mend some pieces as well. That's why I've grown to love, me; I have to be responsible for protecting my heart. I am too old to be assuming, Karen."

"Well put!"

Poking fun, Karen decided to do a little reminiscing. "You're right about assuming Barbara, otherwise, by next month, you'd be calling Gary, and leaving messages asking, *"Why haven't you called, me?"* In a pathetic tone, Karen mimicked.

"Oh, stop it, Karen." Admitting guilt, Barbara broke with laughter.

"Now we know what they were really saying, *"Because I didn't want to talk—to you."* Barbara recollected.

"Ah..., yeah, those were the days. Hey, today that would translate to *"I'm just not—into you."*

"I know!..." Barbara uttered. "It's unfortunate, but that's how things play out when we assume too quickly. Thank God our *esteem levels* are greater than they were in our *younger days."*

"Yeah, it's a harsh lesson, but we have to learn from our *experiences* Barbara. I think too often we get excited too soon when a man shows interest, we instantly assume that he's the one, or we hope he's the one."

"Yeah..., it happens before we realize it, it's easy. Emotions are soaring; you're so happy that you've meet someone, tied with an anticipated end leads to presumptuousness. That's why I'm building up my confidence—level now, girl. So when I see Gary in a little while, and am reminded of my attraction for him; I'll have something to chew on."

"Right, right, as the word say, we have to *renew our mind* daily with *scripture* and our *convictions*."

Realizing the need to reflect daily on the scriptures, Barbara was glad that she was having this conversation with Karen. She felt led to *gird her mind;* knowing her emotions may well become a factor in Gary's presence.

"You hit the nail on the head," Barbara said. "Girl, let me get off this phone and on the road before we start shouting, I'll keep you posted." Barbara whispered a prayer. *"Lord Jesus, give me traveling grace. Give me the strength to stay grounded. Keep me mindful that you have accepted me. In Jesus name, I pray amen."*

Within twenty minutes, Barbara rang Gary's doorbell. "*Merry Christmas* BJ, he greeted her with a wide-mouthed grin."

"*Merry Christmas* to you, Gary! Baffled and cold, BJ watched Gary as he stood smiling, and staring upwards. Glancing up, she caught sight of the *mistletoe*.

"Gary, please!" Smiling, she kissed him on the cheek.

"It's Christmas Gary; I would've greeted you with a holidays cheeks kiss."

"I had to test it, BJ." He said, grinning. Inhaling a snivel of his cologne, *Hmm..., that was Aramis he was wearing at the party, my all-time favorite, stay calm girl.* She'd remained *passionate* with it's fragrance since discovering it in high school.

Dressed for comfort, Gary wore a caramel colored polo trimmed in brown, a pair of khaki Dockers and brown loafers. Staring at the box that she was carrying, "You brought something for me?"

"Yeah, I brought you some of my cinnamon rolls; you seemed to have enjoyed them."

"That's putting it mildly BJ, thanks!" In delight, she admired the spaciousness of his home. After a swift scan of the room, she remarked. "Wow, it's so roomy in here."

"Yeah, more than I care to clean, I have to have help; it's not an option. Would you like some hot apple Cider? Tea? Or Juice?"

"Cider would be great, thank you." Removing her coat, "Oooh..., this fireplace is calling me," as she caressed her hands. He invited her to sit on the fireplace ledge. "Come, sit, I'll get your cider."

Admiring the refinished cherry wood floors that extended to the kitchen area, she took pleasure in the warm setting. Absent a Christmas tree, lighted candles, ornaments and an abundance of poinsettias captured the holiday ambiance. The walls were a light mocha with ivory crown molding. A flat screen TV dressed the wall in front of two oversized beige love seats, and a huge recliner; angled in a circular fashion. The fireplace encompassed the adjacent wall and completed the circle.

For seating comfort, the ledge was equipped with brown custom-built pillows. Above the fireplace hung a sketched portrait of a beautiful southern style home.

Gary returned and sat beside her; placing the cider between them on a tray. Admiring her outfit, "You look lovely as usual BJ; that's a good color on you."

Wearing a burgundy dress, with a string of black buttons in the back, it was her favorite color also. She accessorized it with a two-inch black width belt, and black calf-length boots. Smiling, "Thanks, you're kind as usual." Again, she inhaled the intoxicating aroma of his cologne. *I know this is Aramis.* Inhaling, she inquired. "Is that..., *Aramis* cologne that I smell?"

"Yes! He voiced, exhibiting stimulation. You recognized it, you like *Aramis?*"

"Do I! Gary, you're ahead of your time."

Slapping his knee, he laughed. "I know..., it's old, but I love it; Macy's still carries it." He mentioned, offering an explanation for using it.

"No need to explain or defend, it's an *oldie* but *goodie*; consider it a *good thing*." BJ couldn't resist sharing the story behind the cologne.

"I was in high school when I first discovered it. My girl friend, Virginia and I visited her aunt in Milwaukee for a summer. This guy named, Ronny; aw, he'd smell so—good." Holding a hand to her chest, she voiced it with so much *zeal*, Gary wasn't sure if she was enjoying his scent, or reliving her moments in Ronnie's presence.

"One day, we mustered up enough nerve to ask for the name of it, he said it was *Aramis.* I remember writing it down for safekeeping. Humor me Gary, I was only *seventeen*." Laughing at full volume, he loved every word. "What's wrong with that, it proved that you had—*good taste*, even as a kid. Now, you're not going to be thinking about that guy in Milwaukee tonight, are you?"

Turning her head. "Not a chance!" Only revealing half of her little story, she didn't dare—tell him the safekeeping was for use by her future husband. Just one of many little *trinkets* that she kept stored in her "*mental hope chest*."

"BJ, you have the prettiest brown eyes that I've seen in a while; they're so bright. I wanted to tell you when we were in your back yard. You turned your face toward the sun, and they were like..., *magnetism*, for lack of a better word. You had a baffled expression on your face."

"Yeah, I remember the moment, baffled is correct, you were staring, Gary." She said, laughing.

Gary loved teasing her. "I bet you hear that all the time. We'd just met; I didn't want to appear forward or anything."

Seizing the opportunity, she came back with. "So, are you being forward with me, now? I'm—teasing you." She said smiling, letting him off the hook.

"It's ironic that you used the word, *magnetism*. I was told that exact expression before referencing my eyes, so, forgive me if I don't sound too excited!" She nodded, smiling.

In protest, "Hey, that's no fair!"

"I couldn't resist, Gary; I like to rib, too. I accept your compliment. To answer your question, women comment on my eyes all the time."

"Women!" He spoke, frowning. "That you have pretty eyes?" He voiced, in a suspicious tone.

"Seriously, never—in a sensuous manner Gary. When it comes to men, they only stare. I think the eyes say so much, people don't want to send the wrong signal. Take what you said, *"You didn't want to appear forward."* It's weird; I hesitate too before telling a man that he has pretty eyes.

"You're right; I did say that." BJ didn't bother to tell Gary that his eyes were the first outstanding trait that she'd observed on him in the Home Depot.

"Let's play a game of twenty questions; I think it'll be fun to speed up our acquaintance process."Gary suggested.

"Okay, since we haven't had the chance to talk; I think that's a great—idea."

"You go first," Gary said.

She'd been waiting for this moment to determine if Gary was a Christian. Her question was designed for him to be *specific*. She figured, if she'd asked him "*Do you go to church? or Are you a Christian?*, would be giving him the answer he knew that she *wanted to hear.* From past experiences, she knew a man would say and agree to *anything to get them seven digits from a woman that he liked.*

Bracing herself, she casually asked. "So Gary, how do you *spend* your weekends?"

After brief concentration, "Well..., um...that's a loaded question. Let's see, I generally play things by ear. For some reason or another, on Saturdays, I always end up at the Home Depot or Lowes. I may do breakfast or play golf with a friend. Now Sundays, that's my *rest* day." He responded adamantly, conveying passion.

Feeling a knot in the pit of her stomach that felt the size of a grapefruit; she prayed that the agony wasn't reflective by her facial expression. *Oh, no! He's not a Christian.*

Continuing with his weekend itinerary, "I love Sunday buffet brunches after attending early *morning services*. If nothing else is going on, I'll watch some sports and relax."

Barely restraining her emotions. *Oh, my goodness, he is a Christian after all."* Her facial form was consistent with that of a little kid on Christmas morning.

"As in church worship?" She asked. With a sharp motion of his head, he glanced in her direction, showing a baffled expression, "Is there any other kind?"

"Ah..., No! That's great." Aiming to disguise her excitement didn't go over as cool as she wanted, nonetheless, he was a *Christian.*

Setting her up for a prank question, Gary laughed within; which was sure to get him a *modest* response.

"Okay, it's my turn now. What do you do on Monday mornings, other than pick up *contractors* at the Home Depot?" Jabbing her on her shoulder, he fell over laughing.

Both hands cupping her mouth, she struggled to find her voice, sadly, it remained void; after a brief silence, she finally muttered. "If I get really—lucky; I take them home with me."

"Ah…, you're quick, you're good." Gary remarked, grinning.

"No! You're good, that was pretty clever, Gary." Still laughing. "You got me, good! Oh, I owe you big… time."

Making a gallant effort to soften the blow, he confessed. "Well…, if the truth be told, I actually—picked you up."

"It's too late to be kind now Mr. Russell." Voiced with sarcasm.

"Point me to your powder room please!" She asked, with polite emphasis, and her head held high.

Still blissful, he pointed and mumbled. "Sure, it's right around the corner"

Gary was glad that he'd approached her in the Home Depot. Building the toy chest to him indicated that they'd a common interest. Personifying a woman of strong character, yet, *laced* with an allusion of innocence; he found her to be charming. He adored watching her blush; BJ never disappointed.

Securing the bathroom door shut, with her hand clinched in a victory *fist pump* position; she stole a second to delight in the moment. *Oh my, he is a Christian, is the big test finally here?*

Coaching from the sidelines, counseling, encouraging her daughter, friends and other women on topics of relationship behavior from a Christian perspective; was it possible that she'd finally get the chance to exercise what she'd been advocating?

Leaning against the door, she recalled how it felt to be attracted to a man, the emotions, the desires associated with caring about someone. Recognizing her appeal to Gary was a tiny bit more than she cared it to be, when he looked into her eyes; he gave her goose bumps!

Fond of his sense of humor, his laid-back temperament, the subtle flirtations; she loved it all. BJ could've stood the entire evening dreaming about how she admired Gary Lloyd Russell. In preparation to return, she turned on the faucet to make her trip appear legit; she only needed space to collect her emotions.

"I'm back!"

"Okay, back to twenty questions, it's your turn." Gary said, politely, imitating a kid who'd cheated on a board game while his opponent was away.

"No! You go; I'm still recuperating from your *bombshell* of a question." "Alright, let's see...," he paused. "Do you consider yourself a *committed Christian,* BJ?"

Carefully selecting her words, while twisting a lock of her hair, she responded gently, but stressing importance. "I like to think so...," she paused. "I do classify Christ as the head of my life, and I'm serious about my relationship with him; so, the answer would be a definite, yes!"

"You know BJ; I hear that expression so much, I am not sure who's what? I've never claimed the title. I grew up in the church, but never experienced the relationship that I'm learning about now."

Pleased that his suspicions were correct; he was convinced that she was a Christian also. In the past, it hadn't really mattered to Gary if the women he dated were Christians. After joining the men's ministry at his church; he learned the hard way that it did matter.

He continued to speak softy with his head slightly hung. "When my Mom was alive we had to go to church, my Dad made sure he honored her wishes."

"Aw..., I'm sorry about your, Mom."

"Thanks, I was only fourteen; she died of pneumonia. I am the oldest, so I had to help my Dad raise my sister and brother. We had support from our grandparents, aunts, and cousins, but at the end of the day, it was just us most nights."

"Oh, you were so young," said with affection.

"Yeah, but believe me, I grew up in a hurry; I had no choice in the matter BJ."

"Your church going experience, I can relate, it's identical to mine Gary. My Mom was the same way, thinking back; I can't recall any fundamental teachings on developing a relationship with Christ." In a sincere and convincing voice, Gary shared his thoughts and concerns.

"I've been attending church for about *eight months* now. I'm getting a clearer understanding of what is required of me to grow in Christ. I desire change, and God is becoming more evident in my life. But some days...," he paused, "I find myself becoming frustrated."

Tussling with his words. "I often feel that expression "*committed Christian*" to be debatable, or I'm not sure of its true meaning."

Speaking carefully, "Are you serious about developing your relationship with Christ?"

Flashing a quick but stern look, he convincingly replied. "Absolutely, of course I'm serious."

Reacting fretfully, she uttered. "Sorry! I didn't—mean to offend you."

"No! No! I'm sorry, you didn't." Reassuring her that no offense was taken, he reached, and softly stroked her hand.

"Then you're committed, Gary. I don't know what others mean, but when I refer to the expression; I simply mean that I'm serious and have made up my mind to be obedient to the word. I guess we need to make sure that the expression *committed Christian* doesn't become synonymous with being called "*religious*."

"Hmm..., *state of mind*, good point BJ. Being serious, I like that; I can relate to that. Thanks! Some days I allow myself to become discouraged. I compare the length of time that I've been going to church, to people who've been attending for years. I feel, um..., deficient relative to my spiritual growth; I feel that it's not enough." Leaning forward, with clasped hands, and elbows resting on his knees, he spoke softly with straightforwardness.

"It's somewhat—humbling I guess, at work my day's consist of me pointing, and telling everyone else what to do. He chuckled. " So I guess my lowly feelings are a good—thing."

"Gary, that's the— enemy attempting to discourage you, if your efforts to grow have been sincere in the past eight months, they count as much as someone that's been serving him for eight years. Commitment has to be more than a "*state of mind,"* just as you said. More importantly, to what or whom is the commitment. Is it *God, the pastor, tradition, family or church fellowship?"*

Using bible passages to illustrate her point, she turned to face him. Think on Matt.19:29, 30, Jesus said that the last shall be first when he spoke on inheriting everlasting life. And what about the *thief on the cross,* in Luke 23:43 Jesus assured him that he'd be with him in *Paradise.* In those two instances, *length of time* was not a factor."

"Hmm...yeah! You're right, that helped, thanks BJ."

"If those thoughts come again; meditate on Eph.2:8-9."

To enhance his desire to grow in the Lord; he'd joined a bible study for men in his church, and had a married man for his prayer *partner* and *mento*r. Comparing himself to seasoned Christians often rendered him insecure in his walk with the, Lord.

Reaffirming that it was only a trick of the enemy; he found solace in her efforts to exhort him. Assured that he'd a captive listener in B.J, he spoke with ease. "This is the first time that we've mentioned our Moms, is yours still with us?"

"No! Not since *Mother's Day of 1989."* She said with sadness.

Instantly, her sympathy shifted to him. "I feel guilty; I had my Mom so much longer than you." Stated with compassion.

"Mother's Day BJ, oh that had to be hard." Gary could've remained wordless; the natural sensitive expression on his face expressed his empathy for her. Exhaling a deep sigh. "Yeah! Hard is the word," she nodded. "She died of congestive heart failure; it could've occurred during the night, she wasn't discovered until the morning of Mother's day. My siblings and I were looking forward to taking her out for a *Mother's Day* dinner. Five months prior; she'd a massive heart attack on *Christmas Day.*"

Her voice escalated, followed by laughter. "My Mom, boy, she chose days that you'd remember her by!"

"It certainly seems that way," Gary said, as he shared in her wit.

"Is *Mothers Day* a more tolerable one for you now, BJ?"

"Yeah, the first two years were really hard; I didn't attend worship services on *Mother's Day*. With slumped shoulders, Gary shared.

"I remember ..., it was a tender moment for us also. In the south, the red and white rose distinction was a big deal."

"Oh, yes! Lord!" BJ echoed, smiling

"Our Aunt would bring *huge* fresh cut *white* roses from her garden, looking back; I think they only magnified our sadness." He said, laughing.

"Aw..., you guys were only babies." She paused. "I'm changing the subject Gary, are you familiar with the scripture that talks about *everything working together for the good of those who love the Lord?"*

"Yeah, Romans something."

"Right, right, 8:28, I think it's indicative of your life Gary"

"How so!" He asked, softly.

"As children of praying saints, I think we get to *piggyback* from their prayers until we come into the full knowledge of understanding. When you consider the responsibilities, the decisions that you encountered as a kid caring for your siblings; you were forced into adulthood. Now, look at you. You're still young, and a successful business owner that's thriving in a competitive industry."

"Hmm..., I have to agree with you, girl," nodding. "I often think about the enormous tasks that I faced, and instantly; I am reminded of how it all worked for my good. I was mature beyond boys *my age*."

Airing a surprised expression, she pondered her thought, before saying. "You know..., I'm—really enjoying getting better acquainted with you, Gary." Nodding and smiling.

"I detect a note of surprise there BJ," giving a corner smile, "but I'll take it, the sentiment is mutual; it's taken us long enough. I almost wish they weren't coming. I'd rather continue relaxing, and talking to you. Is that bad of me?" Voiced, in a moping tone.

Smiling in agreement, "Only if you don't mind a bias answer."

Naturally desiring to see his sister, he was equally sincere in his pursuit to learn more about BJ; he sensed something special about her. He looked forward to enjoying the holidays with her, his sister and her friend.

The doorbell rang. "That will be the caterers." He informed. Thrilled with their line of dialogue, she was glad in her decision not to bring the girls; it would've altered their topics of conversation. She admired him for his humbleness and transparency in the area of his spiritual growth.

Generally restricting topics of spiritual inadequacies to his prayer partner, he felt a common bond when he learned that their childhood Christian experience were identical. The empathy expressed concerning their mothers cemented their friendship.

BJ couldn't have imagined a more pleasurable evening. Directing the caterers to the kitchen area, the aroma of the food surrounded the room. Right away, it stimulated her appetite; she recognized that it was Chinese. Carefully uncovering and opening pans and cartons of food, they placed it on the counter top; including cloth napkins and silverware. Gary tipped and thanked them for a job well done.

"C'mon and get some of this good food, woman." Walking to the kitchen to join him, in suspense, "You're going to eat before they arrive?"

"Yes! I'm hungry, how about you? They'll probably get lost a few times anyway. I'm not going to wait; it's more of a buffet style thing anyway; since I couldn't get you to cook."

At a lost for words, her mouth opened, she uttered. "Uh..., you're not letting up on me cooking, are you?"

"Can you blame a bachelor for trying to get a home cooked meal? I've tasted a sampling of your cooking; you had to teach Michelle." He poured on with thickness.

"Aw..., okay, I'm flattered; one home cooked meal coming up for Gary."

"Finally!" He teased.

Ordering from his favorite restaurant, he assured her that the food was delicious. The buffet included entrees and appetizers consisting of eggs rolls, wontons, Mongolian beef, Peking duck, Szechwan beef, garlic, and cashew nut chicken, steamed rice, Chinese greens, and sliced pork. At the counter, they'd prepared their plates and individually said their grace.

"Mmm..., this is good. How'd you know it's my favorite; hot and spicy, just the way I like it." She said, savoring the taste of the Mongolian beef. "Good! I hoped that you'd like at least one of my selections." He muttered, while tearing into the Peking duck.

"I told you it was good," he repeated, mumbling and wiping his mouth. Preferring not to be stuffed when his sister arrived, BJ had small portions.

Between bites, she observed the neatness of his place, it'd a lived in, but tidy look. Pointing to the portrait of the house over the fireplace, she inquired. "Did you build that?"

"I helped; it's our home in Georgia, it's been remodeled several times over."

"Wow, talking about feeling fulfilled, that's mega fulfillment."

"We do," he nodded, speaking for everyone.

"My uncles, and cousins, they all have similar homes; it's what the Russell's do best."

"How neat!"

"For me, it's more than a career, it's ironic that you mentioned that scripture in Romans. Correct me if I'm wrong, but it also talks about your *purpose,* right?"

"Yeah, right," she nodded.

"It's a gift BJ. Since I've gotten back into fellowship, I'm using it as my ministry. There are other contractors at my church also. On alternate weekends; we volunteer our time to help members that's in need of work on their homes. In the beginning, we limited it to the seniors, but we're going to extend it to other members as well."

"Wow! Gary, it doesn't get anymore rewarding than that."

"It's makes perfect sense, I'm only giving of my time and loving what I do. So, you love Chinese I see?" He observed and stuffed his mouth with an egg roll.

"It's my favorite, in years past; I was on this kick preparing Chinese food every day, in a *wok.* In fact, I got pretty good at it." Taking a gulp of his bottled apple juice. "What was your favorite dish to prepare?"

"Michelle loved my, garlic chicken; I guess it's mine also." Dabbing his mouth with his napkin, "Mmm..., sounds good. Do you still remember how to prepare it?"

"Of course, I still cook it, just not on a daily basis as before. If cooked properly, Chinese food is extremely healthy."

"You won't get any arguments from me; I'm a regular customer of theirs, that's why they brought me the cloth napkins and silverware. They knew by the size of my order that I was having guests. I get tired of cooking; well...," he paused. "It's not the cooking as it is the choice of what to prepare."

"Now, that's the problem." She agreed. Walking to the family room, he said, "Let's listen to some Christmas music."

The doorbell rang! Peeking from the window, "it's them." He said, with dissatisfaction in his tone. Swiveling her chair to the face the front door, BJ remained seated.

Opening the door, his sister rushed into his arms shouting "*Merry Christmas!*" Returning to retrieve the remainder of her items, she handed Gary her travel bag. Holding the door open, he shouted. "Do you need help?"

"No, we got it."

In seconds, Connie returned yelling. "Surprise!" Moving aside, Connie's friend stepped in smiling.

Dropping the travel bag to the floor, Gary looked as if he'd seen a ghost. *This can't be Kathy, my goodness; she looks like I remember her, after twenty plus years. But she's married! Where is her husband? What is she doing here?"*

Blaring for Gary to embrace her, Kathy greeted him.

"Hi, Gary, long time no see." Feeling anemic, and in a state of astonishment, "Kathy..., is that you?"

"One and only, don't I at least get a hug? She *leaped* into his arms. Still in shock, his embrace was automatic, lacking in warmth and affection. Not to worry, Kathy's hug packed enough robust for them both. *Ooh, he looks better than I remember. My baby is all grown up. His embrace was a bit wobbly, well, I did—hurt him. Oop's…he has company."*

"I told you it'd be a surprise!" Connie blurted, frolicking like a child waiting to be rewarded for her efforts.

"That's putting it mildly, Connie." Not wavering, with fury in his tone, "C'mon guys, you could've told me something."

"Would you have let us come?" Connie asked, expressing attitude from the dejection of his remark. Gary ignored her question.

For the first time since his childhood, Gary Lloyd Russell found himself in a situation that he'd no control. Kathy was his first love in every way. Four years older than Gary, she'd broken their engagement, and married an older guy while he was away at college.

Never returning home prior to his graduating and moving to California, this was their first time meeting. Because of his maturity level and height, at a young age, Gary became attracted to older women; girls his age he felt were too adolescent.

At age twenty, Kathy found him more fascinating than men her age. Dating many women since her, he never cared for any woman the way he did Kathy, he often thought of her.

Now, suddenly remembering BJ and feeling appropriately embarrassed; he turned to her. *Oh my, Lord, I forgot, BJ. What have my sister done to me.*

"I am so sorry BJ. You can clearly see that I'm totally in the dark; I wasn't aware." He rambled, sounding more like, *you believe me don't you.*

"Ah…BJ, this is my sister Connie and this is Kathy, a friend from back home. This is BJ, well, Barbara to you."

Now standing, BJ, spoke. "Nice to meet you," and extended a hand to greet them.

"Nice to meet you, too." Kathy responded, accepting her handshake. Connie turned to comment on the food, saying only, Hi! Without a handshake.

Fuming, Gary shot Connie a sharp glance. She knew the look; but ignored it. It was comparable to the one his parents used to give them in church when they were misbehaving.

"Something smells good," Connie said, as she sniffed and followed the scent into the kitchen.

"Oooh, I can't wait to change and get into this food." Having in common the same skin complexion and facial features; it was apparent that she was his sister.

At age thirty-six, she was the middle of the three siblings. His younger brother *Tre'* was thirty. Standing at least 6ft, her black wet and wavy hair extended past her shoulders.

Looking as if she'd just stepped off a Vogue runway, she was wearing a black two-piece suit with a gold silk blouse and black boots. Her make-up was excessive, but well applied. Gary mentioned that she frequently modeled.

Kathy, looking good at the age of forty-four, bearing similar physical attributes as BJ; signified a possible pattern for his taste in women. A size smaller, and a shade lighter than BJ, the gold highlights in her hair complimented her red form-fitted sweater dress and black boots; that demanded attention.

"Where will we sleep, big brother? I hope we have our own rooms as we do at your *Bed & Breakfast* in the Valley."

Finally regaining his poise, he turned to BJ and asked her to excuse him. Venting a distressed look, he showed them to their rooms.

With emotions zooming, Barbara speculated, what *in the world happened here? What is she to, Gary?" She has to be an old girlfriend. He literally dropped the bag; she's obviously someone he hasn't seen in ages.* She now understood why he wasn't too excited to see his Sister; she was clearly the brat that BJ had anticipated.

If Kathy's an old flame of Gary's, it would explain Connie's rude behavior toward BJ. She was undoubtedly on a matchmaking mission.

BJ knew that the evening had ended for her and Gary. Sharing pleasure in getting to know him, she couldn't help but think of the impact that Kathy would have on their relationship; she suspected that'd depend on his feelings for her now.

In the midst of the commotion, she did detect a side of Gary that she admired. Voicing his dissatisfaction with their surprise visit assured her that he'd *backbone;* she loathed *spineless* men.

Releasing a deep breath, understandably disappointed to say the least, with sagging shoulders; she slowly gathered her coat and purse from the guest closet. Placing her coat around her shoulders, she leaned against the breakfast bar to wait for Gary's return.

"Where are you going?" Gary asked.

"Surely you're not expecting us to continue with *twenty questions,* Gary?" Replying somewhat harshly. Acknowledging defeat, in a soft-spoken tone, "I guess you're right, I'm sorry BJ."

Taking a softer line, she opted to take the broad shoulder approach, which closely resembled the story of her life. Recognizing his tongue-tied dilemma, her aim was to give him some breathing space.

"Gary, I know Kathy was or is someone special to you. It's okay; you had no clue that she was your sisters traveling companion. You guys have some catching up to do."

In concession, he remarked. "I'll walk you to your car. She's a former girlfriend; actually, we were engaged to be married; it's a long story BJ.

At the door, turning abruptly to retrieve her purse; she ran head on into Gary. Grabbing her around the waist beneath her coat, he pulled her into him. Trying to land what probably would've been a *whopper of a kiss,* BJ was quick; instantly, she leaned her head back; and pushed his shoulders away.

"No! Gary," she voiced, softly, but with firmness. Showing a confused look, he was taken aback by her refusal, but surrendered.

"Well, under the circumstances, I guess...I understand." He spoke, in a faint voice.

"It has nothing to do with the circumstances Gary." Noticing his disappointed look, she remained silent.

"You mean; you're not... attracted to me in that way?" He asked, with sincerity in his tone.

It was *exam* time for Barbara. Time for her to practice the guiding principles that she'd purposed in her heart. Presently, she desired to *leap* into Gary's arms, as Kathy had to validate her attraction to him. This time around would be different.

"No! Gary, that's not what it means, if we'd continued with our twenty questions; we probably would've gotten around to my reason for not reciprocating your kiss." Grabbing her by the arm, he gently pulled her back inside. "C'mon, I need to hear specifically why you didn't kiss me." So out done with BJ rejecting his kiss, for a brief second, he'd forgotten about Kathy's arrival.

"Gary...," she protested. "This could take a while; you do have company, remember?"

"I have the time; they'll be here for a whole week, this wasn't my plan, you were supposed to be my guest for the evening."

Closely resembling a reluctant witness that was about to be interrogated; she returned with restrained emotions. With her coat draped over her shoulders, she sat displaying a pouting posture at the breakfast bar. She desired not to have the ensuing conversation.

Kathy's arrival had tainted the tone and mood for the evening. She knew Gary wasn't going to rest until she satisfied his ego. Gary sat on the edge of his seat, with his legs stretched around her chair. His arms firmly folded, he stared her straight in the eye.

"Now..., talk to me, brown eyes." Before she could reply, demanding to eat; Connie barged in.

"I'm ready to get to that food Gary, I'm starving." Shooting Connie an unkind look, he extended a hand to her, implying *back off,* supported by a firm remark. "Not, now Connie!"

"Excuse me!" Making an about face, she exited the room. Clearing her throat, aiming to take the easy way out; BJ repeated Gary's explanation.

"You were correct, it's the circumstance, that's the reason, it wouldn't be right." She said, smiling.

"You know..., I am not buying that now, BJ." Turning his head, "C'mon, *pony up,* girl."

"Alright, alright," she let loose a long sigh and paused. "I haven't been in a relationship with anyone over sixteen years." She yanked out, experiencing a gamut of emotions.

This was much harder than she'd ever dreamed. Rehearsing this very scene a thousand times in her mind; it was finally a reality. *Why am I telling him this, how do I know that he likes me; this is what I'm supposed to say to someone that I'm starting to date. I guess this is a date, he must be interested, or I wouldn't be here, calm down. You can get through this.* Taking her chin in his hand, he gently lifted her face.

"You're serious, aren't you?" She nodded.

"That would be a yes!" She said, somewhat proudly, displaying a bashful countenance.

Consumed by soaring emotions of affections toward her, and frustration from his at present situation, he confessed. "I'm so... sorry; I apologize for assuming that a kiss was mutual, I seem to have a habit of doing that with you."

Gary could've kicked himself. He should've allowed her to take the lead as he normally did; which generally landed him a kiss. Impressed by his attitude, her lips formed a subdued smile.

"It's fine Gary, actually...,"she paused. "Technically, it was mutual." Exhibiting a generous grin, "I'm intrigued!" *Aw, he's sweet, I can do this.*

Continuing with her explanation, "Some years ago, I resolved that when I meet a man that I'm, she paused.

"That you're what?" He asked, with sensitivity.

"That I'm attracted to emotionally and physically; I'd *abstain* from—kissing him until we've developed a true friendship. That's why I didn't embrace your kiss, there, I said it." She recited, sounding more like a *botched* speech.

Exhaling generously, she'd like nothing better than to head for the front door. Never in her entire adult life had she encountered a more inhibiting moment. Having a light bulb moment, Gary smiled and nodded. "It makes sense BJ; it explains your guarded behavior. When I'm in your space, I can feel you tensing up." *Was it that evident, I tried to be so cool in his presence?*

"Really! Oh my," throwing a hand over her face.

"And I thought I was being so cool, you never reacted, or gave any indication, Gary."

Now feeling self-conscious. He reassured her. "It's okay..., it's a good thing, I tease you to loosen you up."

Pushing him playfully on his shoulders, "Okay! Gary, now you're really starting to—embarrass me."

"As I said before, you're charming." In our men group at church, the single men have pledged to practice *celibacy.*"

Now feeling that she was in good company, she spoke with bulging eyes and an illuminated face. "Are you serious? Don't mess...with me, Gary!"

Nodding in affirmation, he smiled. "Yep! So, I guess you must be some kind of authentication to keep me faithful, girl." He chuckled.

"Wow! Gary, that's interesting, so how're you doing?" She asked, as if she was inquiring about the "*weather.*"

Now conscious of her question, she yelled! "Never mind!" Covering her mouth with her hand. "Don't answer that! Sorry, let me go?"

Dead serious in wanting to know how Gary was doing in the area of abstaining, but realized that she'd no foundation for inquiring. "Your sister is hungry."

Getting up from the chair, she grabbed her purse. "Thanks, BJ!"

"For what?"

"Your frankness and satisfying my ego, I know it wasn't easy for you. I'm sorry if I added to your discomfort. You're *refreshing,* one day I'll share some of my experiences with you." He said warmly, in an appreciative tone.

"Gary, you have company,—remember?" Walking to her car, Gary unleashed distressed sighs.

Receptive to his *plain as the nose on your face emotions,* she spoke. "The feelings for Kathy surfaced, didn't they?"

Pausing briefly, in an apologetic tone, he replied. "If I said no, I'd be lying."

"Gary, at this point it's not an issue. Our friendship was built on honesty; let's keep it that way. Good night, and have a Merry Christmas. Reaching, she kissed him on his cheek.

"Thanks! Good night BJ. You've never used my business card; please let me know when you're home."

"I promise."

She'd planned to stay the night with her girlfriend Christine, since the evening was young, she'd enjoy the drive home. Pulling from the driveway, he yelled. "Wait!" Sprinting into the house; he returned with cards, and boxes of candy.

"I forgot; this is for you and your girls. Tell Jordyn I hope this will help to fill her toy chest, *Merry Christmas."*

"How thoughtful of you Gary, *Merry Christmas* to, you." She responded, with an expression of sincere gratitude and surprise.

Waving goodbye, Gary remained in the driveway until she drove off. *Gee, he's definitely full of surprises. For a dreadful ending, the gifts are definitely a consolation. He is a nice man.*

In route home, Barbara placed a call to share the news worthy event with Michelle. Not surprised, Michelle was calm. Barbara often teased her that her behaviors regarding certain matters were more inline with that of a man. Unlike her Mom, she didn't need the details.

After revealing to Michelle the entire circumstances of Kathy's arrival, she reminded her that Gary had no control of the situation and that she should wait and see how things would play out. Barbara would wait later to tell the girls.

Storming inside, Gary was furious. Swaying to Christmas music being played on a CD, Connie was dishing up mounds of food. With no hesitation, Gary yelled! "Connie, we need to talk, now!" Stuffing her mouth with an egg roll, she gathered a handful more.

"Okay!" She agreed, seeing his apparent irritation.

"In private, please, you can bring your food. Let's go into my office."

Opening the double cherry wood doors to the fourth bedroom that he'd converted to an office lounge; he ordered her to sit. Taking the first chair she saw by the door near a wall of bookshelves, she sat juggling the egg rolls from her hand to her lap. She was reminiscent of a scary child that was caught in an act of bad behavior.

Seeing her frustration, he offered her an alternate seat. "Sit there Connie." Pointing to a roll top writing desk with a chair. Seated in his high back burgundy leather chair behind his 'L' shaped cherry wood desk, he nursed a headache; his hands covered his forehead.

In a calm, but inquisitive tone, "Connie, what the heck is going on here? Why is Kathy here? Why did you think that you could invade my privacy with someone that I haven't heard from; nor seen in over twenty years?"

Not giving her space to answer. By hand gesturing, she indicated, which question do you want me to answer.

Frowning, and clearing her throat. "Well..., to begin, Kathy moved back home a month ago. Eight months prior to his retirement from the military, her husband was killed in an explosion. To cope with her loss for the past six months; she's traveled."

Showing signs of genuine sympathy toward Kathy, he lowered his tone. Pacing the floor with folded arms, "I'm sorry for her loss Connie, but how did she end up here, and without my consent?"

"Well..., let me explain. We started hanging out about two weeks ago. She called, and of course she inquired about you. I told her you lived in California. She said they lived here for a short time, but never had a chance to see any of the sights. She said California would probably be a nice place to spend the holidays. I told her I could show her the ropes in Los Angeles, she agreed."

"Our plan was to checkout some shops on Rodeo Drive, which we did, and visit you." Ravenous from the long flight, she devoured another roll, as she flashed him a well rehearsed phony smile. Rubbing the back of his neck; he continued to stride across the room.

"Is here any particular reason why you couldn't have informed me about her situation? Just because I'm single, I do have a life, and I do not appreciate what happened here this evening. You've gotten away with some pretty clever tricks as a kid Connie, but I will not allow you to dictate my life, and be *rude* to my guest." He ranted, while staring in her face with widened eyes, and a crinkly forehead.

Cringing, and holding tight to the egg rolls, "Is she your girlfriend?" She paused, recalling their last conversation. "I'm sorry, but the last time we talked; you said you didn't have anyone special."

Since Gary wasn't officially in an advertised relationship, Connie assumed Kathy's presence would spark some old flames for him; she was correct in her analysis.

"It's none of your business what she's to me? Connie, do you realize I haven't spoken to Kathy since..." He's without voice. "Since she took off and moved to New York." Venting aggravation, he flung his hands in the air.

"I realize that, but I thought I was doing you a favor. You were in love with her; you asked her to marry you. You're single, I thought you might have another chance with her; she still cares for you."

She pleaded her case with passion and justification. Breathless and defenseless, reaching for something to say, he yelled! "You haven't changed a bit, girl," shouting louder than he'd intended. Having a flair for being dramatic, she tucked her head; as she looked up with sadden eyes.

Divorced from her college English professor, she has a ten-year old Son also. Gary believed that he was too kind in letting her have her way. She's a buyer for a high-end clothing store that afforded her trips to New York, Los Angeles, and often, Europe. Her ex and their father keep her Son while she travels.

"Whose brilliant idea was it to surprise me anyway?" Understanding that she was in hot water, she took a stab to appeal to Gary's soft side. *I guess I'd better come clean. Wow, he's as stern as Daddy now.*

"It was my idea; Kathy said it probably wasn't a good one. I thought you'd show more sympathy Gary, since she's a *widow* and all; I thought you'd be glad to see her."

Chewing on another roll, she tried the flattering approach. "She's excited about seeing you Gary." Knowing that his Dad would've fore warned him, he inquired. "Did Daddy know that you were coming here, Connie?"

"I kinda told him that I was going to Los Angeles, and that I might visit you."

"Does he know that Kathy is traveling with you?"

"Not, really, if you're this upset, then you must still have feelings for her." She said, insultingly.

Not sure of his feelings, he knew when he saw her; he felt a throb in his body. He'd enjoyed BJ's company, now he felt guilty for inviting her.

Disregarding Connie's comment, with his hands resting to his waist, he resumed his pace. "This is the plan for tonight. I am going to spend the night out back; I have an in-law unit. To make your stay comfortable, you guys are welcome to whatever you need."

"Explain to Kathy that I am tired, and in need of some rest. Tell her that I look forward to seeing her in the morning; I'm sure she'll understand." With respect to their intrusive behavior upon his privacy and home; he felt that his actions were defensible.

Standing up, "Wow, you're upset, you used to be so easy—going, you've turned into, Daddy."

"No! I used to let you get your way because you were my *baby sister*."

When they were growing up Gary was extremely protective of his little sister. In the absence of their Mom, he felt compelled to be a soft place for her to fall. Sometimes that meant letting her have her way, often, against his better judgment. Their Dad didn't fall for her tricks. This time, she'd miscalculated her limit for pushing Gary.

"I'm a business owner Connie, and I've paid the cost to be my own boss, I like it that way. I try to make good choices and decisions for everyone involved. You didn't give me a chance to make a decision; you've forced my hand; now I'm playing it the best I know."

"My first thought was to send you packing to a hotel; I'm serious. I need some space to think and sort this through, girl; I'm sorry Connie, good night!"

Always the big brother, a trace of a smile tugged at the corner of his mouth. "By the way Connie, you look nice as usual; it's good to see you."

"Thanks! I'm sorry Gary. For what it's worth, Kathy did suggest a hotel also after finding Barbara here. Running to give him a remorseful hug, "Good night, Gary!" His phone rang; it was BJ letting him know that she'd made it home.

Gathering some pjs from the bedroom; he headed out back and collapsed across the bed. Needing to make some sense of what had occurred, he dialogued with himself and the, *Lord. What in the world happened here? I can't believe this, the only woman that I've ever loved shows up in my home.*

It was close to Christmas the last time he'd seen Kathy. Feeling horrible, he'd just made a break through with BJ, and now this. *What must she be feeling or thinking? Aw, she smelled so good when I embraced her. I like her; she is different. She's actually a challenge. Well, we are only friends so far, thank God for that; this could've been a disaster."*

Being the analytical type, Gary needed to know the whys. Was it finally *destiny* for him and Kathy? He needed some answers. *Lord, what is going on here, you know I've never stopped loving Kathy, she was my first love. I just met BJ, a woman that obviously loves you. She appears to be serious, with the abstaining and all. You know the struggles I've had in that area, even with Christian women. I feel safe with BJ.*

Now Kathy, Good Lord, you—must be testing me big time! Unless she's come to know you since an adult, I'm in for the temptation of my life, Lord. Both of them got that backfield in motion going on. Have mercy, Lord! At ten o'clock p.m., fully clothed, Gary Lloyd Russell fell asleep with his pjs still in his hand.

Barbara Jean Keller fell asleep on the floor by the fireplace, as she often did. Adoring staring into the flames; she found it to be tranquil and therapeutic. Before doing so, she revisited the evening that she'd spent with Gary.

Believing that her Mother's prayers had finally manifested, at her Mother's *Home Going;* her Pastor said that the prayers she'd petitioned would still be answered. Each of her siblings had been married, some three times over. She knew that her Mom wanted to see her baby married. Desiring the same for Michelle; she realized the significance of her prayer.

She was delighted how she'd conducted herself tonight. She'd remained true to her convictions, the standards and the parameters that she'd set. Her attraction for Gary was undisputable, as was the torch he still carried for Kathy.

She thanked God for the increase in her *esteem* level. She praised him for keeping her grounded, and not compromising her *standards* for a *passionate kiss*, a kiss that could've invoked residual affects.

Walter was correct; her gut instincts about him were on target. In spite of Kathy's presence, which rained on her parade, she was happy to learn that they shared a mutual attraction. Only time will reveal the *strength of it.*

In light of Barbara's big disappointment at Gary's, she didn't allow it to dampen her holiday enjoyment entirely. Hosting a Christmas Dinner for her family and a few friends, she waited until Christmas morning before opening the gifts from Gary. Giving Jordyn a gift certificate to *Toys R' Us*, he'd learned that Michelle was an avid reader, giving her a gift certificate to Barnes and Nobles. For BJ, her card read, "*To my Honorary Apprentice, Good luck on your next project. I'm here if you need me.*" Enclosed was a gift certificate to the Home Depot, attached to a box of Sees' chocolates.

Flattered that Gary's gift selections were individually appropriate, clever and generous; she was saddened at the possibility that she may never see him again. In celebration of her forty-seventh birthday, she and Michelle took Jordyn to the snow in Tahoe for three days.

Kim sacrificed time from Walter long enough for a trip home to Maryland to be with her parents for Christmas. In preparation for the *New Millennium*, Walter buried himself in installing security devices for possible *Y2K* glitches in his business office systems.

Karen and Michael spent a quiet Christmas with her parents and relatives, after making a decision to put some space between her and Bill. In the midst of his discontentment, Bill flew to Oregon to be with his parents for Christmas. Bill had no plans to give up on Karen; he'd wait for the perfect opportunity before continuing his pursuit.

Chapter 8

New Years' Eve, Walter Hines was in a good mood. Looking forward to bringing in the *New Millennium* with the new love in his life, he was experiencing a life of abundance and a renewed spirit. He called his mother to wish her a happy New Year. "Good morning, Hines residence."

"Hi Mom, Happy New Year."

"Hi Baby, Happy New Year to you, what time will we see you this evening?"

"You won't Mom, that's why I'm calling. Mom, I can't begin to tell you how God has moved in my life lately. He's blessed me to meet a God-fearing man to mentor me, and I've met a faithful Christian woman in that of Kim."

"Walter, I'm so happy for you, I truly am Baby. Kim is a lovely young lady, the daughter that we never had. Mama's prayed for this day for years." Speaking in a relieved and thankful tone.

"I know you go to Bill's' church before coming to St. Hebrews Baby, you do what you need to do, St. Hebrews is family; you hear me. Sometimes you have to branch away before God can move in your life. What are your plans for this evening?"

"Kim is accompanying me to a business sponsored event in San Francisco. Afterwards, I'll see her safely home, and look forward to my nice warm bed, *alone.* I thank God that I will not be faced with the *temptations* of New Year's Eve past."

"Aw..., Baby, that's so good, your father will be happy to hear the good news. We're praying that she's the one; we're ready for some grandkid's, boy." She voiced, with a friendly jab implying that it's long overdue.

"Satan is not going to let you walk away without a fight. You make sure you keep your armor on. I love you, and I will be praying for you as always, especially tonight." (Eph. 6:11)

"Aw..., thanks Mom, I love you, too." Walter's happy to have such understanding parents. Recalling seeing his Mom kneeled in prayer many days and nights; he knew that she indeed would be praying for him. He needed to call Kim surrounding the details for the evening.

To assist with Kim's dress alterations, Barbara and Karen arrived early. Due to the complexities of their holiday schedules, and each visiting with their family and friends; the girls hadn't gotten together since Barbara's horrendous night at Gray's, therefore, she hadn't disclosed the intimate details.

Greeting with hugs and kisses. "Happy New Year guys!" Barbara greeted.

"Happy New Year to you! How are you really doing?" Karen asked, in sincerity.

Relaxing at the kitchen table in her jeans and royal blue sweater, Barbara answered. "I'm good, the holidays were a bash. Here, I saved this for you." She said, and handed them a container. Her response was anything but convincing.

"What is it?" They asked; tearing into the container wrapped in foil. *"Lumpia!"* They yelled.

"We were hoping that you'd save us some." Kim said.

"Oooh, this will go good with my *hot wings*." Karen added. "Let's heat this up, Mmm...yummy, we got a party."

"The fudge!" Kim recalled. "Mother sent *fudge* for you."

Keeping an alliance front with Barbara, Kim broke the ice regarding Kathy. "I can't wait to hear what Miss Kathy's like, was she nice?" Kim spoke with attitude, as she joined them at the kitchen table.

Stress free in her red terrycloth robe, just one of many Christmas gifts that she'd received. The charm bracelet from Walter dangled from her arm as she placed curlers in her hair.

"Actually, she was, Kim. She's quite attractive also; she looks younger than forty-four. She has a beautiful smooth brown complexion, a well endowed—physique." Using her hands to illustrate curves.

"I was only in her presence for a brief moment; she was pleasant, more than I can say for his sister. You'll get to see her later tonight." Placing a cup of Barbara's favorite cinnamon tea in front of her, Karen started the inquest session.

"So, his sister was a brat?" Karen asked. At eased in her grey jogging suit. She munched on a *lumpia* roll while glancing over the plans for her event.

"Well..., let's just say in her attempt to surprise Gary; she was distastefully surprised to find me there. Her only alternative was rudeness. She's gorgeous; she only wants to get her big brother hitched."

"Poor Gary," Kim remarked."

"Poor Gary is right; I know he didn't orchestrate their visit. We were having such a good time getting to know one another. The atmosphere was ideal, before dinner, we were sitting on the fireplace ledge sipping hot apple cider. We played a game of twenty questions. It's neat; it was Gary's idea to speed up our acquaintance process.

"Sound like you, guys were hitting it off." Kim weighed in.

"Yeah! We were." She paused. Gaping into her tea, her finger softly circled the brim of the cup. Suddenly, raising her head in a jerking motion; she gave the impression of someone coming out of a trance.

"Life's a journey, only time will tell if we're on the same path. Am I disappointed, yes! I have to rest in Pastor's comments "*Things aren't always as they appear.*" She said, with a little less discouragement in her tone.

"It must've been awkward for Gary. How long did you stay? Karen asked, drenched in curiosity.

Laughing uncontrollably, "Awkward is being generous; he was far from the cool and laid-back Gary as you know him. Poor guy, I felt sad for him, really, I did. He went into absolute shock when he saw her." She snickered.

"You are kidding." Kim echoed.

Turning her head to acknowledge, "No, I am not, I thought he was gonna join that bag on the floor. I stayed longer than I wanted. After he returned from showing them to their rooms, I let him off the hook by leaving."

"He walked me to the door, and attempted to lay a *whopper* of a kiss on me. Full of passion I'm certain. I managed to reject him!"

"He tried to kiss you, with her there?"

"Oh, it was fine, it's a huge house, we were at the front door, they were way out of sight and hearing range. He was so flustered, it probably was his way of saying sorry or something, I don't know."

"Could it be he just desired to kiss you, Missy?" Karen noted; with broaden eyes.

"I guess!"

"Rejected him, girl, are you crazy?" Karen said. Immediately, Barbara realized that they were caught up in the excitement; there was no doubt to them why she resisted Gary's advances. She decided to endure them for an instant of fun before she proceeded to explain her actions.

"For obvious reasons guys, c'mon. I certainly didn't want to resist him; it was a dream that came true. His arms reached beneath my coat, and embraced my waist; pulling me close to him."

Acting similar to a scene in a play, she's pretending with her hands, gazing into space with sparkly eyes, as if she's envisioning the very act. Finding her display of theatrics comical, they were pleasantly shocked.

Neither had ever witnessed her in a romantic involvement, this was totally out of character for her. Because of her resilient character, they often teased her that she was too standoffish to men. She always assured them "*when the right stage was set, the curtains would go up.*"

"I thought I'd literally—melt guys." Doubling over with laughter. "I managed to recover in spite of raging emotions. Thoughts of this and that were zooming through my mind. You would've been proud of me; I bounced back with a quickness. Oh, oh, I forgot, he had *mistletoe* over the door, he pointed to it when I arrived. Hmm…, so I guess he did desire to kiss me."

"Did you kiss him then?" Karen asked, bubbling over in suspense.

"Yeah, on his cheek, nothing close to his attempt. Grinning in unbelief, they sat with their mouth wide-open.

"Girl…, I think I would've taken that kiss as a Christmas present." Karen said, and laughed aloud.

"So, how did he take you resisting him?" Kim asked, with eagerness.

Barbara giggled, turning her head, "Not so well, I'm afraid. His ego was—bruised, beaten, so much so, we ended up going back inside, and talking for another fifteen or twenty minutes."

"You, guys went back inside to talk. Oh, he was crushed?" Karen presumed, laughing and flinging her arms. "I know why you resisted; I just don't see the how."

Feeling better than she did when she first arrived, she loved their comical and juvenile behavior, she was bowled over as well. What a difference *being in Christ made*, grown women, ***recapturing their innocence through Christ;*** excited over the thought of a ***kiss.***

"I know your questions are wishful thinking; so I'm going to excuse you. I could've indulged in a *moment of lust;* secure in knowing that it wasn't going any further than a kiss. However, I would've *entertained* that kiss *repeatedly* in my mind. And we know, *"where the mind—goes,"* they said in unison, *"the body—will follow."*

"That's good!" Kim added. "You're right; you'd be focusing on how he—*made you feel,* rather than his present circumstances." Kim clarified.

"It was fun while it lasted, you know we never get any excitement like this amongst us, we had to have some girl fun." Karen added, jokingly.

"Exactly, I concur, it was one of those thoughts that kept darting in and out of my mind at the time."

"You must be pleased with yourself. That took some self-discipline on your part girl, Gary's an attractive man." Kim noted.

"Yeah, it took all sixteen years of dress rehearsal, and then some. After thinking about it, the hardest part wasn't resisting him. I mean, the desire was there, but I knew kissing him would've *violated* my number one principle, *no kissing*. Explaining to him why I didn't kiss him was the task. For some reason I felt *ashamed,* I knew it was the *enemy*, but he was so *kind*, you wouldn't believe. The more I think about it, I really feel that he was relieved that I didn't kiss him, seriously."

"Oh..., really!" Karen grunted. "Why?"

"Yeah, I do, the ego thing was a factor, but that was natural. He did give me the option of bringing you guys, so I knew his intentions were honorable."

"Ah..., that explains it; you didn't tell us that we'd been invited." Kim complained.

"I know!" She paused "I had my reasons guys." She said with shyness, while smiling. After evaluating Barbara's dilemma, Karen knew Barbara went suited in her armor.

"Your pep talk definitely paid off. I tell you, this Christian walk is something else." Karen remarked, turning her head, and releasing a deep breath.

"We have to be on guard at all times. In years past, the *consequence* of a kiss would never be a consideration, even with Christians." Karen added.

"That's because..., in times past, the kiss was the agenda, Karen, even amongst Christians." Barbara reminded, laughing. "Hey, I'm just keeping it real, guys, thank God, that we've come into the knowledge of understanding the origin of our actions. But we do have to be tested, right? Or, how will our growth be measured." Barbara paused. "I mean..., how can we determine our area of weakness?"

Mulling over the thought, Karen spoke. "Yeah! I guess; we do have to be tested."

"My testing days are coming, but for now, you can imagine what it's like for Walter and me. Kissing is not an option for us at this stage, considering his active—love life." She said, with smiles.

"You're playing a major *role*; you're *holding him* to your values." Karen reminded her.

"In all fairness guys, he hasn't made any advances toward me, I mean..., unlike Ralph, I feel and see his attraction for me; but he hasn't put any moves toward me."

"Exactly, because you're bringing him up to your standards, which keeps him in check. He never had a woman to do that. That's why he's so intrigued with you

Kim. His biggest problem was women chasing him; he hadn't acquired the Christ centered life to resist them."

"I feel as if he's saying; if you don't bother me, I will not bother you." She cackled.

"Aw Kim, that's so special. You're so blessed to have *internalized Christ teaching at an early age*. Don't ever be ashamed of your *virginity*, I envy you." Karen encouraged.

"Aw, thanks Karen, I needed that. After hanging with some of my sorority sisters at times; I often feel *alone*. They're Christians too, but haven't embraced the need to *abstain*." Followed with a hug to Karen.

"You had us in mind when you invited him, didn't you?" Kim asked, with a suspicious grin.

"Who? Me!" Echoed Barbara, grinning. Kim's phone rang.

"Hello!"

"Hi, this is Walter"

"Hi, Walter!" She said, smiling and *winking*. They yelled!

"Hi, Walter, Happy New Year!"

"That was Barbara and Karen."

"Will I be picking you up at your place?"

"Yes!"

"Ask them if they want to ride with us."

"Karen, do you want to ride over with us?" Karen yelled, "Yes!"

"What about Barbara Jean, or is she going with Russell?

"Ah..., we're still working out the details, see you later."

"Sounds as if you guys are batting a thousand." Karen surmised.

"I'm not bragging." Kim said. "But we're doing fine; I don't think I'll need to sign up with that dating website. Walter is remarkable; we share the same goals. Bill plays a major role in his life now, he's a God sent. *hint... hint*."

Kim ragged on Karen for her not recognizing Bill's apparent qualities. "What's going on with Bill?" Kim inquired.

"Ah..., I'm exploring my options. My first assignment for the New Year is to sign up with the dating website. I like Bill, but I wanna take things a little slower, relative to Michael; I only want the best situation for him.

"Like I said before, listen to your child." Barbara reminded her.

"Kim, I saw Walter with you at bible study, what did he think of Pastor Rama?"

"Oh, he loved him, I introduced them afterwards. He told Pastor he'd come again. Pastor invited him to the men's retreat."

"The poor man doesn't stand a chance. The women were checking him out at bible study." Karen interjected.

"He does command a second look, I admit to that." Barbara confessed.

"Last year, we thought you were interested in him." Karen pointed out.

"We'd hear you say "*Walter and I ate here and there.*"

"Okay!" Kim agreed, enthusiastically.

"Oh..., girl, the operative word was *eating*. Those were business lunches. The market was—*booming*, plus, he was good for the ego." She smiled. "Nah, I find him attractive, but I don't desire him in the same manner as you." She *winked* at Kim.

"I hear ya!" Karen said. "I find him attractive too; I just think he's a fine specimen of a man."

"Yeah, yeah, exactly, thanks Karen." Barbara remarked. Kim talked openly about her and Walter's attraction.

"We agreed not to entertain in our perspective homes, unless there're others present. When we met, the attraction was *purely physical.* So, when we do get together we make it quality time. We talk on the phone for hours; we take long walks through the park and museums. God forbid me to be an obstacle for him, when he's trying so hard."

"That's insightful of you Kim; I share the same sentiments regarding Bill." Karen said. Barbara's cell phone rang.

"Hello!"

"Hi BJ, Happy New Year!"

"Happy New Year to you, Gary." Barbara greeted, as she glanced in Kim and Karen's direction.

"I left you a message last week, since I didn't hear from you; I figured you'd made alterative arrangements to the event tonight."

"Ah..., yeah, with regard to your guest; I think its best. It was considerate of you to call. Last week, oh, we were in Tahoe when you called, celebrating my birthday."

"I didn't know that, happy late birthday; I wish I'd known. I'll be looking for you tonight."

"Like wise." Giving her a disapproving smile, Kim looked at Barbara in suspense, and asked.

"Why did you let him think that you're going?" After Gary's call, Barbara's countenance appeared saddened. "It's not important. I'll tell him that I changed my mind at the last minute, which I did. It was nice of him to call. That's why I'm not going. He'll feel torn, and go out of his way to recognize my presence. I'm fine; it worked for my good. I can continue with my traditional prayer vigil." She laughed. "I'll just have a longer prayer list."

"Precisely!" Kim said. Getting up to brew more tea. "You're probably right, Barbara. Because he's considerate, he'd be torn; I am claiming him for you." Kim added.

"You can check out the internet at midnight to ensure that we've made a smooth transition into the *New Millennium.*" Kim suggested.

"Yeah! I forgot about that." Barbara agreed.

"Let's lift up prayers of Thanksgiving for this year, traveling grace for tonight, and the men that have come into our lives." Karen suggested. *"Lord we give you praise...*

Finalizing the plans for the limo; Walter wanted Kim to be pleasantly surprised. He knew how to pamper women. Treating women special wasn't limited to Kim only; he'd a reputation for dining his women in style.

Removing his pressed tuxedo that was hanging on the bathroom door, he scanned the room. Admiring the folded back satin comforter, silk sheets, candles by the bedside, and chocolates on the pillows; all compliments of his housekeeper. *Oh, she—thinks I'll be entertaining later tonight, not tonight.* Knowing the routine from past holidays, the housekeeper aimed to please.

The first pickup was Kim. Charmed to see Walter step from the limo; she felt like *Cinderella*. Watching her stride toward the car in her red satin floor length a-line style dress, with and rhinestone accessories; Walter was rendered breathless. It was reminiscent of a teenager picking up his date for his high school prom.

Taking one last twirl in the mirror, Karen struggled to zip her black form-fitted semi-formal dress with a "V" neckline in the back. Loving the attention that her legs draw, she chose black stockings with a rhinestone ankle bracelet, and black satin three-inch pumps.

Assured that Bill would be in attendance; *Um, maybe I should've invited him, no, I'll just leave things as they are.* Feeling justified in her decision to explore her options, she that felt if Bill was the one; it'd be evident soon enough. Spraying on perfume, she reached for her purse, and dashed for the door to wait for Walter.

Securing the delivery of his dates, now comfortable at home, Walter kicked off his shoes after disrobing down to his black boxers in the living room. Getting a bottle of juice from the refrigerator, he heard music coming from the hallway toward his bedroom. Deciding to investigate; he headed down the hallway. *I didn't leave anything on, or did I?*

With hesitation, he carefully opened the double doors to his bedroom. Wearing only a black negligee, a woman lay in the middle of his bed.

"What the heck—are you doing here, and how did you get in here?" Walter shouted.

Looking for something to cover his body, he snatched his robe that hung over the chair. After covering himself, clutching the comforter from the bed; he tossed it over her. It was none other than Deborah Collins, his date on last *New Year's Eve.*

"I thought we could have a repeat performance of last year, Walter. I met you here for lunch a few months ago, and you left the key under the planter, remember?"

Forgetting that he'd left a spare key for her after inviting her to lunch didn't change matters. Deborah worked five minutes from Walter's home. As an outside sale Account Representative, it afforded her the flexibility to meet with him.

"Deborah, you've got to go,—now!" Reaching for her arm to pull her from the bed; she grabbed his arm with both hands, causing him to fall onto the bed.

Walter struggled and pushed her off him, resisting her attempt to caress his body. His forceful push landed her to the floor on the other side of the bed.

"Ouch,—my neck, I can't move it." She cried, *Lord, please help me*" Walter prayed, *silently*. Running to her aid with concern, he sat beside her, "Are you okay?" Jumping into his lap, and locking her legs around him, Walter knew he was in for a tussle.

"Please, don't do this, Deborah. I have a girlfriend now; I'm not the same man." Attempting to kiss him, "Sure you do, I've been watching you Walter, it's a new year, c'mon, you've never resisted me before. I love you Walter."

With emotions raging, he pleaded of her to let go. Literally begging, he reflected on his newfound relationship with the Lord; he prayed within, *Lord, please help me!* Recalling his Mom's advice *"Keep on your armor."*

Walter knew; the time that he'd spent with the, Lord had been real and far outweighed the *meager minutes of pleasure* with Deborah. Gaining strength, he extended his hands behind his back grabbing her legs; enabling him to loosen her clutch from his waist. His harsh stare into her supported his seriousness. Nursing a flattened ego, she surrendered.

While frantically gathering her clothes; she yelled obscenities at Walter. With sunken shoulders and breathless, he leaned against the door facing.

"C'mon, Deborah, we both agreed it was over." Now fully dressed, she tossed his key in his face and left.

"Deborah," walking after her. "I'm not rejecting you; I'm rejecting what we did, I'm sorry if I've hurt you."

Without a word, she stormed out the door. After securing the door locked, he chose a different room to sleep. Feeling thankful, *Thank you Jesus, thank you, Lord.* Owning up to a robust *whip appeal* affect from Deborah, which rendered him helpless in times past, he realized; God's *mercy* was with him.

Highly intelligent and engaging, he enjoyed Deborah's company as well. Like Walter, she lacked applying the word to her life. Sensing her hurt; even though they'd mutually agreed that their relationship was over months ago; somehow, it wasn't giving him any comfort. He wished he'd the strength to resist her initially.

Walter wasn't operating alone; prayers and the *Holy Spirit* were with him. After settling down, being conscious of the late hour, he desired badly to call his Mom to thank her for her prayers. For this type of victory, he knew she was lifting him up before the Lord.

For once in his life, Walter understood the true meaning to *resist temptation*. Recalling biblical stories, he laughed aloud, *this must be how it felt for Joseph trying to get away from Potiphar's wife; I wonder if she was as fine as Deborah."*

Since the hour was late, he anxiously looked forward to sharing his victory with his friend and mentor, Bill. Aware of Bill's affections for Karen, he was stunned to see Bill at the event with Monica, a business associate of theirs. Karen had turned a cold shoulder to Bill, he thought. Exhausted from the evening occurrences, for the first time in his adult life, Walter fell asleep, *alone,* on *New Year's Night.*

Deborah Collins, counting on Walter's past behavior toward her to kick in, she couldn't believe that he'd turned down her advances. Deborah had no way of knowing that the cards were stacked against her in the form of *prayers and the Holy Spirit*. Furious to say the least, she'd been confident that Walter would welcome her into his bed; she remained confused.

Knowing that he'd been spending his nights alone; for safety measures, she'd make trips by his place, therefore, she was puzzled by his excuse of a new girlfriend. She hadn't noticed him bringing anyone to church as well.

Deborah knew that their relationship was physical based and accepted full ownership of that. On the other hand, Walter wasn't mindful of her true feelings for him. Indulging her with extravagant restaurants, plays and movies resulted in mixed signals for Deborah.

Because Walter's a Mama's *Boy,* he possessed a natural sensitivity and generosity toward women. Attending church Sunday after Sunday, like Walter, they'd met while serving on the finance board.

Reminded daily of her disobedience, Deborah often wondered if she'd abstained from sleeping with Walter would've made a difference. Nothing like Walter's church going experience, Deborah was reared in the word, and she knew better.

Moving to the Bay Area from the east coast; she selected a church based on its locality, Walter became her consolation prize. The fact that she got his attention above the other women gave her a reason to hope. She'd held Walter's interest longer than any other woman had.

The fact that she was as cute and shapely as Hallie Berry didn't hurt. There were only a few single men at St. Hebrews, but none with a resume comparable to Walters. Deborah was determined; and would not be giving up so easy.

Chapter 9

January 2000, Karen signed up with the Christian dating website. Different from Barbara, she added a photo to her profile. It read, *Forty-two years old, looking to correspond with committed Christian man, enjoys reading, sports, hiking, and testing new recipes.* Hearing her doorbell ring, she hit the submit button and logged off.

"What's up guys, come on in?" She asked, and invited in Barbara and Kim.

"Michael's getting as handsome as he's tall, we saw him out back shooting hoops." Kim remarked.

"I know, soon I'll be at—war with the girls"

"Soon?" Spoke Kim.

"Oh, the interest is there, thank God for his interest in basketball. It really offers a balance for him."

"Did you forget about the singles meeting after church today?" Kim asked. "Oh, yeah—what do I need to know?"

"I'll e-mail you the details."

"Kim and I were chewing on pastor's sermon from this morning." Barbara said. The scripture in itself was a sermon enough for me. Proverbs 3:5, 6" *Trust in the Lord with all thine heart and lean not unto thy own understanding, in all thy ways acknowledge him and he shall direct thy paths.* With regard to Gary, I found it comforting."

"Yeah, it does offer a sense of hope and comfort." Karen agreed. Needing details of the event, Barbara started the inquisition process.

In anticipation, with her hand under her chin, she was anxious to hear the outcome. "Tell the truth guys, after seeing Gary with Kathy, what are your true assessments? How did he interact with her? What did you think of her?" Karen jumped in. "Well, for starters, she has nothing on you"

"Aw, how loyal of you."

"But, anyway, she was pleasant. I was only in their presence for a short while." Kim gave her play-by-play account. "Walter spotted Gary; he invited Walter to sit at the table next to him. You're correct; Kathy was pleasant, a bit reserved, but polite. Connie was overly friendly, until she figured out that Walter wasn't an option for her. I'd gone to the powder room when we first arrived."

"Yes! Connie was giving Walter the eye." Karen agreed.

"Gary's first words were *"where's, BJ?"* We told him the truth; you had a last minute change of heart. He looked surprised, but accepted it." Secretly admiring Gary's friend, Karen mentioned. "There was another guy with him; he was a cutie also, nice and engaging, like Gary,"

"Oh, that would've been his friend, Tony."

"That's it!" Kim said, "Tony was the designated dancer for Kathy and his sister."

"Is he available?" Karen inquired, in a bashful tone, expressing a sincere interest.

"I don't—know..." Barbara pushed out slowly. "I know he's single, he's an electrical contractor."

"Well, anyway," Kim continued. "Gary remained calm and cool as usual. When he wasn't talking to Walter or other associates, he sat and sipped on punch."

"That's *old man* Gary," Barbara joked.

"You could see that he engaged her in conversation," Kim paused, gesturing with her hands. "But he wasn't all over her, or anything close to it. At one point; she tried to pull him on the dance floor, Gary gently handed her hand to Tony." Kim concluded her report.

"Oh, I forgot, at midnight, he slow danced with her, bringing in the New Year."

"See..., I knew I made the right decision," knocking her fist on the counter top, "Tony wouldn't have been an option for me, for a midnight dance." She stated tenaciously.

Not expecting to receive such a detailed report of the evening, however, she was pleased. It only affirmed her decision to stay home; it would've presented an uncomfortable evening for Gary. After all, it was New Year's Eve, a time of celebration and enjoyment.

"Hey, you know we had your back, girl." Karen responded, with attitude."

Barbara admitted; it had been somewhat of a downer for her. "Thanks, guys. I can't be upset, but I can sure be disappointed. I wish he'd told her to *get lost Kathy, you walked out on me for another man, and now I got me another woman."* Her hands were on her hips, she was moving her head like *Sh neh neh.* Screaming loudly, they found her behavior entertaining and amusing.

"Seriously," She added. "We always have choices." Barbara voiced. "Kathy has the edge," she fussed. "They have a past; they knew each other in the biblical way." She said, sarcastically, boiling over with laughter.

Because of Kathy and Gary's past intimacy involvement, she felt Kathy's presence naturally ignited some smoldering flames for Gary. Paying attention to

Barbara's thoroughness, Kim replied. "You've definitely thought this through, I guess it makes sense; I've never experienced such matters." Kim confessed.

Karen embraced Barbara's idea entirely. "I agree; you're right, it happens. You hear it all the time, people meet, and rekindle relationships with their high school and college sweethearts."

"I'm being silly; I know he has to explore his emotions; I would too. Oh, by the way, he's a *Christian.* You guys ragged me so about that *almost kiss* until I forgot to share the most important information."

"I knew it, I knew it." Kim declared.

"He doesn't classify himself as a committed one."

"What's your take on that?" Karen asked, and mimicked. "He has to be a *seasoned Christian* for me, remember?"

"I was waiting for you to remind me, Karen. Surprisingly, I'm cool. Oh, oh, I forgot, he's—abstaining also. It's a challenge from his men's ministry."

"Really..., for how long?"

"Trust me; I wanted to know, too." Admitted BJ.

"Well that's a huge plus for you." Karen spoke.

"Tell me about it, we talked the commitment thing through, my concern is with *his heart,* his attitude and his feelings toward the, Lord. For the first time since we've met, we had time to talk. It was my reason for not inviting you guys. I needed space to probe his mind, and to hear from his heart. He possesses," she paused. "Um, a tenderized spirit for the, Lord. I like what I heard. I detect seriousness in his desire to grow."

Barbara wasn't too concerned at this point with their involvement, if indeed there was one. Desiring not to minimize the importance of his commitment to God, she judged him on the content of his heart, and not on an *adjective*—which described his relationship with Christ.

She wasn't about to toss Gary in the reject pile, she was a good judge of character; her wisdom assured her that Gary Lloyd Russell had more going for him than meet the eye.

Being frustrated with Karen; Kim asked, "Miss Karen, so, you're gonna just let Bill get away?"

"You're referring to the lady that he was with at the dinner?" Karen asked. "Her name is Monica; Walter said she's a business associate." Kim shared.

In shock, Barbara screamed, with her mouth wide open. "Bill brought another woman?" Karen promptly defended, expressing emphasis with head movement. "No! He—did not come with her." Sulking like a spoiled child. "He did spend some time with her, we never got close, I only saw him from a distance. I have to tell the truth, I was a little jealous."

"A little jealous, huh, please, more like coveting" Kim corrected.

"Oh, hush!" Karen protested.

"Before you came, I signed up with the dating website."

"You didn't?" Barbara scolded.

"Did you upload your photograph? Did you restrict your search to the Bay Area?

"Yes, to both questions."

"C'mon, let's go to Michael's computer; I bet you have a hit." Kim suggested. Since she'd claimed Bill for Karen and Gary for Barbara, she did so with reluctance.

For monitoring purposes, she kept Michael's computer in the family room. After logging in, she discovered that she'd four responses. Kim screamed. "Oh, my goodness, you got four hits. Let's see the photographs first! Ooh, this is so much fun." Opening the first one. "Wow! He's big! " Kim noted.

"We have to read the profiles too, guys." Barbara reminded.

"Ooh..., he's too, old for you Karen. He's seventy-six; did you specify a range girl?" Kim asked.

"Maybe I didn't!" Amazed by her responses, "I can't believe I got this many."

Barbara laughed, before saying. "I can, you included your photograph, Christian man or not, he looks on the outer exterior, before he sees the heart."

Impressed mostly by the one called, *"Rock"* she selected him. His profile read. *"Committed Christian man, thirty seven, divorced, and looking for a committed woman that is seeking to grow in the Lord. Serious about the potential to be married again. Enjoy outdoor activities; love to watch NBA basketball, raising a nine-year-old son.*

Having a striking resemblance to NBA player Derek Fisher, (*Lakers*), 5'11, clean cut, and easy on the eyes; Barbara smiled. Right away, she thought of Gary. "I see Gary's point, what's his name, "*Rock*," he used the expression "*committed Christian*" twice. Are you going to reply to him, Karen?" Barbara asked.

"I'm going to sleep and pray on it."

Kim discussed how Walter's behavior had been in common with that of a brand new Christian lately. "In the past two days, Walter's so excited; he said he'd some kind of victory over something. He didn't go into any details, but it sure has him fired up. He said in due time, he'll tell me."

"I know," Barbara agreed. "He left me a new year's greeting expressing the same sentiments, and thanking me for being there for him over the years. I guess we should just rejoice with him, whatever it is." Karen decided to evaluate their *quest* results.

"Look guys, we're into the *New Millennium;* regarding Mr. Right, Kim is the only one that's on target.

"You might be correct, I mean about him being *Mr. Right*. I won't say I am the only one on track, I think you've met some nice men; you're just facing some obstacles right now. I already told you, Walter is my, husband." Kim reminded them, with no hesitation.

Barbara boldly aired her thoughts about Karen's decision. "I think Karen could be on second base with Bill if she wanted to be." Kim didn't vacillate with her thoughts. "I concur completely."

Getting a brainstorm, Barbara threw it out for comments. "Hey, I like that, *second base*. Let's use the game of baseball as a measuring device to monitor our progress in our relationships. For Gary and me well...," she paused. "I'm still in the batting *cage.*"

Falling over laughing, Karen weighed in. "I'm at bat, with Bill, or could be."

"And, you Kim?"

"Um...," considering the thought, while displaying confidence, she finally replied, *"second base."*

Explaining the rules, Barbara said. "The goal is for us to hit a *home run*."

"Does a home run mean being engaged or married?" Kim asked.

"Alright, you're feeling this, okay, *third base* is engaged, *homerun*, means altar, wedding. What cha' think?"

"I think we're crazy, but I love it." Karen added.

"Hey, we gotta have some…fun! I have to do something to keep from crying." Barbara teased.

"Let's pray guys." Suggested Barbara. Joining hands and lifting their voices unto God, they asked for continued directions and guidance for their lives. Barbara and Kim thought Karen was way *off base* looking for someone else.

Enjoying a relaxing day after the new year, doing what she loved, Barbara's phone rang.

"Hello!"

"Hi, BJ!"

"Hi, what's up?" She said, in a low-key and cool tone.

"No, Hi, Gary?"

"Okay.., Hi, Gary!" Voiced cheery, but unwillingly.

"I'm leaving tonight; I'm going to Atlanta for about four weeks, more or less. My Dad had a stroke two days ago. He's okay, but he'll have limited use on his right side."

"I'm so sorry; I'll place him on my prayer list."

"Thank you, please include me, also. I'm calling to say goodbye, and to see if it'll be okay for me to call you."

"We're friends, aren't we?"

"Without a doubt."

"Then I'll expect your call."

"Are you okay?" He asked, "You're not your usual happy self."

"Um, I confess; I'm not my usual *perky* self." She responded, somewhat gravely. "Ah, you sort of caught me in the middle of something. I was jotting down some thoughts for a *novel* that I hope to finish this year. I guess my mind is a little preoccupied, maybe."

" Well, I'm going to let you get back to your *writing*; maybe you'll share it with me someday."

"Hmm, I can do that." She said reluctantly. *How convenient, he'll get to be with Kathy.*

"I'll check on you later, take care." Her phone rang again. She allowed it to go to the voicemail. "*Where are you? I'm reminding you that we're celebrating my husband's birthday this weekend, your presence is expected.*" It was her big sister, Mildred. Releasing a deep sigh, she saved her document.

After Gary's call, she ceased composing, picked up her pen and wrote in her prayer journal. She hadn't purposely meant to be chilly to Gary; she still nursed the displeasure behind Kathy's appearance. Catching her off guard was a good thing; she wasn't in the mood to masquerade her true feelings.

Envisioning sitting in a batting—cage, without a bat, she ripped into laughter. When things were out of her control, laugher had become a means of therapy.

Thinking of Sober, she returned an e-mail that she'd received from him. Hitting the send button. *Who knows, Sober just might be my, Mr. Right.*

They were slowly becoming good friends. He'd his shortcomings as everyone did in the Lord. She admired his truthfulness; he was a nice distraction. She'd definitely be interested in meeting with him when he returned to the area, if he was interested in her. She'd forgotten; they hadn't exchanged photographs, it was part of her initial request. To their surprise, it'd worked out great, their focus had centered on each other.

Spending the remainder of the day in the *word and prayer*, if God was speaking to her, she wanted to be available to hear him. Later that evening she looked forward to a pleasant evening in the city with her girlfriend Beverly and her husband; they're having dinner and seeing a play. Remembering to pray for Vanessa, Gary and his Dad; she completed her notes in her prayer journal.

Gary boarded a flight to Atlanta with his sister Connie, and his old flame Kathy. Having been assured that his fathers condition was stable; Gary still felt that the trip was necessary. Aware that his Dad was an active and proud man, being laid up wouldn't sit too well with him; he'd use his trade to make things more mobile and comfortable for him.

Still fixed on his conversation with BJ; he felt indifference in her tone. Categorizing the night at his place as being an oxymoron episode; still, he was glad that he'd invited her. Their game of *twenty questions* satisfied curious and inquiring minds for them both, on the other hand, after Kathy's arrival; he regretted BJ having to witness the incident.

Working the entire year without time off, Gary desperately needed a vacation. Knowing that he'd be flooded with administrative work upon his return; he felt blessed to have a reliable foreman to facilitate the day-to-day activities.

Affording him the necessary time to evaluate his life, this trip would provide him the opportunity to get to know Kathy as well. He needed to know if his emotions were genuine for Kathy of today, or Kathy of the *past*. The physical attraction was evident; but he needed to know about the woman she'd become.

Remaining in the in-law unit during their entire stay didn't determine anything for him conclusively. After Kathy's failed attempt to seduce him in the limo after the party, he felt safer there. Without wavering, she expressed her desire to spend the night with him. Alluding to the two cocktails that she'd consumed; he refused her by saying that he was too much of a gentleman to take advantage of her.

Understanding that it was his caring way of refusing her, Kathy would provide him the space he needed before trying again. Gary didn't have the courage or didn't desire to reveal his pledge of celibacy to Kathy as he did BJ.

Many times over, Kathy regretted running off in the manner in which she did, eventually, she grew to love her husband. Being much older than Gary was; her husband was positioned to give her the material things she desired.

Never losing her affection for him, Kathy was elated and surprised that Gary was still single; she felt as if life was giving her a second chance to make things right with him. The mere fact that he chose to stay in the back unit let her know that it wouldn't be a slam-dunk. Older and more experienced when they were dating; she'd the upper hand.

New Years Eve proved to her that he wasn't the young man she'd left. She couldn't dismiss his involvement with BJ either; taking notice of his attentiveness toward her the night of their arrival. For now, Kathy felt that she'd the upper hand; BJ would not be a factor for a while. With that in mind, she relaxed and delighted in the flight.

It's late February, Karen Harding finally agreed to meet Harold *Rock* Banks from the internet dating website. After days and hours of corresponding on the internet and telephone, it was a mutual decision to meet. Raising his nine-year-old Son, Harold teaches a young adult bible class at his church, and is active in their singles ministry.

A leisure walk around the lake would be their first date today. Not wanting her time with him to interfere with her daily walk; it was her idea. While Michael attended basketball practice, she designated that time to herself.

Sharing a similar past with Harold, he was originally from the south. His family moved to California when he was a toddler. Born in the south also, her parents migrated to California while she was a baby. Both classed themselves as natives of California.

After their walk, they stopped at a nearby coffee house until it was time for her to pick up Michael. Before going on a "real date," she wanted to test the waters. They planned to meet later that evening for a movie.

Early picking up Michael, Karen opted to wait for him in the Gym. She hadn't seen or spoken to Bill since the New Year. When she entered, the boys were completing their required laps around the gym.

Dashing by, Bill stopped abruptly sporting a brightly lit smile, expressing gladness in seeing her. Sharing mutual sentiments, she'd missed Bill's company also and his stunning blue eyes.

"Hi, stranger," Bill said, with a broad smile. "It's been a while, how have you been?" Amused by his greeting, she flashed him a short, but pleasant smile.

"Good! Keeping busy as usual, we really enjoyed the gift certificates."

"I got your thank you note and Christmas Card." He said, smiling.

"We should be able to get at least two more dinners." Bill had sent gift certificates to Radio Shack and their favorite Chinese restaurant for Christmas.

"I' m glad you're enjoying it. Well, I'd better go and release your Son to you." Staring into her eyes, "It's really good seeing you Karen." Desiring to tell her how much he'd missed—her, he refrained. Showing shyness, with a quick glance and smile, she uttered. "Likewise!"

Catching her completely off guard, she was reminded of how much she missed him. Streaking across the gym to tell the boys it was their last lap, he wore white shorts, a navy blue sweatshirt and a blue baseball cap.

Closely watching his every step, Karen could've counted them. Still possessing the body of an athlete, he'd done an excellent job in maintaining his toned physique.

Bill knew that he was in love with Karen, believing that she'd feelings for him as well; he was unable to pinpoint her exact objections to their relationship. He wasn't certain, but suspected that it was a racial concern. If so, he knew Ronald had to be the driving force. To avoid a conflict between Michael and his *Father*, he surrendered to her despondency toward him.

Standing with folded arms, and one leg resting against the wall, he watched Michael and Karen walk toward the exit. He reflected on a *Clint Eastwood* movie. Clint and a fellow secret service agent woman were playing cat and mouse.

In this particular scene, the woman was walking away from him. *"Clint said, if she turned and looked back at him, he'd know that she liked him."*

Before taking hold of the door handle to leave, Karen turned and looked in his direction. Smiling, he tipped his baseball cap to her. Bill laughed, aloud, and spoke, "*she likes me... Clint.*"

Michael couldn't wait to get inside the car before he began quizzing his Mom about, Bill.

"Mom, did you talk to coach?"

"Yes, very briefly, now can we get in, please?" She replied, feeling uptight. Throwing his gym bag into the back seat, he continued to cross-examine her. "Are you going to see him again, Mom?"

Releasing her frustration from his interrogation process, she tightened her grip on the stern wheel. "I can't make any promises, Michael." Trying the clever tactic, "He still asks about you," he voiced, with—aggravation and disappointment in his tone.

"Really!"

"Yes, Mom..." Perturbed at Karen's choice to back a way from Bill; he was dissatisfied with her remark. Michael loved Bill as his Coach, and a mentor. He loved his Dad dearly, but felt he was selfish. Becoming aware of his Mom's faithfulness to God, he'd observed that men were never present in the home; she never dated, unlike his father. He felt she deserved some happiness in her life as well.

Karen was happy to learn that Bill still expressed an interest in her. Seeing him required her to admit her true feelings toward him; she'd taken her frustration out on Michael. Until today, he hadn't mentioned Bill, Karen figured that he'd become discouraged after his Dad's behavior.

On several visits to his father's, Ronald would often remind Michael that he was his father, and that no one would be taking his place. Confident in his identify; Michael had no problem with his Mom and Bill. Subsequently, he didn't lend too much attention to his Dad's comments. Not looking for Bill to replace his Dad, whom he loved, he wanted him for *his Mom.* Having his coach and mentor in his home would be an added bonus for him.

Having a movie date with Harold, Karen hurried to drop Michael off with her parents; they were attending a Warriors' game. Right on schedule meeting in front of the theatre, Harold came directly from work. In a grey blazer, black pants and white shirt, he was dressed business casual.

Spotting Karen, Harold yelled to get her attention. "Oh, there you are", Karen spoke.

"Shall we go in?" Harold asked.

Glancing at her watch. "Yes, and not a minute to spare." Expressing admiration with her outfit, he complimented in approval. Karen chose a short denim jacket with pants to match, a cream shell, and matching cream boots. To avoid discomfort or blushing from potential romantic scenes, Karen selected an action-packed Samuel Jackson flick.

After the movie, they walked a couple of blocks for ice cream. Harold's a computer programmer; working close by, he ran into some of his co-workers. Second-guessing before asking, "Karen, would you mind...if we sit with them?" He eased out, slowly with apprehension. "Of course not."

"To her surprise, she actually enjoyed their company. Jim was the prankster; Valerie was somewhat shy, like Karen. Austin and Harold kept them entertained. Impressed by Harold's out going personality, she was happy to see that he interacted well in the company of others.

Eventually stealing some time alone, exchanging horror stories regarding playing taxi for extra-curricular activities for their kids was the height of their conversation. Having married young, apparently his wife wasn't ready for motherhood, nor becoming a wife. Pleased with the idea of raising his Son, he was looking for a *wife,* and not a mother for his Son. Harold could do household chores as well as any woman. As the evening culminated, he asked if they could see each other again, assuring him that it was a possibility; they said good night.

In route home, Karen called to update, Kim. "Hello!"

"Hi dear, what are you up to?"

"I just got off the phone with Barbara; we were talking about you."

"Oh, I can imagine what you were saying."

"Good! So I will not have to repeat my self. How was the date with, Mr. *Rock?"* Hoping it was a *disaster,* She remained loyal to Bill being the one.

"It was pretty good, in fact, we had a great time. We did a movie, ice cream, and met with his co-workers."

"Is he someone that you want to get to know better?"

"Uh..., I'm not sure, I do have to make up my mind up though, he wants to get together again, soon."

"What are your objections?" Carefully itemizing her concerns, she answered. "Hmm..., he's four years younger, that's not a problem. He's extremely mature; I'm sure raising his nine years old Son has helped, he's actually the problem."

"His, Son?"

"Yes!"

"Are you forgetting that you have one, too?"

"No! Michael is fifteen and fully capable of taking care of himself. I've worked hard to get him where I want him, relative to household chores; we divide the duties as roommates. I'm not sure if I'm up to rearing another boy at this point."

"Wouldn't it be primarily Harold's responsibility?"

"No! That wouldn't be right. We'll discuss it in more detail later. I have another call coming through."

After seeing Bill, she had to own up to her true feelings for him. Karen wasn't up to admitting her true reason; the excuse with the nine-year old Son was only a cover-up.

Chapter 10

Logging in to check one of her business e-mails, she found an e-mail from Gary. Since few assignments come from that e-mail address, she rarely checked it. She'd given him the card with the address the day they'd met. Now, February, the e-mail was sent in January.

Hi! BJ, I know I said I would call. I want you to know that I really enjoyed the time that we spent during the holidays. My Dad is coping well. I'm building a wheel chair ramp for the front and back porch, I'm also installing a hot tub to help with his therapy. As for Kathy, we're taking one day at a time; it has been over 20 yrs. I'm glad that you didn't allow us to kiss that night; your reasons make a lot of sense. Intimacy only confuses your emotions. Because of you, we're friends. See you soon, Gary.

Perceiving that Gary had been doing some real soul searching; she also sensed caution. Declaring their relationship as friends didn't bother her, after sixteen years, she didn't expect a man to fall into her arms; if he was worth having, he was worth the wait. Making plans for a trip to New York later in the year, she didn't mean *literally* waiting. Her phone rang.

"Hello!"

"Hi! Barbara, this is Stacee. I only have a minute. I didn't know if you received the e-mail, I wanted to clarify receipt of the theme for the prayer breakfast."

"Yes, I got it; I made a note of it. I'm looking forward to it: my time is fifteen minutes correct?"

"That's the amount allotted to you, if you need more, go for it."

"How have you been?"

"Girl, between work and ministry, I've been swamped." Stacee said.

"The next time you're in the area we'll have to do lunch."

"I look forward to it, Goodnight, Barbara." Logging into her designated dating e-mail account, she had a message from Sober. *"Good evening, Zest, hope all is well with you. I was telling my prayer buddy about you. Sometimes I think we should've uploaded our photos. The lady that I met before I started corresponding with you, well..., my interest level is increasing for her, it appears to be some interest on her part as well. I'm not being shallow minded with looks only, she actually shares many of your ideas and qualities. I guess I'm guilty of being visual.*

How is it going with the guy that you met? You seem to care for him. I certainly want to continue to correspond with you, even though it's only over the internet. I still want to maintain trust and honesty also, it was the basis of our friendship in the beginning. You said you were going to share some of your writing, I'm still interested...Take care.

Sober had become the male friend she never had. In agreement with him, she had to confess, the photo's possibly would've made a difference. Her initial attraction to Gary was visual, so, she totally understood his attraction for the woman that he'd met. Responding, she wrote. *Hi! Sober, all is well with me. Your message was so kind and considerate. I agree, I think our leaving off the photographs possibly changed the course of things for us. There's no denying we accomplished what we intended, a great friendship! I'm feeling the same; I want to know more about the guy that I met. I guess I'm visual oriented also, in my case I'm playing it by ear, I'm not sure of his feelings for me.*

Regarding my writing, now that we've declared our relationship as friends, I'm going to share one of my letters with you, instead of a poem or short story. If all goes well, maybe the four of us can meet some day. I wish you the best. Talk to you soon. "Zest"

A dreamer in the truest sense, inspired by a movie she'd seen, she began writing *letters* to her future husband. She had no name for him, no visual image of how she wanted him to look. Without any false expectations or an expected end, this was her way of enhancing her imagination for writing, and keeping her dream alive. After writing her first letter, it was almost a year before she wrote another one.

Proving to be therapeutic as problems escalated in her life, she found herself emptying her heart through the letters; it was representative of a long distance relationship. With hesitation, before she lost her nerve she composed an e-mail.

Hi Sober, per your request, I'm sending one of my letters in a word attachment. After completing several letters, I told my daughter that I should publish them in poems or some format. She asked if I would be ashamed, I remember saying, probably yes! For inspiration, I'm reminded of a quote from A.W. Tozer, "Sin has played many evil tricks upon us, and one has been the infusion into us a false sense of shame." Remember, this could've been for you. ☺

My Dearest love, ***April 4, 1998***

I know we have yet to meet. I anxiously wait for the moment, the hour, and the year that our paths will cross. In past years, I've substituted others to fill the void. I know now that they were only occupying space, a space that can only be filled by God and you. I know that he's building a bridge for our paths to cross in his own time, not ours. For me, there's still plenty—of molding—shaping, and—twisting before I'm ready to meet you. If you came now, you wouldn't be pleased with me. I'm unaware of all the changes that are needed, but God is, I only know that change—is needed.

When it's our time, it'll be majestic. We'll dance to the melody of "At Last." There'll be an immediate bond; our eyes will speak for us. We'll talk for hours and hours. I want to become your best friend, absent of hugs or kisses. I want to love you for whom you've become, and not how you can make me feel, and vice versa.

When we merge on our bridge of destiny, the Holy Spirit will allow our strengths to compliment our faults, as he continues to mold us as one. Good-bye for now.

My love!

Hitting the send button, "Oh well, we'll probably never meet anyway."

Enjoying the cool morning air at the Marina, Barbara had just finished having early morning tea with her girlfriend Sue. Sue was waiting to meet with her golf club buddies. Barbara spotted a man talking to a woman that looked exactly like Gary. *That can't be, he's still in Atlanta. That is, Gary, um; it is February."*

Writing on a card, the woman handed it back to him after saying a few more words, she walked away. Surprised that Gary had returned without a word to her, after a second thought, she was reminded that they were only friends.

Headed in the opposite direction to start her walk along the course, she heard someone calling her name. Knowing that it was Gary, she took her time turning to look. "Hey, you!" He greeted.

"What are you doing here?" BJ asked.

"Looking for you, no hi, Gary, or it's good to see you, Gary." Softening her expression, and forcing a practiced smile, she mimicked him.

"Hi! Gary, it's good to see you, Gary."

"I knew I'd find you here. You said you come here in the early morning, I took my chances that today would be one of them. Walking side by side, they continued on the course around the Marina.

Meeting the woman in question, he waved and said good-bye to her. Feeling the need to explain, "She's the wife of a roofing contractor; I worked on several projects with him. I lost contact with him; she gave me his cell number."

"So, how is your Dad?"

"Oh,—he's doing exceptionally well. Like a little kid, he's running up and down those ramps that I built. Thanks for your prayers. With intense therapy; they expect him to regain complete mobility."

"Aw, I'm happy for him. It was awfully considerate and smart of you to build those ramps."

"It was needed BJ, I thank God that I do what I do. I hired one guy to help me. My Dad is active; the accessibility and freedom will keep him from becoming depressed. My stepmother, boy, she's enjoying that hot tub; it's a real treat for them."

"Aw, that's good, is she a good stepmother?"

"She is, I wish she'd come along sooner." He smiled. "At first, we gave her a rough time. But my Dad took care of that, real—quick. He told us, "*she was there for—him, and not us.*"

"Now, that's telling you." Buffering her laugh.

"Yeah right," he paused. "We were just kids; we were only reacting out of loyalty—to our Mom. Helping to raise—my two siblings was no joke. By the time I was eighteen; I felt the age of someone twenty-five—or thirty BJ. I couldn't wait to go away to college."

"Ah,—that explains it Gary." Now it was her turn, she was having an *epiphany* moment of his apparent behaviors. "Your mannerisms, your expressions are that of an older man, the *Aramis.*" She teased.

"Because of your elder expressions, your youthfulness often escapes me Gary. Most of the time I feel as if you're the older one, it's a good thing mind you." She encouraged him, with a smile of approval.

"I'm glad it's a good—thing, because I'm *too—old* to try to change now—girl." After sharing a simultaneous glance, they cracked up laughing from his remark.

Believing that Gary was ahead of his time, she also found it charming. Wearing white and navy blue sweats, white sneakers and a navy baseball cap, she was quickly reminded of her attraction for him.

"BJ, how's life treating you?" He asked, tenderly. Thinking before she spoke, "You know, Gary I can't complain."

"Well, you're looking good; we're wearing the same colors." He observed.

"Um, great minds do think alike." They smiled in agreement. Barbara was wearing navy sweat pants, a white polo with a navy sweatshirt tied around her neck. Tossing a rock into the Marina, her facial expression climbed to serious.

"How about you Gary, how has life been for you?" She asked softly, hoping to hear about the events in Atlanta.

"How much time do you have? I'm kidding. Things are okay." *I wonder if she was referring to me and Kathy, she'd ask if she was interested."* Tossing another rock into the water; she dusts the dirt from her hands. *I want to know about him and Kathy* Fussing to herself, realizing Gary wasn't giving up any scoop on him and Kathy, with errands to run; she decided to leave.

"I have things to do Gary; I didn't know that you'd be here." Facing him, displaying a serious demeanor, "You know my number if you want to continue with *twenty questions."*

Walking slowly to her car, she wished he'd call out to her. Seeing a nearby bench, Gary wandered over and took a seat. Staring at the water, he contemplated when he'd tell BJ about the outcome of him and Kathy.

He was glad that she didn't ask about her or them, he wasn't ready to share. He was happy that he'd found her, he did desire to see her; but wasn't ready for a deep conversation. Barbara didn't disappoint.

She was thrilled that Gary remembered that she frequented the Marina, it proved that he'd listened to her. After the initial blow of his return, she was glad to see him.

Dying to know if he and Kathy were an item, she didn't feel comfortable inquiring; she had to respect his privacy. As much as she adored Gary, she had no plans—to *pursue him.* She wouldn't refuse his company; however, she wouldn't initiate any type of activity with him. She'd learned *"If it doesn't—fit, don't force—it."*

Upon her arrival from the Marina, a pleasant surprise awaited her. It'd been a couple of days since sending a copy of her *letter* to Sober; she was curious to get his reaction. Logging in, she had a reply. *"Zest, girl that was special. I would love a woman to present a letter to me like that after we've declared our love for each other, it would serve as confirmation, icing on the cake. I know you'll have a name to put in that salutation one day soon. In need of some alone time, I'm going to my place to retreat. Keep in touch," Sober! P.S.*

"Hey, let's exchange photos for the fun of it. I have to get one on digital. Oh, I loved that A.W. Tozer [shame] quote. "Shame only hinders us from the things that we truly desire." That's my quote. Sober! Pleased to hear his positive comments, she'd definitely made a friend. *Retreat, he needs to be alone, hmm...*

Armed with hotdogs, popcorn and sodas; Walter, Bill and Michael take their seats. It's April, the last game of the Warrior's regular season; they're hosting the Spurs. Having close and upfront seats, Michael was ecstatic. "Wow, what great seats!" Michael voiced.

Walter and Bill were season tickets holders with some of the better seats in the arena, as expected. While shooting the breeze, Bill and Walter spotted Gary returning to his seat from getting popcorn. Bill waved to get his attention; seeing them, Gary walked over, still in work attire; he wore jeans, a caramel sweater, and matching laced boots. Greeting with hi-fives, each gave their take on who they thought would win the game. At tip-off time, Gary motioned to return to his seat.

"Hey man, my friend didn't come tonight, would you like to sit with us; if you're alone?" Bill offered, styling his blue and gold Warrior sweatshirt and jeans.

"Yeah, I'm alone, I'd love to." Gary joined them and sat next to Bill. Fond of their company previously; he was glad that they'd invited him to join them.

Since returning Michael home from practices, and games, Bill had received warmer receptions from Karen; they'd also spent more time talking on the phone. Depending on her schedule after dropping Michael off on several occasions, she'd be home and invite him in for coffee or dinner.

Feeling that it was time to take it to the next level, Bill was planning a cookout for the upcoming playoffs; inviting Karen and her friends were at the top of his guest list.

Entering the parking lot to pick up Michael, Karen saw Bill walking a gorgeous younger Black woman to her car. Before waving goodbye, he leaned in the window and gave her a kiss; unaware of her presence. *Could Barbara and Kim be correct, did I pull back and let Bill get away.*

Had God sent her Mr. Right in the person of Bill, and she refused him because he didn't complete her ideal list of criteria. She knew she didn't want a future with Harold. He would make someone an excellent husband. Harold did support their theory of finding a decent man on the internet. Now feeling guilty, she wished she'd never wasted his time.

Relative to Bill, it wasn't just concerns with Michael; Karen had question marks for them as an item. *I know Bill had Black friends and all, but, could we adapt to each other's culture. How would his parents receive me? He was married to a White, woman. With regard to the friendships that I have with white women, there are some valid cultural differences. Will he like my cooking? Will our differences become a conflict, and could we handle the prejudice of others? It's still a relevant issue, even today."*

After witnessing the kiss; she wondered if it was too late. Barbara joked about being in the batting cage with Gary; Karen wasn't sure if she was playing in the same *ballpark* with Bill.

When she entered the gym the team was taking their routine laps. Seeing Bill enter the building earlier; he was nowhere to be seen. Somewhat relieved; her relief didn't last long. Feeling someone behind her, she turned to see Bill showing that silly grinned which she adored.

"Sneaking up on me, ha?" She said, smiling. Looking into her eyes, "Seems to be the only way that I can get—close, and alone with you these days."Emanating enticement and rendering Karen voiceless. Staring in silence, Bill savored her loss of composure. Finally speaking, she voiced. "That's not true!"

Challenging her sincerity, "Prove me wrong; join me at our favorite restaurant this evening? Just the two of us." He challenged, blaring with persuasiveness.

In replay mode, her emotions ran rampant. *You want to go to dinner with me, who was that woman I just saw you kiss.* Like the *"energizer bunny,"* the image of the kiss and the mystery girl invaded her thoughts.

Bill, sensitive to her awkwardness and surprise; gave her time to pull together her thoughts. "I'm going over to release my boys before they collapse. If you prefer to keep it from—Michael; meet me there around seven o'clock p.m. Taking backward strides, and smiling; he ran across the gym.

Waving goodbye to Michael and her Dad, Karen sat at her Mom's kitchen counter, nibbling on a carrot while she waited in suspense. Mary asked Gilbert to take Michael to dinner so that she could talk to their daughter. Glowing, she told her Mom about Bill inviting her to dinner later that evening. "Are you going?"

"Yes! He said if I didn't want Michael to know, I could meet him there for seven o'clock. Of course I'm going. Why did you want to talk to me, Mom?"

Bending to remove a sheet of cookies from the oven, she handed one to Karen. "Nothing now, you appear to be coming back to your senses. You're Father and I met Bill. Between the two of us, we have over one hundred and twenty five years of life experience. We've managed to keep our marriage together; and we're happy. I think we're pretty good judges of character also, but you, we're starting to wonder."

"I know Mom, you're right, in confusion I got sidetracked. I feel in my heart that we're in God's will, Michael loves Bill."

"You need to listen to your Son, Daughter. You need some guidance, let Michael and God be your *map.*"

Taking a bite of the cookie, she somewhat agreed. "That's what Barbara said. This is tasty Mom.., lots of nuts, you remembered.

"Tell me Mom, what do you make of this. Prior to my picking up Michael; I saw Bill kiss a younger Black woman goodbye after walking her to her car, he didn't see me.

"Karen please..., people kiss friends, my—goodness girl! He invited you to dinner, didn't he? Somehow I don't perceive Bill as being a player." Mary proclaimed, standing with her hands on her hips.

"You're right, let me go, I don't want to be too late."

Mary was happy to hear that Karen was meeting Bill for dinner. It made her job much easier. Trusting Karen's decision and judgments regarding her career pleased Mary and Gilbert, she was always on target, but with her relationships; she sometimes needed a little coaxing. They were proud of how she'd committed her life to God in waiting for him to direct her to her next husband.

***When** Karen* arrived at the restaurant; Bill was waiting in his favorite booth, along with Walter. Standing to give her his seat, Walter kissed her on the cheek.

"This is a pleasant surprise Walter; will you be joining us for dinner?"

"No! I needed some counseling from my mentor."

"You chose a good one, it's been a while, how are you?"

"Too long, it's good to see you too Karen. Bill, I'm taking off now, we'll talk later. Bye Karen, say hi to Barbara Jean."

"Goodbye, Walter."

"I'll call you man." Bill assured him. Smiling and glaring at Karen, Bill reclined as if he was in a lounging chair.

Noticing his persistent stare and smile, "Why the painted on smiley face?" Slowly turning his head. "I'm just so glad you came."

Glad that he'd trusted his instincts, or more to the point, the *Holy Spirit*. Believing in his heart that his discernment was correct, he knew their relationship was in line with God's will for his life.

"You know, I'm happy I came too Bill." Signaling harmony, she nodded and smiled. "I'm also hungry, let's order."

Wondering if he'd ever see her, his faith had wavered. Karen apologized for pulling away explaining that she needed time and space to sort out her feelings. After assuring Bill that it'd nothing to do with him personally, nor had he done anything to invoke her despondency, both agreed that they'd take one day at a time.

Chapter 11

It's the month of May, and the NBA Playoffs are in full swing. Keeping true to his word, Bill hosted a cookout. Riding together to Bill's, Karen became the designated driver. Barbara met Karen as she entered her driveway in her black Range Rover.

"Where's Kim? I thought she was riding with us?" Pointing to the back seat. Karen shared, "She's worn out; trying to hang with Bill and Walter. After work, they're taking a kickboxing class. The problem is, her shift starts at 7:00 a.m., and they can go in at their leisure." Barbara climbed into the front seat along side Karen.

"I love your jean skirt." Karen complimented.

"Thanks, it's comfy." Desiring to feel relaxed, to complete her outfit, she wore a cotton turquoise blouse, white sneakers and socks. Feeling self-assured lately, she wore the blouse tucked in.

"You seem to really be feeling Bill lately, no more objections? Oooh, he'll love your legs in those yellow shorts." She teased.

"Stop it! You know how I am, my Mom talked to me. I took into account the things that you'd said. I think I over reacted, it's been a while since I've been in a relationship."

"Oh, really, so what else is new?" They both laughed.

"You had some valid concerns Karen, having you and your friends over is a good idea. He probably wants to secure your comfort on his turf, as he was at your parents place."

"Yeah! He said it's time for me to meet some of his friends and family."

"What's up with, Gary?"

"You tell me, I haven't spoken to him in weeks."

"What are your feelings toward him, now?"

"Hmm..., controlled, until I'm in his presence, then I get butterflies..., I hate it!"

Grinning, Karen interrogated her. "Why do you hate the feelings?"

"Because...," she paused. "I have to try and pretend they don't exist, while maintaining a straight face."

"I feel ya, Barbara." Kim yelled.

"Thanks, Kim!" Pulling into Bill's circular driveway, she saw parking spaces along side the retaining wall. Finally, sitting up, Kim looked and shouted. "Is that Gary's car, the black Hummer?

"Did Bill mention that he'd invited him?" Barbara asked, with restlessness in her voice.

"You sound disappointed!" Karen noted.

"No...," pondering the idea of seeing Gary, "No, its ok, really, I'm...," she paused. Tripping over her tongue. "Just taken aback."

Nudging Barbara while pointing, Karen spoke, quietly. "There..., that's the lady that I saw Bill kiss."

"You're kidding." Barbara acknowledged, who wore a suspenseful look with her mouth dropped open, and eyes bulging.

Hurriedly gathering her items and whispering, Barbara ordered. "C'mon; let's get out of this car, we'll know in a few minutes who she is; it has to be a friend or relative, right, anyone else wouldn't make sense?"

Around the corner, they walked onto an outsized terracotta colored patio, bearing a southwestern appeal. Along one wall were four black wrought iron tables and chairs, a hot tub that encompassed one entire corner, adjacent to the basketball court.

Filled with chickens, steaks, ribs, and burgers, Bill attended to a huge built in BBQ grill that was stationed near the kitchen entrance and family room. Becoming aware of their arrival, Bill waved for them to come over.

"Welcome!" Bill said, with his hand extended, he signaled and called to the woman in suspense.

"Dena, come here please. Sporting a hot pink short set, and a bright smile, setting off her mocha complexion, and shapely figure; Dena appeared. Dena, this is my friend Karen, and these are her, friends Barbara and Kim. Guys, this is my sister in-law, Dena."

"Come, I'll show you where to put your desserts, Dena offered, after engaging in small talk and pleasantries."

Barbara brought her famous sweet potato pie, Kim baked a pound cake with a lemon glaze; Karen made double chocolate chip cookies and brownies.

Karen, now feeling silly, it was only a friendly kiss, just as her mother had said. Directing them into the kitchen area, they placed the desserts on the counter top.

Staying behind to chat with Bill, Kim informed him that Walter was in Tahoe on another one of his solo retreats. Bill told her Walter might return in time to stop by.

Glancing in the family room, they saw a blonde haired guy, and Gary watching one of the playoff games. After seeing them, walking poised in his black shorts, white tee shirt, and white sneakers; he greeted, showing all thirty-two.

"Hi BJ! Hi Karen!"

"Well, hello to you, Gary."

"You're a welcome surprise." Karen remarked.

"Bill didn't mention that he'd invited me?" Turning their heads, both smiled, and said. "No!"

"I saw them at the Warriors game last month, we exchanged phone numbers. I called to invite you to the game BJ; it was last minute, but I got no answer, or recording."

"Oh..., it was probably the night that I turned off my phone, entirely."

"Ah, didn't want to be bothered, huh?"

"No! It'd been a hectic day, I did watch the game."

"I'm going to go and check the scores." Karen conveniently announced.

"How've you been, BJ?"

"Good, keeping busy."

"What about you, how is business?"

"I'm finally caught up with the administrative work." He nodded to the TV screen. "In the evening, I crash while watching the playoffs.

"Let's see whose winning." BJ suggested.

Allowing her to walk ahead of him, BJ sat on the couch next to Karen. Gary introduced them to the blonde haired guy, whose name was Todd. Sitting on the arm of the couch, Gary extended his arm across the back of the couch behind BJ.

Racing to reclaim his seat, a tall slender Black guy in jeans, and a Warrior tee shirt slumped into the recliner. Once noticing their arrival, he introduced himself as Kenny, Bill's brother-in-law. Inquiring about the game status, Todd updated him with the scores and plays. Raising eyebrows between Barbara and Karen, they ex-changed a puzzled glance.

Dena is Black; Bill said Dena was his sister-in-law, causing them to assume that Dena was married to a brother of Bill. Instantly remembering, Bill didn't have a brother. Moments later, another couple arrived.

"Come on in, guys." Todd welcomed. "Guys, this is Shari and Jamie, Shari and Jamie, this is everybody." Sporting a stunning tan, Shari looked as if they'd just left Cancun.

Grinning, Shari remarked. "We get it Todd; we'll get to know everyone before the days over, I'm sure." Shari's eye-catching blonde hair, and green eyes were a great contrast to her white two-piece short set. Her petite frame was a perfect fit for sitting on the lap of Jamie's buffed and masculine frame.

Admiring Bill's masculine décor, Barbara loved his dark cherry blend furniture. A cabinet with sliding doors housed the wide-screen television that they were viewing. Behind the couch was an entrance that led to a mini theater, complete with trimmings for a media center; available for use if the family room became over crowded.

A wedding portrait of a White man, and a *fine looking* Black woman caught Barbara's attention. The man, looking familiar prompted her to take a closer look; to her amazement, it was Bill. The woman in the portrait bore a resemblance to Dena, mocha skin tone, physique, hair, everything.

Finally solving the puzzle with Dena and Kenny, Dena was Bill's deceased wife Sister. Bill's wife was *Black!* Scuffling to get Karen's attention, she was competing with the game and the surrounding commotion. The Kings and the Lakers were playing, creating a high volume atmosphere, and loud speaking voices.

Cautioning Karen to remain quiet, Barbara discreetly asked her to check out the wedding portrait, Karen behaved accordingly.

Leaning and whispering into Gary's ear, "Which way is the powder room?" As she stole a quick swift of his cologne. Eyes fixed on the game, Gary pointed her down the hallway, Karen followed.

Stepping into a spacious guest bathroom complete with double cream pedestal sinks, a matching décor of cream towels and candles, and a baby-changing table; they were happy to find it empty.

Standing with her hands resting on her hips, "Now, don't we feel a little silly? You were so concerned that he wouldn't fit into our *culture,* it appears that he's quite f*amiliar* with it."

Discovering that Bill's marriage had been *interracial* sent Karen into shock. Drooping into the chair by the door, "I should've trusted God and my, Son as you told me. She was so beautiful, he must miss her some terrible." Karen voiced, in compassion.

"Without a doubt, I am sure." Knowing this information early on would've alleviated many of Karen's concerns. Bill, having a Black Son whom he assisted in rearing obviously gave her comfort.

"To quote Dr. Washington "*God is so smart*." You availed yourself to be open-minded to all possibilities to meet your mate Karen. God knew you had issues concerning his race, he sent you a *trailblazer,* that's the *awesomeness* of God."

"I wonder why he never mentioned this to me." Moving her head, as she contemplated the thought.

"Considering your concerns; it's probably best that he didn't."

"Why?" Karen asked, looking bewildered.

"Oh, just let it be food for thought." Getting together her emotions before rejoining the others, Karen checked out another group who'd assembled on the patio.

Seeing Kim in a swing in the garden, Barbara joined her.

"Are you asleep?" She asked.

"No! Just resting my eyes. It's so nice and relaxing out here." Kim commented.

"Bill's a nice person; I sure hope Karen has her head on straight, now."

"Oh..., I think she does." Barbara said, with confidence. She'd let Karen announce her new reveal to Kim. Kim encouraged Barbara to sit.

"Here, you partake, I have to go and change, I'm going to my girlfriend Tara's church this evening; their singles ministry is having an event. Bill tells me Walter may get back in time to stop by."

Sitting down, Barbara inquired, "His returning won't interfere with your plans, will it?"

"No! Not at all, he's welcome to join us."

"Oooh, it is nice sitting here, ah..."

"Enjoy, see you later." Heading back in her flowery sundress and brown sandals, she changed into a pair of jeans and a blouse. Delighting in the satisfaction of a beautiful spring day, with her eyes closed; Barbara used her foot to propel the swing in motion.

Savoring the cool breeze, she was aware that someone was present.

"Mmm...," she drew in the scent, knowing that it was Gary. Taking pleasure in his cologne, she inhaled deeply. With her eyes still closed, she acknowledged his presence by smiling, "Hi! Gary!"

"So, this is where you ran off." In abruptness, she sat up, "I followed Kim out here, she left, it was so inviting I couldn't resist." Inviting him to sit beside her, she patted her hand on the swing.

"I think I will, how did you know that it was me, you had your eyes shut?" Snickering softly, "Um..., I smelled you."

"I don't know if I like the sound of that, BJ." Slapping him on his knee, "You know I was referring to your cologne."

"I knew what you meant; I enjoy your reactions. Maybe we can finish with our *twenty questions?"* Gary suggested.

Startled by his suggestion, she decided to get comfy. With one leg resting in the swing, she faced him. "Are you sure you want to continue with *twenty questions*?" She asked, with great importance.

Getting excited, she knew if he was asking to play *twenty questions*, he must be ready to discuss Atlanta and Kathy. The rule was complete honesty.

Gary saw Bill waving a dishcloth indicating chow time; extending his hand, he helped her up. "Let's go eat." He said.

"To be continued," BJ remarked. Allowing him to help her stand, she let go of his hand as they walked back to the patio.

Employing magnificent grilling skills, Bill's ribs, chickens and steaks, were firm, yet succulent and juicy. Topping off the menu, Dena made pasta, potato, and green salads.

Gary pitched in his delicious corn on the cob, brushed with butter and seasoned lemon pepper. Todd brought a variety basket of fresh baked breads from the world renowned Fisherman's Wharf. Kenny made old-fashioned churn style ice cream. Ice, bottled water and juices in every flavor filled a country style tin washtub.

After a long, yet relaxing day of good food, good fellowship, and action packed basketball; the evening hour had approached, and the crowd had thinned. Earning the title of the perfect host, Bill and Karen were finally able to steal some time alone.

Kim's friend Tara had come for her; Walter had showed up and joined them. Seeing BJ's exhaustion, Gary offered to give her a ride home, without any objections, she agreed. Still present, Kenny, Jamie, Shari, and Dena raided Bill's old movie classic collection from the media center.

After pouring glasses of lemonade, Bill and Karen headed for the patio. Exhaling noisily, Bill lay stretched onto a lounging chair, his overlapping long legs caught Karen's eye. *Gosh, he's tall, just like my Dad.*" Wearing white shorts revealed his hairy tanned thighs and legs, a yellow polo, and white sneakers, ironically it matched Karen's yellow shorts and white blouse.

"This turned out pretty good!" He said, in a pat yourself on the back sort of way, while folding his hands behind his neck.

Seated in a chair directly beside him, "This was better than good Bill, you're an excellent cook and host."

"Thanks! Sherrie and I used to entertain all the time, everyone loved coming to our home. She was a great cook; she taught me all that my Mom didn't teach me."

"Of all the times we've talked, you've never mentioned her; please feel free to talk about her anytime."

"Aw, thanks! That's nice to know; I'm especially reminded of her today. Throwing his head back with laughter, "I'm sorry; Sherrie had a great sense of humor. Her passing wasn't a complete surprise; we'd months to prepare. Her main request was for me *not* to be telling another woman how much I miss her."

"Oh, okay..., now I get it. Wow! She was a class act."

"She left me a video full of *do's* and *don'ts*, all in a comical manner. It was her way of letting me know that she was okay, and she wanted me to be as well. It did help, generally when I think about her; it's always something to make me laugh. We met in a psych class in college, Sherrie was the *brain;* I was the dumb Jock."

"Oh, I don't know about that, but opposites do attract you know." Smiling, he said, "For us, there were many opposites."

"Speaking of opposites, I saw your wedding portrait, she was gorgeous."

"Hmm...,"he paused. "I guess seeing that helped you to put Dena and Kenny into perspective?"

"Precisely!" Showing a restricted smile, "Why haven't you mentioned that you had an interracial marriage?" With sincerity and meekness in his tone, he looked into her, "Why? To absolve you of the objections that you'd concerning us? I knew you had them."

Following a deep sigh, and arched eyebrows, she mumbled. "Touché*!* I guess I asked for that." Changing positions, he sat up to face her, as his legs encircled her chair.

"No worries, I didn't want you to find—comfort for us in the obstacles that Sherrie and I overcame, Karen. I needed you to take comfort in the fact that if God put us together, we too can overcome the impediments that the world may bring upon us."

Taking hold of her hand, "That's why I gave you your space. When you came to the gym that evening, and later had dinner with me; your mannerisms were altogether different. You talked freely; you looked me in the eye, without turning your head; I felt that you were giving me the *green light*. How am I doing?"

"Don't stop, you're on a roll. Wow! How perceptive of you. You certainly captured my sentiments; I did feel content and secure; I'm glad I conveyed the proper signal." *The truth is in the eyes. I feel as though I'm hearing him through his eyes."*

The wisdom demonstrated by Bill in withholding that information had to be God inspired; his explanation was confirmation that they were in the will of God.

"Everyone was on your side from day one, Barbara, Kim, and my parents."

"I love them; your parents are terrific."

"It's mutual, my Dad is happy to have someone that he can finally look in the face while talking to them." She laughed. "He grew up during a time when 6'6 wasn't the average height; he said he often felt awkward, because people stared."

"Um, I can relate, I've experienced a little discomfort on occasion myself."

"I love your masculine décor; did you re-decorate?" Bill came apart with laughter. "Oh, you think this is the home we lived in."

"What did I say so, funny?"

"I'm so sorry; remember I told you that Sherrie gave me some do's and don'ts, well..., and I'm quoting her. *"I don't know where you guys will live, it will not be in my house, she can have you, but not my kitchen."* Both busted out with laughter.

In addition to his wealth from his business, at the age of thirty, they each purchased twenty-year-level term policies; with a face value of *one-million*. Sherrie was confident that her request wouldn't pose a *financial strain* or burden for Bill; she found it amusing.

"I have to agree with her on that one, Bill." Giggling, softly."

"My Son, Tilmon and his wife Denise live in our home.
She'd a plaque in the kitchen with a prayer and an inscription that reads *"Sherrie's Kitchen."* It'll be handed down to generations in honor of her. Removing the plaque wasn't an option." He said, grinning.

"Absolutely! What a thoughtful memorial." Still smiling, he commented. "I didn't have much of a choice. I think it was her way of making sure that Tilmon would fill it up with grandkids. C'mon, let's see what these guys are doing." Karen and Bill joined Dena, Kenny, Shari, and Jamie in the media center.

Defined as a good day, it'd set the course to their *destiny*. Karen acceptance in embracing Sherrie's humor provided him to vent freely without guilt.

This was the first year since her death that his heart didn't ache with pain as he thought of her. Desiring to wait until he'd grieved to a point of satisfaction and contentment from the Lord; he didn't want to camouflage his hurt and loneliness with empty relationships with women. Finding comfort in *Phil 4:7 and the peace of God, which passeth all understanding shall keep your hearts and minds through Christ Jesus."*

Driving home without music, Karen's thoughts were consumed with reflections of Bill. She couldn't have wished for a better day. She thanked God for the mercy he'd extended to her in letting Bill remain patient with her.

Gary headed to his Pleasanton home after dropping off BJ. Happy that he'd gone to the cookout; Gary knew that his good friend BJ would be there also. Always taking pleasure in her presence; BJ had fallen asleep in route to her home before seizing the opportunity to ask questions about Kathy and their involvement in Atlanta.

Since they'd defined their relationship as friends; Gary didn't know what was expected of him to share, or if she was even interested in knowing what had transpired with them.

Recapping the day as she logged on to her computer, Barbara Jean was happy for Karen and Bill; bringing her to his home was a good thing. She smiled when she focused on their *baseball analogy.* Karen was at *bat,* closer to *first base*. Kim had definitely secured a safe spot on *second base* with Walter. As for Barbara, she was not sure if she was even in the same *ballpark* as Gary. If she was, it was a *foul ball,* way out in *left field.*

Invoking the *twenty-question* game, she could've asked anything that she wanted to know about Gary and Kathy. She kicked herself a hundred times over for falling asleep before doing so. Deep down, was she ready to hear the truth? She was confident that she did have a friend.

***At** eleven-fifty-five p.m.*, a warm *August night*. Kimberly Denise Montgomery, registered nurse; was working the graveyard shift at Carson General. Because of a power outage nearby, County General were routing their patients to Carson's.

After working the day shift, to help with the overflow of patients, she volunteered to return to help with the third shift. Since the beginning of her shift, it'd been a steady pace of patients.

While updating a chart from a previous patient; the attending physician asked Kim for her assistance. Her hair in ponytail, wearing blue scrubs, she hurried over to assist with a young Black woman who was being helped on to a gurney.

Nurse Campbell, the triage nurse, favoring Rose from the Golden Girls, asked for her medical card. "It's in my purse; *my boyfriend* went to get it from the car. I can't lose my baby," she voiced, sobbing.

Administering and performing various procedures ordered by the attending physician; Kim moved rapidly. Stepping to the side of the gurney as they waited for the elevator, she offered comfort and compassion to her patient.

Scurrying in, the alleged *boyfriend* handed the purse to Nurse Campbell, it was Walter. Kim heard him say *"Here's her purse; I don't know what you need."*

Walter turned and almost fainted as his eyes became glued on Kim. Recognizing it was impossible to speak with her at that moment; he sprinted for the exit.

For a brief second, losing her focus, Kim could've used some medical attention of her own. Always the skillful professional, Kim took hold of the IV bag as she walked along side of the gurney into the elevator.

Admiring her beautiful brown skin, thick eyelashes, and manicured nails; Kim was soaking with curiosity, she checked the ladies wristband; her name was, Tonya Robinson.

"Did he bring my purse?" Tonya asked.

"Yes, he did." Kim responded, warmly. *What is he to you, and is he the father of your baby?* Her professional capacity at the time prevented her from satisfying her most painful suspicion.

Walter couldn't dismiss the vision of Kim from his memory; it was a steady replay of the hurt and confused look on her face. Breaking into a sweat, he rubbed his hand across his head as he walked to his car.

Seeing Kim was a major shock to say the least. *This is not her regular shift, what is she doing here this time of night?* Kim hadn't spoken to Walter after she'd signed up for a third shift. She knew he'd an early morning flight to catch; therefore, she didn't want to risk awakening him. Realizing that he'd no chance of speaking to her tonight, Walter went home.

Her shift ended at seven o'clock the next morning, he was attending a workshop in Vegas, and would be boarding his flight at seven o'clock a.m. Praying, he whispered. *"Lord, please let Kim understand. Have her to know I love her. Father give her the strength to get through her shift Lord, please don't let her make any mistakes that would endanger the lives of others. In Jesus name, I pray. Amen"*

At four o'clock a.m., Kim headed for the nurses lounge. She noticed that Thomas Martin talking to Nurse Campbell, and then getting on the elevator. She was too tired, frustrated and angry to speculate and make small talk with Thomas Martin. *What is Vanessa's man doing here?*

Happy to find the lounge empty, except for another nurse who looked as fatigued as she was. Kim was exhausted, but not from a lack of sleep. Curled in a recliner, she reflected on Tonya Robinson. Her baby boy was born premature, and with a blood clot. Come morning he'd be transported to County General.

The entire night she'd been haunted by Tonya's words. *My boyfriend went to get my purse,* in conjunction with the look of surprise, and shock on Walter's face. Now doubting the level of trust that she'd placed in him, he obviously hadn't given up his *womanizing*. Now feeling betrayal and humiliation, she'd let her guard down wanting him to be her, *Mr. Right*.

Believing that he was God inspired, her heart, mind, soul and spirit were all in unity. Missing her parents dearly, she wished she was close to them; it'd been her reason for desiring a man *like her father.*

Thankful that the dreadful night finally ended, Kim was happy to be home and in her comfortable bed. Noticing that her message light was blinking, she hesitated in checking; knowing it was Walter. She wondered what lie he'd be telling. "*Kim, by the time you get this message, I will be in Vegas. I'm begging for a chance to explain, I love you, Kim. You're the only woman that has commanded love from me. Please call and tell me you'll meet with me when I return later today. I love you Kim."*

Acknowledging his sincerity, it didn't provide her with what she needed to hear. The fact that he needed to explain implied that there was a problem. Before taking her nap, she called her Mom to tell her what'd occurred.

Being a Pastor's wife and a co-pastor, Jackie had learned to look for the good first. She assured Kim that she'd valid reasons to be upset; but she needed to hear his side before drawing any foregoing conclusions.

Unfailing in making her feel better; she told her she would have her Dad call her later. Giving permission to Jackie to tell Barbara, Kim was too tired to repeat the drama.

The doorbell rang, Kim wavered before answering. Peeking to see a delivery truck, she opened the door, and was handed a white box of long stemmed red roses tied in a big red bow. A separate box contained a crystal vase. *Oh, he's rotten with guilt.*

They were the most beautiful roses she'd ever seen. The card read, *"Since I can't be there, this is a small way of letting you know that you're in my thoughts. I will call you later. Love, Walter.* Assured of Walter's love for her, her concerns became a *trust* issue. After putting the flowers in water, she laid down to rest.

After sleeping for eight hours, her phone rang. "Hello!" She answered, groggily.

"Hi! Kim, this is Walter. Kim..., can you hold on please." Returning to the line, "Kim can I call you right back?" Clicking back to his call, he was unaware that he hadn't released Kim from the call.

Getting comfortable, her ears were finely tuned.... *"Walter, you know we share something that neither of us can deny. I don't know why you were so cold to me New Year's Eve, but I'm willing to give you another chance. I gave you your space. I watch you go home at night; you never have another woman with you."* Walter cut in, *"Deborah, I..."*

"Let me finish, Walter. I understand that you've been trying to get into the word, maybe we can study together. Let me come over tonight, please?"

"Deborah, I ...have a call, I have to go, Deborah" Unable to access the call, it dropped. Deciding not to accept any more calls while talking to Kim, he re-dialed her.

"Hello!"

"I'm sorry for the interruption, Kim."

"No! I'm sorry about this interruption; you didn't release my call Walter. You can let, *Deborah* come over tonight." ***Dial tone!***

Past angry, Kim was unable to identify the exact type of temptation that Walter always found himself facing, she believed that he was growing stronger in the Lord, but felt his love for the Lord should've constrained him from the advances of other women.

Unable to forget Deborah's comments, they played repeatedly in her mind. *Deborah said she was over New Year's Eve night, which means she came over after he dropped me off.*

Now, horrified, the Tonya Robinson mystery, and now, a Deborah. Lowering her e*xpectations, and standards* to consider him, he was slowly proving to be undeserving of her love for him. *The nerve of him, nothing he could say would get him out of this.* Pulling the covers over her head; she cried herself to sleep again.

Realizing that he wouldn't be seeing Kim; Walter took his time as he drove a rental car home from the airport. He'd hoped to try and mend things by calling; unfortunately, the phone call only compounded matters.

Things were going so great for him and Kim; at present, he resented his past. He knew it would catch up with—him; he fussed. *"You can't continue to transgress without reaping consequences. A good understanding giveth favor, but the way of transgressors is hard."(Prov.13:15) Considering the circumstances, I think I need to give Kim some space.*

Walter knew Kim was a special gift from God, he also knew he wasn't deserving of a woman as sweet and innocent as her. Determined to uphold his *vow* to God, he'd prove worthy of his blessings.

Later that evening, Kim's phone rang, "Hello!"

"Hi, Kim! This is Vanessa; I heard you pulled two shifts on yesterday." "Boy, did I, it felt like three."

"I'm off tomorrow if you need me to cover for you."

"No! Thanks, I'm off too, that was one of the conditions.

That was very considerate of you Vanessa. By the way, I saw your friend Thomas last evening; does he have a sick relative at Carson?"

"You saw Thomas, here, at the hospital last night? He's supposed to be on a business trip."

"It was closer to morning, around three or four o'clock."

"That's strange; I don't know who he could've been visiting at that hour." Distracting to Vanessa, Kim's news of Thomas had altered her thought process.

"Oh yeah, thank you Kim you for talking to me regarding this relationship. You said some things that got me thinking; I know I deserve better than him, it was wrong for me to get involved with him knowing he was married."

"Aw, you're welcome, you can't change your prior actions, but you still have some choices, Vanessa; it's up to you, God is forgiving."

"I was wondering if I can go to church with you on Sunday."

"I may take a short trip home for a few days. If I do, Barbara or Karen will be happy to have you join them. I had an episode last evening; I'll tell you about it once I have a clearer understanding of it myself."

"Thank you for praying for me, Kim."

"You're welcome. Good night! Five minutes later, Vanessa called, again.

"Hello"

"Kim, this is Vanessa, remember you said you saw Thomas at the hospital last evening."

"Yes!"

"Do you have any idea what floor he visited?"

"No! But Nurse Campbell probably can help you. She was on duty. Tell her the time, she'll remember.

"Thanks, Kim, she's here now. I'm here late working on a report. I will be talking to her. I think Thomas is seeing someone else; he's been behaving awfully strange and secretive lately."

"If he is, you need to know."

"I will keep you posted. Goodbye!" Kim turned on her laptop to check for possible flights. She felt the need to escape, once online, she checked her messages and found one from Barbara.

"Hi dear, you know Jackie called. I'm so sorry, Kim; I know you must be past exhaustion and frustration, mental more than physical. It's why I chose not to call. I want you to know that I'm praying for discernment and strength. I want ask you to believe as I do, but I know things are not as they appear. Since Bill is his mentor, he probably won't be calling me; he probably thinks I'm angry with him.

I'm with your Mom; give him the benefit of the doubt until you talk it over. Love ya.

Kim wasn't surprised with Barbara's response. She'd opted to stay home, and face her *giants.* Ready to talk, she placed a call to her buddies. "Hello!"

"Hi Barbara, hold on, I'm bringing on Karen.

"I'm here, Kim." Kim had called and gave the entire scoop to Karen, including the Deborah call.

"I got your e-mail Barbara, but you and Mom haven't heard the latest."

"You mean; there's more." Cried Barbara.

"Yeah, I'm afraid so." Kim told Barbara about the conversation that she'd heard between Walter and Deborah.

"Oh, my! I'm—speechless."

"That was my response." Karen told her.

"In all fairness Kim, from what you've told us, it doesn't sound like any *hanky—panky* occurred—on New Year' Eve."

"Yeah, I agree, sounds like she got—*rejected* to me, Kim."

"Yeah, still..., we could analyze and speculate until the cows come home, and we'd still come up short. I still believe—in Walter, let's get together for prayer soon, and dump this in God's hands." Barbara suggested.

"Amen!" Karen said.

"I agree guys." Kim said. "Well, I'm going to start worrying the Lord right now! I didn't see this coming. Good night!" Kim did just as she said; she went before the Lord in prayer. *"Lord Jesus...*

Vanessa approached Nurse Campbell and repeated the exact words spoken by Kim.

Holding her pin under her chin, and looking upward, "I remember it was late; he said he was looking for his girlfriend who'd just had a baby or in labor. There was only one pregnant woman that came in last night. He gave me her name; I looked it up, and told him where to go. Let's see..., of course I can't recall her name." Flipping through charts, "Here we go. Tonya Robinson, here you can see for yourself." Gently handing her the chart.

"I have work to do." The chart stated, *Tonya Robinson, twenty-six, single, Medical Sales, HP 222.2422 WK 334.2211 resided in Alameda County. Baby was born six weeks premature. Critical, but currently stable, should remain in intensive care. Baby will be moved to County General for further treatment and observation.*

Vanessa's investigating had paid off, medical sales was probably her connection to Thomas. Nurse Campbell said he referred to her as his, *girlfriend*. She knew if she wanted the truth, she'd have to find it on her own. Other than his wife, Vanessa knew of Thomas deceitfulness better than anyone. Many days and nights she sat and listened while he lied to his wife; often times she was in his arms.

Because of her affiliations, she knew several nurses and doctors at County General. She'd have no problem getting the information she needed. Sadly, it'd have to wait.

Thomas wanted to buy and sell real estate as an investor; consequently, they were leaving to attend a two day seminar. Her search would have to be put on the back burner until they returned. Vanessa would hold off mentioning her findings to Kim.

Vanessa wasn't afraid to tell Kim if she found that Thomas had been cheating on her, she knew Kim would be there for her. Finally admitting the things Kim said to her were true, she wished she'd *loosen* her lips to Kim or someone relative to Thomas's marital status; realizing it was the enemy's way of keeping her isolated, and in bondage. Forever protecting Thomas, the thought of him cheating on her was making her queasy in the stomach.

Returning from their two-day seminar, Vanessa was back on the trail of Tonya Robinson. At County General, dressed in her blue scrubs, she approached the front desk of the ICU maternity ward.

"Hi, I'm Vanessa Webster, an RN at Carson General. Last week a patient by the name of Tonya Robinson gave birth to a premature baby boy that was in critical condition. I was in the area and thought I'd check to see how he's doing."

"Let me see, Tonya Robinson," thumbing through the charts, she informed.

"Oh..., I' m so sorry, he didn't make it."

"Oh, no! How sad! Thank you so much for your help." Vanessa managed to speak, considering his condition, she wasn't surprised.

"No problem, Dear!" Taken aback, she was back to square one. Vanessa desperately needed to know the baby's father. Too recent to have a birth certificate; she couldn't bear waiting thirty days. Getting a brainstorm, she called County General from her cell phone.

"County General, how may I help you?"

"The morgue please!"

"County Morgue, Henry speaking."

"I'm Vanessa Webster over at Carson's General. I'm calling regarding the Robinson's baby boy; can you please tell me the name of the mortuary that picked up his body? I want to send my condolences."

"Sure, let me check..., that would've been, Taylor's Mortuary."

"Thanks, Henry!" This was her last resort, or she'd have to wait the remainder of the thirty days for the birth certificate.

"Taylor's Mortuary, Clyde speaking."

"Yes! Clyde, I'd like to send a card for you to forward to the parents of the Robinson's baby. May I have their name; I'd like to address it to both of them."

"No problem, I'll check the file..., Tonya Robinson is the only name that's listed, and she's the mother."

"That's great, thank you so much, Clyde." Striking out again. Lately, she hadn't been able to get a concrete reading on Thomas, he'd been so moody, quiet and keeping to himself. On two occasions he'd hung up his cell as soon as she entered the room.

Never stopping to consider what his wife might have been going through, Vanessa was finally experiencing how things must've been for Thomas wife. Looking back, she'd been too busy gloating and thinking that Thomas preferred her to his wife. *How could I have been so stupid and naive? I helped break up a marriage, and it looks as if Thomas has been two-timing me. Did he really want a baby that bad? If he's the father of her baby boy, that means he still needs me to come through for him, I don't think so!"*

Insisting that she should get off the pill two months ago, he said since they'd be married soon, it'd be like getting a head start with their baby. Naturally, she was in agreement. Praying that it wasn't too late, if she wasn't pregnant; she was going to safeguard for the future.

Placing a call to her gynecologist to write her a prescription for some birth control pills; she was at the pharmacy pronto. Normally it would've required a visit to the doctor, but since Vanessa had recently visited her, and the fact that she's an RN; she'd no problem getting the prescription.

She knew she'd to keep Thomas at bay for a while, traveling at least three days out of the week; she knew she'd it made. Confronting Thomas wasn't an option; she'd wait out the remaining weeks for the birth certificate. With the baby being deceased, she needed something in black and white to put in his face when she approached him.

Sorting through photographs that she'd taken during the holidays; Barbara was looking for one to send to Sober. Preferring the casual look, she figured that the holiday pictures were too flashy. So she settled on one that she'd taken with Jordyn at the Marina, wearing a burgundy sweater, black jeans and boots.

Scanning the photograph, she attached it to an e-mail. *Hi! Sober, it's time we put a face to our name. Attached is a photograph of me. Hope all is well with you and your lady friend. Let me know if I look like I talk, or should I say write. ☺ Zest.*

Remembering Kim, she sent an e-mail to her also. "*Hi, Kim, just a note to let you know that I'm praying for you and Walter. I know it's going to work out for your good. Love, ya." (Rom.8:28)*

Before signing off, she checked her e-mails, and found one from Walter. *"Hi, Barbara Jean, I know you're disappointed in me. I want you to know how much I miss our talks, and that I love Kim. I'm serious about my walk with the Lord. Love, Walter"* Barbara's phone rang. "Hello!"

"Hi, Barbara, this is Vanessa."

"Hi! Vanessa, it's good to hear from you, how have you been?"

"Things could be better, but I'm hanging in there. Do you mind if I attend early morning services with you on Sunday, Kim said she may be out of town?"

"Sure, do you need me to pick you up?"

"No! Since it's so early, I'll meet you in the front of the sanctuary; I don't wanna go in alone.

"I felt the exact same way; I'll see you on Sunday."

Four weeks since Kim's horrifying night, while lounging and thumbing through magazines, her phone rang; it was Barbara. "Hi Honey, just checking in. You know your parents are on their way here for the conference. Have you talked to, Walter?"

"No! I'm letting him think about his actions."

"Kim, you've got to sit down and talk to him; you owe him the opportunity to explain. In the past, he would've called me, now he has Bill. Walter loves you and would never deliberately do anything to hurt you. He sent me an e-mail saying how much he loves you."

"Really!'

"Yes! Sometimes people force their way into your life Kim, and you have to deal with it. Take Gary for instance, his privacy was *violated and invaded* by his sister and Kathy. I *believe* in Walter, or I never would've encouraged you in the relationship. I know things look a little bad for him right now, I have a feeling that *it's not as bad as it looks*, Kim."

"That's become your *slogan!* I'm trying, Barbara. What about, Sober, what's going on there?"

"Stop changing the subject, it's so ironic; we both are interested in someone that we've physically met."

"It must be good to a have a male friend, especially a Christian one; it helps to get their perspective on relationships and life in general." Kim remarked.

"You can't rely on circumstances only, or your emotions, Kim. If you feel that you're in God's will with Walter, then you've got to exercise some faith. Beside, you haven't heard his side of the story.

"Have you talked to Gary, today?" Barbara laughed.

"No! That's why that *slogan* works well for me. Get up and get dressed, I'm having a little get together for your parents."

Kim joined her with laughter. "Well, you succeeded in making me laugh."

"I'm signing off, see you soon!" Plotting to engage in some *risky business,* Barbara invited Walter to the fellowship at her home. Knowing Robert and Jackie desired to see him, even if Kim didn't.

Chapter 12

Robert and Jackie Montgomery checked into their hotel room at the Marriott Courtyard in Pleasanton. Since Kim resided in her two-bedroom condominium, instead of her four-bedroom home, Jackie felt it'd be more convenient for them to stay in a hotel.

Coming for a weeklong conference, the height of their focus was their baby girl. For this reason, they planned to stay an extra week. Robert longed to meet the man who'd stolen his baby's heart, and to offer support. Jackie immediately put a call in to Kim. "Hello!"

"Hi, Baby!"

"Hi, Mom, are you guys, here?"

"Yes! We just checked in, we're in Pleasanton. Barbara invited us over for coffee and dessert. We'll see you there."

"Sounds, good!"

Barbara was excited to see her long time friends Jackie and Robert. Sharing the same moral and Christian values; they'd reared their daughters together. Kim was older than Michelle was, but they played well together as kids. They were thankful that both of them had embraced, and internalized Christ as savior and Lord.

Being wiser and four years older than Barbara, Jackie was confident that Barbara would re-dedicate her life to Christ when she returned to the *world* to" *have her fun.*" She and Jackie maintained a close relationship.

The doorbell rang; "How come I'm always the first to arrive? Karen asked, looking carefree in a brown sweater dress, and boots. Relaxed in a black sheath dress, and mules, Barbara commented smugly, while smiling. "Maybe you like coming to my home?"

"I guess."

"You know I invited Bill, he's coming after he's done with practice." Barbara informed

"Yeah! He's going to drop Michael off at my parents. It was nice of you to invite him."

"You know Jackie is as *nosy* as we are, she knows history is in the making for a husband for one of us, she needed to inspect the prospects."

"How are things going with you and Bill?"

"Surprisingly well, I told you that we've been having dinner together. It was a little tense in the beginning, but I'm back to feeling my comfort level with him again."

"What did you do about poor, Harold?"

"I talked to him and told him that I wasn't ready to take it to the next level. He was disappointed, but he understood. He's really a nice man; it's good to know there are still some good ones. Did you invite, Gary?"

"No! Way!" She replied, in a matter of fact tone." Barbara was adamant concerning not pursuing Gary.

"I told you that I'm letting Gary initiate our getting together. Until I know where things are with him and Kathy; I'm going to take it slow. You know we talked about this; assuming is not an option. I could tell he wanted to talk; he was ..., um reluctant. Maybe they're engaged, or maybe nothing."

"You're right; let the ball stay in his court."

"I invited, Walter"

"You did?" Karen replied, grinning.

"Yes! And he's scared to death; I told him that Kim's parents want to meet him, I assured him that I believed in him, and that Bill would be here to help keep Kim's Dad off him."

"You're crazy; did you really say that to him?" She laughed.

"I sure did. He knew that it was my way of taking the edge off." Removing trays of spinach-cheese appetizers and mini sausage quiches from the oven.

"He thought it was funny." Barbara shared.

"Yum, yum, that looks good"

"Here, try them."

"Mmm..., tasty, there're delicious. Are you having a party?"

"No! Just a few appetizers and dessert." To tie off the menu, she'd prepared a tray of boneless chicken strips in a bourbon sauce and a veggie tray. For dessert, she purchased a red velvet cake from a local bakery, and baked homemade apple pie to serve with vanilla ice cream.

"Vanessa's going to be joining us for Sunday services."

"That's terrific! Prayer works, you know, she's really opened up since that little talk that she'd with Kim. She feels free; her secret is out, and the healing has begun."

"Speaking of healing," Barbara said. "Mrs. Martin must be devastated; I sure hope she's on her way to healing."

"I know," Karen said, in a sadden voice.

Vanessa Webster was about to find the information that she needed. It'd been over thirty days since the birth of the baby; she'd made contact with an RN that she'd met while taking her state boards, who would supply her with the information that she needed. She was waiting for Millie's phone call. "Hello!"

"Vanessa, this is Millie; I have the information from the birth certificate that you requested. The mother is, Tonya Robinson and the father is, Thomas Martin." Voiceless, she held the phone in silence. "Vanessa! Vanessa! Are you there?"

"Yes, I'm sorry Millie, thank you so much."

"No problem, take care!"

Feeling brittle, she needed to sit. She'd given this man two years of life. Lying to her friends and family, never enjoying a holiday, fibbing to her parents, ducking and dodging from church members when they were out; driving to out of the way movies, and eateries in fear of being recognized.

Always camped by the phone in case he called. It didn't take long for her to deduce that he'd been cheating on *his wife* and *her at the same—time.*

Needing to dump her nauseating information on someone; she called to tell the news to Kim, confident that she'd find a listening ear.

"Hello!" Kim answered, *Dead silence!* "Hello! Is anyone there?"

"Kim, this is Vanessa...," speaking softly.

"What's wrong, Vanessa? Are you alright?" Kim pressed, in a distressed tone."

"I took your advice; I followed up with Nurse Campbell. Thomas was there that evening visiting the woman who'd just had his baby. Her name is, Tonya Robinson." Now, sobbing.

"What?—Who—? Did you say, Tonya Robinson?"

"You know her? Vanessa asked. Kim disclosed the exact events that'd occurred regarding the night that Tonya Robinson arrived at Carson General.

"What is...," searching for words?" Vanessa stuttered. "What's Walter's affiliation with her, and why in the heck did she refer to him as her, *boyfriend.*"

"That's the *million dollar* question, Vanessa; I had to put some space between us, Girl; it was too many back-to-back incidents that suggested indiscretions to me. You've cleared him on the baby question, but he still needs to explain his involvement and bringing her to the hospital.

My parents are in town, we're meeting at Barbara's for dessert and coffee. I'd love it if you'd join us, ah..., I don't think you need to be alone right now."

"Thomas's out of town, I guess I should wait until he return before confronting him. Sure, I'll be right over and ride with you." Happy that she was able to clear up one less concern for Kim, she prayed that it'd d be enough.

She'd met Walter and thought that he was a good man; she also sensed his love for Kim was genuine. She now felt honored to have Kim for a friend.

Arriving at Barbara's, Kim and Vanessa were the second guest to arrive. Her parents, Walter and Bill were in attendance; Bill and Walter were running an errand for Barbara. Jackie greeted her at the door. Embracing with hugs and kisses, Robert ran over to complete the circle, looking GQ in his grey blazer, black turtleneck, and black slacks.

As always, Jackie exuded class and grace. Maintaining her sized ten dress size, the royal blue silk form-fitted dress draped with a multicolored scarf and matching pumps revealed how she'd also preserved her curvy figure. The three-inch-matching belt accented her petite waistline.

Rushing from the airport to the hotel, she only had time for a ponytail, which highlighted her youthful facial features? Extending hugs and greetings to Vanessa as well, they'd met her on a previous trip.

Anxious to update her parents with Vanessa's recent findings, Kim asked Barbara if they could use her office to chat. Feeling relieved after hearing the good news, Robert echoed. "Well, that's one foot out of the dog house" He said, snickering.

"Girl..., I told you that you needed to talk to that man. We met him briefly, he was scared to death." Jackie added, laughing. Kim leaned against the desk; Jackie was seated in a chair by the desk.

Today was the first time that she'd seen her father since meeting Walter; their resemblance was impressive. At fifty-two, Robert's tall, lean, and buffed frame rested against the facing of the doorway.

Having the same skin tone as Walters, the graying around the temple heightens his handsome and distinguished appeal; it also kept him on the defense with the women.

Defending Walter, Jackie testified. "The mere fact he came here today suggests that he has nothing to hide."

"As your father Kim; I have to agree with your Mom. I haven't always been the man that you know as a father. I've had my days of indiscretions as well. It's more important to consider where we are now in, Christ. God has a way of using our past to confound the present circumstances that exist in our lives" Nodding in agreement, Jackie stood to her feet, with her arms folded.

"I see something in this—one baby girl." Robert said with assurance. That something was—himself. It was assurance from God that his *baby girl* was safe with Walter. Turning to face Kim, Jackie re-affirmed Robert. "I agree with your Dad, Babe! If I'd focused on your Dad's past, I would've missed out, *big time*. We've prayed for your husband since you were a baby; we both can't be wrong."

Releasing a long sigh, Kim caved. "I guess he's suffered long enough, thanks for sharing Dad, you didn't have to, I appreciate it."

"Anything for my baby."

Jackie and Robert joined the others. Robert told Walter that Kim would like to speak with him, and pointed him to Barbara's office. After recognizing Bill, Robert and Bill got busy talking about basketball.

Vanessa brought Barbara and Karen up to speed regarding the Tonya Robinson saga. They were happy to learn that Walter wasn't the father; however, they were sad for Tonya and Vanessa.

Vanessa, now totally ready to be rid of Thomas; Jackie walked into the room just in time to get the entire scoop.

"Vanessa!" Jackie uttered.

"Do you want complete *healing* and *restoration* from God for your part in this?"

"I do, I really am sorry!" Kim and Barbara traded surprised glances. This was new dialogue and *attitude* for Vanessa.

"I am going to suggest that you do something; it isn't going to be easy. Considering the damage perpetrated by you and this man, it bears some degree of sacrifice and complete remorse on your part. Is it necessary? No! Will God honor it? Yes! You need to *apologize and ask forgiveness from his wife.* This will start the healing process for you; it will be true *repentance.* You'll see; you'll be a better woman for doing it." Staring intently, looking reserved in her grey pants suit; Vanessa sat quietly.

"Being a co-pastor as well a Pastor's wife, I've dealt with these situations more than I care to admit; they normally end in destruction for everyone involved. Thank God, there are no kids to consider." Jackie preached, with crossed legs and folded arms, as she sat in a chair at a writing desk.

For privacy from the men, the ladies had migrated to the bedroom. The atmosphere was quiet, but thick. Barbara and Karen occupied the futon. Vanessa, seated at the end of the bed released several deep breaths.

She exhaled generously, before saying, "Oh, my..., I'm not opposed to apologizing, I'm just afraid that she won't give me the time of day." Said, innocently.

Talking about a *ninety-degree turn*, Vanessa's attitude had taken one. Amazed at her transformation from *rebellion to submission,* they stared on in astonishment. Elbowing—Barbara, Karen did so when she noticed Barbara sat with her mouth partially open.

Meeting her match in that of Jackie Rose Montgomery; Vanessa was defenseless. She'd counseled many women who'd found themselves involved in inappropriate relationships. This wasn't new terrain for her; and it was evident in her mannerisms and boldness. This was definitely a turning point in Vanessa's life.

"You'll be blessed, Vanessa. I've witnessed both scenarios. The women who humble themselves usually become strong dogmatic women of God. We'll pray and ask God to soften her heart to you. Now, to rid yourself of him," Jackie carried on. "Do you have any bank accounts, or anything held jointly with him?"

"No!"

"Good, mind you, these are only suggestions. He's living in your home right. That needs to end; now, it's time for him to feel some *discomfort* from something."

"Oh, he will; the information that I got today is all I needed."

"Great! Since he recently moved in, he shouldn't have too many possessions there. Go home, pack up his things, and take them to a nearby economy motel; pay in advance for a day.

An e-mail is all he deserves; tell him of your findings today, include the motel name and room number. Leave the key in an envelope at his workplace, address it, *personal for Thomas Martin.* How am I doing?"

"Great, I was thinking along those lines, but his belongings would've been outside."

"Give me a hug." Jackie reached and embraced Vanessa with a motherly hug. Looking on with admiration, Barbara and Kim relaxed shoulders was an indication that *tension* had been released.

"Leaving his belongings outside wouldn't be a wise thing to do; he's going to be angry enough as it is. Losing you and his *baby boy* in the same month may take him over the edge. You don't want to appear vengeful, Vanessa." She said, touching her shoulders.

"He'll understand that your actions are valid; he'll also appreciate your *tactfulness in securing his property.*" Jackie admonished.

Thomas would be returning the next day, paying for a day or two at a motel was no big deal for Vanessa, she and Kim made more than a comfortable living as RN's. The plan was in motion; the girls would help her remove his possessions. After praying for God's favor to be with Mrs. Martin, they re-joined the others. Barbara would attempt to make contact with Mrs. Martin.

Completely out of character for Vanessa, she was thankful that Jackie was available to counsel with her. Finding out that Thomas had cheated on her along with his wife, forced her into submission to God, and counsel from Jackie.

Since high school, Vanessa remained the tough exterior type; always dominating her peers. She wished she'd a Christian friend that was bold enough to challenge her before Kim.

Entering the room, Walter commented. "Girl..., I can't tell you how much I've missed you. When Barbara Jean invited me here today, the only thing came to mind was "*thank you Jesus.*"

"Jesus, is good, you can also thank Vanessa. I am sure God directed her actions." Kim remarked calmly; noticing his sharp appeal, sporting a grey shirt, and pants, with a short black leather jacket.

"There are still unanswered questions Walter." Revealing the mystery that linked Thomas to the triangle with Tonya; Kim shared Vanessa findings with Walter. Becoming ecstatic, before handing Kim the letter, Walter commented. "See, I told you I was innocent." He said with excitement.

"Well, why did she refer to you as her, *boyfriend?*"

"What? When? I didn't know that. She had to be speaking in the past tense if she was referring to me. Here, read this. I was prepared to give it to someone to give to you if you'd refused to talk to me today."

Leaned against the front of the desk, she opened it and began to read. Walking slowly behind the desk, she sat in the chair. Treading back and forth across the room, with his hands buried deep within his pockets; Walter admired Kim's presence in her hunter green pant suit.

My Dearest Kim, ***September 1, 2000***

It brings tears to my eyes every time I envision the look on your face from that night at Carson General. I felt your hurt and I saw your disappointment. Because you're a skilled professional, you maintained your composure; I prayed and asked God to help you make it through the night.

It's been approximately one year ago since my involvement with Tonya. I met her at her church; my company funded a loan to their church, she was on the finance committee. It was never anything serious; I'm ashamed to admit. After being at her home one evening, I left my palm pilot. Insisting that she would bring it to me, she never did. I gave up after realizing it was her way of getting me over again.

Learning of my trip to the conference in Vegas, I knew that I needed it, plus, it was a gift from my parents. Talking to Bill about it first, she offered me no recourse but to visit her home. Calling ahead the night in question, I asked her to place it in the planter box by her door before retiring. Knowing that I would be coming through late, I figured she'd be asleep; I'd grab it and leave.

Leaving my engine running, I ran to get it, and it was there. As I turned to leave, the door opened, holding her stomach and crying; she asked me to drive her to the hospital. Suggesting 911 and an ambulance would be better, she said, no, it'd be too late. Feeling trapped, I said, okay. Grabbing her purse and coat I helped her to the car. Except for her moaning and groaning, we rode in silence. Taking comfort in the fact that this couldn't possibly be my baby for several reasons, I settled down.

After arriving at County General we were instructed to go to Carson General. Immediately thinking of you, I suddenly remembered that you didn't work the night shift. Pulling up to the emergency entrance, she was assisted by hospital staff. Forgetting her purse and needing to clear the entrance for an Ambulance, I had to park. Turning to leave after giving her purse to the head nurse, I saw you. With God as my witness Kim, I needed a gurney myself; the rest is history.

Relative to the phone conversation you overheard, Deborah is a woman I previously dated; it's been over for us months ago. Meeting at my place for lunch, I'd leave the key under a planter for her, forgetting it was still there, she was waiting for me New Years Eve. With God as my witness, Kim, I wrestled with her until she knew I was serious. I do mean literally wrestled with her. After the incident was over; I offered up lots of Praise and thanksgiving. Remember, I kept telling you I had the victory, that's what I was referencing. I didn't succumb to her advances Kim. One day I will tell you the significance of that victory on New Year's Eve.

Bill can confirm everything I've told you, it's the truth, Kim. For your information, I practiced—protected sex, always. I may have been called weak, but I've never been called ***stupid****. I value the family environment that my parents provided to me. I've always desired the same for the child that I— bring into this world. For precaution sake, I plan to initiate HIV/AIDS and STDs testing for the next year.* ***Love, Walter***

Extending her arms to both side of the chair, with the letter in her hand; Kim glared at Walter with an expression he was unable to read. Walters's letter had reminded her of one of Abraham Lincoln's expression; she felt he'd truly presented her with a *"long faced letter."*

"Talk to me Kim," he pleaded.

"I'm sorry Walter, it's..., I'm having difficulty understanding these casual relationships with other Christian women. Not judging, but the reality is overwhelming Walter. I've never encountered situations like this, I mean... I've witnessed it from other women and men in the church all my life."

Staring on with compassion for her, he was frustrated with his actions. Seeing the hurt and pain he'd brought on her, he walked to the desk, and kneeled in front of her.

Staring intently, he watched the tears settle in her eyes. "Is the reality of who I used to be too much for you, Kim? And I do mean the past tense? I'm not the same man, Kim." Lowering his head,

"I accept complete responsibility for the women as well. I should've been the *bigger one* and exercised restraint. Until I met Barbara Jean and then Bill, I had no accountability. I hadn't been taught that my primary responsibility was to develop a relationship with Christ.

I'm not making excuses, but I didn't grow up with the teachings as you. St. Hebrews was it for me. I know it'd would've made a difference, *as it has now."*

Seeing the hurt and dismay in her countenance, he knew his past life style was out of her league. He was forced to consider *"Will love be enough."* For once, he identified with the song, *"What's love got to do with it"* Recognizing that his past behavior was the big issue now, could she *trust* him.

Remaining silent and looking steady into his eyes, Barbara's expressions paraded through her mind. *The truth is in the eyes.* Finally speaking, "I believe in your sincerity Walter, more importantly, I believe that you've truly developed a relationship with Christ."

"It's the only reason that I believe in you. Loving me *only* would never be enough; I know your love for Christ will constrain you. *(2 Corth.5:14)* My parents see something in you also, especially my Dad. They think highly of you."

Blinking back the tears, he placed his head in his hands. "I hold them in high regard too. I knew I had to face them, but I was consumed with embarrassment and guilt. The guilt that I feel is for my *past mistakes*. I'm *free*—now Kim, God has *delivered* me. In time, I will prove your love for me will not be in vain."

"I realize that there are many men that's been more faithful and deserving of you, but there's *no one,* and I mean *no one* who'll love, and cover you the way I will." Staring her straight in the eye, "do you believe that Kim?"

Wiping her eyes, "I do Walter, I do." In affirmation, she nodded. Releasing a deep sigh. "Can we join the others, now?" Reaching for her hand; he escorted her from behind the desk. Before leaving, he gave her a hug and a kiss on her forehead. Rejoining the others, everyone yelled. "Yay! Yay! Followed with cheers and laughter.

Joining them just in time for the conclusion of the video, Barbara had showed Jackie and Robert the video from Mary's and Gilbert's Christmas party. Observing Gary from the video, and getting the take on why he wasn't present from Karen, Jackie cornered Barbara. "Girl, Gary is a welcome sight. You're doing the right thing, being anxious is not an option. I'm only doing a heat check from the last time we talked." She reminded her giggling.

"You don't have to sell me, you're preaching to the choir."

"I know," Jackie said. "The women in our church know you and Karen by name. I use you guys when I'm talking to my singles. Girl, women need to know that there are faithful and God-fearing women in other—churches and states. Satan would have you to think that you're the only one."

"This is true, as single Christian women we are the *majority,* but, it's time for us to become the majority of *Godly women.*"

"You are so right Barbara, I hear the comments that men make. Girl,—these men—know that they're *out numbered*; they can afford to be *selective*.

When they get through *gettin* that free *milk*, they get right with God, and then they go and buy them some milk." Holding out her hand, she pointed to her *wedding ring.*

"It's the truth, Barbara, men haven't changed. We've *changed—to accommodate, them.*" Nodding and grinning, "Again, Amen! Amen!" Barbara echoed.

Recalling how fun it'd been for Robert to chase her during their courtship, Jackie believed men still possessed that *hunter's instinct* today. She believed that women have taken their fun—from them.

Moseying over to Walter, wearing a mischief smile, Robert asked. "Are you okay?" Chuckling softly, Walter replied."That's refreshing; you're asking me if I'm okay; I'm better than I was before I came."

"That's because I know my baby girl, I raised a little *tiger!* Walking toward the balcony from the living room, Robert beckoned for Walter, "C'mon, let's share a little."

Bending over the balcony rail with their backs facing the door, Robert gawked toward the view of the hills.

"I hear you've had a bit more indiscretions than you probably care to allow for, or admit." Robert remarked, and exhaled a deep breath.

"You need to know that you're not alone, man. I haven't been a Pastor so long that I can't recollect how God delivered me. If the truth be told, I'm certain that I behaved worse than you ever have." Robert said, and looked to the sky.

Holding his teeth clinched, as if to prevent them from falling out; Walter prayed that he'd heard him correctly.

God's amazing," Robert added.

Wonderfully inspired; Walter was choking from unbelief. Turning his head and looking downward, Walter finally uttered. "Pastor Montgomery."

Quickly reprimanding him, "Call me Robert, Please!" He spoke firmly, with a smile.

"Robert, you'll never know how much your candor means to me, more than ever today."

Bobbing his head, and laughing, "Oh, I know..., trust me that I know. I was ordered to tell you." He pointed upward.

"You know that expression "*what goes around comes around*." It's pay back time for me. I chased and slept with many women before I met Jackie. I did the chasing. I was in church, a Christian, serving Satan breakfast, lunch and dinner."

Unleashing a nervous laugh, he confessed. "My baby, she's *smitten* with a man just *like her Dad*." Robert exhaled noisily. With all smiles, Walter anxiously waited to hear more of his prophetic wisdom.

"Walter, I believe the Lord has a calling on your life. I do not—profess to have the *gift of prophecy*," he said, and extended his hand.

"But I do have the *gift of discernment*. God will let you know without a doubt, no one will need to tell you. You see Walter; you'll always have women wanting you. They'll become a *thorn in your side*. God won't stop women from desiring or chasing you." Gaping Walter directly in the eye, he continued his admonishing.

From sheer disbelief, Walter was having a tough time concentrating. *Kim's Dad had women issues like me, she can't know this. God, you are awesome."*

"Once you *submit* your life to him, *completely*." Robert said. He'll give you *buffers* to resist their advances, such as his *grace*, the *word*, the *Holy Spirit*, and the wisdom to know how to handle them. And a fine *foxy wife* to remind you of his grace. That's what Jackie is to me, my "*buffer.*" He said, flaunting a wide-mouthed grin.

"She's God's amazing grace, I call her my shield; you know when in warfare you keep your shield close to you. I thank God for her everyday."

Robert's goal was to convey to Walter the importance of surrendering his—life to God. Realizing that God was his ultimate *shield,* he referenced Jackie *metaphorically* to show how much he loved—her. He keeps her close because he desired her near him. His love for God—keeps him from submitting to the advances—of other women.

"Wow!" Echoed, Walter. Thanking God for the rail that was giving him the support to remain standing, Walter was flabbergasted with Roberts's admission.

Before coming today he felt hopeless; he'd gave way to the enemy to discourage him. *You might as well go back to your Deborah's and Tonya's, Kim is, too good for you. You knew your past would catch up with you. That girl's Father is a Pastor; he would never let his daughter marry someone like, you.*

Walter knew in his heart that God was changing him daily. Acknowledging Roberts comment regarding a calling on his life, "you're the second person that has said that to me, my Mom told me it's time to stop running. She said God is getting ready to use me to do his work. I never would've thought to write Kim a letter that came to me this morning. I had no clue I would be seeing her today."

Holding back the tears, Walter looked upward. Gazing on in admiration—and compassion, Walter reminded Robert *so much* of—him in his younger day. Believing that Walter would be faithful to God also, he could be assured that Kim would be the recipient.

Clearing his throat, "Walter, you probably think I'm crazy with the humorous disposition that I've shown in my exchange of words. I'm sorry, but I'm just amazed at God's sense of humor.

Now, regarding Kim, she used to say that she didn't want to marry a preacher. So, if God has called you to the ministry, do not expect her to run into your—arms shouting *Hal le lu jah."* Walter's knees *buckled.*

"However...," he paused, "she wants a husband *just like her—Dad.* I hope she's gained enough wisdom as an adult to know for him to be like me, that he'll probably be a preacher, pastor or both." *Kim did pick a man just like me, Walter reminds me so much of me, his humble spirit and all, after God broke me."*

Walter's facial expressing screamed, Oh, no! Amused by Walter's pitiful looking face, Robert couldn't help but grin. To ease his conscious, he assured him that if it was God's will for her to be his wife; Kim would come around.

Instantly, Kim appeared at the door, "You guys are being rude; get in here." Walter and Robert joined them with a look of camaraderie.

Vanessa Louise Webster, finishing an unusually busy shift, she couldn't wait to get into her little red Miata as she headed for home. Coming near to her car, suited in a navy blue suit and white shirt; Thomas leaned on the driver side door. Stopping within a few feet of her car, "Thomas, what do you want?"

"I got your e-mail, and the key to the motel. Is this the way you want to end it, Vanessa? You could've waited until I returned for us to talk. What are you doing girl?"

"Certainly you don't need a definition, Thomas. You got your nerve. For the past month I've walked around on pins and needles not knowing if you're the father of Tonya's baby. I knew you'd never admit to it; I've been the other woman remember, Thomas." She said, with passion as she moved closer to him.

"I know you; you'd lie your way out of the gospel if you had to."

"I messed up, what can I say Vanessa."

"You can start by explaining to me why you got involved with her in the first place? The two of us wasn't—sufficient for you, you needed *three?*"

"It just happened Vanessa; He said, and leaned on the hood of her car, with his head down."I met her at a church anniversary that we attended, then we met again at a medical convention. She's in medical sales; she wanted to branch into the pharmaceutical industry. We had lunch a few times, and so on. I didn't ask her to have a baby for me, it just happened."

"*Unprotected—sex*, it just happened, also. You need therapy more than I do. I am so sorry that I hurt your wife, and I take full ownership for my part; you didn't force me to do anything with you. Like a fool, I trusted you Thomas." She yelled! In astonishment, he stood quietly accepting defeat.

"Men like you love to prey on young women with *low self-esteem* like, Tonya and myself. Yeah, I said it, but I stand corrected, that *had* low—*self-esteem.* I'm serving you notice, if your wife will let me; I'm going to beg for her forgiveness.

God has already forgiven me; I suggest you do the same. I thank God that he's surrounded me with Godly women, with God's help I'll get through this Thomas."

"I'm sorry, Vanessa; I can see that you're going to be alright. I did desire to have a baby with you. I planned to marry you Vanessa. You never challenge me on anything before; I respect how you've handled things Nessa; here, let me reimburse you for your trouble." Handing her two hundred dollars.

"I thought you wanted to be married, Nessa? His nickname for her when he was frustrated. "I do, but not to you. I was silly to think that you'd be faithful to me. The *vows* haven't changed, Thomas. Why would you respect ours?" Pushing past him to get into her car. He mumbled, *Boy, have she changed, I've met my match."*

"Get out of my way Thomas. I don't want or need your respect." Before getting into her car, she asked. "Can we agree to stay out of each other's life?"

"Are you giving me a choice, Vanessa?"

"By the way," she said. "Before you over inflate that ego of yours, this anger is directed more toward—myself, for my foolishness." Dropping his head, he stood lifeless as Vanessa sped from the parking lot. Riding with the top let down, she needed to enjoy the freshness of the air, which corresponded with the freedom she was experiencing. The freedom that came from knowing that she was free from the *bondage of lust, and false expectations.*

"Hello!"

"Mrs. Martin, my name is Barbara Jean Keller. I'm going to ask that you please hear me out before hanging up."

"I'm listening."

"I have a woman who'd like to apologize and would like the opportunity to ask for your forgiveness. Her name is Vanessa Webster...." Barbara paused.

"I am familiar with the name." She said with coolness in her tone.

"She wants to apologize for her role in helping to destroy your marriage." Barbara heard a snicker on the line.

"Tell her she can call, but the marriage was destroyed by many more before her." She said, in a matter of fact tone.

"Mrs. Martin, I'm sorry, thank you so much for talking to me. I will let her know, is this time of the evening, okay?"

"Yes! That'll be fine, please call me, Jo. Tell Vanessa she's blessed to have a friend like you."

"For the record Jo, I recently became acquainted with her."

"Thank you; I do appreciate you telling me that. You have a nice evening, Barbara." Jo hesitated before inquiring.

"Ah Barbara, may I ask what church you attend? She heaved out, slowly. "I must say I'm impressed, no, surprised is a better word; you're calling to clear the way for a woman to apologize to me."

Barbara chuckled. "Can I assume that's it's a good thing, Jo?"

"Absolutely, you must be sitting under some kind of *new theology*. I'm not accustomed to this kind of behavior from women in the church."

"Oh, I get you now. Well, you're right about the teaching. We're just trying to be doers of what we're hearing. I must confess that the idea came from a friend of mine who's a co-Pastor out of state. However, I attend Wisdom Fellowship,

Pastor Rama; I'm confident that this would've been his *prescription* as well. As sisters in Christ, it's time for us to stop hurting each other. "

"I've heard of your church, and the teaching; now your actions are making sense. Look, the location is kind of far for me, can you recommend a church in this area with similar teachings. I can give you my e-mail address. I'd certainly like to visit your church, someday."

"I'd be happy to, there's Corinth, Pastor Crenshaw, I'll send you the link to their website."

"I've heard of him."

"Thanks Barbara, as you can imagine, I'm definitely in need of a new church home. I'm moving on with my life; I even signed up with a Christian dating website."

"No, kidding." Barbara responded, in surprise.

"If you don't mind Jo, can I also send you the dating website link we used, we found some decent Christian men on it."

"I think I'd like that, thanks Barbara, you have a nice evening."

"Goodbye Jo!" Barbara made it a matter of importance to assure Jo that she'd no knowledge or influence in Vanessa's indiscretions with her husband.

She was stunned to hear Jo inquire of her Church location, but pleased to know that they'd did the right thing. They owed it all to Jackie's wisdom and her experience. Overjoyed by Jo's receptive spirit, Barbara promptly placed a call to Vanessa. God had truly extended his favor in the matter.

"Hello!"

"Hi! Vanessa, I spoke with Jo, she's willing to talk to you; she said early evening is the best time."

"Thank you so much, Barbara. I'll give her a call tomorrow."

"I'll be praying for your strength, she's a sweet lady; I didn't detect a hint of bitterness."

"Thanks Barbara!" Following prayers of thanksgiving, Barbara retired early for the evening. She chose to keep Jo's shared information private from Vanessa.

Following Vanessa's recent life decisions, her esteem level had increased immensely. She'd met and spoken with Jo Martin two days ago. To her surprise, Jo was a vibrant, intelligent and attractive woman. Judging by Jo's appearance, it was obvious that she wasn't losing any sleep moping over Thomas.

Her bold red suit and matching accessories proved that. With respect to her short statue, she didn't lack confidence in showing off her newly colored blonde shoulder-length hair that contrasted with her light skin tone.

Since meeting Jo, and observing her outer as well as her inner beauty, Vanessa couldn't resist invoking the tired old *cliché "Why would he cheat on a wife like her."* In awe of how God had spared her from Jo's deserving wrath; she was thankful for Jo's vindication. Having only pity for Vanessa, Jo informed her that she knew about Tonya Robinson's baby, also. She thanked Vanessa for her remorseful spirit, and hoped that she'd learned a valuable lesson from her *insensitivity* to her as a *Sister in Christ.*

Reiterating that she didn't have the right to magnify the problems in their marriage; she also seized the opportunity to impart some wisdom to Vanessa; some of it resonated heavily within her spirit. *"If a married man breaks his vows with God and his wife, he wouldn't think twice before he cheats on the other woman."* After assessing Jo's statement, Vanessa owned up to the fool that she'd been.

Early morning service had concluded at Wisdom Fellowship. The Praise and Worship team had led the congregation in songs that exemplified the true meaning of Praise and Worship. Pastor Rama had delivered an encouraging message; he'd taught from *1John 1:9 if we confess our sins, he's faithful and just to cleanse us from all unrighteousness.*

After pouring her heart out to Jo, and asking for her forgiveness; Vanessa had sincerely repented, making it a message of confirmation. God had honored her humble efforts toward Jo. Vanessa knew this was going to be her new place of worship. Kim, Karen, and Barbara escorted Vanessa to the singles table to sign up for their singles conference.

Chapter 13

Still enjoying nice weather in California, it was an unusually warm October day. Attending a late dinner date and business meeting with friends, Bill offered the use of his "*hot tub*" to Karen and the girls for the evening. Prowling the kitchen for items to take to Bill's; they planned to meet for six-thirty p.m.

Arriving within ten minutes of the other, Karen was turning on the grill when Barbara arrived. Changing into their shorts and tank tops, Barbara was glad that they were alone; a tank top in the presence of male company would be a no, no; for Karen, her built in bra was sufficient.

For their convenience, Bill provided a basket of large towels, slippers, lotions, and magazines. Two rib eye steaks, zucchini squash and red peppers completed Barbara's contributions.

Karen added two salmon steaks that she'd thawed for dinner; along with some fettuccini with Alfredo sauce left over from the previous evening meal. Between the two of them they had a meal fit for a king.

Compliments of Bill, he'd made a pitcher of raspberry ice tea. After locating the controls to transfer the music outside; they found a non-commercial Jazz station. Within minutes; the steaks were on the grill.

Barbara found a stack of cedar planks below the grill, a sure fire enhancement for grilling. The grill was no joke, in minutes the steaks were medium well; the cedar plank was hot and ready for the salmon; it only needed about five minutes.

"What happen to Kim?" Karen inquired.

"She went to the City (S.F.) with some of her sorority sisters; they're having dinner and seeing a play."

"What about, Walter?"

"She said Walter is driving up to his time share in Tahoe, he needed some alone time."

"He's needed a lot of that lately, whatever he's doing, it appears to be working. I'm amazed at the turn around that has occurred in his life; he gives a completely new meaning to *repentance.* " Barbara remarked.

"Your faith never wavered with him during the questionable incidents; you did provide a certain level of comfort."

"I've known Walter longer; and I've witnessed his transformation. My *gut* instinct assured me that he was sincere about his newfound relationship with the, Lord."

"You know, Vanessa is another one that's moving at a fast pace, she was at bible study on Wednesday; she's definitely a changed woman. *Another repented one."* Karen said.

Creating a small feast, their food was ready. Barbara was glad that they were eating somewhat healthy, the next day she was attending a BBQ at her sisters.

"I need to eat light tonight." Barbara said. "My brother-in law, Sullivan will be spreading the grill with ribs, chicken, burgers and links tomorrow. Girl..., his BBQ is screaming; he makes the best sauce." She licked her lips from thinking about it. "Am I invited?'

"Of course, he prepares enough to feed the entire block."

"Did you taste the salmon, Mmm..., the cedar makes all the difference, girl." Karen took a bite.

"Mmm..., it does, this is good, Barbara."

"This was a good idea." Barbara said. "How are things moving with you and Bill? I know that you've been spending time together."

"Things are going great; he tries to do things to include Michael also. We've had some alone time, too, not alone, but alone from Michael, but with other people."

Barbara smiled, and nodded. "I knew what you meant."

"He did kiss me good night the last two times he dropped me off at the door, just a peck on the cheek, nothing mushy." She crossed her legs and laughed.

"Aw, that's sweet." Twirling the fork in her fettuccini, Barbara took a bite, and remarked. "This is your first involvement since your divorce, isn't it?"

Taking a gulp of tea before saying. "Yes, it is. Lord knows it's taken long enough. I thought about you and Gary's—almost kiss. We'll have to set some boundaries as these feelings intensify."

Pushing back her plate, Barbara replied. "Yeah, you can count on them intensifying. That was delicious Karen; I'm ready for the hot tub."

Gathering their beverage glasses, they climbed into the hot tub. Laughing while enjoying the water; like little kids in a pool they made sounds of... Ooohs, and ah's.... "You haven't mentioned Gary, lately."

"Huh..., there's nothing to mention, I did see his name on my caller ID earlier this week, there was no message"

"You didn't call him back?"

"No! She voiced with attitude. "Technically, he didn't call. I still like him. I have a special place reserved for him in my heart. When we're together, I feel..., he's being cautious. If it's for my protection, I certainly do not want to defeat the purpose."

"Are you okay with that?"

"Of course, it's not that serious, we've never kissed, remember?" Enjoying the fellowship, they didn't realize the lateness of the hour. Seeing car lights, Barbara yelled! "Here comes, Bill." Rushing, she jumped from the tub clutching a towel as she raced to the bathroom to change. Barbara wasn't about to let Bill see her top half all wet and clinging.

Failing miserably at shielding her laughter, Bill walked over to the hot tub, "What's..., what is so, funny? He stuttered, and where is she going in such a hurry?" Grinning, as he turned and looked in Barbara's direction.

"She just remembered she needed to confirm a consultation with a client in the morning, and she doesn't have their phone number with her." That part was the truth. Shortly, Barbara appeared dressed in street attire. Thanking bill for his generous gesture of hospitality, she said, goodnight.

"You're welcome, Barbara; you can come over anytime that you like."

"Thanks, Bill! You're a sweet heart. Karen, I'll call you."

"I am out of here in a few." Karen said.

Embracing her chest area with her arms, she was chilly, the air was past *nippy*. Pulling a chair close to the tub, Bill crossed his legs to chat. "So, did you have a nice time?"

"We did, we had a great time; you're welcome to what's left."

"Aw, thanks, I'm stuffed, but tomorrow sound good. You know I love a home cooked meal."

Feeling a little uncomfortable, but not for the same reasons as Barbara, just uneasy. While making small talk regarding their evening, the air became increasingly *chilly—and—windy*.

Stepping from the tub, "Will you please pass me a towel?" Bill grabbed her hand to assist her. With clinched teeth, she made uttering sounds of discomfort. Unfolding the towel, Bill wrapped it around her.

"Is that better," he asked, holding the towel around her. Sensing his stare to her face, in braveness, she acknowledged it against her better judgment. With her height, Bill didn't need to lean far before he was kissing her on the lips.

As the kiss progressed, it took on more steam than the hot tub. Not bothered that her wetness was soaking his clothes, he tightened his embrace; Karen offered no resistance. Bill whispered, "I love you, Karen." Remaining silent, in a gesture of acceptance she strengthened her hold; assuring Bill that they were on mutual ground.

It'd been over *three years* since he'd kissed or held a woman, for Karen, it'd been her ex, eight years ago. Reacting to the other loneliness; their desire to be held was in common.

In spite of their warm *clasp,* her body felt—chilled from *the cold wind;* prompting her to bring back her thoughts and actions. *Oh my, goodness, this is getting out of control.*

Continuing to respond to his touch, she ignored her conscious. Finally, simultaneously they let go of their hold; knowing that they'd *flirted with forbidden—behavior.*

Taking her by the hand, "Come inside out of the cold." Profusely apologizing, he gathered a blanket from the hall closet and wrapped it around her.

"Karen, I'm so—sorry, can you please forgive me?"

Concerned only with getting dry and warm, "No worries Bill, please..., let me go and get changed into some dry clothes." As she headed for the guest bathroom.

Upon her returning to the family room, Bill had changed into a dry set of clothes also. Receptive to Bill's awkwardness and remorseful spirit; Karen made a bold effort to *levy* the blame. "Bill, I'm equally—responsible. We're both adults here, no apologies are necessary. Your attitude is appreciated and honorable. However, it's not your fault entirely; we knew what we were doing. We both chose to indulge in a brief moment of lust."

With drooped shoulders, "I just don't want you to get the wrong impression of me, Karen."

Laughing loudly, "Huh..., I could be—guilty of the same implication, Bill. Let's just say we're equally at fault. We know now..., she paused. "We can't engage in embraced kissing anymore. In all fairness Bill, this wasn't planned." Finally smiling, she ultimately convinced him that she didn't think less of him.

"I'm glad that you don't think I was trying to take advantage of you." Nudging him on the arm, "I' m betting that you've remained *celibate* also, right!"

"That would be a yes!" Bill admitted, softly.

"Bill, we were once married, now we find ourselves single and alone; we let our guard down. I'm fine, the girls and I talk about this all the time. Will we be able to *abstain* in the midst of a *temptation*? It's examination time, Bill." She said, laughing loudly.

"We didn't *ace the exam*, but I think we passed it."

Overcome with laughter, "You're funny, thanks Karen. You made this bearable. I've never had this type of conversation with anyone since Sherrie; there's been no attraction for anyone."

"Aw...I'm thrilled; the sentiments are mine as well."

"It's more than an attraction on my part Karen; until you, there hasn't been any desirability for anyone. I don't mean physical appeal only. At the risk of moving too fast, I was showing my love for you Karen. I meant it when I whispered I love you, it was not an *in-the-moment* kinda thing."

"Wow, I like the way you worded that." Purposely looking into his eyes. "I'll say this; you are in the right, *ballpark*."

"Is Michael spending the night with your parents?"

"Yes, he is."

"Let me follow you back, and we can stop at the coffee house near your place. I want to make sure that you get home safe; we have some strategizing to do. I want us to *ace our next exam."* He said, smiling."

"I like that analogy Bill; you—catch on quick, sounds like a plan; let's go."

In route home, unable to stop thinking of his moment with Karen, Bill reflected on scriptures as he dialogued with the, Lord. *"There is none righteous, no not one." Lord, it's because of your amazing grace that keeps us from falling. Tonight was evident Father; we're all just* ***one decision away*** *from falling. (Rom 3:10)*

Bill was pleased to discover that she hadn't been involved in a recent relationship. He was also happy that she was agreeable to setting guidelines for their time spent together.

Being introduced to Christ by his wife Sherrie; Bill took his walk with the Lord serious! After tonight, he knew Karen possessed the qualities that he desired in his next mate. Knowing that he took a chance on telling her that he loved her; the statement relating to the *ballpark* assured him that he was on *base.*

Obviously enjoying a challenge, he'd forgotten the fun it'd been to *pursue a woman,* she reminded him of his courtship with Sherrie. Bill had no problem meeting women in college; he was a star basketball player. While the girls chased him; he chased Sherrie. Once drafted into the *NBA*, women followed Bill on every road trip before his injury.

Observing the attention that women gave to him, Bill had a hard time convincing Sherrie to marry him; especially since he wasn't saved. Both being determined in their convictions, he eventually gave his life to Christ, ultimately, winning her over. Presently, he was ready for a— repeat with Karen.

"At Last"

Taking pleasure in a peaceful evening with popcorn and cranberry juice, Barbara Jean Keller was set to watch a double hitter NBA game. Equipped with her caller ID feature, she was prepared to ignore all calls except emergency ones.

Her phone rang minutes to tip-off time. Grunting and fussing, *who is this?"* The screen revealed Gary's name. *What a surprise!* Assured that it would be a short conversation, picking up the phone, "Hi, Gary!"

Surprising him, "Hi! To you, look, I know you're watching the game. How would you like to go the Arco Center tomorrow; the King's are hosting the Lakers?"

"Don't mess with me, Gary! Are you serious?"

"Yeah!"

"I'd love that. What time should I be ready?" Boiling over in delight.

"I'll call you tomorrow; we're going in a limo, Tony will be joining us. Enjoy the game."

"Thanks!" *Wow, he is full of surprises.* Blissful at the idea of going to the Arco Center, she was never up for the long drive, not to mention the hustle and bustle in parking.

Famous for being one of the *thunderous* arena's in the NBA; the King's games were always sell-outs. She didn't view going in a limo as being flashy; she felt it was being *smart.*

The doorbell rang, Barbara made a quick dash by the mirror, checking the fit on her new purple cropped sweater, and straight legged jeans; she opened the door to find the entire gang, plus a new member; it was Vanessa. Karen had a weeklong conference in Vegas; BJ had attended a seminar in LA, therefore, Karen and BJ hadn't talked about their recent dates with Bill, and Gary. Karen's hot tub kiss was at the top of their list of conversation, followed by Barbara's basketball game.

"I know you have some juicy stuff to tell us, a long ride to Sacramento, and dinner." Karen teased, showing off her new lime green silk blouse, and navy pants that she'd purchased in Vegas.

"You guys..., get in here. I'm just about done with dinner."

Karen purchased her favorite cheesecake with a lemon glaze. Kim brought a dozen of Mrs. Fields chocolate cookies and chocolate mint ice cream. Vanessa brought a tray of jumbo shrimps and cocktail sauce. The girls came loaded with their favorite goodies anticipating a good time.

This was their time to kick back, shoot the breeze, and offer support and encouragement if needed. Today would the first time that Vanessa would be joining them for their "*heart to heart session.*"

Trying desperately to maintain her weight loss, and eat healthy, Barbara knew the girls would be bad and bring irresistible desserts, therefore, to lessen the caloric intake, she served grilled chicken breasts with a jerk sauce, and a tossed salad.

Looking for carb's, Karen surveyed the stove and counter tops. "Where's the pasta, the bread? Girl, I need some carb's." She complained.

Looking at her in unbelief, Barbara remarked. "And just what food category do you consider those sinful desserts that you brought?" She interjected with passion, while resting her hands on her hips.

Laughing, Karen admitted being busted. "That's dessert, it doesn't count, I need some bread." She begged.

Throwing her hands up in surrender. "Alright, I aim to please." Removing a loaf of sour dough from the fridge and to the oven; in minute's bread and butter was on the table, along with grilled chicken, a broccoli salad and a tossed green salad.

Seated at the dining room table; they were raring to go. "Okay, who wants to go first? Let's save you for last Karen, you need the most counseling." Kim teased, looking carefree in her black velour leisure suit.

"We need to build and altar for her, and throw her on it." Kim joked. Exploding with laughter, Karen complained, and stuffed her mouth with bread.

"It's Barbara's fault; she ran off and left me there." Pausing to swallow her bread "I guess neither of us realized that we were so hungry for passion." She smiled, and lowered her head, pretending to be ashamed. "I surprised myself." Karen admitted. "I didn't know that I still had it in me, I guess passion is like riding a bike."

"No, more like a match when it's *ignited.*" Barbara corrected her.

"You got that right!" Karen agreed, hollowing with laughter.

"What started out to be an innocent kiss ended up being a prelude to a lovemaking scene for a *Lifetime Movie!* Can you believe that?"

On the edge of her seat, listening intently, and grinning like a teenager, Kim asked. "So, what stopped you, or did you?"

Glaring in Kim's direction with a look of protest, she countered. "Of course we stopped! Uh..., we did have a little help; thank God. I kid you not, it became *so chilly.* This cold wave of *wind blew directly on us;* we both pulled back; it was evidence of God's grace."

Breaking to snicker. "Bill was drenched with embarrassment; he became profusely apologetic. I kept telling him I was equally as guilty, he wasn't having it; he wanted to shoulder all—the blame." She smiled, waving her hand. "To top it off, he declared his love for me; I was speechless." Unanimously, they yelled.

"He did! Wow!"

"Yes! After we checked ourselves and dried off; Bill suggested that we go for coffee to discuss plans on how we're going to interact going forth. We have this little analogy going, we want to *ace our next exam."*

Barbara sat quietly smiling at Karen. She reflected on her incident at Gary's. Now it was Karen's turn, they hadn't realized the temptations would come so quickly, and with such intensity.

"You know guys, for years, we've wondered how will we respond, we know the scriptures; *"Put on the whole Armor of God, there's no temptation except that is common to man,"* it's easier said than done isn't it?" Barbara confessed, with sincerity.

"Granted, in this situation Karen was partly innocent." Barbara admitted, smiling. "We stayed longer than we should've, I did leave her alone; it obviously became a compromising position for her."

Now that relationships were in place, it became apparent that they would be faced with similar temptations going forth. Barbara created dialogue for behavioral ideas and solutions for *future encounters*.

"Question guys, could that kiss have been—avoided, in spite of my leaving?" Pausing to think, Kim uttered.

"Um, she could've said, it's cold, I need to get dressed, and dashed inside, I don't know."

"I guess, I agree with Kim, I should—not have kissed him at that moment." Karen confessed.

Laughing within, Vanessa remarked. "No, comments from me." *Surely, they are joking?*

"I'm the student today. I don't see anything wrong so far, it was only a—kiss." Vanessa spoke, displaying coolness, in her gold jumpsuit.

"A kiss which could've led to serious—indulges." Karen voiced. Continuing with her take on the matter, Barbara added. "I don't think they could've—avoided a kiss that evening, seriously." Positioning her posture to a straight position, she used her hands to illustrate her point.

"It was destined to happen, the mere fact that they were alone and it was unplanned. If she'd gotten dressed, he would've joined her inside, it was his home, remember; which could've been far more dangerous?"

Enjoying the exchange of ideas and the food. In suspense, Vanessa asked, as she tossed her salad. "How so, what's the difference, inside or outside?"

"Well, they would've had easier access to couches and bedrooms, a cozier atmosphere." With shoulders swaying from side to side, Barbara continued her point.

"There wouldn't have been anything to distract them. Think about it, I think the kiss happened in the right spot, at the right time. For it to have progressed any further, they would've needed to disengage, then walk into the house, by that time, some conviction should've taken place from one of you." She said hopeful, while grinning

Staring on in bewilderment, Vanessa was intrigued with their line of reasoning.

"You're right," Karen interjected. "The operative word is *should've.* At that moment, uh..., we did desire to *sleep together.*" Karen caught glimpse of Kim's facial expression, with expanded eyes, Karen clarified.

"It's true, we did, Kim." Shyly defending,

"I didn't say a word." Kim blurted, grinning. Kim had managed to escape—such temptations, before Ralph, she'd never seriously dated. In college she'd focused on getting her degrees. Plus the fact, Christian men on campus were far and few. Consequently, the conversation unleashed her innocence.

"Now, you're talking." Vanessa jumped in, and stated.

"I was beginning to wonder if you and Bill were human." She stated, displaying humor.

"Girl,—you talking about some *cold wind* distracted you, huh..., I would've suggested going inside. It would've taken a *tornado*—to distract—us." Vanessa said, and fell to her lap laughing. Vanessa's candor and humor was well received by everyone.

"Thanks Vanessa, for keeping it real." Karen replied.

"This is a good discussion," Kim noted, and further expounded. "Kissing heighten your awareness. It also served as a warning for you going forth. Walter knows better than any of you regarding temptation. That's why he's being so careful."

"You are so right, Kim." Karen said. Rehearsing the scene in her mind, until Barbara's analysis of the episode; Karen hadn't fully comprehended the impact of that kiss, or the possible consequences.

"Just now, I hit the rewind button, you're right about being inside, Barbara. I could've become pregnant." The thought brought back the chills."

"God is merciful and just; he knew the intent of your hearts. The *cold wind* was *I Corth 10:13* in action." He provided a way of escape." Barbara shouted.

"On the way to the coffee house to meet Bill, I kept saying *"thank you, Lord for that wind."* Bill said he thanked God for the wind, also. *I Corth 10:13* was one of the scriptures we talked about, along with *Eph. 6:11*, *Phil 4:13."*

Munching on a cookie, Barbara spoke. "Don't be too hard on yourself; until recently you hadn't defined your relationship; there were no rules in place."

Non-stop with the teasing, Kim inserted. "So, I guess this clears up any *culture barriers* or concerns." Karen had no choice but to come clean.

"Okay, I confess. I did use Michael as a concern, but I had issues that were doubtful to me. However, they're no longer of consequence now. He and his wife raised a well-rounded young Black man and Bill played a major role in it."

"Withholding the fact the he'd been married to a Black woman forced you to do some serious consideration of what you really wanted." Kim evaluated.

"I agree, Kim"

Since Vanessa had never abstained from sexual interactions; she couldn't identify with their concern over *"a kiss."* She was slowly grasping the importance of not being placed in compromising positions. She knew Kim was a *virgin*; she didn't understand why, but had accepted it. She had no clue that Karen and Barbara had been abstaining as well.

Vanessa silently dialogued to her lonesome. *Maybe God gave me my job at Carson's to meet, Kim. I've read and heard about Christian women abstaining, I never believed they really existed. If they did, I figured them to be those homely looking women that wore no lipstick, and that were [perceived] as unattractive. I never imagined attractive and sensual women like them [not] to be gettin it on with somebody. No sex, no kissing? Um, I don't... know about this type of dating."*

Curiosity getting the best of Vanessa, with disbelief in her tone and displaying a cute frown, she posed the question. "Going forth Karen, you mean you guys won't be kissing anymore?"

"Not if we can help it, maybe a peck on the cheek, but no more *tongue wrestling* for sure." Karen turned her head to express emphasis. They roared with laughter. Maintaining her composure, Vanessa was dumbfounded.

Bending forward in her chair, with her hands extended, she asked. "Well...," at a loss for words. "How do you plan to show your affections to each other?" She asked innocently, with nosiness in her tone.

Behaving shyly, and shrugging her shoulders, "Um...we'll participate in corporate fellowship, go to the theatre; engage in outdoor recreation and activities that include Michael." Vanessa sighed, and smiled. Motioning her head in bewilderment. "I'm sorry, but this is all *new* to me, guys." Vanessa confessed. "I can't say everyone, but the women that I know in my church; huh, they're sleeping with their boyfriends."

"Most of the men they date ain't even Christians, and the men that are Christians..., huh, they expect you to give it up just like the men in the world." She voiced in a frustrated tone, and flopped her arms by her side.

"And you, know I'm telling the truth guys. Look at Thomas and Tonya, and," she stuttered. "what's her name, ah, Deborah, and—Walter," flinging her hands, she spoke passionately.

Dead silence in the room, Vanessa got—no objections from the girls, they countered with a reassuring peek in her direction. Speaking a different language, Vanessa brought candor, honesty, and the opportunity for self-evaluating.

"How do you attract a Bill, a Gary or a new Walter, anyway?" Vanessa asked, with sincerity, while smiling. "I mean...you've been seeing them on a regular basis now; I can't believe you haven't slept with them. Don't they pressure you to sleep with them?"

Giving her an endearing smile, sensing her genuine spirit, Vanessa's boldness had warmed their hearts; Barbara pointed to Kim to answer her. "You weren't kidding when you said you're the student today." Kim joked.

"The best answer that I can give," she paused; looking downward to collect her thoughts.

"For starters, you're an extremely attractive woman Vanessa, so, getting the attention of a good man is the *easy* part. Doesn't matter whether they're good, saved, or not, they all check out your physical attributes first." Kim chuckled, and made a motion with her hand.

"Amen to that!" Cheered the *peanut gallery*.

"The problem starts after you meet him..., how will you conduct—yourself? The night that Walter and I met, it was all *physical*, with God as my witness. I could've chose to let go of my inhabitations and swarmed over him like bee's on honey, which I—desired." She admitted, smiling.

"However, since I've—submitted my life to Christ, I had to behave accordingly, in turn; he was compelled to treat me with—respect." Vanessa nodded, expressing acceptance.

"Your actions will determine the direction for the relationship. For us, I—chose the *course*, especially after I learned that he was lacking in the exact qualities that I desired."

Speaking with caution, she continued. "The first step is to *submit—your life to Christ completely;* make him Lord over every area of your life. Once you take on his *mindset*, you'll desire things that are good for you. You'll desire a more Christ—centered life." *(Phil.2:5)*

On the edge of her seat, Vanessa clinched to every word as Kim zealously attempted to enlighten her sister. "As men come into your life, you'll be able to distinguish a Bill, from someone that's not—good for you." Vanessa nodded in agreement, bearing a facial expression as if she was getting a new revelation.

Pointing her finger, Vanessa remarked. "Now that's the difference; that personal relationship was *lacking*." She spoke, and savored the taste from a bite of cheesecake.

"I never had that, and neither did Thomas. The women that I've hung out with in the past, they tell you "*Girl, God is a forgiving God; and don't be telling your business to those church women, they just want your man for themselves.*" That's how I learned to be so secretive, in addition to the fact I knew that I was behaving wrong." She gurgled.

"Well, you don't have to be *secretive* anymore, we won't let you." Kim assured her with a smile.

"Vanessa, a man will only go as far as you let him, we all know that." Barbara reminded.

"If you resist him, he'll leave you alone, providing you want to resist him. If he's serious about you, he'll accept your standards. The choice is yours, the main point is to look for someone with the same *values and principles*, otherwise, if you're *unequally yoked*, the *dominate one always win.*"

Continuing to enlighten her, Barbara shared, "With Kim and Walter, she became the dominate *one*. Women have more power over men then we realize, in most cases we lack the high level of *self-esteem* that's needed to call their *bluff*."

"Now, ain't that the truth." Karen agreed.

"We cave in thinking he'll leave—us, and he—will, eventually. But, do we have to let them take a part of us every time they walk?" Barbara expressed.

"My, Dad told me that a woman can't keep a man—with her body only." Kim voiced.

"Amen!" They yelled!

"Often times, good will men test women to see how far they can go with them. Seriously, I've had men friends and brothers to admit to that." Barbara continued to share. "We should always maintain obedience relative to sleeping with someone, but keep in mind, there is a *shortage* of men. Since we never know when a potential husband is testing us, doesn't it make sense to always be prepared to pass the *test?* When you go to a job interview, you know you're not the only applicant, so, you bring your 'A' game."

"Wow! That's deep, Barbara." Echoed Vanessa. "Boy! I'm sure I've flunked a few tests."

"You're not the *Long Ranger.*" Karen threw in.

"You're in good company, Vanessa." Barbara declared. "I behaved exactly like you at one point. When I became pregnant with Michelle, I was in church every Sunday, greeting people as an usher.

So don't be discouraged; when we learn better, we have a choice to behave better." Continuing to encourage Vanessa, Barbara expanded on her past life as a carnal Christian.

"The challenge to grow didn't exist for me. To be honest, foundational and new member's classes were not an option. Sadly, it's still a reality today for many churches; like Walter's for instance.

"For real?" Vanessa replied, with inflated eyes. "I kid you not," Barbara confirmed.

"True commitment doesn't occur over night, Vanessa, it's an overnight decision to make the commitment, but that's when the test of faith begins; it's a process."

"Well..., since it's *testimony* time, I guess I should jump in," Karen replied, grinning.

"That's right, tell it, tell it! Kim edged.

"Before I was married, I fornicated and went to church, also." Nodding her head. "I knew it was wrong, but I never heard anything from the pulpit or any teachings to the contrary. It was during my marriage that I came to know Christ as, Lord; that's why I've been able to sustain since my divorce. Otherwise, I would've fornicated as before." Karen voiced, and continued sharing.

"It's why I was so taken aback with Bill and me kissing. I knew where we were *headed;* I do not want to be a stumbling block for men anymore. I know better now, I just Praise God that Bill owns my principles and love the, Lord too." Karen voiced in sincerity, looking downward.

Because of Karen and Barbara's candor, Vanessa was on an emotional high, she felt that she was in good company; gaining a new perspective on Christian growth.

"Thanks guys, maybe this Christian walk is attainable after all. I've never had anyone to own up to their past, I assumed you guys were reared in the *word* like, Kim."

"Critically, that's the problem, huh..., I wish, Vanessa. We see people in their present state, but rarely do we get to know from where God brought us. That's why we're supposed to *broadcast our testimony.* " Karen clarified.

"I have a testimony also, Vanessa." Kim said. "God has kept his hands on me during some tempting times as well. I can't relate to the experiences that they've had, but to me, that's evidence of how God *has kept me*. Away at college, I had the freedom from my parents, but God assured me in a mighty way that he is *omni present*." She spoke with conviction.

"Thanks, Kim." Vanessa said, softly. Not thinking too highly of Kim's decision to remain a *virgin*, she now respects, and appreciates her choice to *abstain.*

"Okay Barbara, inquiry minds wants to know, what happened after the game with you and Mr. Russell?" Kim asked.

They yelled! "Yeah, gives us the dirt."

"It was an innocent evening, too innocent. I'm kidding, sorry, no kissing scenes to report. You must bear in mind; Gary and I are still in the friendship stage, only." Coming to her rescue, Karen reminded them. "Remember, she showed Gary that night at his house that she wasn't down with the kissing."

"Oh, Yeah, I forgot about that. Gary is the—man as far as I'm concerned." Kim declared.

"We had a great time, it wasn't just the two of us; Tony went also."

"Oh, did he." Karen remarked, glowing.

"Yes..., Karen, we went to the Arco Center in Sacramento. We stopped along the way and had some yummy Vietnamese Cuisine."

"Why did Tony have to go?" Kim fussed.

"Probably because it was a planned event for them. We went in a limo, another guy from his men's class was supposed to go, but he came down with the flu. I was a *wild card;* I'm sure.

"That was nice of him to take you along." Kim added.

"He said he knew that I could hang with him and Tony when it came to basketball topics. We made up trivia questions."

Gary had bragged on BJ's knowledge of the game so, Tony elected to test it. Asking her to name the starting five of the Detroit Pistons "*Bad Boys;*" she named the five starters and the off the bench players as well. Tony was speechless. Gary cheered her on and relished the moment.

"What's going on with Kathy?" Karen asked, anticipating getting the entire scoop. Scanning the room with *a long face,* Barbara uttered. "Uh..., would you believe I still don't know?"

In a motherly fashion, Karen scolded her. "What do you mean? You spend an entire evening with the man; and you still don't know what's up with Kathy."

Smiling, with hunched shoulders. "Sorry!" She answered, regrettably showing signs of defeat in her posture, and tone.

"I couldn't bring myself to ask about his relationship with Kathy. It didn't seem proper..., I mean..., you're forgetting Tony was present."

Exhibiting frustration, she swung her arms as she pleaded her case. "It was more like a night out with the, boys, okay, literally. I felt that if he wanted me to know; he'd tell me. After all guys, the man—wasn't putting any—moves on me that would justify me demanding an explanation about them or us. What was I to do?" Throwing up her hands.

Karen passed. "I guess; you have a point."

"If he doesn't hurry and get off his pot," Kim said. "I'm gonna ask him a couple of questions, myself. For starters, what are your intentions with my friend, Mr. Russell?"

"I might have to hold you to that Kim." Barbara smiled, and nodded in agreement.

"Okay, enough about, me. Where are we with our *baseball* concept? Vanessa, you're going to love this. Kim, have you told Vanessa how wacky we can get during our "*heart to heart*" share times?"

Kim snickered. "Nope, I thought it'd be more effective if she saw first hand."

In a boastful fashion, Karen led out. "I know; I'm on *first base* with Bill." Voiced with confidence, and grinning from ear to ear.

"I guess, I'll say *second base.*" Kim reported, posing with crossed legs, and a hand under her chin. "Speak of the devil; Walter wants to meet with me later today, he sounded serious." She added, wearing an inquisitive expression.

"Let's see...,"Barbara said. "I guess...," she paused, "hey guys, you must keep in mind that my situation is a little different. With everything said, I'm going to exercise some faith; I'm *at bat, in the name of Jesus.*" That stirred another round of laughter. "But keep in mind," she added. "I could hit a *homerun,* and pass both of you." Giving them two snaps up, and a seductive smile.

"Excuse—me!" They screamed!

"Kim never could've convinced me that you were this hilarious, I've never had so much fun with a group of women, and didn't have anything to share." Vanessa spoke.

"Oh, yes you did, you said more than you realize, girl. You reminded me of God's grace and his mercy. I have no reason to boast." *(Eph. 2:8,9)*

"I agree with Barbara, Vanessa. After our "*hot tub*" run in, I'm feeling incredibly blessed.

"I forgot, Barbara," Vanessa remarked. "As my shift was ending; I saw your friend, Joyce. She was in the cafeteria, her Son; he'd been shot. He's in ICU in stable condition. I'm so sorry to be so late telling you, she said she was going to call you."

"Oh, No! She must be a basket case, no problem Vanessa. I have to go and see her." Instructing them to lock up, she reached for her keys and left.

They'd a good *heart to heart* session. Meeting with the girls would become a momentous occasion for Vanessa; bringing to light new views on Christian principles in dating.

Excited about her newfound friends; she was glad they'd included her in their most intimate topics of conversations. Recognizing that she wasn't ready for an involvement now in her life; she was confident that she wouldn't be repeating that kind of mistake again.

Chapter 14

Entering the IC unit of Jerold's room, Barbara found Joyce leaning on the foot of his bed. From the door, she stood and watched Jerold's wide body lie in absolute stillness. Recently returning from surgery, he was still sedated. Jerold appeared to be attached to every life saving device that was available. At the age of thirty, he gave the impression of a big kid. His features and skin color resembled Joyce.

According to his, Mom, Jerold had been a football player in high school; Barbara hadn't known them at the time. Joyce said he could've gotten a scholarship to college, instead; he chose to move out, and get his own place.

The money from the death of his father rendered him anxious. His poor choices in selecting friends constantly made his life vulnerable to tragic incidents. This time wasn't a surprise for Joyce.

Hitting him in his back, the bullet narrowly escaped his kidney. Having been successfully removed; the details of the occurrence were still inconclusive. The gunshot was reported as being the result of a drive by shooting. Joyce thanked God for sparing his life; she was fearful that he was the target.

As she moved closer to the bed, Joyce raised her head and jumped into Barbara's arms. Sobbing frenziedly, "Thank you so much for coming, I was going to call and ask you, and the girls for prayer. I was so hysterical; they gave me a sedative to get me through his surgery." Helping her back into her seat, Barbara gave her assurance. "You're going to be fine, and so is Jerold. The nurse said his status is altogether stable; someone has already been praying."

"Me, I cried out to the Lord like I've never done before, I begged for his mercy." With bloodshot eyes from crying, she stared at her now broken friend. Wearing no make-up, this was a cardinal sin for Joyce. Displaying signs of aging, her hair was pulled back in a bun, revealing strands of grey that is generally well hidden.

Instead of Capri's and mules, she wore grey sweats, and sneakers. In desperate need of a jolt of caffeine; she wrestled with sleep deprivation.

"I called Pastor Moore; he sent Deacon Derrick and Deacon Byron. I hadn't been to church in a while, but they still came."

"Of course they came; they love you, just as Jesus loves you." She said gently, while rubbing her back.

"His love for us is unconditional; and for that we can be grateful."

"I kept saying, Lord, you took my husband, are you going to take my baby, too? I would've just died."

"Thank God he extended his mercy, just as you asked him. This is, ICU; I can't be here long, c'mon, let's pray. "*Lord, Jesus, we confess our sins and ask that you cleanse us from all unrighteousness, Father, we give you Praise today for sparing Jerold's life. Thank you, Father for honoring Joyce's cry for mercy. Thank you for her church family assuring her that your love is unconditional. We ask for a speedy and complete healing for his body. We pray that you'll fill them with the knowledge and spiritual understanding of your will for their lives. Free her from worrying that they may attack him again. Let his spared life be assurance that you are in control. In Jesus name, we pray. Amen."*

"I'm going to go now, I'll check on you later, you have my numbers, please use them." Scribbling a couple of scriptures on the back of her business card, Barbara handed it to her. "I think you'll find comfort in these verses."

She kissed and hugged her goodbye. Barbara gave Joyce Heb. 4:16 *Therefore, we can come boldly to the throne of grace, that we may obtain mercy and find grace in the time of need.* Ex.34:7a *Keeping mercy for thousands, forgiving iniquity and transgression and sin.* Since Joyce begged for his mercy, Barbara would pray that the scriptures would magnify the mercy that he'd extended to her and Jerold.

Walter Douglas Hines was a changed man. Certain that it is the will of God for him to minister in the area of preaching the gospel; he's excited. He'd learned first hand how you can have a life altering change when we surrender our lives to God.

His paramount of concern now rest with Kim, will she accept God's plan for his life. He's also certain that he's in God's will with Kim.

On a cool November day, Walter left work to visit his parents. Having a competent, and reliable office manager afforded him the flexibility to come and go as he pleased.

Knowing that his parents would be home today; he decided to pay them a visit. His Mom is a retired schoolteacher, his father is a manager for the rapid transit system; he's home sick with the flu.

"*Walter*, come in, Baby!"

"Hi, Mom!" Pearlie greeted. Looking polished in her black pants and pink sweater. Her salt and pepper wavy hair was in a French roll. Towering over his short, and pleasingly plump Mom; he reached and gave her a tight hug.

"I'm making some lunch for your Dad," she said and returned to the stove to attend to her lunch preparation. Walter followed her into the kitchen. Lounging in his burgundy terrycloth robe and pants; Arthur, Walter's Dad sat at the table reading the newspaper.

Recently renovating their kitchen, since it's only the two of them, they settled on a corner booth and table; they enjoyed the restaurant style setting.

Sliding into the booth across from his Dad, "Hi, Pop, how are you feeling today?"

Placing the newspaper on the table, "I think I'll live Son, your Mom is taking good care of me." Walter's features were identical to his fathers, in height, body frame, and skin color. Pearlie often said that he sounded like Arthur as well.

"What's new with you, Son?" Sipping on his orange juice. Walter sat with his elbows on the table, and the palms of his hand on his temples.

"Oh..., Dad! So much is going on in my life right now; I don't know where to begin?"

Abruptly, Pearlie asked. "I hope everything is good with you and, Kim, she's a keeper."

"Amen to that!" Arthur repeated in agreement.

"Kim and I are fine, guys..., I've made a decision to work in the ministry of preaching the gospel, I believe God is leading me in that direction."

"Well, Praise God, you've finally stopped running, we knew it. Does Bill know, how is, Bill?" Pearlie inquired.

"Yes, he does know, he's great; he wants more of your sweet potato pie. Between you and Barbara Jean, you've spoiled him. I'll be seeing him later this evening; we're attending a business dinner.

"Great, I'll send him a pie, he's a good man, I'm so glad that the two of you finally got together after working so close. How is Barbara Jean doing, ask her to give me a call?"

"She's great, I'll tell her."

"Does Kim know anything about this?" Arthur asked.

"Nope, I am telling her later today."

Refilling Arthur's juice glass, Pearlie asked. "Son, when are you going to tell, Pastor Scott and the congregation?"

"I'm going to be talking to him this week."

"That's your cousin, he'll be happy to know you'll be joining him in the pulpit. I can hear him now." Pearlie mimicked her Pastor Cousin. *"We got a long blood line now to carry on the ministry."*

Decisively aware that he had plans that he wasn't quite ready to reveal, even to his parents, Walter sat quietly.

"Lunch is ready," Pearlie announced. Bringing a tureen of split pea soup to the table filled with smoked turkey, followed by a basket of hot buttered corn bread, and a tossed green salad; made with Pearlie's special dressing. To satisfy the sweet tooth, a potato pie awaited them. Walter knew he was in for a treat.

Kim opened her door; holding a long stemmed red rose, Walter greeted. "A pretty rose, for a pretty lady."

"Thanks! Walter, you're so sweet. Oooh, I love your sweater, the cream blends so nice with your complexion."

"Thanks! It was a gift from my parents."

"Come on in, what's your pleasure, coffee, tea, or *me*?" She said giggling. I couldn't resist Walter; I recently watched an old movie classic, and heard that line; I thought it was so catchy."

"I'm telling your Dad on you, bottled water will be fine. How was your day?" He said with a wide mouth grin.

"It was great, I just left the girls; we had one of our *"heart to heart"* sessions."

"Oh, Lord, what's commonly known as men bashing sessions."

"No, way! Sit down," she ordered. "You look sad, what's wrong, Walter?

Taking a seat at the kitchen table, "I need to tell you something that's happening to me," he murmured, softly.

Kim looked on with a worried expression, responding in a panic tone, "You're not sick, are you?" Handing him the bottle of water.

He eagerly assured her. "No! No! It's nothing like that." Kim breathed a sigh of relief, and sat across from him at the kitchen table.

"Kim, you know that I've had a lot of alone time lately. I recently returned from my cabin in Lake Tahoe on a two day retreat of praying and reading the scriptures. I'll just say it, I know without a shred of doubt that God is leading me into the preaching ministry."

Closely observing her face, Kim returned his stare with a blank expression. Fighting to keep a straight face, the words of her father continued to inhabit his thoughts. *Don't expect her to run into your arms."*

"Are you being receptive to his prompting?"

"Yes!" He answered, timidly.

"Well, that's a good thing. My Dad said he didn't want to go into the ministry; he went kicking and screaming."

"I must say; I'm elated and excited about sharing his word from a ministry perspective. Kim..., surely you know how I feel about you. I mean, you have to know that I want you to become my wife." Taking hold of her hand, he stared deep into her eyes.

In a shy and edgy kind of tone, "I guess," smiling, as she twirled her thumb around his.

"Kim, scripture doesn't support everyone that preaches the gospel should *ultimately* become a *Pastor.* I don't know what God has in store for me; however, would you be opposed to being my wife if I later became a Pastor?"

Drawing in a deep breath, and releasing it, she laughed. "Boy!—you really did want—to talk, didn't you?" Walter laughed, and squeezed her hand.

"My Dad became a Pastor when I was a preteen. I remember he had to attend a convention, and I didn't want him to go. I told them I didn't want a *Pastor* for a husband. Shortly after that, my Mom joined him in the ministry."

"When he was in the corporate segment, before going full time in ministry; he had to travel at least once a month, sometimes more. I recall not liking that either." She jabbered on, expressing her feelings regarding his news.

"His traveling was my only objection. In the same breath, I always said; I want to marry a man *just like my Daddy.* As a child I didn't have the wisdom to know to be *like my Dad,* he'd probably be a preacher, pastor or both. With that said, I guess my prayer was—answered, Walter Douglas Hines." *Did I just agree to marry him?*

In seventh heaven, Walter wanted to jump across the table and give her a big hug, instead, in a humble tone, "Wow! Kim, I take that as a compliment. I had a long talk with your Dad that day at Barbara Jean's; he's a remarkable man. I attended that workshop with them the next day after we met. I observed your Dad, he sat with your Mom at lunch and during the class sessions; it's obvious that he enjoys her presence. Yo, mama is fine, girl." He sneaked in, with a broad smile.

Smiling in agreement, she affirmed. "That, she is, my Dad thinks so too."

"I want to be just like him when I grow up; I want you by my side in the ministry and everything I do."

Continuing to caress her hand. "You have some tall boots to fill, Mr. Hines; I know he told you about his weakness with women. You know, I see a lot of my father in you. You have this sincere and humble spirit about you, like my, Dad. I feel protected when I'm with you." *Based on what I've learned about my, Dad, Walter is just like my Dad.*

"Girl..., don't you make me cry up in here?"

"You! Cry? Aw..., I love a man that cries. My Dad cries, and he ain't no *whimp.*"

"Thanks Kim, man or woman, we *can't* be like Jesus until we—*weep*, right?"

"Yeah, you're right, he did cry!"

"How was it being a *PK*?" (Preachers Kid)

"Hmm..., it was okay, him being a Pastor didn't alter my Dad's commitment to me and my, Mom. Working in management I guess he'd learned to delegate. When I went to college, he'd surprise me."

"Ah, checking up on you, ha?"

"Right! Right! We'd take vacations; he'd be home for dinner. He made us feel special."

"That's what I'm talking about, he's a remarkable man." Walter added. *God, you changed him, you can change me.*

"I know that I have plenty to learn, Kim. He said your Mom was eager to move to Maryland."

"She was; she said God assured her that this was his will for them. I guess the kids don't get a vote; I sure wasn't ready." She added, grinning.

"I would never make a decision without prayer and discussing it with you. If it's God's will, I have to believe he'd at least give you a *hint*." He said, grinning.

"Walter Douglas Hines, is this your *pathetic* way of proposing to me? If it is, you'd better be packing a *diamond*."

"Ah..., ah, yes, no, I mean..., yes. It's a proposal, but no, I do not have the ring, Kim. I was so anxious to get your response regarding my ministry, until I forgot all about the ring. I was too worried that you'd say no; a ring wouldn've mattered. I'll let you pick any ring that you desire." He said, with non-stop grinning.

"Oh, no you will not, I'm an old-fashioned girl, that's your department." Adjusting to a relieved and relaxed posture, he sat in amazement. "That's why I love you so, you keep me on track, Barbara Jean was right."

After getting Kim's ring size, they prayed and asked God's blessing upon their relationship; their future, and to know his will for their lives as husband and wife. Before leaving, he kissed her on the forehead and invited her to join him at St. Hebrews for Sunday worship service. He left focusing on one of her Dad's comments, *God will give you a fine foxy, woman."* He was elated.

Delighted that things had gone well with Kim; he was confident that he'd regained her *trust*. The moment he laid eyes on Kim, he knew she was *one*. The *prey* had captured her *hunter*.

Walter needed to secure her parents blessing before running off to a jewelry store. Sharing their conversation to Robert, he was happy to hear that Walter had gotten the confirmation regarding the ministry. Giving Walter their sincere blessings; the call ended with a word of prayer.

His next call would be to his dear friend, Barbara Jean. "Hello!"

"Hi! Barbara Jean, this is, Walter. I don't know what to tell first. I guess I'll start with God is leading me into the preaching ministry, and that Kim has agreed to marry me. There, I said it."

"Oh, my goodness Walter, you are full with *good news* this evening, no *punt* intended. That's great, hold on, I have another call." Barbara clicked over, it was Kim, she asked her to hold.

"Okay, Walter, I'm back."

"Will you join us at services at my, church on Sunday?"

"My pleasure, I'll see you then." Bringing Kim back on the line. "Hi! Kim, what's up?"

"Don't what's up me; I know you were talking to Walter."

"You're correct, and congratulations! Best Wishes! And all that good stuff. You're *on third base*, girl."

"Not officially," she kinda of fussed.

"He has to get the ring, it happened in such an unorthodox fashion, but the sentiments were the same. Looks like I'll be following in Mom and Dad's footsteps."

"You mean the ministry?"

"Yeah!

"You'll be great, Kim. You'll be a blessing to many young girls and women, some older ones, if they'll listen. Wow, after only eleven months you've met and secured your husband, oh..., my, goodness."

"We owe it all to you, Barbara. You invited him to the party."

"Maybe it was *destiny*, just as he said that night."

"Let's get destiny rolling; I will see you at his church on Sunday. I know he invited you. Goodnight!"

Barbara Jean couldn't be happier for Kim and Walter. Her phone rang. "Hello!"

"Hi, BJ, do you have a minute?"

"Hi! Gary, the way this phone keeps ringing, a minute sounds about right. What's happening?"

"How does brunch sound after early worship services Sunday?"

"Um..., its sounds real good..., but we're visiting Walter's church on Sunday. He's sharing his testimony on God leading him into the ministry."

"No, kidding, what good news. He left me a message; I bet it was to share this."

"Would you care to join us; I'm sure we'll be eating somewhere afterwards?"
"I would be honored, let me pick you up."
"Thanks, parking is hideous around there."
"I'll call you later, BJ."

Sunday school had adjourned, it was a typical Sunday morning at St. Hebrews; children were dashing to the neighborhood store to stock up on their favorite goodies. At 10:45 the parking lot looked filled, an usher waved to Barbara and Gary that there was one more space. While crossing the street from the parking lot, Gary spotted Bill and Karen parking a block away. "Let's wait for them." Gary suggested.

St. Hebrews was a well-maintained traditional building, complete with a towering steeple. A crowd of people had gathered in the foyer preparing to enter the sanctuary.

Diversely blended in age; the congregants consisted of babies to elder adults. The teenagers laughed and joked as they made their way into the sanctuary. In royal splendor, the older women wore beautiful "crowns" and matching fall colored dresses.

Standing tall, the deacons were decked in their dark suits and polished shoes. Like a sore thumb, you could tell who the single women were, in their *take a second look* form-fitted suits and three-inch heels; with freshly styled hair and manicured nails. As customary, the women disproportionately *out numbered* the men.

An elderly usher that could've passed for Grady's twin brother on *Sanford* and *Son* greeted them; appearing proud in his neatly pressed navy blue suit and white gloves, his beaming smile validated his warm welcome.

Once inside, Barbara and Gary saw Kim seated in the middle pew. Kim spotted her and indicated for her to join them; Bill and Karen followed. Karen was seated next to Walters's mother. Pearlie was radiant in her rose-colored two-piece suit, with matching accessories, and a pillbox hat.

Taking pleasure in answered prayers for God to intervene and turn Walters's life around; this was a proud day for his parents, they weren't expecting anything close to this magnitude. God had blessed exceedingly abundantly above their expectations. *(Eph. 3:20)*

Walters's father, Arthur proudly took his seat on the deacon's row to the left of the pulpit. Walter was nowhere to be seen, a seat was reserved for him between Pearlie and Kim. Within seconds, Pastor Scott, dressed in his black robe entered from a door on the left side of the pulpit, Walter was behind him; taking a seat on the deacon's row. Sporting a "GQ" look, Walter wore a three-piece black and white pin stripped suit, white shirt, a red, black and white tie. Peering into the congregation, he made eye contact with Kim.

With raised hands, Pastor Scott instructed the congregation to stand to receive the choir. The organ struck a cord to the tune of "*We are Soldiers,*" commencing the choir processional down the center aisle.

Wearing navy blue robes with white collars; they were swaying from side to side. Some marched in attention as if they were in a military platoon; others were strutting and rocking resembling a jazz band on Bourbon Street.

Consisting of men, women and children, it looked to be a forty-member choir. Hands were clapping; feet were stomping, and Tam Bo urines shaking. The congregation was fired up, it was filled to the capacity seating of three hundred and fifty.

Pastor Scott, tall, dark, and heavy in stature, graying slightly around the temple, served as the cheerleader waving his white handkerchief to the beat of the music. Motioning for the congregants to be seated, he proclaimed. "Let the church say amen," in his somewhat husky voice.

Pastor Scott, like his cousin Walter constantly found himself on the defensive end when it came to the women. They loved his appeal as well as his pulpit status.

Walter had informed his Pastor of the announcement that was to follow. "This morning, St. Hebrews, and on a more personal note, the Scott family; have been smiled on yet again by the, Lord. He's given us another Son in the ministry, and if he's a true Scott, he can speak for himself.

I give you none other than Walter Douglas Hines, the "baby boy" of Pearlie and Arthur Hines. Let's receive him with a warm welcome this morning, St. Hebrews."

Heads were turning with surprised looks; the sanctuary *buzzed* with sounds of whispers; yet, they managed to render handclaps, Hal le lu jah's, and praise the Lord.

Walter stood in front of the collection table; he was given a hand held mic by a deacon. After battling back the tears, he composed himself. Well-wishers audibly whispered sweet prayers of "*Help him Holy Spirit, use him Lord.*" Walter proceeded with a faint smile, acknowledging them for their shouts of exhortations.

"All praises to my, Lord and Savior Jesus Christ. Thanks to my Pastor and cousin," he smiled, and turned to recognize him. "For giving me this time, at this hour to say to you what the Lord has placed on my heart. I thank God for my parents, without their prayers, love and support, I wouldn't be here today. I thank you, St. Hebrew's for your support, I especially thank you for the trust that you've invested in my business and me."

"The mortgage industry is competitive; I value your trust."Offering appreciativeness, he continued.

"The end of last year the Lord placed a heaviness upon my heart. It was regarding some behaviors and relationships that were inconsistent with his will and plans for my life; more to the point, behaviors that were in direct contradiction to his word."

Making a brave effort, he choked back the tears. "I stand here today to ask for your forgiveness, forgiveness for my indiscretions, and *forgiveness of every woman* whose relationship with Christ was—hindered because of my influence, or interaction in their lives."

Pearlie yelled! "Thank, you Jesus!" Others shouted. "*That's alright Son, take ya time, let him use ya.*" Sucking in a deep breath to keep from crying, he exhaled loudly. Identifying with their brother, sounds of quiet sobbing could be heard, along with amen's, and chants of "*Thank, you Jesus.*"

"I'm reminded of the *Psalmist* David, when he said, *"Blessed is he whose transgression is forgiven, whose sin is covered. Blessed is the man unto whom the Lord imputeth not iniquity, and in whose spirit there is no guile. When I kept silence, my bones waxed old through my roaring all the day long."*

Tears, now tumbling down his cheeks. Desperate to keep their brother exalted, his tears summoned the need for more shouts of "*use him, Lord, say it Walter, it's alright Son.*"

He continued to recite the Psalms. *For day and night thy hand was heavy upon me, my moisture is turned into the drought of summer. I acknowledge my sin unto thee, and mine iniquity have I not hid. I said, I will confess my transgressions unto the, Lord; and thou forgavest the iniquity of my sin." (Ps. 32:1-5).*

Unable to find a dry eye in the sanctuary; the ushers walked the aisles with boxes of tissues, as they zealously supported their brother in his ***humble and unprecedented*** attempt to obey God. When his emotions subsided, Walter came to his close.

"That was my prayer daily, Church; which brings me here today; to share with my church family, that the spirit of the Lord hath anointed me to preach good tidings to the meek. As the prophet Isaiah wrote, *God has truly given me beauty for my ashes. I have taken on the garment of praise, for the removal of heaviness that was upon me."(Is.61:1-3)*

"I believe that everyone needs a Nathan; I thank God for sending me mine in that of William Hansen, on a more familiar basis, he's known as Bill. Bill, will you please stand. I also have a *Nathanette,* Barbara Jean, will you stand, also." He said, laughing. With handclaps and amen's, they were warmly welcomed by the congregation.

"The Lord has used them significantly to help get me to this moment in my life. I know most of you have seen me running in late on Sunday mornings for some time now; I've been sneaking off to my mentor Bill's church for early morning worship services. During the week, I will be attending classes two nights a week." He shared in excitement.

"They have a curriculum of classes designed to equip you for a more Christ centered life, they're available to assist anyone as you desire to grow in the Lord."

"Amen!" They shouted.

"If the, Lord is willing, I've estimated; that it will take me about two years to complete them. Effective immediately, I will be attending on a regular basis."

The sanctuary was filled with chants of ah's, and no's, Walter extended his hand to quiet them. "Hold on, this will only be a temporary arrangement; I've cleared it with Pastor. Our plan is for me to return and implement a new teaching curriculum here, one that will challenge us in our daily walk, and spiritual growth."

The murmuring changed to, "Amen! Thank, you Jesus." They were happy to know that Walter wouldn't be leaving them. They loved him dearly. His testimony today cemented that love; they knew God's anointing was upon him.

"I've saved the best for last, y'all," he grinned.

"God has been good to, me. Talking about *unmerited gifts*. Once I got out of self, God allowed my path to cross with the woman that I believe he wants as my wife, and partner in the ministry. As soon as I can put a ring on her finger, that is. When God works, he moves fast." He said with a big grin, and chuckled.

"Only God could've brought us together. I pray that you'll receive and love her as you have me. We'll be visiting here on a periodic basis. Kim, will you stand please."

Standing, and flaunting a bright smile, she greeted the congregation with a slight nod of her head. Desiring to look special in her clothing selection, but with subtlety; similar to Walter, she chose a grey two-piece pinstriped suit, with a white blouse with matching accessories. For a relaxed look, her hair draped her shoulders in a loose body curl. Kim was no stranger to large capacity crowds, being the daughter of a Pastor, she and her Mom had acquired a natural grace for public introductions. Walter was overjoyed with the handclaps, and praise the Lord's that went forth in acknowledgment of Kim.

After thanking them, he also asked for God's blessing upon their relationship. Placing the mic on the table; he took his seat between his Mom and Kim.

Returning to the podium, Pastor Scott wiped his forehead with his now *wet* and *limp* handkerchief. It wasn't wet from sweat residue alone; it caught a few *teardrops* also. Releasing a long sigh. "I don't know what y'all thank, but Walter has preached his first sermon here, today." Everyone responded in agreement. "Amen! Amen! Pastor."

"Walter told me he needed me to give him space to say what thus said the, Lord. I must say, I wasn't prepared for the spirit led testimony we heard here today, church. He's *emptied* himself." Spoken with heart-felt emotions, now, in a softer tone.

"He would've been free in God's eyesight if he'd restricted his confession to his prayer closet. Nevertheless, he chose to confess before *man*. No need for running and gossiping. Oh, we like to dress it up and call it *sharing*. If you read your bible, what he did here today is biblical." He admonished, displaying pulpit humor. (*James 5:16)*

"When he takes his rightful place in the pulpit, he can stand boldly and proclaim God's word. Without compromising, he'll be able to teach from *Genesis to Revelation.* If you were listening, it was a testimony with a two edged sword, and I'm not above it." He surveyed the sanctuary for reactions. "Amen, Pastor." They shouted.

"That's why I tell you, church, search the scriptures—for yourself. Walter did, with that said. *Shamefully*, Walter had to seek outside help to get to this moment today." A silence ensued.

"There will be some changes here at, St. Hebrews. God is using Walter to bring relief to the captives, as it relates to study and teaching. What he demonstrated here today can only be done by a man that's been broken and have surrendered his life to, Christ."

"Amen, say it, Pastor." They cheered.

At age forty-eight, married with four children ranging in the ages of six to thirteen, Pastor Scott was keenly aware of the need for change. Scuffling with pride, justifiably so, nevertheless, his desire to be obedient to God's people *trumped* satisfying traditions and expectations—from others.

"That type of brokenness and submission can only be achieved by knowing Christ for yourself. For years, we've done the same old thang, church, handed down from generations to generations, believing that we're doing fine. Well, church, I'm here to tell you, we're not—doing fine."

"Walter's testimony has existed far too, long and by too, many over the years at St. Hebrews. Oh, I can stand here and make excuses, and say, *this is the order of service and ministry that was handed down to me.* Gaining strength from their receptive expressions, he continued.

"I'm happy that God is—intervening on my *watch*. I consider it a good thing. As Walter stated, he'll be coming back to head up our teaching ministry. What he didn't tell you; I'm going to be joining him in taking *some of the classes."* The church erupted, hollering, *Thank, you Jesus, amen, ha le lu jah.*

"You see church, in the kingdom of God, submission and surrender has to come from the *top down*. Between the two of us, we'll be better equipped to train the other ministers and teachers." The congregation continued to explode with cries and shouts in agreement.

"In the spirit of frankness, we have received what we came here for today. To worship God, to be encouraged, edified, and convicted if needed. We've been challenged church; if you were paying attention. On that note, is there anyone else who care to share his or her heart today?"

Little by little members began to stand and give testimonies of Praise, thanking God for Walters's boldness, and the humility that he'd shown.

He'd allowed the *Holy Spirit* to use him to create an atmosphere filled with attitudes of confession and praise.

Returning to the podium, Pastor Scott joked. "The only thing that he didn't do was take *Jesus to the cross* and offer up his *whoop.* Amused by his own comment, Pastor Scott used the support of the podium, as he leaned over with laughter. The sanctuary murmured in disbelief of his sense of humor and candor.

Pastor Scott announced. "We're gonna offer up a couple selections from the choir, and open the doors of the church. Unless there's other business, we're going home, can I get an amen, church?"

In astonishment, the congregation hummed with *"Praise the Lord, Pastor."* This would be the first time in history for St. Hebrews to conclude a worship service at twelve-thirty.

Appearing that Walter's testimony had resonated to the pulpit as well; the Lord had used Pearlie and Arthur's baby boy to nudge the spirit of their cousin and Pastor.

As they exited the sanctuary, Walter extended humble good-byes to well-wishers. Once outside, men and women thanked him for his bold heartfelt testimony. Some were touched and convicted in a manner that wasn't appropriate for public testifying; they resorted to whispering how they'd identified.

Initially, the women were standoffish with Kim, until one woman broke the ice. One by one, they came. The *icebreaker* was none other than Deborah Collins, his *New Year's Eve Nightmare.* Approaching them with extended hands, in a black two piece suit; she offered best wishes to, Kim. With a firm handshake, she thanked Walter for his remorseful words of expressions.

Out of respect for her feelings, Walter had notified Deborah informing her of the day's event, and his engagement; giving her the choice not to attend. To his surprise, through the grapevine, Deborah had learned of Kim.

Subsequently, to avoid discomfort and distractions amongst the three of them, Deborah made the decision to leave St. Hebrews. Harboring no hard feelings for Walter, she had one regret; she wished that she'd remained *faithful* to God and the teachings of which she was accustomed.

In her pursuit to secure Walter as her prize; she'd broke fellowship with Christ, ultimately allowing *lack* in her principles, standards and convictions. Now conscious of the fact that this was Deborah's way of accepting his apology; Walter couldn't have been more pleased; his public confession hadn't been in *vain."*

Deborah would never know the consequences of her actions on that New Year's Eve night; it gave Walter the *assurance of victory over temptation.* No longer the *cats meow*, he desired the women of St. Hebrews to know that he was committed to Kim. By the manner in which Kim was welcomed, he was successful in his attempts.

The occasion was celebrated with everyone going to Skate's, one of Walter's favorite restaurants. With Thanksgiving only a week away, there were many reasons to be thankful.

Thanksgiving week, returning from San Francisco, Walter dropped Barbara Jean back at his office to retrieve her car. He knew she'd be the best person to help him select Kim's ring. Impressed, Barbara Jean wasn't surprised of the ring Walter had purchased for Kim.

Instructing her not to look or ask the jeweler for the price, he'd her to select five styles that she thought Kim would like. Honoring his request, he settled on a one and a half caret princess cut in platinum. Dying of curiosity, she resisted peeking to see the prices. A forever class act, he knew she would keep his transaction confidential.

Stopping by Carson General to check on Jerold. Barbara found that he'd been released. Since she was there, she decided she'd look for Kim. Boiling over with anxiety to share with her; she found Kim in the nurse's lounge. Glancing up from reading a magazine, Kim spotted Barbara, and waved to her to join her.

"You're here to see, Joyce's, Son; You know that he was released?"

"Yes, I was, this is good news."

"I checked at the beginning of my shift this morning, he was released on yesterday with a prognosis for a successful recovery."

"I spoke to Joyce a few days ago, girl, you wouldn't believe the change that's come over that woman. She thanked me repeatedly for some scriptures I'd given her. She can't stop talking about God and his mercy."

"That's encouraging," Kim said.

"So it took one tragedy to turn her away from God and another to bring her back. God was merciful to Jerold. It's nice of you to include her in your fellowships Barbara."

Barbara smiled. "Yeah, especially since we hardly agree on anything. I like her; she's having what she think is *fun,* just as I did."

"Girl, I couldn't wait to tell you how happy I am for you and Walter. Pastor Scott was right; he did preach his first sermon. God did use him; St. Hebrews will never be the same. There wasn't a dry eye in that sanctuary when he was done." Barbara babbled.

"I know!" Kim said, glowing. "I wanted to run up there and hug him. I was so proud of him, specifically when he apologized to the church and particularly the women. I couldn't help but cry; he is a *diamond in the rough*."

"So, what did you think of Deborah Collins, Kim?"

"I was impressed; she led the way for the other women, poor Walter. The girl's got it going on, I'm serious, nobody but—Jesus could help him *resist her."* She fell over laughing.

"And Tonya Robinson, uh... she's no *chop liver either, s*he was pregnant at the time, but maintained her appeal." Kim informed.

"You're so crazy; Deborah is a doll, definitely a woman with class."

"I'm glad that I didn't let him get away because of his weakness for women; I guess we need to be careful when we pray. I had no idea that my Dad had been a *womanizer.* He's a good Dad."

"I think so, he's a good husband also, this did happen before they were married. It only proves; all things are possible when we surrender."

"It wasn't easy Barbara, but I know God allowed me to be the *anchor* in this relationship."

"Indeed he did, that's why I wasn't concerned. You were just what he needed during that stage of his life, someone who wasn't going to chase and make advances to him. Walter really wasn't the womanizer, they chased him, he was guilty of yielding." Barbara said, giggling.

"Seems that way, ha."

"I don't know his cousin, Pastor Scott, but I felt he was doing some confessing of his own."

"I think you maybe right Kim; he certainly had a humble spirit about him. He was correct, Walter is free."

"God is so awesome; he used Walter who was once considered a womanizer to bring about change and healing for those people. It all started by you, and then Bill, believing in him, Miss *Nathanette."*

"Wasn't that cute..., you're right, he only needed someone to challenge him." Barbara agreed.

"Pastor Scott had the right attitude, he was thankful that God would use Walter on his *watch.* It was wise of Walter not to tell Pastor everything the Lord gave him to say."

"I know, you're right Barbara, that—courage came from Walter's brokenness."

"Wow, when you guys first met, he'd just surrendered his life to God." Barbara reflected on her and Gary. "Your relationship with Walter has caused me to look at things differently."

"How so?"

"Remember our preconceived notions of how we want our mates to be, the length of time they've been a Christian, committed, know the scriptures, go to church every Sunday. Be black, white, tall, buffed, slender, handsome, a professional, financially equal, polished and so on."

Kim smiled, sensing antennas of re-valuation rising in Barbara's mind. "Are you thinking about Gary, because he recently recommitted?"

"Yeah!" Barbara agreed, soberly.

Pushing aside the magazine. "Going forth, I'm going to dispense with some of my so called criteria, be more open-minded. I'm going to let God direct my decisions when the time comes, as you did. I'm not going to compromise scripture; um..., but be less *rigid* in my choices." Barbara voiced, in sincerity.

"Well..., I can't take any credit; you know I was ready to dump, Walter after those incidents."

"Yeah, but you gave him a chance to come clean. I'm older than you;" Barbara added. "I have a little more latitude in certain areas. You have to be concerned with finding a man who'll be a potentially good father, as well as a good husband, and a good provider. My primary focus will be on him being a good husband and obedient to God. There's more, but those are the major—concerns."

"That's good, Barbara, you're correct, I will need to concentrate on more areas, hmm..."

"Look at Karen;" Kim said. "She almost lost a good man, and a good mentor for Michael because of a *culture* concern."

"My point, about being *rigid.* It's a harsh reality Kim, but because we out number men in general, the number for *Christian* men is greater. In the *mega* churches, they are filled with *mega* women."

Holding back laughter, Kim added. "Sad, but true."

"Kim, remember we talked about the income ratio, we said that we'd be open to negotiate the income percentages. It appears that women are excelling in all areas over men, including Christianity."

Barbara thoughtfully made her case. "My argument is, if we're willing to lower our *expectations* economically for a mate consideration, should we be willing to adjust our spiritual criteria for the consideration of a mate, also?"

Still concentrating, Kim uttered. "Um..., I guess."

"Not to be confused with *compromising*." Barbara assured her. "Oh, you mean like a Gary, someone who has less Christian experience, yet possess the same levels of [standards and values]."

"Yeah...Yeah," Barbara said, and paused. "I mean, what are the chances of me finding a Christian man my age that's been *celibate* for as long as me, Kim, or for *any number of years*, c'mon."

"Huh,—about as much chance of me finding one at my age. I had my doubts about Walter, after ongoing conversations with my, Mom and my, Dad, now I understand their sensitivity—to him.

Dad said the exact thing that you told, Vanessa "*A man will only do what you let him.*" Mom told me not to compromise my relationship with the, Lord, *keep my knees closed* and let the, Lord work in him." Barbara snickered

"You're laughing because you said the same thing to Michelle, well, she listened too. You, guys used to crack us up with some of your expressions."

"Hey..., whatever worked. I don't know where this is going with Gary, if anywhere, Kim."

Pausing to reflect. "I just realized something Kim; each of us met men that didn't fit our original *criteria.* In consideration of our *quest*, we agreed to be open-minded, I guess we were."

"You're right, Bill's white, but Christian and a serious one, I might add. Gary's younger, a Christian with less experience, nonetheless serious. Walter's Christian, but wasn't taking his walk serious, but submitted, yeah." Kim nodded. "I'd say we did alter our criteria, and without compromise.

"Girl..., you got my *imagination* running now, I need to go and journal this conversation. I'm going to let you get back to your break."

"I'm cool." Kim replied. "I'm having Thanksgiving dinner at, Walters parents, are you coming."

"No! My family will be out of town, it's going be my NBA day, it's a double-hitter. I'll talk to you later."

Chapter 15

The night before Thanksgiving, Karen and Michael were enjoying a quiet evening alone. Bill called to inform her that he'd picked his parents up from the airport, and his mother Carol was dying to meet her. Karen assured Bill that it was okay to bring her by.

Spending the day preparing her contributions to take to Bills on Thanksgiving, Karen took some time to freshen up. She slipped into a grey knee length skirt, a red turtleneck sweater and black mules. She was pleased with her reflection in the mirror; she loved the way the skirt contoured her shapely physique.

Experiencing a twinge of anxiety in meeting Bill's parents, she found comfort in Bill's remarks. Bill assured her that his parents weren't the type of in-laws that you fear, in-laws were his exact words. Hearing the doorbell ring, Michael yelled! "I'll get it, Mom." Getting ready to take a trip to the snow with Karen's parents, Michael was in a good mood. "Hi, Michael," Bill said.

"Hi, Come on in, my Mom's in the kitchen."

"Michael, these are my parents, Carol and Howard."

"Nice to meet you." Michael said, extending a handshake.

"The pleasure is ours," they replied.

"We've heard so much about you, Michael; looks like you're coaching a future NBA star, Bill." Howard remarked, referring to his height.

"He definitely has the potential." Bill said smiling, admiring Michael with fatherly aspirations.

Appearing smiling, Karen entered with arms extended for hugs. "Welcome, I'm Karen."

"I'm, Carol and I'm, Howard." Reaching, Howard joined the embrace. Previously seeing a portrait of them, it did them justice. Coming directly from the airport; they both were at ease in their matching grey jogging suits. Carol's short stature and medium cut auburn hair with specks of grey bore a slight resemblance to First Lady Rosalyn Carter. Bill could pass for Howard's younger brother; he'd totally dominated Carol's genes. About two inches shorter than Bill, at age sixty-eight, he remained physically fit. His once blonde hair had turned a silver grey.

In the family room Michael was busy watching a previously taped NBA game, Bill and Howard eagerly joined him. Karen invited Carol into the kitchen for some girl talk.

"How was your flight?"

"Oh, it was fine; we were here before we got comfortable. Something smells delicious," inhaling the aroma.

"I hope they're okay, I'm baking sweet potato and pecan pies."

"Oh my, they're Bill, and Howard's favorite, I love them too. I can't indulge myself as much as I'd like; I'm a diabetic. I'm able to function without the use of insulin, thank God."

"Terrific, that's a blessing."

Admiring Karen's beauty, "Bill talks about you so much, I couldn't wait until tomorrow before meeting you; I hope I'm not imposing too, much."

Removing a pie from the oven, "Mrs. Hansen, please, I'm delighted to have you here. Would you like some tea?"

"That sounds nice, call me Carol, please." Seated at the counter in Karen's kitchen; the men were in the family room, and out of hearing range of their conversation.

"Mmm! Now you're talking," Carol spoke, as Karen placed a hot cup of cinnamon tea and a cinnamon stick in front of her.

"I love that robust flavor from the sticks." Hesitating, with apprehension in her voice, Carol softly asked. "Karen, has Bill ever talked to you about, Sherrie?"

Turning her undivided attention to Carol, "You know, it took a while." Contemplating the thought, she added, "Just recent, as a matter of fact."

Placing a hand over her chest, Carol let loose sighs of relief. "Until he met you, he'd sort of shut down as it related to Sherrie. After meeting you, he began mentioning her name. This is good; it sounds as if the grieving process is ending."

Carol knew that if Bill was talking to Karen about, Sherrie, she was confident that he was okay. He'd taken Sherrie's death extremely hard: at one point they were worried for him. Carol was happy to meet the woman who'd put a smile back into her baby's eyes.

"I encouraged him that it was fine to talk to me about her, he quoted some excerpts from her video; she was something."

Carol laughed, before saying. "Wasn't that something, he's just now embracing them in the manner in which she intended."

"I get the impression that he's experiencing some peace; it was an unselfish act on her part." Karen said, with genuine affections.

"Thank you so much for discussing this with me, Karen. No matter how old your child get, you still worry about their well being."

"No problem, Carol, I can see by the glow in your eyes that you feel better, now."

"You're a doll, exactly as Bill described you, come sit." Carol said, beckoning for Karen to sit beside her.

"Tell me about your business, I think being an event planner is so... exciting." Karen and Carol sat and talked for an hour before being interrupted by Bill. Bill was correct in his assessment of his parents. They were not people that you fear. Carol was a retired HR director and Howard was a retired branch manager of a bank. Excited with meeting Karen, for the first time in three years, they saw a look of genuine happiness on their Son's face.

"Is the kitchen off limits to males?" Bill asked, charging in.

"Of course not!" Karen assured.

"I'm so sorry; I've hogged her all to myself. Let me go and spend some time with Michael before he leaves." Carol voiced.

Taking his Mom's seat, Bill and Karen sat facing the other. Grabbing her hands, their fingers locked; looking like kids getting ready to play ring around the roses. "So, what do you think of them?"

"They're exactly as you described them."

"I told you, you'd no reason to fear them. I can't wait for you to meet my Son on tomorrow; he's excited to meet you, guys."

"Really!"

"Yes! You sound surprised, Karen."

"Well..., you know how kids can be with their parent's new friend, that *loyalty* thing to their, Mom..., you know."

"The operative word here is, *kid*, Tilmon is a man who understands the joy of being in love, and to be needed; that's why he's married. Michael!" Bill recalled. "Michael will be leaving before meeting him tomorrow. Do you mind if I take him to meet Tilmon tonight?"

"Sure, my parents are coming shortly; this will afford them some time to chat with your parents.

"It appears we both have the *green light* from our families." Karen voiced.

"I'm not surprised, when God is in the *center* of a relationship as he is with us, who can be against us; Ronald included. I meant to tell you, he speaks to me now; we even talked after the last game. He offered kudos's to me on my time that I take to mentor the boys."

"For real! As Barbara would say, don't mess with me Bill!"

"Seriously!"

"Ronald isn't a bad person; he's a good Dad too. Actually, he was a good husband, provider; he just felt the need to share himself with others." She laughed.

"I'm not shocked Karen, a woman of your intellect and character had to see his *good points*."

"Oh my, aren't we insightful tonight."

Gazing deep into her eyes, "I guess I'd better let insightfulness run its course. Let's enjoy the holidays with our families, at the beginning of the year, if God's willing; let's consider making some more permanent arrangements."

"Sounds like a plan." Letting go of hands, they stood and embraced with an affectionate hug before joining the others.

The Pines had just sat down to par take in the luscious Thanksgiving meal prepared by Pearlie. Mr. Hines offered a prayer of Thanksgiving.

"Father we have so much to be thankful for today and everyday. Lord we feel so blessed when we see what you've done in our lives, how you kept your hand on our Baby. Lord, we just praise you. We thank you for Kim, the daughter we have always wanted. Thank you for extending your mercy to, Walter by sending a jewel of a woman as, Kim. Thank you for her God fearing parents who raised her to be a Godly woman. We thank you for the food prepared so lovingly by Pearlie. We ask that you bless the food and her, Father. I ask all these things in, Jesus name, Amen!

Feeling acceptance from Pearlie and Arthur, Kim commented. "What a sweet prayer, Mr. Hines. You've made me feel so, special. God's grace has indeed kept me because of the prayers of my, parents, just as you've prayed for Walter; I feel equally blessed to have him. You played a major role in the man he's become."

Kim couldn't confess how she'd almost rejected their Son because he fell short of her ideal dream man.

With an adoring smile, "That's kind of you to say Kim. We tried; Walter was a sweet child growing up." She giggled. "I guess you can say he's a "*Mama's Boy.*" Walter would come into the kitchen and get one of my aprons; he wanted to learn everything he saw me doing."

"Mama!" Walter cried.

"Don't tell her all my secrets." Urging Mrs. Hines to continue, Kim pressed.

"Oh,—do tell Mrs. Hines, this is major."

"He can clean house too, don't allow him to fool you. I'm a retired teacher. Arriving home before me; Walter loved to come home to clean his room and wash the dishes if there were any left from breakfast." Kim took mental notes.

"He didn't do it without expectations mind you; we rewarded him with extra privileges, and increased allowances. No matter the incentive, the results were the same; Walter became a good housekeeper." Glaring at Walter in approval, Kim was grateful to Mrs. Hines.

"Well, thank you, Mrs. Hines." Walter's expression depicted a little boy who'd lost his dog. Seeing Walter's expression, Mrs. Hines defended her actions. "We, girls have to support each other Walter." Pearlie said, as she united with Kim.

"Walter, will you do the honors and carve the meat today, Son."

"Sure, Mama!" Mr. Hines wasn't in the mood for turkey this year. He wanted a duck with lots of cornbread stuffing. This was fine with Pearlie; she wasn't up for preparing a big turkey. To become better acquainted with Kim; they chose to limit the dinner to the four of them.

Standing beside his father at the head of the table, Walter carved the duck; Pearlie carved the roast. Dressed casual, Walter wore a white polo, which highlighted his smooth dark complexion, and black slacks.

In her crisp white and flowered apron, draped over a blue sweater and a grey skirt, Pearlie was reminiscent of a Black Aunt Bea. Passing the platter of duck to Kim, Mr. Hines sat snug in his blue-checkered flannel shirt and jeans.

After cutting the roast, Pearlie brought the remainder of her spread.

"Oh, my goodness, Mrs. Hines, did you prepare all this?" Gazing at the food with eager anticipation, Kim was comfy in her blue jeans and a cream sweater

In addition to the duck and standing rib roast, she'd prepared cornbread stuffing, mashed potatoes, gravy, turnip greens, cornbread muffins, a corn, okra and tomato dish, homemade cranberry sauce, sweet potato pie and German chocolate cake for dessert.

"I would've loved to come and help you."

"Nonsense child, this is nothing," Pausing from cutting the roast. Pearlie laughed.

"Actually, this is half—of what I usually prepare." Walter nodded his head, grinning, as he piled his plate with food.

"She's right, she comes from a huge family, she'd be sick if she didn't get to grace the table with a Thanksgiving meal."

Loving Pearlie's cooking; Arthur commended her. "Pearlie, you got down with this stuffing, girl, it's so moist and spicy; just the way I like it."

"Mmm..., he's right Mrs. Hines; this stuffing is slamming. It's extremely moist, how did you get it that way?"

"Duck is very fat," Pearlie explained. "Therefore, the duck broth gives you a richer, and a more moist consistency."

Accustomed to good cooking by her Mom, Kim was thankful that Pearlie was a first-rate cook also. Not too surprised, since she and Walter had conducted their cook off; Kim was pleasantly impressed with his culinary skills.

Glowing like a little boy, Walter's mouth was shut and filled to the brim with food. With a look that said, *I told you she was a good cook*. Everyone assisted in clearing the table. Arthur loved football, Walter and Kim loved basketball, Pearlie cared for neither. Compromising, they watched one of each.

Always the perfect host, for their enjoyment pleasure during the game, Pearlie wheeled in a cart of cake, pie, coffee, and cider.

In a scolding fashion, Arthur asked. "Walter, I've been watching Kim's hand all day, where is her ring, boy?"

"Okay...," in her most cynical tone, Kim agreed.

"Uh..., well, you know..., I was planning this elaborate evening to present it to her. It appears that everything involving us have occurred in a non-traditional mode, even the proposal."

Glaring at Kim with a cavernous stare, Walter walked over to the couch where she was seated. On bended knee, he removed a black velvet box from his pocket.

"Hold it, hold it right there!" Pearlie ordered, dashing off, she came back with her Camcorder.

"Okay, proceed."

Taking hold of her hand, "Kimberly Denise Montgomery, *will you be my wife and life time friend?"*

Showing a modest smile, "I will! I will! Walter Douglas Hines." She extended her hand to receive the ring.

"My goodness Walter, your generosity is overwhelming, I guess I..." Walter interrupted her with a kiss, a kiss with so much *passion*; it drew the attention of Mr. Hines.

"Pearlie, I think you're gonna need to edit this video to a "*G" rating before* our grand kids can view it."

Bursting into laughter, Pearlie held her focus, "Ain't that the truth?" The comment distracted their moment, Kim prudishly uttered. "Oh, my, I am so sorry, Mr. & Mrs. Hines."

"I'm not, this is the first *real* kiss we've shared since we began dating, I've been so—*cautious."* Walter interjected, with a naughty laugh, after giving Kim a big hug. Blushing, Kim defended with embarrassment. "He's right,—guys, Walter's been a perfect *gentleman with me.* This ring, I guess I should've gone with you." She knew it cost him a small fortune. Kim was the fugal one, but big on investing.

Capturing it all on video, Pearlie and Arthur were a couple of happy parents. Walter would plan an extravagant event later. They'd taken pleasure in a blessed and happy Thanksgiving day; *Norman Rockwell* couldn't have painted a lovelier picture.

Since Barbara's sister and family had gone to Arizona for Thanksgiving, she opted to watch some NBA action. Featuring a double hitter, the Lakers and Kings, Spurs and the Nets were playing. Given the absence of their Mom, and their older brother Albert, who'd moved his family to Missouri; the effort to get together every holiday didn't register high on a priority list anymore.

After Michelle married and moved to Texas, holidays became her favorite time to spend alone. At one point in her career she'd worked every Saturday, so, she looked forward to enjoying sports or having movie marathons on three and four day weekends

She referred to it as her favorite time to spend with *me, myself and I.* To keep her social skills sharpened, she'd host holiday's events or brunches on alternate years.

Learning that she'd be spending the day alone, Gary asked if he could come and watch the games. She was happy to have a guest that loved the game as much as she did, she didn't bother to mention to Gary that there would be no stuffed bird on the table.

In lieu of the traditional turkey dinner, she was preparing pasta with a sauce that would tantalize the salivary glands of the most discriminating taste buds.

Ecstatic; that one of her wishes were finally coming to fruition, she'd finally get the opportunity to relax and enjoy her favorite sport with someone she deemed special. Declaring it to be a good day, for added comfort she piled on more wood to the fireplace; generating a warm and relaxed atmosphere.

Keeping it simple, yet comfortable, she selected a high neckline gold cotton blouse, and a pair of black lounging pants with a cummerbund waist, black mules and knee hi's; her favorite shoes for kicking off later.

Planning to give God a little help; she'd purposely decided to behave with *mischief.* Before Kathy's arrival, she was confident that Gary was interested in her, but because of his despondency; she now lacked assurance. She knew that he enjoyed her company, but so did Karen and Kim.

Keeping company for just shy of a year now, Gary hadn't attempted to kiss her anymore, or mouth anything to suggest that he wanted to take their friendship to the next level. Arriving at three o'clock sharp, she scurried to open the door holding a wooden spoon.

"Hi, Gary! Come on in," she invited, and dashed back to attend to her simmering sauce. Carrying an armful of goodies from *Trader Joes's,* Gary inhaled the aroma of her sauce.

Wearing brown cords, a hunter green polo, brown loafers, and a brown leather jacket, he sniffed, "Whatever I smell, it smells delicious, but it ain't turkey." He commented grinning, while placing the bag on the counter top.

Frowning and turning her head, "you are correct; I wasn't feeling the turkey thing, Gary. We can go by Walters's parents later if you want some stuffing and all the trimmings." Explained in an apologetic tone.

"No! Thank you," displaying a boyish grin. In front of your television set is as far as I want to go, today. Whatever you're preparing will be fine with me."

"My sentiments exactly!" Behaving like an excited kid, with curiosity getting the best of her, she peeked in the bag. "What did you bring?"

"Let's see," reaching in, he removed peanut brittle, caramel popcorn, cashew nuts, pomegranates, and bottled cranberry juice."

"Wow, game snacks, ooh, I love pomegranates. These are big and juicy ones." Pausing to reflect. "I ate these things all the time as a kid, Gary."

"Really! I did, too." Showing a surprise grin.

"I wasn't sure if you'd like them; they can get a little messy."

"Who cares, I have soap and water. I love everything that you brought. The peanut brittle, oh boy," she smiled, "My, Mom used to tear this stuff up, she loved everything with nuts. Oh! I can kiss calorie counting goodbye today." She waved her hand.

After informing Gary of the dinner menu, "Mmm! I love—pasta, please tell me that we're having extra-sour dough bread, BJ?"

"But of course!" Eager with the expectation of a good time, he spoke. "I'm going to go and get the game going; do you need my help with anything before I take off?"

"No! But thanks for asking." Happy as a kid in a candy store, Gary was delighted that BJ had agreed to let him come over. He was prepared to stay home and enjoy the games alone. Having several invites to homes of church members and business associates, today, his focus was basketball; confident that it was BJ's as well, or so he thought.

"I'll join you shortly, Gary." The sauce was simmering; she'd boil the pasta later. Seated on a love seat near the fireplace, Barbara joined Gary in the living room. From the window view, the trees stirred, evidence that the wind blew vigorously. Leaves in shades of orange, yellow, and brown covered the ground; it was a perfect autumn day for inside relaxation.

Taking her favorite seat, she loved to sit on the floor in front of the couch with her back resting against it. Seated closer to the TV, Gary was seated across the room. Kicking off her shoes, in a gesture to make him feel at home; she invited him to do the same. Since both were avid basketball fans, their conversation was limited to comments about the game.

"Who do you want to win?" Gary asked

"The Kings! She answered, with command.

"And you?"

"The Lakers"

"I should've known," she said, tilting her head.

"That's okay; it makes the game more exciting this way." She pointed to the table and remarked. "There's a box of tissues on that table near you; you'll need them when the game is over."

"Yeah, right, in your dreams."

Loving her competitive spirit and game knowledge, he couldn't be more comfortable than if he was with his friend, Tony. "You're correct, BJ; this is going to be fun."

Gary snacked on nuts while BJ wrestled with a pomegranate. After two and a half hours, they'd watched their first game.

Barbara announced. "It's pasta time." Gary joined her at the table; sitting him at the head, she sat on the side closest to him.

In the center of the table was a platter of fettuccini covered with a pasta sauce, of tomatoes, vodka, fresh garlic, chunks of garlic sausage, sprinkled with shaved parmesan cheese. Lettuce, shredded carrots, spinach, tomatoes, and radishes filled a crystal bowl. She'd tossed and mixed the salad with her own special blend of creamy garlic dressing.

To his right was a basket of warm extra sour dough soft bread sticks, brushed with melted butter. Two crystal goblets were filled with sparkling grape cider. The center of the table was decorated with a crystal vase of flowers, and two lighted candles.

With widened nostrils, Gary inhaled, attempting to swallow up the aroma.

"BJ, this looks and smells delicious."

"You said I had to show you that I could cook better than, Michelle, remember." Aiming straight for Gary's heart.

"Oh, Yes! We'll know in a little bit." Asking for seconds of everything proved that he enjoyed the meal; including begging her for the recipe.

Upon completing their dinner, the second game was under-way. Gary retreated to his original spot. After dining sufficiently, for added relaxation he lay stretched on the floor with a pillow. BJ resumed her previous position.

Sliding her photo album across the room to Gary, she figured this would be an appropriate time to show off her cruise photographs.

"Check this out," she said, and continued to view the game. After a few pages, "oh, this is your cruise." BJ remained silent as he proceeded to look. Turning several more pages, he was blissful. "Is this an NBA cruise or something."

"Yep!"

"Aw..., man, you went on one of those cruises. You took pictures with Will Purdue, Jamison of the Warriors, and here's one with Elvin Hays and Alex English, that's Leon Woods; the referee." He ranted.

"You actually got to meet these, guys? How cool was that?"

Taking pleasure in his child like behavior, it was a rare treat for her. She instantly thought of him as a kid, and wondered if he'd ever experienced the excitement that he was now showing.

She finally remarked. "Yeah, it was pretty cool, Gary." Seeing his enthusiasm, she heightens it by tossing him a miniature basketball; filled with autographs of all the players, referees and commentators.

"Wow, you got their autographs, too." Breaking for a moment, he expounded about his work. "You know, I heard about these cruises, and every time I tried to book one; work always became a factor. Woman, I'm impressed; no, I'm jealous!" Relaxing in silence, she gloated in his envy.

Noticing only her in the arrival photo, in a tone filled with hesitation and suspense, he asked. "You went, alone?"

"I did, Gary and it was one of the best decisions I've ever made. Becoming excited from the thought caused her to sit in an up right position. "People were drawn to, me because—I was alone.

Prior to Michelle graduating college, I took her on a cruise. We didn't meet half the people or have half the fun as I did on this one. I'm still in touch with some of them." Suddenly, her voice reduced to a sadden tone. I received an e-mail from the family of one of my friends that she'd passed away. She lost her battle to cancer."

"Aw…, I am so sorry!"

"I met her while waiting in line for an excursion in Cancun. She was alone, and noticed that I was. She walked up to me, and said "*We're going to be partners' today."* In shock, I responded with a surprised, Okay!"

"How neat!" Gary said.

"It was an instantaneous bond, she was traveling with her in-laws; her husband had to work. She had the prettiest green eyes and red hair that was thinning from her radiation treatments."

"The lady in the cabin next to me was a Pastor and single, also. We went shopping together; at dinner time, we'd take turns visiting each other's table. God made sure I was in good company."

"The players, were they friendly, or standoffish?

"No! Not at all, they were in the same dining rooms as everyone else, some dined in their cabins on given days. There were scheduled events to meet with them and play games. There were interview sessions; we were able to ask questions. They were enjoying themselves with their families as well.

"Sounds like you had a ball."

"I did," she voiced with glistening eyes, as if she was reliving the moment. "Traveling alone, I had to pay for double occupancy, but it was worth every penny, Gary. To top it off, the Spurs had just won the *championship*, and to see, Malik Rose, ah man…, I was past excited. I got a photo shot of him, too."

Moving across the room, she searched the album to find Malik's picture. "Let's see…, here, it is."

"Wow! You did, and that's Brent Price and Rick Barry. Is that, Kenny Smith?

"Yeah, Kenny was one of the Host Commentators.

"You went to *Clyde the Glide"* BBQ place, too. Did you meet him; he's one of my favorite?

"Yes! I went, No! I didn't get that lucky." She replied, with a *long face."*

"You know he brought his Cougars to the Coliseum last year?" Gary informed.

"I know; I was there." She nodded. "I went in April also, for his last game before retiring."

"You were there?" He asked in excitement.

"You—know it, *side court*. I did get to meet his *brother and mother;* they were—so friendly and sweet. It was a warm and family type atmosphere; it reminded me of an eatery from my hometown. I piled up on BBQ and desserts to take back to the hotel. The ship docked in Galveston; I went a day early, spent the night in Houston, and decided to seize the moment."

"You're not kidding when you say you enjoy being, alone."

"Yeah..., I guess, the entire trip was adventurous. It forced me to step beyond my comfort zone."

Smiling heavily, and staring into space, "I wanna do it again, alone!" Placing added emphasis on alone. *Hmm...she' certainly not fishing for a cabin buddy.*

"The news of people disappearing from cruise ships didn't scare you?"

"No! Not— at— all, it did heighten my level of awareness." She laughed, before saying, "I didn't believe that I'd be tossed overboard or anything close to that, unless I got into an altercation with someone."

"Oh, I carefully explored the possibilities. Since I'd cruised before, I could definitely see someone disappearing after disembarking at a *Port of Call.* It's the only alternative that's makes any sense, outside of being thrown overboard; where would you go?"

"Huh, you're—right, it ain't too, many choices."

"When on an excursion or shopping, I remained close to people from my ship. Everyone wore NCL nametags. I made it a point to return within two to three hours before we were scheduled to launch."

"You certainly have the right attitude. We only live once; longevity—isn't promised to all of us."

"Yep, we just have to make wise choices, and go for it." She agreed.

Falling asleep in the middle of the third quarter had become part of her ritual; like clockwork, she'd awake just in time to catch the best part, the *fourth quarter*.

Opening her eyes, she became conscious of Gary's presence and glanced across the room. With his faced turned toward her; Gary was out for the kill. She stole a moment to appreciate the allure and his apparent peacefulness. Exhibiting signs of contentment, he quivered his lips. *No drooling Gary, that will not be cute.* To muffle her snickering, she placed her hand over her mouth.

Aware that they were missing the fourth quarter, she knew he'd want her to wake him. Sliding across the room, she gave him a soft jab to his shoulder. Getting no reaction, she chose a more sensitive area. Gently touching his face prompted him to flip his body, causing her to flinch.

With opened eyes, he was stunned to discover that he'd fallen asleep. Sitting up with a disappointed look, "Is it over? Did I miss the game?" Attempting to hide her laughter, she found his actions entertaining. Gary's behavior was identical with someone who'd overslept for work. "No! Only the third quarter, we both fell asleep."

Seeing her snickering, "you're laughing at me, aren't you? I know, I can look pretty foolish—when I wake up sometimes. I guess I was comfortable." She smiled.

"I fell asleep too, Gary," she repeated, in assurance that it was okay.

"It's fine, I'm glad that you felt so relaxed. I understand, it's takes a lot—out of me too when my team gets—*spanked,* like yours did."

Sighing heavily, with an unwilling smile, "oh..., you're brutal, BJ." When the game concluded, she brought out the dessert.

The afternoon had turned into evening. Retreating to the breakfast bar for dessert was her favorite place to chat with the girls. In front of two chairs, she placed a bowl of juicy jumbo strawberries and a dish of melted milk chocolate, with two glasses of bubbling sparkling apple cider, and a dish of chocolate cream mints. Returning from freshening up, Gary was seated at the counter.

"Do you like chocolate dipped strawberries, Gary?"

"Indeed, they're really good if someone feeds them to you." BJ smiled. Bordering on her fantasy that was about to ensue, his remark shocked her. "Hey, you're messing up my fantasy." She whined, somewhat bashfully.

"Oh, do forgive me!" He mocked her.

"Since this is my, *fantasy,* you only get to participate per my instructions."

Blushing, BJ instructed him that he was only to have half of the chocolate mint. Placing the mint to his mouth, she bit her portion from his lips. As their lips slightly touch. "Mmm...! That was sweet." Gary uttered.

"Yeah, it was, just as I imagined." *So why didn't he kiss, me."* Gently dipping a strawberry in chocolate, she placed it in her mouth.

With a surprised look, "Hey, I thought that was for me." He voiced, imitating a spoiled kid. Feeling let down that her little coaxing didn't land her a kiss; she retreated.

The biting of the mint was supposed to initiate a kiss. The strawberries were their dessert to eat individually.

"The strawberries weren't part of the *fantasy,* Gary."

"Is the, *fantasy* over?"

"Yes!" She nodded with certainty and a grin.

"I thought you were seducing, me." Now teasing her, he commented smiling.

"Was it working?" She asked, with coolness, and lifted eyebrows.

"Uh..., why don't you continue and find out. That's the shortest *fantasy* that I've ever experienced."

Amused by his sense of humor. She laughed hilariously, before responding. "Probably, because it wasn't your "*fantasy*."

Picking up another strawberry, she dipped and ate it. Finally, reaching for one, Gary realized it was the only way that he'd get a strawberry. *Hmm..., would she have kissed me, this time?"*

Happy that Gary had humored her in her little "*fantasy*" episode, by his reaction, she was confident that she could've gotten her little kiss if she had initiated it.

Dying to know about him and Kathy, she refrained from asking. Since everything was going so nice and smoothly, the mention of Kathy may have altered the atmosphere. She opted to peek into his future instead.

Savoring a strawberry, "Gary, do you want to have children?" Rendering a sad expression, he motioned his head from side to side. Wondering if she'd asked a sensitive question of him, she was now regretful. In light of her growing attraction to him; she felt her question was timely.

Dipping another strawberry, "I do not want any kids, BJ"

"Really"

"Yes, really," while admiring the strawberry he was about to devour. "Remember, I told you I had to help raise my siblings. That was enough for me. Any fatherly instincts that I may have possessed, I've used them up." He smiled, as he reminisced.

"Girl, I've changed—enough *peed pants, given baths, fixed lunches, helped with homework,* no—thank, you, BJ!"

"Okay—you've convinced, me."

"My, Dad was right there helping me. I love children, BJ. My nieces and nephews, I spoil them to death when they come here."

"You're still young Gary, what if you meet a woman who wants children?"

Letting off a mischief cackle, "I'll introduce her to one of my, friends. In the past, all the women that I've dated wanted to have kids."

"Yeah, that would be considered natural, Gary."

"Yeah, I guess, I find the older that I get, the better my chances are looking. You said you've never been married, BJ, why?" Turning to face him, she looked him squarely in the eyes.

"That's easy! No one ever proposed, for starters."

"No, way!"

"With God as my, witness."

"That's hard to believe, BJ."

"Aw!—you're so kind, here, have a strawberry on me." After drenching it in chocolate, she placed it to his mouth.

"Thanks! I didn't say it to be kind, BJ" He spoke softly, slowly chewing the strawberry.

"Did you desire to be married? I don't mean did you want to marry any of the, guys you dated." He asked softly, with a look of expectancy.

"Thanks for the clarification, but of course I desired to be married, most *women do."*

"The average woman would never admit to a man that she'd never received a proposal, she'd say, *"I was proposed to three or four times, but they were never the right man for me."* Grinning and gesturing with his hands, Gary did a pathetic dramatization of mimicking a woman.

"You're funny, Gary." Falling onto the counter, she laughed at full volume. Lost in her emotions, she slapped him on his knee. "You're so right, Gary; I'm sure I've used that line a few times in the past."

"Trust me; I've heard it more than a few times, BJ." Studying her with an attentive stare, he asked, softly. "So, why the honesty with me, BJ?"

The fact that she'd never been married used to be a tender subject for her. At one point, she'd developed a complex. She felt that something had to be wrong with her; every woman in her inner circle was or had been married.

Through the word of God, She'd gained awareness of her God—given *identity and purpose.* she'd discovered her God given gifts and talents. She no longer desired to be like this person or that person for whatever—reason.

"Why am I being so honest with, you? Um..., that's a good question, Gary." With slightly folded arms, she stood with her back resting against the breakfast bar.

Carefully measuring her words, she spoke with self assuredness. "For starters, it's the truth." She hunched her shoulders, before saying, "I'm comfortable talking to you."

Smiling, while absorbing the thought, she added. "I guess I've come to realize...,"she paused. "That I'm not *defined* by anyone's—*perception* of—me, or my past. Again, through the word of God, I grew to *love, me*."

Holding his stare, she nodded with poise. He smiled and nodded in approval. "You've certainly come to terms with yourself." *She could— careless what I think of her non-proposal.*

"I wasn't always this confident, Gary." She confessed quietly. "The *word* challenged me to be true to, *myself.* I recognized that it wasn't anything wrong with me. Years later, I read Iyanla Vanzant *"In The Meantime,"* which allowed me to put my past relationships in their proper context. The men in my past were my "*mean time men.*" I was not the women for them."

"Maybe they weren't the men for—you."

"Oh..., I'm certain that it was a little of both." She chuckled. "I'm trying to take the *high road*, Gary, they were nice guys."

"Do forgive me, for infringing on your act of diplomacy."

BJ's admission of never receiving a proposal wasn't to imply that she would've accepted one on any *terms.* The truth of the matter, she *had not* received one for whatever reason. She injected it into the conversation for her—*benefit*; it validated the fact that it was no longer an *issue to her.*

"In hind sight, I didn't possess the wisdom needed to pick a husband anyway; so it worked out fine."

"That's interesting, BJ, I guess I've had a few "*meantime* "relationships of my own. Question, now that you know your identity, what's one thing that you'll look for in a man?"

"No fair, Gary, you've had two questions in a row. I've *completely unveiled,* can't a girl at least keep her shoes on."

Tilting over with laughter, "No! You don't need shoes, you're at home." He joked, and laughed. "Okay! She conceded. "Considering our topics, I guess it's appropriate, let me think...Gary. Now that you know my inner most feelings, my answer should make sense to you. Um...I should be able to—see some of *me in him,* does that make sense?" Looking to him with elevated eyebrows, she waited for his response.

With his fist propped under his chin, he leaned on the counter. Stroking his chin with his fingers, still mulling her comment; he sat in an upright position, "Girl, you're making me think, that makes a lot of sense. Let me see if I've got this. I hear you saying, he should possess some of your qualities, principles or characteristics right?

"Basically, Yes! Now, it's my turn," she voiced quickly, halting any attempt for Gary to get in another question. "What's one attribute that you desire in a woman, Gary?"

"Hmm..., you're good, this is hard."

"No, not—hard, perhaps I've had more time to spend on self evaluating than you."

"Okay, she'll have to be *"cling free."*

"You don't want her touching, you?" She asked, softy, with suspense in her tone. "No! Not physically, but, emotionally. I'm sorry," he said, chuckling. "That wasn't a good analogy. Let me share this." Gary shared: To stay on top of his industry he'd frequently attend trade shows and seminars. In previous relationships, the women tended to be too, *clingy*, not wanting him to attend; instead, they preferred him to spend time with them.

"Those events are important to me; I need her to respect my time away from her, my interest." Stated with coolness and a smile.

"Sounds like you need her to have *purpose,* like you."

"Exactly! When I'm with her, I'm all hers." With folded arms, and nodding in approval, BJ smiled. Not recalling having this level of candor ever with a man, this time was different; she felt an extraordinary sense of *liberty and freedom.* She enjoyed being *her,* absent of an agenda to impress.

Returning to his earlier position, his hand rested under his chin, anxious to learn more about her. "Have we made it to question number *twenty*? Gary asked.

"Hold that thought, my cell phone's ringing." She took off in a slow trot. Using the time to reflect over their conversation, he found her self-expressions pleasantly refreshing. Feeling challenged to divulge his volatile side; she'd created an atmosphere for trust, reminiscent of the night that they shared about their Moms. He pondered what he should say. S*he's so honest with me, I should tell her about me and Kathy, when I explain it, she'll understand; she knows Kathy was my first love."* BJ and Gary continued with their version of twenty questions.

Chapter 16

At 9:00 a.m. the morning after Thanksgiving, Karen arrived at Barbara's. Being aware that she's an early riser, she showed up an hour early anxious to give the details of meeting Bill's family. After receiving no answer on the first doorbell ring, she rang it a second time.

"Good morning, Karen."

"Ah..., ah, good morning to you, too, Gary, she managed to release after almost choking. *I guess I am too early after all. Boy, do we have something to talk about."*

"Come on in, I think BJ's in the shower. I have coffee made, would you like some?"

"Yeah! I could really use a cup. I hope it's strong." *Boy, do I need a cup of something.*

Examining the area with a critical eye, she searched to find evidence of what had happened on last evening. *Wow, they must've really taken it to another level, not possible! Maybe he came this morning, No, he's in his socks. Their shoes are scattered in the floor. The pillows are on the floor in front of the fireplace, a bowl of strawberries are all gone but two, only scrapings of melted chocolate."*

Continuing to inspect the area, she desperately sought justification for Gary still being over at morning time. At 10:00, they'd planned to meet to discuss their Thanksgiving day dinner.

Placing a steaming cup of coffee in front of her, Gary asked. "How was your Thanksgiving, Karen?"

"It was better than I could've ever imagined."

"What about, you?"

"Aw, I had a—ball, we watched back-to-back basketball. I have a new basketball buddy. We ate, we laughed, we talked, and we ate again." Bearing signs of contentment, he wore a huge smile. "We didn't have turkey, but it was the best thanksgiving meal that I've had in a long while. Have you had that pasta sauce that she makes?"

"Oh,—yes! What are you making?" Karen asked.

"I volunteered to prepare a Cajun Omelet; I have it down pretty good." Karen noticed the sound of running water had stopped. *He's right, she was in the shower. I am an hour early, hmm...* "Do you like hot and spicy food, Karen?"

"Yes! I love spicy foods." Looking for seasoning, he was opening and closing cabinet doors. "Try that, one." She pointed.

"Thanks! Karen," Slumping his shoulders in relief; "I am completely lost in her kitchen."

"Have no fear, BJ to the rescue. Surprised at seeing Karen, she spoke. "Good morning Karen, you're early!"

"You look bright eyed and bushy tail this morning." Karen noted, flaring an uneasy smile in her direction. Totally oblivious to any implied comments or gestures that Karen was attempting to convey; BJ dismissed her efforts.

"That's great, because I do feel energized; I got a recuperative night of rest; we turned in fairly early." Giving attention to her straight faced expression. *She said, we turned in early; am I dreaming or better yet, sleepwalking."*

At ease in her green army pants, BJ wore a tee shirt and socks. Moving closer to inspect Gary's cooking skills, BJ rested her arm on his shoulder, "Mmm..., Gary, that looks yummy."

"Oh thanks, wait until you taste it." He turned, giving her a *wink,* and a smile.

"Are you finding everything you need, Gary?" She asked, and sat beside Karen.

"Yeah! Thanks to Karen. Would you like a cup of coffee, BJ?"

"No, thank you, I'm good!"

Rubbing and blinking her eyes, Karen needed to ensure that her vision wasn't impaired after witnessing Gary's wink at BJ. Looking from Gary to Barbara, she tried to get a clue of what had happened; regrettably, she remained in suspense.

Showing no signs of awkwardness, *guilt or conviction*, Barbara was busy admiring Gary's culinary skills. Failing to make eye contact with Barbara, Karen gave up.

"Wow, Gary, are those home fried potatoes that I smell?"

"Yes! And wait until you taste them" He bragged. "Careful, a girl could become spoiled." Voiced smiling, in a flirtatious tone.

"With the hospitality that you've shown, anytime." Karen concluded that she'd enough; turning to Barbara, "What in the ..." Gary interrupted her speaking, and announced. "You can tell the others that it will be ready in ten."

"Good morning everyone, Mmm..., something smells awfully good. You didn't have to call me." Walter spoke. "I know Kim's up, I heard her in the shower."

"Wait..., ah, minute." Karen yelled!

"What in the world is going on, here? Did I miss an invite to a *slumber party*?" She screamed, with an array of emotions. After exchanging fleeting looks, they suddenly realized that she was unaware that they'd spent the night. The laughter erupted. Kim appeared, dying of curiosity, "did I miss a joke?"

Attempting to clarify her confusion to Kim, Karen explained. "I get here earlier than I'm expected. Gary answered the door, and told me that Barbara was in the shower. He's in the kitchen preparing breakfast, in his *socks."*

Motioning her head from side to side. "I should've known by Gary's hearty welcome that nothing was going on. He was his usual happy laid-back self. When people are caught while *sneaking*, they generally get nervous and *combative."*

"Girl, you're too, funny." Barbara observed.

"I'm sorry Karen; Kim mentioned that she was going to phone you last evening. I assumed you knew that they were staying the night, I wondered why you were behaving so strange."

"I intended to, I was too tired and sleepy." Kim confessed.

"Karen, I wish I had a camera," Walter said. "When you saw me, and then Kim, Girl, the look on your face, I thought Kim would have to administer CPR to you." He fell over laughing, as everyone joined him.

"You got that right!" Karen agreed. "More to the point, when Gary answered that door; I needed more than that cup of coffee he placed in front of me."

"This was a classic scene, straight from" *Three's Company"* Barbara noted.

"You're right!" Everyone agreed enthusiastically.

"Jack, Chrissie, and Janet were never on the same page.

"I loved that show," Gary remarked, deviating a moment to get in on the fun.

"Let me see if I can clarify this for, you." Barbara offered.

Barbara shared: Around eight-thirty or so, Walter called to ask if he and Kim could drop by; they had something to show her. Walter and Gary were recapping the games; Walter only saw one of the basketball games.

Since Barbara and Gary had taped both games, Walter wanted to see the other one also. Around ten o'clock, p.m. Kim and Barbara became sleepy. Walter and Gary were having such a good time; Kim didn't have the heart to insist that they leave.

Since Gary had the longest commute, she invited everyone to spend the night. Kim bunked in Barbara's room on her futon. Walter slept in the guest room; Gary stayed in Jordyn's room. In appreciation for not having to drive to Pleasanton or Walnut Creek; Gary agreed to make omelets for everyone.

"There, you have it." Barbara concluded.

"Thinking back, I was completely unaware of your suspicions Karen," Gary commented, soberly. "I did notice that you were somewhat sedate, I assumed that you and BJ had communicated before you came. The idea of you thinking that I'd spent the night, alone..., with BJ, in my dreams." He chuckled, this played out better than any *three's company* episode. Well, breakfast is ready, guys."

Gary's omelet was a hit along with his home fried potatoes with green onions, and cheese toast. They ate until their hearts were content, and stomachs stuffed.

Working with only a skeleton crew on a site in the Contra Costa area; Gary needed to leave to check on them. He invited Walter to ride with him. Before doing so, they drove by Bill's to meet his parents, then to Gary's office to check his messages. This afforded the girl's time to continue with their initial plans.

"Oh my, goodness Kim, you got your ring, it's beautiful."Karen screamed with excitement. With all the "*Three's company*" drama earlier, Karen hadn't noticed Kim's ring. Barbara Jean smiled; Kim was clueless that she knew. Upon their arrival last evening, Barbara screamed and admired it in pretense.

"Can you believe it?" Kim said, with a sigh of delight.

"When did you get it?" Karen asked, gazing with admiration, still holding Kim's hand.

"Yesterday, it wasn't planned; Mr. Hines put him on the spot. Walter had it with him; he got down on bended knee. Girl, Mrs. Hines got it all on video; she actually had him to pause while she ran to get her camcorder; is that neat or what?"

"You can show it to your parents and children, that was fast thinking on her part." Karen said. Bending forward giggling, Kim shared. "Girl, Walter laid one of your *hot tub* kisses on me."

"What, where? Karen asked, bursting with excitement.

"On his knee, in front of his parents, I was mortified; he felt justified. Walter said that we'd waited long enough. I'm glad it was in front of his parents and not mine, thank you Jesus."

"I have to agree with my friend, he has denied *his flesh,* for him, that's a miracle." They rolled in laughter, as they huddled on the floor by the fireplace.

"His parents are—fantastic, they were cool with it. I feel as though they're my parents."

"What are Bill's, parents like?" Barbara asked, anxiously waiting to hear the report, lying belly down on the floor, with her hands under her chin.

"They're precious; I felt I was warmly received. They stopped by on their way from the airport the night before. His mother is very personable, like Bill; she loves to touch your hands, or put her arms around your shoulder if she's close to you. His Dad's a character; he's the comic. Bill gets his looks and height from him."

"What about his Son and his wife? Kim asked. "Were they there?"

"Yes, Tilmon and Denise, Sherrie dominated in skin complexion, his features are closer to Bill, but he's more handsome than Bill." She added smiling.

"Denise is a doll; she has those big pretty *blue* eyes, not like Bills of course." Karen said, cheerfully, raising her eyebrows. Talking about opposites attracting, they have a three-year-old daughter named, Marissa, the most darling little girl you ever want to lay eyes on.

"In route to Lake Tahoe, my parents stopped by for Michael. Tilmon's in love with Michael, he said he's the little brother that he never had. Carol and my, Mom have made plans to go Christmas shopping; they made an instant connection. My Dad has two friends now that he can look in the eye while talking."

"Sounds like a match made in heaven to me." Barbara added.

Meeting Bill's parents was the needed ingredient for Karen to put closure to her previous concerns, and objections. She felt their genuine love and acceptance.

"Since you've met his parents and family, how do you see you guys progressing?" Kim asked.

"We've had some serious topics in the past few weeks." Nodding, as she sipped on a cup of tea. "We both have properties and children, therefore, we've definitely discussed estate planning, church preference, schools for Michael, and so forth.

But the other night...," she paused, waving her hand and smiling. "Girl,—he said after the holidays he wants us to discuss, and I'm quoting him, *"more permanent arrangements."* She nodded, with a wide-mouth grin.

"Wow, I guess we don't need a *weatherman* to tell us which way the *wind is blowing*." Kim teased.

"Isn't that something, it gets better; Ronald has settled down. I think he finally found him a new love. Bill said he spoke and talked to him at the last game."

"Well, Praise the Lord! Yelled, Kim and Barbara.

"With respect to our *baseball concept*, this would put me on *second base*, right?" Karen asked.

"Oh, oh, I forgot. He asked my, Mom for my ring size. She was too excited to keep it a secret."

"Oh my, Lord, yes, that would put you on *second base."* Barbara agreed, and "Kim's on *third base*." Hey, we got some prayers of thanksgiving to offer up before you, guys leave here today." Barbara added. They both said a hearty, "Amen!"

Barbara's phone rang; checking the caller I.D., she saw it was Gary and let it went to voicemail.

"It was Gary," she announced.

"So why didn't you answer it ?" Kim questioned, frowning.

" Because we're talking."

"So!" Karen and Kim pressed.

"Excuse me..., let's see what he said...." *"Hi BJ, its three o'clock, I'm just now heading out to the site. I know my crew is gone; but I need to check things for myself. I was tied up with paperwork and messages. I want to thank you for a fun filled Thanksgiving Day. It was so neat watching the games with you.*

I'm envious of your NBA Cruise and Memorabilia, girl. You were the perfect host. It was kind of you to let us stay the night. I guess I should be thanking Walter and Kim for coming by; I know they made it possible.

Oh, I enjoyed your fantasy; it was as refreshing as you. I'll be out of town for few days on business. Talk to you when I return. Take care!"

"You were the perfect host" Barbara mimicked.

"I thought that was considerate of him." Kim protested. Kim liked Gary and believed in her heart that his feelings were mutual for Barbara. Barbara mimicked Gary out of frustration for not satisfying her *fleshly curiosity*.

"It really was considerate of him, I simply can't read him completely," she admitted quietly, from aggravation.

"You just don't feel in control, you don't know where it's going, and it's frustrating for you." Kim interjected.

Jerking her head in Kim's direction, Barbara nodded slowly, while concentrating. She confessed. "You're probably right, thanks, Dr. Phil, so how do I overcome my anxieties, Dr.?" She inquired, in a gracious but mocking tone.

"Tell her, Karen," Kim remarked, laughing. Kim had exhausted all her philosophical views; she threw the ball to Karen. "What are your feelings for him now?" Karen asked, with compassion.

"I have to admit; I've definitely grown to *love, him*." She said, cradling a pillow to her chest. "I love that expression, *"grown to love, him,"* Karen repeated.

"Some years back, I heard Chuck Swindoll say, "*we don't fall in love, we grow in love*." Fall, refers to decreasing in value, to drop, decline."

Karen contemplated the idea. "Um, so it makes more sense to say I fell—out of love than in—love."

"I guess, the word grow means to increase, develop, produce, sprout. My feelings for Gary are definitely not falling or decreasing."

"By the sound of his voice, and the message he left you, I think his feelings are ascending for you as well." Karen concluded.

"I agree," Kim, said.

"Did you pick up on his "*In your dreams comment?*"

"Don't forget the *wink* at breakfast, I saw that. I thought I'd fall off that stool." Karen said.

"It appears you're on, *first base,"* Kim cheered!

"If everyone gets *to third base* as planned, Pastor Rama will have to expand his calendar for *premarital* counseling sessions." Barbara said, jokingly.

"Okay!" They said, in agreement.

"Inquiring minds wants to hear about that, *fantasy* he was referring to in his message." Kim commented, teasing. "Um…I wonder if it'd anything to do with those strawberries and chocolate we polished off last night."

"Well, I guess it's obvious that we didn't do the *nasty,* as some people thought, turning her head away from Karen, smiling.

"Hey…, give me a break; my mind didn't go that far, you guys pulled a fast on me. It proved a picture is worth a thousand words…, but I did think he'd spent the night; that could've been possible; without doing the *nasty*." Karen made her case, grinning.

"Alright…,I would've thought the same thing, we were flirting heavily. That's what I meant when I said I can't read him." Bringing them up to speed, she gave them a play-by-play account of her little "fantasy incident."

"No,—you didn't, Kim remarked, with her hands cupping her mouth, and grinning. Barbara joined in the amusement.

"I certainly did, I thought it was cute, I wouldn't advise it—for you, guys." Barbara admonished, with naughtiness. "I was confident that the outcome would be safe. You know how a good attorney never ask a *question of a witness* unless he knows the *witness response.* I knew my witness; and I knew he'd humor me."

"All that, and no, kiss," Karen stated." With her hands extended outward.

"I know; that's what I mean, I feel extremely comfortable in his company. You would not believe how I poured out my inner most feelings and thoughts to him on last evening. I don't know if it's a *true love connection,* but it's something there, we've definitely become friends."

"That's good, that was the goal, to be friends, first, right? Karen asked. "Exactly!"

"To be fair," BJ nodded. "If I'd kissed him when I bit the mint, he would've kissed me. I didn't want it that way." She moped.

"Girl, you have way more restraint than me." Admitted Karen.

"I would've grabbed the *mint and the lips*, all at the same time." Enjoying a burst of giggles. "Seriously, I like the mint thing; I'll have to remember that on my, *honeymoon.* I'm just having fun. Bill and I have limited ourselves to only a peck on the cheek when we greet and depart. We're not so trusting anymore." She chuckled.

"That makes sense." Barbara agreed. "Now that you've declared your feelings for each other;" she said, dramatizing with her hands and head motion. "It's only natural for you to desire each other." Barbara added.

"What if Gary had embraced you and laid a passionate kiss on you." Karen asked, in suspense.

With widened eyes, Barbara uttered. "Ah..., ah...truthfully, I would've kissed him, that was the agenda, remember. I believe God would've extended the—same grace—for us, as he did for you and Bill." Barbara remarked, with her hands held in the *prayer position, looking upwards*.

"Remember, my safeguards, God knew my intentions were innocent; the girl was just trying to get a *long awaited kiss*."

"That's right," Kim shouted.

"He would've used our phone call as your way of *escape*." She said, laughing hilariously. Right, right, thanks Kim, for the vote of faith and confidence."

"What about you, Kim, how has it been for you and Mr. Hines?" Inquired Karen.

"Child please, same as you, guys. Walter treats me like a *"china doll."* That's not a complaint mind you. He's on a mission to prove to me that he's changed; he's in another zone. I'm not so confident—to think that we couldn't fall to temptation if we place ourselves in a compromising position now. He ain't *walked* on water yet, for now, he's too excited about his relationship with the, Lord. I can't miss what I haven't had."

"That's right, babe..., you just keep thinking that way." Barbara exhorted, poking fun.

"It works out great," Kim added. "He's busy doing his thing. We don't feel the need to be with each other so, it takes the pressure off us desiring to be alone with each other. Outside of work, I'm busy laying the foundation for my preteen girl's ministry."

"Have you come up with a name?"

"No, we've kicked around a few names, *Virgins for Christ,* I'm sure we'll think of something soon. Barbara, I think Gary's respecting the foundation that you set in place the first time he tried to kiss you." Kim reminded.

"I think you're correct, Kim, it has been a year. I don't mean to be shallow and think that a kiss would tell me how he feels; its just a little fleshly *ego* thing. I'd really prefer to hear him say, "*I really miss you when I'm away from you;*" She dramatized, using hand gestures. Or, *"we've been friends now for over a year, how about we take our friendship to another level or something along those lines."*

Barbara was assured that Gary liked her as a person, but his flirtatious remarks were inconsistent with his actions; consequently, giving her mixed signals. She did have reasons for hope.

"You, guys, excuse me for a moment; I need to check my e-mails for some documents." Barbara announced. Checking her dating website e-mail as well, she'd finally heard from Sober after sending her photograph.

"I hope you had a happy Thanksgiving, Zest. After seeing your photograph, I wish we'd posted them in the beginning. I don't mean to complicate your life; however, I would welcome the opportunity to meet with you. I know you're interested in someone else, and it's okay.

My birthday's a week away; I'd be honored if you'd celebrate it with me when I return. One of my favorite places to dine is Scott's Seafood Restaurant in Jack London Square.

We can make it a special occasion since it's the holidays; let's dress for the occasion. I realize that you don't know me, for safety considerations you can meet me there. Please think about it before you respond. I have no expectations in mind, just a night of good food, and entertainment with a dear, friend. Sincerely, Sober P.S. I will try to get a photograph uploaded to send to you before we meet.

Thrilled that Sober obviously found her attractive, with the thought of no *expectations* in mind; she concluded that she'd love to celebrate his birthday with him. Before allowing Kim to protest, she replied. "I *would love to celebrate your birthday with you. You're correct, I'm interested in someone else, but we're only friends. I'm well acquainted with Scott's. You can e-mail me the details. It was good to hear from you. I look forward to meeting you." Zest*

Printing it to show to Karen and Kim, she picked up some Thanksgiving cards that she hadn't opened. "Look, guys, check this out. Oh, Michelle said to say hi. I placed a call to her while checking my e-mails. She said she'll call you later Kim with best wishes." Handing the e-mail to them, she opened the cards while giving them time to read it.

"Seems to me that someone's had a change of heart after seeing your photo. Well, at least we know that he liked you based on your person first." Kim noted.

"I agree," Karen said.

"You—still interested in him?" Kim asked, with cynicism in her tone.

"I like him as a, friend. I love his personality; he's funny, and sensitive, *kinda like Gary*. Like Gary, he calls me, girl. He was so sweet when he responded to one of my *"letters to my husband."* He could've been my, *Mr. Right;* he's going to make some woman a good—*husband.* "

"The *letters*, have you shown any of them to, Gary?" Karen inquired.

"No, way! I didn't want to scare him away. He'll only see them if he's the one. They're written to my future husband. I only sent one to Sober after we agreed that we were going to remain friends. I wanted a man's reaction."

"Will you celebrate his birthday with him?" Kim asked, with a disappointing look. Adamant in expressing her disapproval of Barbara meeting Sober, she felt Barbara needed to wait and exercise a little more faith.

"Ah...yeah! I responded before giving you the opportunity to change my mind. Michelle thought it was a good idea, like you, Kim, she's still holding out for Gary."

"Well, you can do what you please; my money is still on Gary." She commented, and sulked."

"My heart agrees with you guys. Kim, I'm not throwing in the towel with Gary. I see a lot of *me in him*. He embodies everything that I'm looking for in a man. I'm meeting with Sober out of curiosity; to see what could've been; plus, we are *good friends*."

"Just watch..., she'll go to Scotts, and find this *hunk* of a man that she can't resist; she'll be saying "*Gary who*?" Karen teased.

"Ha-ha!" Looking at the cards, she remarked. "Hey guys, they're from Joyce and Vanessa. She must've mailed it before she left for Jersey.

Happy Thanksgiving Barbara, *I want to thank the three of you for being there for me. This time last year, I had a boyfriend who belonged to someone else. I allowed Satan to keep me in bondage by keeping my little secret to myself. I have learned the true meaning of what goes around comes around.*

I Praise God for your Mom, Kim, for admonishing me to apologize to Jo. It was the beginning of God's healing process for me. I still feel bad for what I've done, but there's an underlying feeling of peace, I know it's from God. I want to thank the three of you for reaching out to me and not judging me. I don't know what I would've done if I'd been rejected by Thomas and you guys, too; I'm glad I didn't have to find out. Rom. 6:1, "Shall we continue in sin that grace may abound." That was significant for me, Kim; I didn't know that the scripture existed.

Thank you for introducing me to a wonderful church and Pastor, I look forward to growing in Christ. I'm also going to take a pledge of celibacy along with you, if I stick close to you, I know I can do this. Love, Vanessa

***P.S.** I ran into Thomas last week. He said my apology to Jo challenged him to do some serious self-evaluation regarding his relationship with the, Lord. He said that he stepped down from his leadership roles.*

"Oh my, goodness, is that a testimony or what?" Barbara acknowledged.

"That was so thoughtful of her. I'm sure yours is in your mailboxes."

"I was afraid to approach her," Kim acknowledged. "It took every ounce of strength and courage in me. I didn't get any peace until I confronted her."

"You know, we just can't take the attitude because a person is grown that it's *none of your business;* especially when they've *professed to be—a Christian,* in church, in service, it is our business." Karen expressed.

"It's called showing *"tough love."* The enemy is so crafty, he convinces us that we'll lose them as a friend, or they'll be offended. Consequently, they continue to lead a *defeated—Christian life.*"

"It's also called *restoring a sister or brother that's been over-taken in a fault.* According *to Gal.6:1,"* we're commanded to do what you did, Kim. You did it with love and compassion, and left the results up to God."

"A little too, late for Jo and Thomas, but Vanessa's obedience forced him to look at his, life." Karen observed.

"Right, a double whammy, it's unfortunate," Barbara spoke. Sometimes we'll lose friends. As Christians, we have to accept the alone seasons in life as well. Jo is going to be fine. I received an e-mail from her thanking me for the dating website, and that she'd be visiting Corinth Baptist soon."

"Alright, Jo!" Yelled, Kim.

Vanessa needed a Nathanette to challenge her and stand in the gap with her. Kim's confronting Vanessa produced a positive impact on *three* individuals.

"Let's see what Miss, Joyce is saying."

Dear Barbara,

I can't imagine Thanksgiving coming and going without me expressing to you how much I appreciate you. Over the years you've always included me in your fellowships. I especially thank you for those scriptures on mercy. God has truly transformed me from those scriptures alone.

Jerold and I gave our lives back to, Christ. I was so sad to hear my son tell me he—stopped going to—church because I stopped going. That was devastating for me to hear. When I think of the role that I played in the direction of my child's life, it makes me sick. All day long, I thank him for the mercy he extended to us.

We're both in bible study and Sunday school. Oh, girl, men just don't seem to be a priority right now. I think I'm finally experiencing some of that contentment you mentioned. You know the mind is a powerful thing." That little expression you guys say, "where the mind goes, the body will follow" Well, I've found that to be so true. Since I've gotten back in this—word, as Blanch from the Golden Girls would say, I don't give—into those—urges anymore. ☺ Sincerely, Joyce.

Mystified, they all responded with *"Wow."*

"Let's pray!" Karen suggested, as they joined hands. *"Lord, we thank, you for the grace you've extended to each and every one of us through out this year...*

Exhausted, Barbara needed some alone time with the, Lord. She'd two fun filled days of Thanksgiving. *"Good evening, Father, today was a good day. The past two days have been great. Thank you for, Karen and Kim. Thank you for, Gary; he's so much fun. I can be myself; he seems to appreciate me for it. I don't feel the need try to impress him. Thank you for residing in me. Thank you for loving me as I have learned to love myself. Thank you for blessing Kim with Walter and Karen with Bill. Their coming together is evident that you're still in control.*

I don't know what your will is for Gary, and me. I have grown to love, him; I just don't know how he really feels toward, me. Forgive me for trying to intervene with my little fleshly tricks; and still came up short. You gave him those cute lips; I just wanted to see if they were as sweet as they look, sorry, Lord. Thank you for my friend, Sober. I' m assured that I have two friends. Thank you for the peace and contentment that I feel right now. I ask that you continue to direct me daily. In Jesus name, I pray. Amen!

Chapter 17

It's Friday, Barbara Jean's looking forward to finally meeting with Sober. A year ago, the girls went on their *quest* to find their mates. In spite of their zeal to meet Mr. Right, they never wavered from trusting God for the outcome.

In keeping with their *baseball analogy*, Kim leads out on *third base,* secured with a diamond from Walter. Karen is *tagged at second base,* just waiting for Kim to free up third base as she moves to home plate.

Barbara Jean is confident that she's finally secured a spot on *first base* with Gary. She believed in her heart that he's the man that her *letters* were intended. Gary expressed interest, but had yet to say the words that she needed to hear; the words that would reveal to her that he felt the same. Still haunted by the *ghost of Kathy,* in the meantime, she's getting ready for a birthday celebration with her internet friend Sober.

Tussling with what to wear, she stared at her reflection in the mirror. Dressed in a form-fitted black velvet two-piece formal suit., she's pleased with the fit. Often troubled by her rear end, she'd have *flashbacks* of her childhood. She was forever conscious of her *butt.* Having a well developed physique since the age of ten, she was constantly called "*high booty, big booty, and sway back,* including from little boys, which made it worst. To add fuel to the flame, an older lady in the neighborhood would tease," *Look at them Mae West hips."*

At the age of ten, in the south, she had *no clue* of the existence of a *Mae West.* Because she *detested* the expression and the attention, she refused to inquire. Always voiced in an endearing manner, and with a smiley face, Barbara concluded that it must've been a good thing. Nonetheless, she didn't realize that her compliments to the little girl that she adored had contributed to her developing one *huge complex* of her rear end.

After having to repeat the 3rd grade, or more to the point, in the south it was called " *flunked,"* which earned you the inauspicious title of being called *"dummy."* Now combating two *complexes*, she attempted to rid her self of the excess baggage on her bottom.

When no one was home, Barbara Jean would *literally* bump her butt against the door facing or wall fifty to a hundred times, hoping to reduce it; only to discover that she'd succeeded in getting a bruised rear.

By the time she was in high school, she'd lived down the *dummy* tag. Still puzzled why she'd flunked the 3rd grade, she did recall not liking her *banana-*

eating teacher, she also felt that it was mutual. Since she'd *crossed over,* she hopes that her *destination* was *heaven;* she planned to ask her someday.

Unfortunately, her butt increased with age. After becoming an adult, she discovered that she was in good company with many women, making it less of an issue for her. Because of the *flashback* from her reflection in the mirror, she felt more secure and comfortable in her second choice. She settled on a black satin dress with a column collar, fitted waistline, knee length skirt with a flair tail.

Her phone rang. Disrobing from the velvet skirt, that'd slid to her ankles; she scrambled to answer it.

"Hello!"

"Hey girl, this is Janice. I know it's a late invite, but we're sponsoring our annual Christmas play, would you like to go with me?"

"Sorry! I've got a date this evening, can you—believe it, Janice?" She screamed with excitement, as she lay across the bed swinging her feet.

"Is it with, what's his name?"

"Gary! No, it's with the other guy, the one from the internet."

"Oh, yes! The one that you've never seen."

"Yes, he invited me to celebrate his birthday with him, at Scott's tonight."

"This turned out to be your year after all, girl. I'm not surprised."

"You're not...! Why?" She asked in curiosity, causing her to sit in a straight posture on the bed. "No! You haven't been watching your "pot cook."

"What! My pot cook… oh, you mean that expression, "*watching a pot while it's cooking will never get done*" or something like that."

"Yeah, yeah, it's true, ever since I've known you, you been busy getting a license for this and that or, pursing some career. You never complained about the fact that you didn't have a husband."

"Well..., it wasn't by design, Janice. I kept trying to fit into occupations that conflicted with my *strengths and talents,* or I was trying to go with the flow of the economy. Just because I didn't openly complain, it didn't mean that the desire wasn't there."

"Well, I'm happy for you.

"It was a good year, Janice, I can't complain. It's been especially good for Kim and Karen, too.

"I should've joined you, guys in your *New Millennium Quest* at the beginning of the year. I guess I need to submit to God, and develop that personal relationship with Christ that you guys shared about last year." She expressed, lowering her tone as she reminisced on their topics from last year's brunch.

"Wow," Barbara expressed, "you still remember. Hey, it's never too, late; it'd be a good way to start the New Year."

"Yeah..., I'm going to let you get ready; you've definitely given me reasons to keep *"hope alive."* She laughed.

"Hey, Janice, I have another call coming through."

"Okay, call me, or I'll see you at the brunch, goodbye!"

"Hello!"

"Hi Mom, I wanted to get catch you before you left. Are you excited to meet Sober?"

"Yeah, um..., more curious than excited, I think."

"Well, I'm with Kim, we feel that Gary is the one; did Sober send his photograph as promised?

"No, he didn't, I'll check before leaving. Look, I haven't given up on, Gary, okay—" Barbara assured her.

"I gotta run; my flight leaves Saturday morning. See you then, keep me posted, have fun."

Since she and Sober were only friends, she told her family about the date. Concerned that she was meeting someone that she'd never seen, she consented to letting her brother James drive her. Meeting Sober inside of an upscale restaurant, full of patrons, and...valet parking, she didn't share in their anxiety.

At seven-thirty p.m., Barbara arrived at Scotts. Complete with a brightly lit moon, the evening was gorgeous. The air was stimulating, but not cold. Her silver shawl draped across her shoulders was sufficient for warmth. The ambiance was spectacular for romance, the decorations added to its splendor. Secretly, she wished she was meeting with Gary.

Dressed in festive attire, couples and groups of people were chauffeured in by limo's. Red, black and white were the most fashionable colors. Neighboring restaurants were swamped by the hustle and bustle of eager patrons. Families brought their children to see Santa, and the Gigantic Christmas Tree.

Blaring loudly, the chiming of the Salvation Army Bell infused a sense of *nostalgia*. Across the way, people stormed into Barnes and Nobles to make purchases and enjoy the coffee bar.

A leisure walk along the pier to see the fleet of boats used to be a favorite past time for her. Failing to remember the elaborate décor of the square at Christmas time; she was delighted that she'd made the decision to come.

Greeted by the host as she entered the restaurant, "Good evening, how may I serve you?"

"Yes! Can you direct me to the Turner table, please?" Per Sober, she was told to ask for the Turner table; she'd guessed it was his last name. So caught up in the names of Zest and Sober; they never mentioned their real names.

"One moment please," returning to his post to check the name, she enjoyed the music played by the handsome man on the piano. Returning, the host instructed. "Right this way, please!" Reciprocating his smile, she nodded to the piano player as she walked by. Escorting her to a table in the back, she had a window view of the water and boats.

"What can I get for you; I've been instructed to satisfy your every need."

"A bottle of Perrier water, please."

"Coming, right up."

Since she was early, she sat relaxed as she took pleasure in the sight, and speculated on her *mystery* date. The waiter returned with her water, and handed her an envelope; her anxiety exploded.

Pouring the water into a glass, she gazed at the letter before slowly opening it. Out of curiosity, she looked behind her only to see the waiter and other patrons that were seated nearby. It was addressed, Zest; she knew it was from Sober. *Is he telling me he's late, or better yet, not coming.*

On beautiful white linen stationary, she carefully opened it. Before unfolding the paper, she took a deep sigh to steady her nerve. *Why am I so nervous, I know it's nothing bad? Ah, maybe the relationship with the woman he liked progressed, and he's bringing her, and doesn't know how to tell me. I did tell him I'd love for all of us to get together one day. Oh well, I can deal with that. We're just friend, it can't be any worse than that dreadful—night at Gary's home with Kathy. Stop it! Girl, just open it.*

Dear Zest,

Writing is not one of my strongest points. Oh, I can respond to an e-mail, but things of a personal nature, I fall short. I can only hope that I'm clearly conveying the sentiments of my heart. We both agreed we shared similar life styles, and qualities of life. We both desired to grow in the Lord.

As a people, we've become a society of visual individuals, both male and female. We both found ourselves drawn to someone else, and vision played a major role in that attraction. When you sent me your letter, I immediately printed it for safekeeping, why, I don't know, after all; it was intended for your future husband. I want you to focus on the contents of our e-mails, the friendship that we've established, which was our main objective before any further involvement.

Now, I want you to focus on the friendship and your feelings that you have for the other guy in question. You said you were playing it by ear, because you weren't certain of his feelings for you. Well, you can be assured of my feelings toward you.

When I opened my e-mail, and was able to put a face to the name, Zest, the doubts that I held no longer existed. I concur; God did build a bridge for our paths to cross, just as you stated in the letter. Regarding the other woman, I'll freely discuss her more in detail when I see you; I can only pray that she'll understand.

Sincerely, "Sober"

For clarification purposes, she re-read it. *Is Sober declaring his love for, me? Is he saying that he's my God sent husband? How could that be Lord, you wouldn't do this to me at this late date; would you? I like Sober, but—Lord, its Gary that I love. I feel that he's beginning to care for me. He's shown me such kindness and affection, maybe not love.*

Maybe Kim was right; I shouldn't have accepted—this date. I've never seen Sober. I forgot to check my e-mail; he said he was going to send his photograph. Stop it, girl. I'm not supposed to be looking on the outward anyway, that's what he meant when he said we both were attracted to others.

He's right, it can't be all—about looks. No fair, he only reconsidered me when he saw my photograph. Oh well, he definitely has the upper hand. Lord, I know you work in mysteries ways, but this is too much. For a year now, I've had my sights on Gary, whom I've seen.

No, this Sober is only playing games. He never attempted to meet, me before now. Well, if this is you Lord, he'd better be carrying lots—of confirmations. Let me brace myself, I'm certain I'll know shortly. Placing the letter on the table, in a relaxed position she enjoyed the music, and waited for Sober to arrive.

At eleven o'clock p.m. Sober is dropping off Zest from his birthday celebration. At her door, she turned to him. "This was the best evening that I've spent in my—entire lifetime as an adult. My wildest dream or fantasy could never have captured this moment, and the outcome that we've experienced tonight."

Lowering his head, he looked into her eyes, in a sorrowful but mellow tone, "I feel the exact same way, my only wish is that we'd ex-changed photographs in the beginning; I feel that we've lost so much time." Feeling his attraction for her, the thought made her knees tremble.

"I know, and to think I only sent my photograph after your request." Gently cupping her face with his hand, he planted soft kisses on her cheeks. "This has to be *destiny*, thanks for not being angry that I didn't get my photograph to you in time."

"It's okay, it was a great reveal."

"Goodnight! Sober."

"Goodnight! Zest." Leaning against the door for support; she was still in a state of amazement. Afraid to go to sleep, she feared that the night might have only been a figment of her *wild imagination* come morning. Instead, she called the *girls* for a reality check.

Feeling energized, at seven o'clock a.m. Saturday, she literally *pinched* herself to ensure that she wasn't dreaming. Convinced that the events of last evening were not a dream; she rolled over and looked from the window. *Wow, it's a beautiful morning for a walk at my favorite place.* Glad that she'd put a call in to Michelle, Kim and Karen last night, she didn't expect them to rejoice in her happiness that early in the morning.

At eight-thirty a.m., after offering up some *Thank you, Jesus, Praise the Lord time,* she was headed to the Marina. In route, she reflected on how fast the year had come and gone.

It was a beautiful crisp and clear day, perfect for watching the planes decrease their altitude as they prepare for landing at the nearby Oakland Airport.

Often, the planes would fly so low, they looked as if they were going to land in the Marina. A popular spot for walking and jogging, you'd always find a trail of faithful walkers. Completing her three mile walk; Barbara rushed to claim her favorite secluded bench near the water.

Seated in the middle of the bench, to each side of her, she placed her jacket, cell phone and journal to discourage a potential visitor from sitting. Thankful that she'd completed her shopping for the brunch; she felt relief.

Thrilled that Jackie and Michelle were coming to town; this would be the biggest brunch thus far. Having so much to share, if everyone maintained their *"journal"* as agreed, she just might have her ***Novel;*** the thought gave her goose bumps. Before rushing home to begin preparations, she needed some time to process last evening's events.

Comfortable in her black and white sweats, she tilted her head and rested it on the bench. Lost in her *thoughts*, she reflected on her meeting with *Sober.* She recalled being extremely nervous and confused while waiting for him to arrive...

After reading the letter handed to her from Sober; she attempted to remain calm. From her table she could hear the piano playing softly, the music became conducive to releasing the fretfulness that she was experiencing.

Suddenly, the tune changed, at once, she recognized it. It was the medley to *"At Last."* Taking hold of the table, she was fearful of falling from her chair.

*"Oh no, this is too, much; they're playing my favorite song. Maybe it's a coincidence, No! I mentioned in my letter to my husband that we'd dance to the tune of "**At Last**." He took everything in my letter and used it to his advantage. Oh, he's a clever one, I guess some things never change; men are the same yesterday as today. Well, I've changed and that's all that matters."*

Endeavoring to remain poised, she saw Gary being seated at the table across the way. Seeing her, he walked over. *Hmm..., so he does have someone else.*

What a blow to BJ's ego; she'd just given him high praises while talking to the, *Lord.*

"Hi BJ, it's a pleasure finding you here."

"Hi Gary, it's good seeing you." She forced. Aiming to remain calm, she hoped she looked as cool as she tried to sound. Taking a seat at her table, BJ squirmed in her chair; fearful of Sober's arrival.

"Mind if I sit, and keep you company for a moment?" *What choice are you giving me, Gary; you're already seated.*

With a confused look, she answered. "Sure, what brings you here?" Knowing he was due back the weekend; he was the last person she expected to see.

"I'm meeting a dear, friend." He said. *Uh, he's never mentioned a dear friend to, me."*

"And you?" he asked, with a smile.

"I'm meeting a dear friend, also," she announced, proudly. *A friend that'll be here in a minute, Gary, you're a welcome sight, but your timing is horrible. Sober knows about Gary. Um..., maybe this is a good thing. This may be the vehicle needed to get some reaction or emotions out of Gary.*

"You're looking extremely lovely this evening."

"You're looking pretty sharp yourself, Mr. Russell, in your pinstriped suit." She commented, with coolness.

"Did you have a productive trip?"

"Absolutely, you wouldn't believe the things that I accomplished this week; I'm happy everything came together." Showing signs of nervousness, he nodded. *BJ's behaving indifferent, if I didn't know any better, I'd think she's trying to get rid of me. She's pleasant, but I get a sense that I'm only being tolerated. I'm used to her guarded behavior, but this is different. Stop the complaining Gary; you've had numerous opportunities to come clean with her.*

I should've done it last week after her brave reveal. I knew she'd to be a little curious about Kathy and me. I recall being thankful that she didn't inquire, now I wish she had.

Mr. decision maker uh; well, I'm in a corner now, and I don't have all night to get out of it. If I've been sending her mixed signals, then I have to take responsibility. I have to rely on her being the compassionate and understanding woman that I've come to know. I've got to ease into this."

Positioning himself to a more comfortable posture, he leaned forward with his elbows on the table, and hands clasped. "I know I mentioned it on the voice mail; but I want to reiterate what a good time I had at your place on Thanksgiving." He said quietly, displaying a warm and sincere smile.

"I'm glad; I really enjoyed having you Gary." Knowing Sober could walk up at any moment; she found it difficult to focus in his presence.

"Oh my goodness, Gary will know that this is someone I don't really know. Maybe I should go to the powder room; with a bit of luck, I'll meet him in the lobby. Then I can introduce him as my dear friend, not with my luck. Why did I say that I was meeting a dear friend; he'll know in one second that Sober's someone I'm meeting for the first time. Oh, so be it, I forgot; my game playing days are gone.

Looking directly into her eyes, "are you saving the other half of your *fantasy* for your husband, as you're saving your *letters?"*

With her arms loosely folded, "Did you say, *"letters,"* that I'm saving for my husband?" She asked inquisitively, showing a confused countenance. *My letters to my husband, I never mentioned those letters to Gary, I was afraid that I'd scare him away. There was never an opportunity for him to see them.*

Focusing intently and wearing a serious frown, when she spoke she was calm, but doubtful. "I never mentioned my letters to you, or did I ?"

"Yes, and no, you told, Sober. Looking confused, *Sober,* you know, Sober?"

"Don't you recall e-mailing him, *Zest?"*

Dropping her hands to her side, "What? Are you telling me that you're, Sober? Don't you mess with me, Gary!"

"One in the same," he said, with a warm and proud smile. Bending forward with an in your face look, filled with anger and bafflement in her eyes, "You've been—stringing me along, Gary, pretending to be *two* people?"

Getting a hunch that this wasn't going over as smooth as he'd imagined, he needed to do some damage control, and quick. It was evident that she was hurt and angry; he'd never witnessed this side of her.

In spite of her anger, he was *pleased;* he knew she cared about one of them. Tilting closer, with sincerity in his tone, "BJ, I haven't been stringing you along, you know me better than that. I'm not equipped with my desktop to pull up e-mails to assist me in defending myself, so you're going to have to trust that I'm telling you the truth." In light of her frustration, she felt his earnestness. He'd never responded to her in that tone. It was equal to the voice that she'd heard him use on Connie, the night Kathy arrived.

She knew him well enough to know that game playing wasn't characteristic of him. Lastly, she'd gathered her emotions and thoughts. Looking him directly in the eyes, she'd to invoke her *slogan. "The truth is in the eyes."*

"I believe you Gary, really, I do. *He never mentioned he was corresponding with anyone over the internet."* Showing her sincerity, her lips formed a smile.

Opting to play the *old person card*, "Give me a minute Gary, my mind is in catch-up mode; I'm not as young as you, remember? It takes longer for me to process surprises like this." She said, grinning.

"Here, I did print this." Handing her a copy of the dated e-mail that he'd opened after seeing her photograph; BJ knew she'd sent it to Sober a month ago.

"Okay, I believed you anyway, but, thanks!

"Why were you being seated over there, Gary?" She asked innocently and looking confused.

"Oh, that..., I needed to ease into this, BJ, and with good reasons, girl." He said, showing an edgy smile and look.

"You never mentioned that you were corresponding with anyone from the internet." She cross-examined, while smiling.

"Well..., I guess we're both guilty." She laughed, before saying, *"Touché!"*

"This is so ironic." Gary said. "The very thing that drew me to your profile is the very thing that kept us a part. I loved the idea of not—providing a photograph. Plus the fact, I hate taking pictures. Remember I said I'm a visual kind of guy; I'm guilty. When I responded to Zest, that was my way of getting to know someone based on their character rather than their looks."

"Well, you didn't do so good did, you? You dumped poor Zest." She said, smiling. "Yeah! I dumped her for, you."

"Oh, I forgot; she's me. Gary, when it comes to meeting people I think we're all guilty of being visual to some extent; it was a nice effort on our part. "

He chuckled."This is true, but Zest and Sober did develop a meaningful *friendship*. BJ, I just remembered, when I was leaving for Atlanta, you said you'd share your *writing* with me; you shared them with Sober." Feeling deprived.

"I had my reasons, it's sort of complicated. I intended to let you read my, manuscript."

"Oh, but not your *letters,* I'm jealous, sharing your *letter* definitely would've been a sign."

"A sign, more—like a *proposal* Gary."

Smiling, "you should've followed your heart, so how is your *novel* coming?"

"Actually quite well, I'm counting on the girls from the brunch to give me some more ideas."

"Maybe I can earn a *cameo*—character?"

"How does my *leading man* sound?"

"Aw...you have a sharp imagination woman. Yeah, you definitely possess characteristics of a *writer*, your love for being alone. At one point, I was feeling bad for not enjoying myself as you do, alone. Then I remembered my aunt, who writes short stories, she'd always tell us *"Leave me alone with my imagination and thoughts."*

"Aw, that's cute. Before realizing why I enjoyed being alone, I used to feel guilty. Um..., I' m not sure if I'm a *writer* Gary, but when I'm alone with my thoughts; my imagination do *run—wild."* She voiced, with *modesty and humility.*

"See, that's what I mean. I liked both of you for different reasons." Gary expounded. "I loved the transparency that Zest shared in her letters, her desires, and the things that she longed for in a relationship. She admitted to having flaws; she said God needed to work *on her before he sent—her husband,* I thought, what honesty."

"I admired your frankness on Thanksgiving night when you said you'd never had a *proposal,* and how you'd come to terms with *your identity*. You have a way of," he paused, "bringing *me back to basics.* I didn't say it then, but I was thinking, what courage."

He's aiming straight for my heart. Blushing, "Wow!" Gary never ceased to amaze her. "That's exactly how I felt about you and Sober. He was considerate and understanding. Whatever I shared, he always responded with positive remarks. He didn't play games; he was upfront about his attraction for another woman. (*me*)" Gary smiled and nodded, agreeing she was the other woman.

"And you, aw..., you have this non-threatening approach about you. The girls refer to you as being, *laid back and cool.*" With raised eyebrows, displaying a happy but surprised look. He smiled, "Oh..., really!"

"When I talk to you, you listen, and always with an *attentive posture*. I love it when you behave like and *old man;* It tells me that you know your*—identity.* I appreciated the sincere and humble manner when you spoke of feeling spiritually inadequate."

"I feel like you, Wow! BJ. God had a lot of work to do in me, also. I didn't recognize it until I met you." He said softly, while smiling.

"When I opened your e-mail, and uploaded your photograph; I almost fell from the chair; I was just as astonished as you are now. I got a little jealous for a moment, until I reminded myself that I was Sober, also." He admitted, with a boyish grin.

"To clarify matters, I went and re-read all your e-mails." By her mannerisms, he felt he'd gained BJ's confidence and breathed a sigh of relief. Familiar with her body language, she was being guarded, but in a more serene manner.

Pretending to be relaxed, in fact, BJ was still in a state of disbelief. Her thoughts conveyed it. *Gary has declared his love for me, not Sober. I'm still having difficulty with this. If he's Sober, that means he wrote the letter; Gary is really in love with me after all. Calm down.*

"I need you to clarify some things in your e-mails." Gary remarked. "You said that you were in—doubt regarding the other guy's true feelings for you; the other guy was (me) Gary, correct." He nodded; looking to her for confirmation." Finally acknowledging him, she nodded and said, "that's correct." He let loose a sigh of relief.

"It appears that BJ and Gary weren't communicating too well." She remarked, with absolute certainty and regret. Coming clean, "I'm sure it was entirely my fault." Her firm reprimand tone forced Gary to take ownership of his actions.

"I think I'm going to let you shoulder this one Gary. When you returned from Atlanta, you never mentioned the outcome of you and Kathy." BJ remembered all too well the weeks she endured wondering if he was still in love with Kathy.

Continuing to scold him, "I wasn't hearing anything from you that remotely suggested that you wanted to take our friendship to the next level. I needed you to say something, Gary. Compliment my eyes again," she paused and stuttered while motioning with her hands from being annoyed. "Or something, I felt compelled to guard my feelings by letting you initiate our time spent together."

"You certainly did a good job of guarding yourself." He reacted in protest, with a pouting expression. Observing him closely, for once she saw him as being the *younger* of them. His present state of vulnerability showed evidence of his youthful side.

"You're correct; I wanted to tell you on Thanksgiving when you were being so candid with me. Since I'd admitted that Kathy and I were once—engaged, I figured you'd understand my attempt to see if it was *destiny* for, us. Then, I..., I felt—silly," he paused. "After I discovered that it wasn't. I allowed my emotions and *ego* to get the best of me. Thinking of the past, I was hoping for the chance to recapture it. You and I had recently met; *since we hadn't developed any—ties;*

it became easy for me to travel down *memory lane* with her." Giving him her full attention; she aired an expression of indulgency.

"When I returned, I figured you weren't interested anymore, BJ. After all, I'd openly admitted to you that I still had feelings—for another woman." Lowering his voice, and head, "I thought I did."

Dropping his arms to his side, he expressed aggravation. "I didn't know what you were thinking BJ, you never asked about Kathy; I assumed you cared less." Gary was so absorbed in beating himself up for the Kathy mistake; he hadn't realized how BJ really felt about him.

Repeating past mistakes was the height of her focus. She'd put up a shield, a safeguard that was keeping away the man that she loved. She wished she'd been her *nosy* self early on.

Desiring greatly to know about Kathy, she could never get up the nerve to inquire. *Oooh, he's looking so—handsome.* Dressed for the occasion, he wore a black pinstriped suit, a white shirt with a silver and grey tie.

Gawking, with puppy dog eyes, "I'm not boasting mind you, but I'm a contractor, and you know that. I can fix and build anything that I desire. You never once asked me to *repair* anything for you. Other women drive me crazy, BJ; they use my craft to get up and close—to me. Can you fix this or that for, me? I've had women to literally pry loose cabinet hinges just for me to come over to fix." Laughing uncontrollably, she softly screamed. "Gary, stop it!"

"I kid you not, BJ." Grinning, he added. "That would've been an obvious sign to me, you never came through, girl."

Turning her head, and laughing, "I did—think along those lines Gary, that's why it's so, *funny*. The problem is; I'm not used to playing the *damsel in distress role*. I'd love to, but after *umpteen* years of being alone, when you know that no one's coming home for dinner; you get up and *fix it yourself*. I'd played that *card* Gary, the day that I took you home with me, remember?"

"Nah..., I knew that you wanted and needed—my help that day."

"Well, that type of kindness can be misleading to a woman; particularly if she likes the man. I needed to know that when you were in my presence, that it was because you *desired* to be with me; especially after Kathy."

"I can appreciate that, but after I learned of your position on kissing BJ; and the challenge that my men class was imposing; I couldn't take you in my arms and show you how I felt. You'd pushed me back once." Just as Kim had alluded, Gary was trying to respect BJ's standards, more importantly; he really didn't know how she felt about him.

Laughing, she said. "Wow! Gary, so you guarded yourself from being *rejected,* by not making any more advances toward me?"

"Yep!"

Staring on in disbelief, she smiled. "This is too funny Gary, the strawberries, the chocolate mint, *my fantasy;* we've known each other for a year now. My aim that night was to show you that I was still interested."

Softly tapping her hand on the table, she added. "When I said you could only participate as instructed; that was my *security mechanism* to keep it from getting out of control. When I bit the *mint from your lips,* I was kinda hoping gravity would do the rest. When you didn't respond, I assumed you were no longer interested, so I conceded." Doubling over with laughter, "oh my, Lord, we've got another *Three's company* thang going on here. I was confused."

Turning his head, he admitted. "I don't take rejection well BJ; I was torn, so I did nothing. Leaning forward, with a silly boyish look, "If you'd kissed me, I would've relented." Almost wordless, "I..., kinda figured that... Gary," she voiced, confidently. "I needed it to be initiated by, you." Sounding like kids on a play-ground.

"I sure hope I didn't bruise your ego, as you did mine. I wanted to kiss you so bad, girl. I told you to continue with your *fantasy,* and you started eating the strawberries. You said it was your *fantasy,* so I *respected* it." Being wise in selecting a semi private area, they erupted with laughter. "I need to answer a question for you. Remember you asked how I was doing with my, *abstaining* that night; you were kind, but I knew you were dying... to know, but time was a factor that night."

She nodded, grinning. "Um...hum..."

"It hasn't been easy, and I'm talking about with *Christian women* BJ. You go to their home to watch a movie or some sports with them," he paused, and smiled. "Let's just say I was glad to find you *fully clothed* that day."

"What do you mean?" Looking puzzled, and partially offended. "Wait, back up; I know that didn't sound right. You were completely covered, *no cleavage showing, no splits;* they try to seduce me, BJ." Inside, BJ was cracking up at Gary's attempt to be discreet. "I was teasing you when I asked you if you were *seducing* me, I knew you weren't trying to get me in your *bed.*"

"No!" She voiced rapidly, while turning her head, "just a *kiss.*" She spoke assuredly. *Wow! Thank God he read me correctly.*

"This is all new terrain for me, BJ. I try to do my part and make good choices; Unlike before, I'm mindful of what I watch now, no more *"R" rated movies, with sex scenes.* And you should see me at home BJ," He chuckled softly, while blushing. "I keep the remote in my hand, if I'm watching a movie, and they kiss too long, *change the channel.* I'm serious, men are *visual creatures, it doesn't take much for us.* It wasn't easy finding women of the same *mindset*, BJ."

"Poor Gary," she teased, laughing. BJ was laughing with Gary, and not at him. Having implemented the same practices years ago, she totally *identified*, but was amused by his candor and *innocent spirit.*

"It's called being *equally yoked;* it is hard to find Christians that are willing to submit to becoming *spiritual virgins,* including women. Women are visual too Gary; trust me on that one." *(2 Corth.6"14)*

"You don't have to convince me, I knew you—were embarrassed that night, but your sharing was a source of *encouragement,* and *conviction* for me. God is amazing; meeting you was no accident. He knew that Kathy was coming. If I hadn't met you, I might have, correction; I would've fallen to her advances. Learning how you'd abstained for so long; it became food for thought. If I had slept with Kathy, the results for us would've been the same. I was—tempted."

"Aw, Gary, that was expected, you have a past with her." She cackled, before saying, "I saw her Gary, if I was a man, I would've been tempted too, she's an attractive lady. "

Blushing heavily. "You're being silly, but thanks, I know what you mean. Intimacy confuses the emotions; your openness kept me grounded, woman."

"I'm happy for you, see, you're committed to your walk with the Lord more than you realized, resisting Kathy proved it." BJ jumped up and down on the inside. *Yay! He didn't sleep with her.* Leaning closer to her, "*Question # 20 BJ*, by any chance, do you see any of ***you in, me***?"

"You remembered, of course I do, I see myself in Sober also." She joked. Feeling relieved, he added. "After you told me what you were looking for in a man; I had to ask. I might be stretching it a bit, but if our character and interests could be painted onto a canvas, I think they could be painted with *similar* brushes." He said, smiling and nodding, sounding poetic.

"Oooh..., I like that analogy Gary." She smiled, and nodded, in agreement.

"Can we agree that our feelings are *mutual,* BJ?"

"Without a doubt, so, where do we go from here, Mr. Russell?" Sounding more like, *let's get this show on the road.* He signaled to the waiter. "Remember BJ, I don't take rejection well."

Lifting her shoulders, with her hands extended outward, in a sarcastic tone, and smiling. "So, are you getting ready to kiss me or something?" Smiling and turning his head, he was flattered by her flip remark. The waiter brought Gary a black velvet box, tied with a red ribbon, and a single long stemmed red rose.

"Keep in mind the contents of our e-mails." He reminded. The box was in the shape and size of one that's designed for a necklace or bracelet. Carefully removing the ribbon, she slowly pried it open. Embedded in the center of the box was an engagement ring; it was identical to one that she'd admired while helping Walter pick Kim's.

Lapsing into another state of surprise, she patted her chest area, *"heart be still,"* she mumbled. Knowing that she was in shock; Gary broke the silence. Not giving chance to any—more *Three's Company scenarios,* taking hold of her hand, he stated.

"I'm not making any more assumptions, *will you marry me, BJ*?" Seated quietly, she displayed a timid and inquisitive look on her countenance. Gary's heart appeared to have stopped. Per Gary's instructions to the waiter, the piano player softly played. ***"At Last."***

Both would kill to have a hand held *brain scanner* about now, as they dialogued to their lonesome. "*Oh, my ,Lord, there're playing my song. Lord, you're full of surprises. Wow, I got the man that I love and my friend, all in one." "Is she rejecting me? No! She wouldn't."*

What appeared to be a delay of minutes to Gary, it was only seconds. Finally, speaking. "Is this where I'm *supposed* to say, yes?" He nodded, smiling. *Today BJ! Do I have to get on my knees, or what?*

"Yeah! Yes! I think I will." Taking hold of her hand, he placed the ring on her finger; it fit perfectly with room to grow. *"At Last,"* he faintly, mumbled. Bending over, he kissed her gently on the lips. *Mmm..., yes Lord, his lips are sweet, and he smells so...good!* With her hand stretched outward, she gazed at the ring. "Look like you visited Walter's jeweler."

"Maybe!"

"How did you know my ring size?"

"I took a guess; those shoes you kicked off were a size, *eight*."

"My mules, on Thanksgiving," he nodded.

"At the risk of sounding interrogative, what were the deciding factors that brought you to this conclusion? When did you plan tonight's events, and the ring? Bursting with anticipation.

"Not at all, I planned it all this week. Remember, I said you'd not believe the things that I'd accomplished this week. Well, Thanksgiving night *confirmed* what actually occurred the evening in my home. I'm glad you asked. Promise me you want be offended, it won't sound too *romantic* or anything, but it's the truth. "

"It's okay; I like how the storey ended."

"Great, the minute that I realized you and Zest were the same person, I called you and said I would be out of town, remember? I lied, I'm sorry; I needed time to re-read our e-mails. I felt it was better to say that I was out of town rather than talk to you and *pretend* that I didn't know that you were Zest; I would've been guilty of leading you on."

"I agree; aw..., Gary, your—motives were pure."

"I' m sorry for not telling you about Kathy and me. The night that Kathy arrived, I knew that I was being disobedient. In our men's ministry..." Gary shared that the married men in his men ministry said that no matter the love that they had for their wives, or how *pretty, sexy, skinny, fine, fat, endowed top, bottom, big legs, intelligent* or whatever; that *she alone* could not guarantee them remaining faithful to her.

The key to their faithfulness to their wives is the result of them making Christ their ***Lord***, after making him, Savior.

"That's it in a *nutshell.* I tell you, it took me a while to wrap my mind around that, BJ. They *love* their wives, don't get me wrong, but they were upfront, and sincere with their testimonies; I discovered that they were no different from me regarding the challenges and temptations that I'd faced with Christian women. Eventually, after some serious reasoning, it made sense." *(1Cor.10:13)*

"The expression on your face, BJ, you don't look as if I shared anything newsworthy to you." Gary had no way of knowing that the information that he'd shared had *underscored* and *confirmed* the little *nuggets of wisdom* that Robert had instilled in Kim and her over the years.

In addition, she'd received admonishment from an elderly saint to seek a man who *loved God*, he said it'd been the key to the faithfulness to his wife of *sixty years.*

As Gary listed the physical attributes of a woman's anatomy, images of *beautiful* faithful Christian women began to appear in her mind, whose husbands that were Christians, but had cheated on them; whether it was the *local church*, or on the national scene.

To avoid disclosing too much information regarding close associates, and their marriages; she spoke with carefulness. "Maybe what you shared wasn't news-worthy to me, but it was definitely confirmations. I don't mean to be vague, but in the near future, um..., it'll make a good pillow talk discussion." She nodded.

Gary's facial expression, and smile signified that he realized he'd touched on a sensitive topic to her.

Forever the analytical type, and having been *burned* a few times by women; Gary felt that complete *submission* to God wasn't limited to men only. "From past experience BJ, I'm sorry, but women haven't proven to be *naturally faithful*, not to me anyway."

"No kidding! She teased, aiming to restore some humor back into their conversation. "Continue, I'm hearing you Gary, this is good, I'm taking mental notes, trust me."

"When I made that pledge of *celibacy*, it was to *please* God; it sure wasn't for, *me*." He gave a robust chuckle. "I desire a woman that loves *God first too*, which brings me back to *you.* After you shared your testimony, it became obvious; it'd to be your *love for God* that kept you, c'mon; I know you had *choices,* BJ." Lifting her eye-brows, and smiling, implied agreement.

"So, absent the *romance*, I could've married you that night, and *grew to love* you, confident that I had a *faithful* wife."

The refusal to kiss Gary the night of Kathy's arrival was the *catalyst* Gary used to draw his conclusion that she was the kind of woman that he desired, especially after he'd committed to *celibacy*. Gary knew that if he was going to remain obedient to the, w*ord and his pledge,* he needed someone that *believed* as he did.

"Wow!" Speechless! "That was too, *romantic* Gary. I'm getting *misty*..., just thinking about it. It's called *romance* in the kingdom of God; we're used to Hollywood style romance."

"Whatever it's called, it's the truth, BJ." He nodded.

"It's fair, you're right, *submission* to God should come from the woman as well; we're certainly not *immune* to falling to *temptation, you've* proved that." She'd never attended Gary's church, but she ⌈loved⌋ that *men's ministry*.

Earlier, Gary mentioned being disobedient, deciding to turn the tables; she wanted to enjoy him *blush* for a change. Getting comfortable, she stated. "Looking back Gary, so I guess you should've *rushed* me off to the *justice of the peace* that evening, before giving chance to confuse *your lust* for Kathy, for *love*?" She voiced in a jabbing tone, showing a smiley face.

"Ouch...! I sure hope you brought some band aids girl, you're brutal, but correct." Leaning over, he used his hand to muffle his laughter. Mission accomplished, so outdone by her comment; Gary could only resort to humor.

"Okay, you got me. It's confession time, I knew that I was in trouble the minute you left that night BJ; that's why I stayed in my in-law unit."

"Really!" Smiling broadly, in surprise.

"Yep, their entire stay, I knew I was being *tested,* but I gave way to my, *flesh.*" Motioning his head, he admitted guilt. "Knowing that my Dad was okay, I felt that I needed to help with his recovery efforts, and I figured it was perfect timing to get re-acquainted with Kathy. [Not!] I was a—kid back then, a mature kid, but still a youngster. She's still trying to find her identity; especially after the death of her husband. Later I realized that my emotions were more sympathetic in nature."

Turning his head in disbelief that he'd misread things. "To quote you, I didn't see any of *me in her."* Nodding in agreement, with all smiles, BJ sat with her arms slightly folded; enjoying his candor and feeling blessed that the *wilderness experience of suspense* hadn't been in vain.

Reaching for her hand, he voiced. "To use a school days analogy, my assignment was done *sloppy*, but I did pass the *test* BJ, and God used you to help me." Gary decided to perform a heat check, "After discovering that you were a seasoned Christian, I figured that you were probably holding out for a *preacher* or some sort."

Laughing, somewhat loudly. "Oh..., please! Well, since you were so candid with me, I'll confess." Clearing her throat. "You did *fall short* in the number of year's category Gary, but nothing close to your thinking." Showing a remorseful smile, she spoke with sincerity.

"I had to accept my advice that I gave to you." She said, caressing his hand. "Remember, *sincerity of the heart*, verses *length of time*? The thief on the cross, the first shall be last."

"Yeah! Yeah! He recalled. BJ had to invoke her previous advice to Gary. She'd desired a more *seasoned Christian* relative to years in service, however, she couldn't deny Gary's sincerity in his commitment to God.

"Well, we both appear to have been on one accord in our decision making factors, relative to *abstaining* Gary. I mean..., pledging to allow God to control the *zipper* on your *pants*..., said to me that you're probably serious about your Christian walk." She spoke with a straight face. "The attempt alone spoke to the sincerity of your heart. To me, that *outweighed* number of years in *church attendance* any day." BJ had definitely received a lesson in matters of the heart. Turning his head, *blushing* and *smiling*, his facial expression conveyed his discomfort."

Being receptive, she piled it on. "What? Your *zipper*, well..., it's true!" Heavy with emphasis, and grinning. Knowing that she was embarrassing him; it was payback time for his bombshell of a question at his home.

Smiling, "I'm changing the subject BJ, and yes, I am being forward. Speaking of colognes, you've been *killing me softly* with your *fragrance*, what is it?"

"Aw, you like my *Tresor*' ?" He nodded, unveiling a passionate smile. "It's by *Lancôme,* and Macy's carries it also."

"I'll remember that."

Deciding to tell the second half of her *Aramis* story; revealing it the night at his place could've been perceived as presumptuous. "Remember my, *Aramis* story, Gary?"

He laughed. "How can I forget, some Donny or Ronny, guy. I'd hoped that you like it on me as much as you did him."

Brushing him off with her hand, and laughing. "Oh, stop it; he's insignificant to my story. I told you I wrote it down for safe keeping, well, I didn't mention that I was actually saving it to purchase for my future *husband*." She eased out, bashfully.

Smirking, "so you didn't want to put any ideas in my head, ha. Well, I would never deny you the opportunity of fulfilling your childhood *dream;* my *Aramis* bottle is almost empty; you can make my next purchase."

Giving him a controlled smile, "Cute, Gary! You can tease me; I know that I am a *hopeless romantic,* that's hungry. Let's eat; I'm—starved. "

When leaving the restaurant, "Gary, you had me to ask for the Turner table, who's, Turner."

Grinning, "Ike and Tina?"

Standing in the lobby waiting to retrieve Gary's car, the piano player smiled, and softly played *"At Last,* prompting them to cozy up."

Once outside, BJ requested. "Can we take a walk to see the water and boats?"

"Sure!" This was a favorite and familiar spot for her. Her girl friend docked her boat, *Brown Sugar* there. Holding hands, they strolled along the waterfront. The air was cold, but tolerable.

After a short distance of walking in utter silence, they stopped to enjoy the beauty of the moonlight that reflected on the water.

Dreaming of this chance, Gary's hands enveloped her face; imparting the kiss that he wanted to give to her when she said yes to his *proposal.*

Kissing her on one cheek, he spoke. "This is from me," kissing her on the other one, "this is from Sober."

Whispering, "*I love you BJ;* I've loved you for a long time."

Shocked by his expression, she was voiceless. *Oh my, goodness, I just realized, I'm on third base with Kim. Gary's declaring his love for me, and I'm thinking about a baseball analogy.*

Continuing to plant soft kisses on her lips and cheeks, after harnessing her emotions and thoughts, she reciprocated his sentiment. "I've *loved you longer,*" as tears surged down her cheeks.

Noticing the tears, he gave her a bear *hug,* in his attempt to comfort.

"Aw..., I'm sorry that I kept you in suspense for so, long. I should get you home out of the cold..."

Chapter 18

Lost in her reflections of last evening events, BJ sat with her head resting on a bench. Smiling, with her eyes shut, she'd forgotten that she was sitting on a park bench; she'd probably been an amusing site for passing walkers and joggers.

Disturbing her reflecting, her cell phone rang. Fumbling to locate it from the bench, she yelled! "Hello! Hello!"

"Girl, where are you, and what is wrong…with you? Karen asked, referring to her deafening greeting. "Oh…, it's you," she said, in a relieved tone. "I'm sitting in my favorite spot at the Marina, *day dreaming."*

"I should've known; I had to make sure our conversation last night wasn't a dream. So, Sober is really Gary?"

"Yep! I'm still trying to process the reality of it myself, that's why I was so distracted by the phone ringing, I was revisiting the moment."

"How could you not have known that Sober was also, Gary; I mean, how many general contractor's did you meet?

"You're forgetting, Miss *"smarty-pants,"* we didn't disclose our—occupations; remember. But you have a point, there were clues that I missed."

"Oh! That's right; you purposely didn't exchange career information, my bad!"

"Sober said he'd be out of the area for six months or longer, only coming home on some weekends. Gary, who's Sober, explained that it was to keep Zest from asking to meet him. He said he'd previously dated women from the internet; and they were always too eager to meet.

He said he only desired someone to correspond with at the time; he'd met me and wanted to see how things would go with us before committing to anyone else."

"I see, didn't he mention his Dad's stroke? And his visit to see him? And what about Kathy's surprise visit?"

"Keep in mind, Sober supposedly was out of the area anyway; we were not seeing each other, therefore, there was no need for him to announce to me that he was leaving to go to Atlanta. He did casually mention in an e-mail that he was visiting his family in the south and that his Dad had been ill, but it was much later from the time he actually became ill. As for Kathy, uh," she laughed "Child, please! He was too ashamed to share that mistake with anyone; I had to drag it from him."

"You guys were *destined* to be together, think about it; you developed a friendship over the internet with Sober; you connected on a physical level when you met Gary, then you and Gary developed a friendship."

"Now you got it," Barbara replied.

"I have to let you read the letter he wrote, it was so sweet. He alluded to the sentiments that established the foundation for the friendship with Sober, then he correlated the feelings I had for him. I guess this is, *destiny.* Hang on," Barbara said.

"Hello!"

"Now do you believe me, I knew Gary was the one." Kim screamed, with excitement.

"I'm sorry Kim, you were right, your *faith* never wavered. Oh, I forgot, I have Karen holding. Kim, hang up. I'll call you, back."

"Hello!" Kim said.

"Hold on, let me bring on Karen.

"Karen, are you, there?"

"Karen's in the house. Kim, can you believe this?"

"Yes! I knew Gary was the one. I had no clue that Gary was Sober," Kim stated.

"Gary is just as excited as you." He called Walter last evening after he got home."

"You're kidding!" Barbara said.

"Walter called me this morning. You're not going to believe this. Gary confided in Walter—and Bill after seeing your photograph that morning after Thanksgiving."

"Are you serious, they knew?" BJ asked.

"I kid you not, men aren't like us, we can't hold water."

"Let me play it out for you." Kim informed her.

"According to Walter, Gary was thrilled by the fact that you and *Zest were one in the same.*

"He did go to the jobsite as he mentioned; he invited Walter to ride with him. They sort of bonded watching basketball. Anyway, Walter asked if he could tell the good news to Bill, and of course Gary said, yes."

"Wow," Karen remarked. "They're becoming friends. Pastor Rama invited Walter to the men's retreat, and he invited Gary and Bill."

"How neat, well, I can certainly understand his need to tell someone. I wanted to run and call you guys while we were still at Scott's."

"Walter was at the office with him, before going to the jobsite. I had a hard time comprehending it at first, but he explained it in detail. Apparently, Gary printed all your emails, that's why he was late going. Walter said Gary had to be sure that he was the *other guy.* Bill and Walter assured him that they'd never seen you in the company of another man; so he became convinced."

"That explains his boldness; he was definitely prepared, ring and all."

"Right on Gary, "Kim said, "You've wasted enough time."

"Isn't that the truth, you're *on third base* with Kim." Karen screamed.

"You did pass me up!"

"I am not surprised." Kim remarked, boasting. "Michelle believed it too."

"Speak of the devil." Barbara said, jokingly. "Here comes Gary now, in his jeans and Raiders sweat shirt. I bet you can't guess who's on the phone." She yelled to Gary.

"Kim and Karen. Ah, goodness, you know." He smiled, and made an about face to leave.

"I was going to tell you that I'd solicited the help of Walter and Bill, I'm busted." He said, laughing."

"Good morning, Sober." Yelled, Kim and Karen.

"Hi! Ladies, do I need to give you more time and privacy."

"No! I'm signing off guys, come by later to help with the *brunch* details." Moving her jacket, she made room for him to join her on the bench.

"I knew I'd find you, here." Bending, he kissed her on the cheek.

"All night, I've been pressing the rewind button in my mind trying to find the missed clues with, you and Sober."

"You, too!"

"I did find two." BJ recalled.

"The voicemail telling me about your place of retreat in the Valley, and Connie calling it a *bed & breakfast."*

"Oh, yeah, that was after the Christmas party."

"Then, a few weeks ago, in Sober's email, he said he needed some rest, and he was going to *retreat*, plus, he referred to me as, girl."

"You're right, I did mention that in my e-mail. I missed a big clue; your writing. Zest said she wrote *poems,* you said you were writing a *novel*, it threw me."

Gary's cell phone rang. "Someone wants to talk to, you." He handed her the phone. "Hello!"

"Hi Barbara, this is Connie." Turning to him, she flashed a surprised and suspicious look.

"Hi Connie!" Spoken cheerfully, in suspense.

"I want to extend best wishes to you, and I want to apologize for any discomfort that I may have imposed upon you. I'm the baby in the family, and I can still be a *brat* sometimes."

"From one brat to another, I'm the baby in the family also. I understand, no offense taken. You were only trying to help the *old man* get *hitched."* Glancing at Gary, BJ *winked*. "I appreciate and accept your apology."

"I'll be listening for the details."

"Great! I look forward to sharing them with, you."

"Goodbye, Connie! You didn't beat her up too, bad did you?"

"The night after you left, yes! Mam! No, this was her idea. She's a brat, but she's my baby sister, I spoiled her."

Connie was regretful of her actions to Barbara. She realized that she was out of line in bringing Kathy without her brother's consent. To prove her actions weren't personally motivated toward BJ; she felt the need to apologize for her conduct.

"Having the piano guy play ***"At Last,"*** that was over the top Gary; you really did read my letter."

"For sure, please tell me that you don't want a long engagement, BJ."

"Not a chance, we'll need to factor in some time for premarital counseling."

"Oh, that's right; I don't foresee any problems, do you? He asked, innocently. "No, none that I can think of, we've been obedient to one of the *main requirements."*

"What's that? Oh, remaining *celibate*. "Right, we're *"serious"* about our relationship with the, Lord. I did say serious, and not committed," she added, poking fun.

"I got that, thanks. I think I can afford to add another dependent to my payroll," he joked.

"I think we'll be fine once we implement some dating rules," BJ stated, smiling.

"Ah, yeah, like your buddies, especially if we plan on remaining *celibate* until we're married; unless you're ready to *break the pledge*," he said, with a mischievous laugh. "In our dreams," she remarked, smiling.

"Oooh..., she's not a prude after all." He ragged.

"Ah..., " startled, "that's absurd, Gary." Giving him a jab to his side. "Ouch! Sorry! On a serious note, you can drop your barriers now BJ, no more holding back." He voiced, exhibiting a serious expression.

"Um, hum..., well, on that note. I know you said you're adamant about not wanting any kids, but you're only forty, people change their minds regarding such matters all the time."

Gary's age often eluded BJ because of his elder demeanor, even so, he was young enough to desire children later in life. She was open to meeting a younger man; however, it wasn't her *only* preference. She wanted Gary to give some serious consideration to the issue; she was certain that it'd come up in counseling. Still producing eggs, yet, at her age; a baby was not an option.

"You're right; a person can change their mind. In my line of work I can't keep changing my mind, nor can I afford hasty decision making. I try to apply the same principles to my personal life when applicable. Now that you're going to be my wife, I guess I need to go into more detail about me."

"Having reared Michelle, I figured that you'd become content with an empty *nest*"

"You figured correctly." Facing her, he said. "I'm forty, and I think I know what I want. Everyone tells me that I should marry and have kids, "*you're good daddy material Gary.* I don't agree." *Oh no! What is he going to say? Is he a transvestite, whatever it is; he's serious, stop being, silly?*

Holding her hand, and squeezing it to express emphasis, "This daddy had his *material—cut.*" Shocked, she looked with a happy but uncertain expression. "Yes! BJ, I had *a vasectomy,* at the tender age of *thirty-eight.*" Glowing, she drew a deep sigh.

"Don't mess with me, Gary; you're—serious, aren't you?"

"Seriously! I knew I didn't have to; I could've played the fantasy game like everyone else. Get married and think that *love would change my mind*; my wife would end up rearing the kids, alone, with me right there in the home. I've seen too many of my friends marry with *false expectations,* for whatever reasons, and the kids suffer. Is that convincing enough for you BJ?"

"I think..., so." She finally uttered, after almost swallowing her tongue. Noticing her tense facial expression, "What did you think I was going to say?"

Feeling busted and silly, she unleashed an edgy laugh, "Um...something along those lines. Talking about me coming to terms, you've done some careful evaluations of your own Mr. Russell. How insightful of you; that was purely an unselfish act." As a signal of approval, she brushed her hand across his back.

"I'm sorry for not telling with you earlier BJ, your concerns were legitimate. I wanted to tell you Thanksgiving Day."

"That infamous day." She interrupted. "Yeah, right," he paused. "That information was being reserved for my wife; now you have to marry me; only my Dad know."

"I understand Gary, your discretion is well founded, what was your Dad's reaction?"

"Actually, he had a lot to say. He said that it was the best decision that I could've made."

"Really, why?"

"Yeah! I was stunned too, he said that I'd been dealt a *heavy hand* as a kid, but it was God's will, and beyond our control. He told me that he was proud of me, and my, Mom would be too. He feels that I've already proved that I'm a man in the manner that I've established my business. To my surprise, he said I didn't need kids to *validate—my manhood*."

"He's right, that had to be encouraging for you." With his arms resting on his legs, he stared at the ground. "It was, it really, was. The *"Russell's,"* huh..., we believe in large—families." He smiled. "And if you knew my Dad, he's borderline *macho*." Grinning. "He advised me to make sure that the woman I choose feel the exact same way."

"Aw..., your Dad is a wise and thoughtful man; I can't wait to meet him. He appreciated your sacrifice as a child."

"He can't wait to meet, you. He's a good man, losing *our Mom* so young; he did a good job with us. Life can be short for some of us, look at my Mom BJ; she was only *thirty-eight*. I was referring to her when I said longevity is not promised to—everyone; we have to seize the opportunity, as you did with your cruise." BJ nodded, with a look of compassion and understanding.

"I observed how he and my stepmother enjoy themselves, now; they travel, they come and go as they please. I choose that type of freedom in life *now*."

Shifting his posture to sitting upright. "I can't imagine loving you any more *because of kids*, BJ. We're *complete together*, children are a creation of their parents and not vice versa."

BJ smiled, in deep concentration, "That's good Gary, a thought provoking perspective for sure. If any of those fatherly instincts surface, Jordyn will be around to satisfy them for you."

Laughing, "I'm counting on it; my brother Tre' and his wife are coming and bringing their kids for Christmas."

"Speaking of families," BJ said. "Are you ready to meet mine? You're invited to Christmas dinner at my Sister's, and your brother. I'm glad you find humor in being teased Gary; talking about *"three's company"* episodes, meeting them will be a pleasant surprise version of *"Guess who's coming to dinner."*

"I'm ready, *bring em' on*. They can't be any—worse than my sister—and friends when it comes to *match making.* I feel *society* puts too..., much pressure on people. " He voiced, in a passionate and restless tone.

"Especially when it comes to *marriage*. It's not right BJ, it's not gonna happen for every one; obviously God didn't intend for it. People shouldn't be scrutinized."

"I agree, you'll get no arguments from me."

"BJ, I can't began to tell you how tired I get of people trying to hook me up. Their logic is that I'm over the age to be married according to their timetable; I'm sure you've had your portion of friends, and family interrogations."

"Yes,—Lord, at least they don't call women, *Old Maids* anymore." She said, giggling.

"Old Maid," he smiled, *"contre."* Remember we talked about having *purpose*."

Nodding, "um..., hum."

"That's you, I would never have to worry about you *clinging* to me. I mean, you have your friends, family, church family and ministry; you love sports, your career, you travel, and you *write.* When I met you, you were preparing to take on a building project; that excited me. You weren't sitting around waiting on *me*, nor *Sober*." He said, laughing loudly.

Amazed by Gary's insightfulness, she knew it was something special about him, he was unveiling before her very eyes; and she was enjoying the *formation.*

Speaking in an unusual soft spoken tone, it was apparent that Gary had done some careful assessments of his past and future life. Mesmerized by his openness, her facial expression said, *"tell me, more."*

"I honestly believe that if our paths had never *crossed,* you would've been just fine, BJ."

Moments earlier, she'd rested her head on his shoulder, sitting up; with a look of disbelief, she gazed into his face. Her thoughts were; *I can't believe that I've found someone who's captured and connected with the true essence of my identity, he does know me."*

Finally speaking "Gary, you're extraordinary, you really have been listening to me. You're correct on every consideration. Now that our paths have crossed; I know that I never want to be without you."

"The sentiments are *mutual*!" Pulling her close, he cradled her head on his chest and whispered. "To quote your letter *"God had to build a bridge for our paths to cross."*

Barbara Jean Keller just arrived home from early morning worship services. Putting on the final touches for her 3rd consecutive *Christmas Sunday Brunch;* she stole a second to admire her engagement ring. With her hand extended, she reflected on Christmas past. No more dreams of *next year Barbara Jean, next year.*

Finally having the opportunity to include a member of the opposite sex; this year's brunch would be different, and she's ecstatic. The girls attended early morning services, accompanied by Jackie and Michelle. Robert and Mitchell, Michelle's husband attended eleven o'clock services at Walter's church; joined by Bill and Gary.

The brunch menu would be closer to a continental breakfast, consisting of fresh baked cinnamon rolls, fresh fruit, coffee, tea, and juice. After the conclusion of worship services at St. Hebrews; the men will take to the golf course. Joining them later for an early dinner; this will provide space for the girl's to share their journals, and play catch up from last year.

Busy into the night; Barbara and Michelle were like *super-woman*, working their magic, only to have it defused by *kryptonite* come morning; in the form of *fatigue*. Stealing a well-deserved rest, Michelle napped while Barbara turned up the heat on the crock-pots for the red beans and collard greens.

Comfy in her jeans, tee shirt and socks; Barbara Jean diced the sausages, chicken, peppers, and onions in preparation for her *Cajun* theme dinner of seafood gumbo, jambalaya, red beans and rice, crab cakes, whole fried catfish, spicy collard greens, and hush puppies. To satisfy the sweet craving, she tied it off with Michelle's famous four-layer pineapple cream cheese coconut cake, cinnamon swirled bread pudding, served with heavy cream and vanilla ice cream.

Now that everything met her approval, she dialogued and prayed to the Lord. *Well, Lord as always, you had your agenda for our lives; we were busy looking to the internet. Thank you for guiding and directing our path, and testing our faithfulness, and obedience to you. Give us a new and fresh anointing of your grace that you may continue to be glorified by our behavior. In Jesus name, I pray, Amen!*

The doorbell rang, as always, Karen was the first to arrive. "Merry Christmas, *Mrs. Hansen,* I love that red sweater dress on you." Barbara teased, and complimented. "Merry Christmas to you, *Mrs. Russell*; it turned out to be *our year* after all." Karen zealously commented, in a thankful tone. Responding in complete agreement, Barbara spoke, "***Okay!... At Last!...***"

~ Discussion Questions ~

1. When the girls shared their Quest Itinerary during the brunch. How open-minded are you willing to become to find your mate.
   A. Will you date a younger man? If so, how young?
   B. Will you date outside of your race? Yes, or No. Discuss your answer.

2. As Joyce stated, should we be looking further than the church for our mates? A. Why or Why not? B. What are some options?

3. When singles come together in support, fellowship, church worship, as Karen, Kim and Barbara, can we find peace and avoid sexual frustration? Yes or No,

4. What are your views on marrying a man with a lower income? What ratios would you except.
   A. 50-50, 70-30, 30-70, 60-40, make up your own
   B. If yes, what other factors would he need for a balance.

5. When was the last time you shared where God delivered you, in order to encourage someone?
6. Since Bill was genuine in his walk the, Lord, should that have lessened some of Karen's concerns for him as a potential father to her Son.

7. Bill said that he was convinced that he was in the will of God with Karen. He withheld the knowledge of his interracial marriage because he didn't want her to make decisions based on them, and the obstacles he'd overcame with Sherrie his deceased wife.
   A. Was that a fair assessment from Bill?

8. The *hot tub scene:* The girls analyzed it their "heart to heart" session.
   A. Should the *kiss* have been avoided? How? Why? Make it personal for you.

9. After Bill and Karen identified and declared their feelings for each other; they strategically put a plan in motion to safeguard them from future temptations.
   A. If you're a single Christian couple, are you safeguarding your relationship as the characters portrayed in "At Last?" B. Do you believe that it's necessary in order to remain obedient to scripture? Discuss

10. From a Christian perspective, should BJ have kissed Gary at his place, the night of Kathy's arrival? It was just a kiss. Yes or No

11. BJ was somewhat embarrassed in revealing her years of celibacy to Gary; he later attributed her to keeping him grounded. Being a Christian, should she have been embarrassed?

12. Barbara Jean broke the curse of sex and pregnancy before marriage and higher education with her daughter.

A. What curse, if there be any are you striving to break with your children, or yourself?

13. If you're a seasoned Christian like BJ, would a Gary interest you, since he'd only been back in church attendance for eight months? Discuss!

A. Should length of time in service be a factor?

B. With respect to being "equally yoked" what factors should be taken into consideration.

C. Did she compromise her standards and principles?

14. Because of BJ's sixteen years of celibacy, signifying faithfulness to God. Gary said that he could've married her and grew to love her.

A. Lacking in romance, as we're accustomed, what were your thoughts?

15. Zest, (BJ) shared in her "love letter" to her future husband that God had more work to do on her before sending her mate.

A. What about you, are you ready? On the other hand, are like "Zest" and have identified that you have issues, and are allowing God to prepare you for your mate. **Thought question.**

16. Shouldn't it be considered a realistic expectation that Kim was still a *virgin* at age twenty-eight? Why or Why not? What does the scripture say?

17. With respect to the vast amount of Christians that attend church on a given Sunday, why aren't there more ***young adult virgins.*** Where are we missing the mark? Discuss!

18. Is Walter considered typical in our churches today?

A. Were the Christian women an obstacle for Walter?

B. Did he own all the responsibility to resist?

19. Kim prayed for a husband "just like he father;" Her prayer was answered accordingly.

A. Should we be careful how we pray?

B. How can we be sure if we have "diamond in the rough?" like Walter?

C. Did Kim compromise her standards by choosing Walter?

20. Walter's apology to the church was ***unprecedented*** to say the least.

A. How do you think God would honor our outward confessions and repentance today, if we shared like, Walter? Discuss!

B. What impact would it have on other Christians walk with the, Lord?

C. Do you think that it'd serve as a stumbling block or a source of strength?

21. Kim said that God made her the anchor in the relationship with Walter.

A. Are you secure enough in your commitment to Christ to set the course in a relationship for a man that is less committed?

22. Vanessa and Thomas were in church every Sunday, why was she able to commit this act and have such a cavalier attitude regarding Mrs. Martin?

A. As a sister in Christ, why did she experience such a false sense of happiness, when she knew that she was causing pain to a sister in Christ? Did she care?

23. When Vanessa discovered Thomas had cheated on her, only then did she realize the *hurt and pain* that she'd caused his wife.

A. Was she blinded by low self-esteem, were her motives purely selfish? Was she a *victim or a villain?*

24. As sisters in Christ, can we learn to "*restore in love,*" as Kim and the girls. Where should our loyalty lie?

25. Jackie Montgomery believed that "true healing" occurs when we apologize to the person we've harmed or wronged. A. What do you think> B. What does scripture say?

26. What *attracts* Christian women to leaders in the church, such as pastors, ministers, deacons, elders? A. What do we really, really want? Discuss in dept.

Disclaimer: *BJ's mint fantasy was strictly for entertaining purposes guys, as Karen stated; save it for your honeymoon.* ☺

~ *Model Prayers for Characters* ~

Dear God, ***Model Prayer for Kim***

I identify with the character Kim, depicted in this novel. Lord, Jesus thank you for the encouragement in knowing that I am not alone in my desire to remain a virgin until marriage. Thank you Jesus for my parents, and a church curriculum that serves as a constant motivator to keep me on the right path.

Give me the courage not to be ashamed, but to be a beacon of light for young girls and other women which desire to re-commit their lives to Christ in the form of abstaining. Give me the wisdom and discernment to hear your voice as I make my choice to choose my husband. Keep me mindful of your word. In Jesus name, I pray, Amen! **Ps 119: 11, 1 Cor 10:13, Phil 4:13**

Dear God, ***Model Prayer for Karen***

Thank you for the character of Karen. I so believed that I would have been re-married after all of these years. I praise you for keeping me near the cross. Thank you for the grace that you've extended to me in rearing my children. Thank for the extended family of other sisters and couples in Christ who have been there for me.

Unlike Karen, I have yet to identify with my purpose in your kingdom. Speak to me Father as I prepare to seek your will, and purpose for my life. Magnify the gifts and talents that you deposited in me at birth. I invite your mind to continue to dwell in me. Restore unto me joy, and contentment daily, as I meet with you in our secret place. In Jesus name I pray. Amen! **Phil. 2:5, Col.1:9-10, Ps.119:9-11**

Dear God, ***Model Prayer for Barbara Jean-BJ***

Thank you Lord for the encouragement that I received from the character of Barbara Jean. Lord, I too have been celibate and faithful for years. I desire a husband, but my desire to please you gives me the contentment that I need. Fill me daily with knowledge and wisdom for your will for my life. Thank you Lord for letting me know that there are other sisters in Christ who share my commitment to you. If I do meet my Gary, thank you for the dating principles shared amongst the characters.

I pray for someone who owns my principles and standards also. Thank you for the confidence in knowing that nothing is wrong with me, but that I chose you over self. If I **do not** meet my, Gary, through your word, I have the confidence in knowing that as I abide in your word, you will continue to abide in me. **Ps.119: 11, John 15:7, Phil.4:6-7, Phil.2:5, Phil.4:13**

Dear God, ***Model Prayer for Joyce***

Joyce's character was an eye opener for me. Each day you watch over me and my child. You have kept us safe as we watch other kids that have not been so blessed. Thank you Lord for the neighborhood church that picks up my kids on Sunday.

Thank you for the mercy that you have extended to me .Forgive me for my transgressions. Receive me as I prepare to join my kids in Sunday worship services. **Ex.34:7a, Ps.51:1-19**

Dear God, ***Model Prayer for Thomas***

I confess to being a Thomas and a Walter. Forgive me for using the church as a platform to satisfy my ego. Forgive me for using my leadership role as an enticement to prey upon my sisters in Christ. Forgive me for not loving you and not submitting to you as Lord and Savior.

Forgive me for abusing the union of my marriage, which opened the door for the enemy to attack my family. Lord, Jesus, I confess my transgressions and ask for your mercy as I pray for your forgiveness. In Jesus name I pray, Amen! **Ps. 51:1-19 Prvb: 32:1-5, Eph.5:23-33, Ps.119:9-11.**

Dear God, ***Model Prayer for Vanessa***

I am guilty of Vanessa's behavior. I confess to knowing that what I'm doing is wrong and disobedient to your will for my life. I also confess to desiring to remain in my state of defiance. Sunday after Sunday, I listen to your word, but rarely hear it. God, I pray that I will begin to take on your mind set. I ask that you will direct me to women that have the boldness to challenge me. Give me the strength to resist my sisters in Christ who encourage me in my presence, and rebuke and talk about me behind my back. Lord, please help me to accept your love for me.

Help me to love me as Barbara Jean grew to love self. Lastly, Father, forgive me for the pain that I've brought upon my sister. Through this story, thanks for letting me know you can't obtain happiness at the expense of others. Please receive the sentiments expressed in these Scriptures as the desires of my heart. **Ps. 51:1-19 Phil.2:5, Ps.119:-9-11**

Dear God, ***Model Prayer for Walter***

I so identify with my brother, Walter. Unlike him, I have been taught the Word. Forgive me for taking advantage of my sisters in Christ. I confess to using the men shortage to my advantage, allowing them to chase me. Forgive me, Lord. Give me the strength to resist the temptation as I re-commit and submit my Christian walk unto you. Lord, direct me to a God fearing woman that will bring me up to her standards, as I endeavor to take on your mindset.

Lord please send me a mentor like a Bill, or someone that I may be accountable. The enemy encourages me to remain isolated; desiring the companionship of only women. May the words of **Ps. 32:1-5 & Ps.51:1-19** be received as the sentiments of my heart unto you. In Jesus name, I pray. Amen!

Dear God, ***Model prayer for Gary***

Like the character Gary, I too struggle with the act of remaining celibate. Like him, I grew up in the church but lacked the teachings on developing a personal relationship with you.

I confess to adopting the double standard practice that men are not expected to abstain. I know the scriptures apply to men as well. I too am a visual person, I pray for strength as I attempt to implement changes in my choices of entertainment pleasures, movies, TV, music magazines, etc.

I now, fully understand and realize Father that the thoughts and visions that I entertain in my mind will ultimately manifest within my body. Lastly, Father, please give me the wisdom to choose a woman that loves you. Give me the strength and the desire to resist the temptations of women who have yet to submit their lives unto you. As I pray back the following scriptures, I pray that you will receive them as sentiments of expressions from my heart. In Jesus name I pray, Amen. **Phil.2:5, Ps.119:11, Phil.4:13, ICor.10:13,Prvb.32:1-5**

Dear God, ***Model Prayer for Bill***

Because you do not make mistakes; like Bill, I miss the love once shared with the love of my life. Thank you for comforting me during the lonely times. Thank you for guarding my mind, and my heart.

Unlike Bill, I came to know you after my wedding vows. I praise you for the mercy and grace that you extended to our union as we committed our lives to you.

Until now, I have never had to practice abstaining. I count it joy that I have already made you Lord and Savior of my life. In your time, I pray that you will direct me to another woman that loves you. As I begin to date, help me to resist the notion of confusing lust and loneness with love. Until that time, I will continue to abide in your word that you may continue to abide in me. In Jesus name I pray, Amen. **John 15:7, Ps. 119:11, Eph. 6:11, Phil. 4:6-8, Phil, 4:13, Phil, 2:5**

www.ingramcontent.com/pod-product-compliance
Lightning Source LLC
LaVergne TN
LVHW091032080826
845145LV00002B/463

* 9 7 8 0 6 1 5 3 3 2 6 9 7 *